TRAPPED WITH YOU

"You and I, in this lifetime and
all the ones to come, *mo chuisle*."

MARZY OPAL

Trapped With You (Remastered)

Paperback ISBN: 978-1-7383050-3-2
Hardcover ISBN: 978-1-7383050-4-9

Published by Marzy Opal www.marzyopal.com

Editor: Emily A. Lawrence (Lawrence Editing)
Cover & Formatting: Qamber Designs

WARNING

This book contains strong language, sexual content, graphic scenes, and
other dark themes that may be triggering to some.
Reader discretion is advised.

For a full list of triggers, check out my website:
www.marzyopal.com

Please note: Montardor is a fictional city based in Central Canada.

For all the queens who wanted a dark prince that would die,
kill, and live for them…

AUTHOR'S NOTE

Dear Reader,

Thank you so much for picking up Trapped With You (Remastered). If you've been following my publishing journey from the start, then you already know that I first released Cade and Ella's book in 2021 as my debut. Three years later and I've decided to give new life to this story because I felt like these characters deserved so much more!

This version is darker, steamier, and angstier. Since this is a dark new adult mafia romance, both characters are morally grey and absolutely crazy and obsessed with each other. If you enjoy the second chance trope with mystery, present/past timelines, and a ride-or-die couple, then I hope you love Cade and Ella's story. Rewriting this book was such a fun and challenging experience at times, and I'm so happy to finally be sharing it with the world <3

This book remains dedicated to my amazing readership. I wouldn't be here without your support and love for my characters and story world. I hope you know that everything I write, I write with you in mind.

Happy reading, queens!

Love always,

Marzy

Spotify Playlist

PLAYLIST

Adele – Set Fire To The Rain
Artic Monkeys – I Wanna Be Yours
Ariana Grande – Bad Decision, Best Mistake (ft. Big Sean), The Boy Is Mine
Ava Max – Sweet But Psycho
Bad Bunny – Mia (ft. Drake)
Beyoncé – All Up In Your Mind, America Has A Problem, Daughter, I Miss
You, Mine (ft. Drake)
Billie Eilish – Ocean Eyes
Calvin Harris & Disciples – How Deep Is Your Love
Chase Atlantic & Maggie Lindemann – Ohmami
Drake – Find Your Love
G-Eazy & Halsey – Him & I
Isabel LaRosa – I'm Yours
Jay Z – '03 Bonnie & Clyde (ft. Beyoncé),
Part II/On The Run (ft. Beyoncé)
Jhené Aiko – 3:16 AM, Stay Ready/What A Life (ft. Kendrick Lamar)
Justin Bieber – All That Matters
Jordan Adetunji – Kehlani
Kali Uchis – Moonlight
Kehlani – Gangsta
Labrinth – Formula
Madison Beer – Make You Mine
Mariah Carey – #Beautiful (ft. Miguel)
Maroon 5 – Animals
M.I.A – Bad Girls
Nelly Furtado – All Good Things (Come To An End)
Nicki Minaj – Grand Piano
One Direction – You & I
Rihanna – Desperado, Disturbia, Skin, Woo
SZA – Snooze
The Weekend – Die For You (Remix with Ariana Grande), Call Out My Name
Travis Scott – Goosebumps
Twenty One Pilots – Heathens
Zayn – Pillowtalk
Zion & Lennox – Yo Voy (ft. Daddy Yankee)

Ella Ximena Cordova

Nineteen. South Side's princess. Cade's pretty girl.

"He was my beginning, my middle, my end."

CADE KILLIAN REMINGTON

Nineteen. South Side's princepin. Ella's querido.

"She was my match made in heaven and hell."

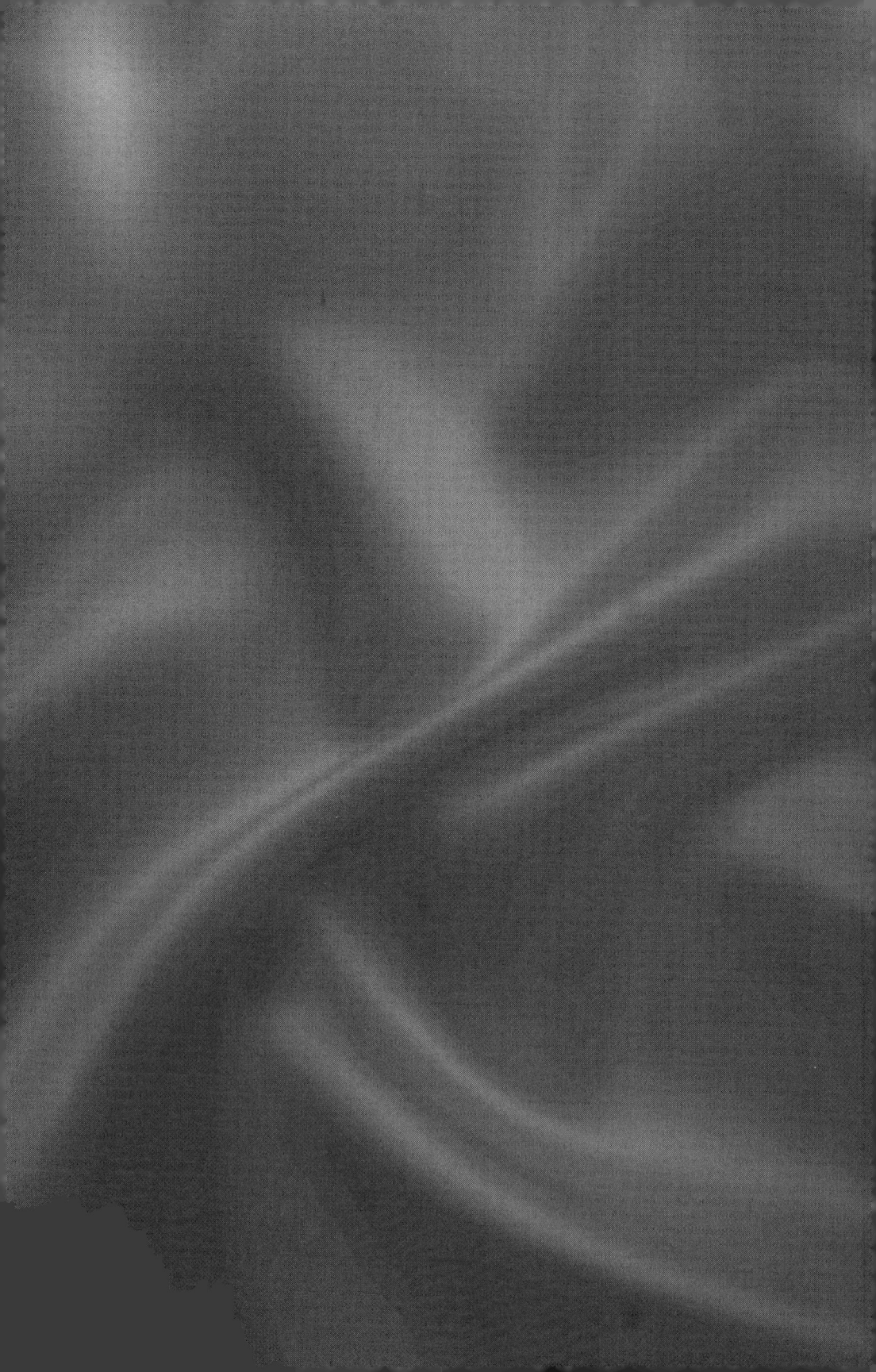

PROLOGUE

CADE

The Past

I was sixteen years old when I met the love of my life.

It was a hot summer evening in August and I was in the car with my new adoptive family, the Remingtons. We were headed over to the Cordovas—long-time family friends of theirs.

Growing up in the rougher side of Montardor, I wasn't accustomed to the rich society of this lavish and corrupted city. It was composed of many immoral individuals and old money families.

The Remingtons were one of them. They were affluent, connected, and known for being key players in the underworld. Classy gangsters in suits and ties, ruling over South Side, Montardor. Their money was long and dirty, stemming from stolen artifacts, illicit substances, and the many art galleries they owned across the city.

Even though I was recently adopted, I still had Remington blood coursing through my veins.

And once my scars healed, I knew they'd want me to join the family business, including all the *extracurricular activities* associated with it.

Blood, drugs, and violence were already a dime a dozen in the life I was forced to lead for the last year. In the past, I'd worked for bad people, dealing coke, ecstasy, and weed to the frivolous teens of Montardor. Unethical by certain standards, but I never claimed to be perfect—especially when I had two mouths to feed.

Though everything changed nine weeks ago when tragedy struck, and the Remingtons swooped in like white knights to rescue my little cousin Olivia and me from our nightmare.

Once upon a time, we were used to stale cereal for breakfast and raggedy clothes with more holes in the fabric than we could count. Now Olivia and I ate hefty three-course meals and our closets were decked out with designer items. Going from a run-down townhouse to a sprawling mansion on the richest side of South Side still felt surreal, but we were doing our best to adapt.

Adapting also meant getting dragged to a hoity-toity dinner on a Thursday night to please our new family, who was extremely adamant on introducing us to the Cordovas.

The bulletproof Escalade we rode in stopped in front of iron-wrought gates. A guard opened them and we drove forward into a circular driveway that looked straight out of a Hollywood movie.

Suddenly, a wave of nervousness washed over me. This world was still so new. Having dinner with a bunch of random people was not my scene. What if I used the wrong cutlery? What if they asked me questions I wasn't prepared to answer? What if they regarded Oliva and me with judgement?

Just because we dressed like them didn't mean we were one of them.

I unclenched my fist and drummed my fingers against my thigh in a quick beat.

Fuck, I need a cigarette so bad.

Olivia, my three-year-old cousin turned adoptive sister now, sensed my unease. She reached forward to rest her small hand over my fingers, halting their movement.

She sat on a booster seat between me and my other cousin—well, *brother* now— Josh, who was pensively gazing out the window, lost in his own world.

Olivia didn't say much with words, but her expression spoke volumes. Dark curls framed her chubby face and her big, gentle eyes watched me with intent. She was silently telling me to 'stop' and 'take a deep breath'.

So I did and inched her a reassuring smile.

Satisfied, she pulled her hand away and settled into her seat more comfortably.

I pressed a kiss to her forehead and mumbled, "I'm okay, Livvy."

Her feet did a little happy dance.

The car parked and our bodyguard stepped out to open the doors.

I stared up in awe at the French Neoclassical style, cream-coloured mansion. The courtyard was picture perfect with a blue water fountain, landscaping lights, manicured greenery, and loads of orange blooms.

At the front porch, their staff stood to greet us.

My stomach sank, dreading a dinner that hadn't even begun.

I smoothed my hands down the front of my black suit jacket, the need to smoke getting worse by the second. Before we entered the house, I asked, "May I be excused? I need to smoke."

Aunt Julia—my adoptive mom—paused in her steps, Olivia held in the cradle of her arms. They were a starkly contrasting pair, with my sister having black curls and dark eyes and Aunt Julia having blond hair and blue eyes.

"It's ill-mannered to keep them waiting, Cade," she said with a frown and a gentle smile, imploring me to understand. "We're already late as it is."

What she really wanted to say was: *Why haven't you stopped smoking yet?*

It'd been seven weeks since they officially adopted us. Paperwork that should have taken them months—hell, even years—to achieve in Canada, they did within weeks. Money was power and living with them had its perks, but it was clear we had a rulebook of bullshit etiquette to follow at home and in public.

One of them being the no-smoking rule.

Yet it was the only way I could cope with everything. The stress. The nightmares. The aftermath of it all.

I almost added that we wouldn't have been late if Uncle Vance—my new adoptive dad—hadn't insisted on fucking his wife in the cigar lounge before we departed. I was walking to the kitchen for a snack before dinner—how uncultured of me, I know—when I heard them going at it like frenzied animals. Unfortunately, I lost my appetite and learned that my new parental unit had a breeding kink. Thankfully, no one besides their butler caught me dry heaving outside the door. So, last I checked, being late was all on them.

Instead of saying that, I answered, "If I don't smoke now, I'm going to be cranky when we get inside, and I'm sure you don't want me to embarrass you in front of your friends."

Josh came to stand beside his mom and ruffled Olivia's hair in an adoring manner, while the latter smiled at him toothily. I liked how quick they got along and how affectionate Josh was towards my little sister. After what we'd been through, she deserved all the love in the world.

"Cade, please." Aunt Julia sighed and cast her husband a look of concern as he rounded the front of the car to join us.

Based on his unimpressed expression, he heard the smoking part.

Vance Remington, South Side's notorious kingpin, could be best described as robustly muscular, very tall, and a charming but scary motherfucker. We had the same features with dark hair and blue eyes and I suspected, once I turned forty-two, I'd be a carbon copy of him. Aunt Julia claimed I already looked like a teenage version of her husband.

Uncle Vance was intimidating without verbalizing it. A lesser man would have cowered in his presence. I just stood my ground, hell-bent on smoking at least one cigarette before going inside.

"The answer is *no*, Cade." He cracked his neck on either side and adjusted the button of his suit, which effectively concealed all his weapons. "I asked you to stop smoking and you refuse to even try. I don't care if you start to get irritable during dinner. We are going in now."

And what he really wanted to say was: *Why are you so ungrateful? I've given you a roof over your head, food on the table, a stable home, and you refuse to follow my one crucial rule.*

Uncle Vance growled one, "Let's go," and impelled everyone to head in the direction of the awaiting Cordova staff.

But I was already walking backwards in the opposite way. "Sorry, Uncle Vance. What did you say? You're cool with me smoking? Thanks. I'll be right back."

I ignored the chilling way he hollered my name and stole to the side of the mansion, towards a secluded garden filled with roses and fancy angel statues. I pulled out a cigarette from my pocket, lit it with a flick of my Zippo, and sat down on an ornate iron bench.

And that's when I saw *her*.

Standing in her stone balcony, she perused the gardens with an otherworldly expression on her face, as if searching for something intangible in the far distance.

Instantly, I felt breathless by the sight she created.

She was beautiful like a summer night sky scattered with thousands of little stars. Long black hair billowing softly in the air, dewy tan skin, and slender frame donned in a short white dress that made her resemble a folklore goddess.

As though I'd spoken those thoughts aloud, she finally saw me.

Our gazes clashed from afar like a magnetic force beckoned us.

Tilting her head, she eyed me with a hint of curiosity and... mischievousness. A joint was neatly tucked between her fingers and she brought it to her pouty lips, taking a slow hit as she watched me in a way that could only be described as intimate.

It made me feel bare and raw. Like all my scars were visible for her to see.

Maybe she wondered what a strange guy in an all-black suit was doing sitting in her garden, watching her like she had created the very universe we lived in.

I couldn't take my eyes off her.

This moment felt sacrosanct. A fated tryst between lovers in a dark fairy tale.

We continued to watch each other as we smoked. Her, as a challenge. Me, as I tried to figure out where I'd seen her before.

There was something familiar about her. She looked to be sixteen years old too, but we definitely didn't run in the same circles.

Before fate handed me new cards, I was a pauper.

And she was a rich princess, living in the proverbial ivory tower.

But when she smirked knowingly and leaned forward, bracing her forearms on the balcony railing, it struck me like a thunderbolt.

5

Oh, fuck.

It was *her*.

The girl I'd sold marijuana to last week in MacGregor's alleyway.

The one who captivated me at first glance, making my heart race embarrassingly fast.

Instead of freaking out and running inside to tell her parents that one of the dinner guests was her drug dealer, she simply arched an eyebrow at my speechlessness. A flirtatious grin played across her lips.

Utterly entranced by this girl, I hissed when ash from my cigarette tumbled onto my hand.

I caught her chuckling and my cheeks flushed.

She quickly finished her joint, threw me a saucy wink, then disappeared inside.

I wistfully stared at the place she vacated, my eyes conjuring her body and the air of confidence she left behind.

There was something about her that sparked a flame in my heart. It lit me up from within, eradicating the darkness looming over my being like a thick, suffocating cloud.

Her playfulness and the fact that she was the first person to stare at me without an ounce of pity—unbeknown to my sob story—had me unexpectedly smiling.

She made me feel like a normal sixteen-year-old rather than a broken boy whose skin bore more lacerations than she could count on her pretty fingers.

There was a bounce to my step after I finished my cigarette and went to join my family, who waited for me on the front porch. Aunt Julia looked resigned, Olivia confused, Josh bored, and I entirely ignored Uncle Vance's angry expression as we entered the residence.

Quiet excitement simmered in my gut at the prospect of seeing her again.

I couldn't have known then that Ella Ximena Cordova would be the first girl I'd ever love.

Or that she'd be the first one to rip out my heart.

Three years later...

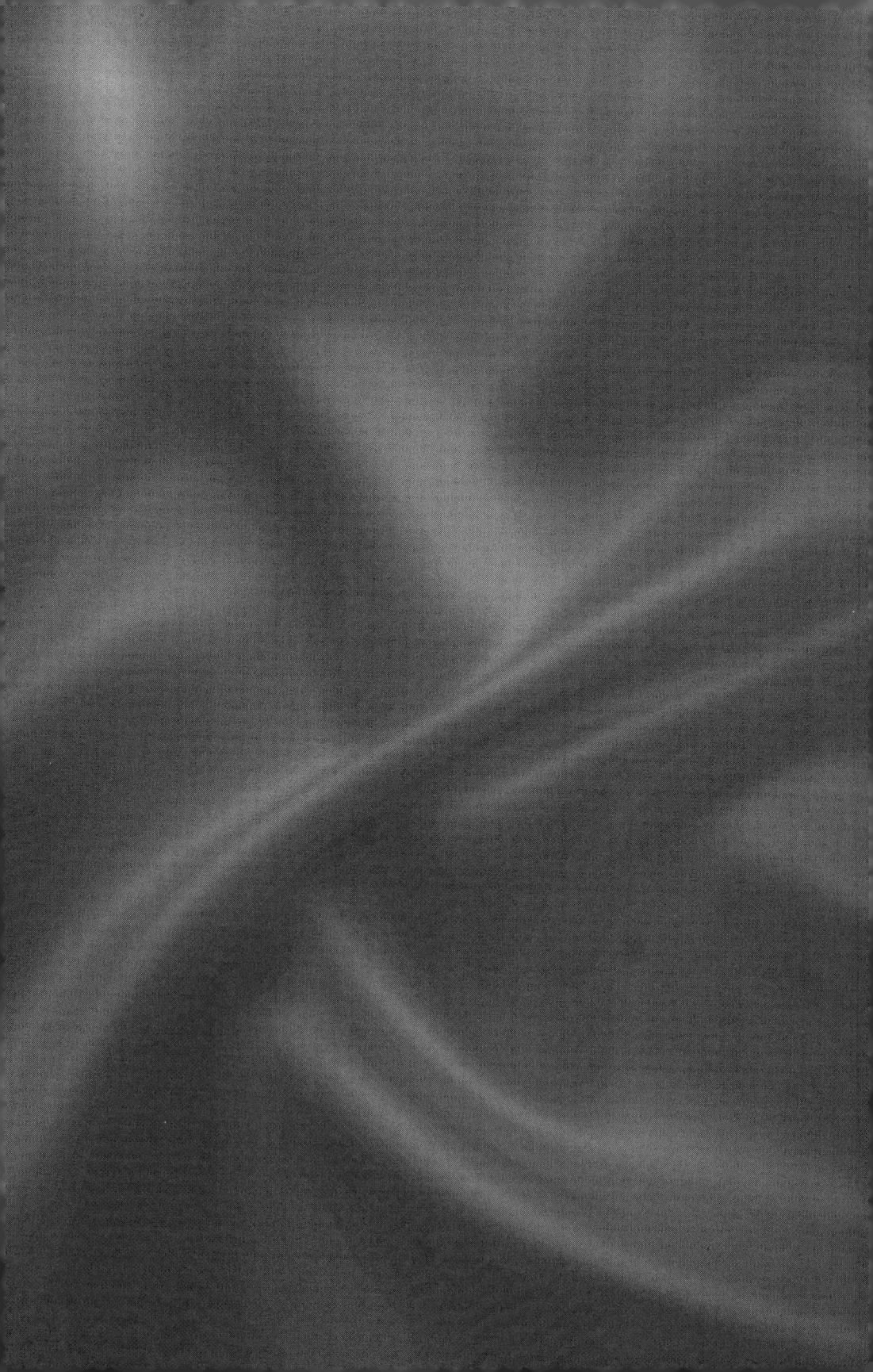

CHAPTER 1

Ghost of You

CADE

The Present

Cupping my hands together under the faucet, I gathered water and splashed it on my face. Rivulets sluiced down the slopes of my cheeks as I glanced at my reflection, a blank expression staring back at me.

On the outside, everything appeared status quo. Dark hair, blue eyes, skin a hint tan —marred with a fading bruise near my jaw from my last fight. It seemed these days my canvas always harboured a wound or two, my body decorated with the story of my rougher days.

But it was never the scars visible to the naked eye that hurt.

No.

The most painful scars were the ones hidden under our armour, like black mold sequestered beneath a shiny surface. Those always took longer to heal. *If* they ever did.

These days, I barely recognized myself. I'd forgotten what living meant. I was simply surviving, going through the motions with an autopilot-like quality and no zeal.

I learned the hard way that sometimes it only took one prominent moment to forever alter you. That so-called moment fundamentally changed something inside me—like a final cog clicking into place—and there was no going back.

I was nineteen years old, but some days I felt beyond that number.

My cell phone vibrated on the bathroom counter and I was pulled out of my train wreck musings. Taking a washcloth, I patted my face and hands before grabbing it.

It was a text message from one of my best friends.

Are you coming tonight? —Shaun

My rational side screamed that I shouldn't go when I had other issues to resolve, other demons to fight, other feelings to numb.

Yet my fingers had a mind of their own as they typed a reply.

I'll be there. —Cade

The boys from the team are meeting in St. Victoria's woods. Pre-gaming before Initiation Night begins. —Shaun

Sounds good. I'll text you when I arrive. —Cade

Shaun sent a thumbs-up emoji.

Tonight was Initiation Night at St. Victoria high school. A twisted tradition that took place on the third Friday night of every October to induct new students on the hockey and cheerleading teams.

I graduated high school a few months ago and was now attending Vesta University since September. However, first year alumni were always invited every single year for one last competition.

To be completely transparent, I didn't give a rat's ass about this tradition. If you asked me, it was just an excuse for trust fund teenagers to do something else besides attend a boozefest and pop pills.

The only reason I agreed to participate tonight was because I knew *she* would be there.

South Side's very own princess.

The bane of my existence.

My unhealthy little obsession.

And my fucking ex-girlfriend.

We were no longer together for reasons I refused to acknowledge.

But I was obviously a masochist who still tortured himself with thoughts of her.

Ella Ximena Cordova was the kind of beautiful that transcended time. Never in my life had I seen such a stunning individual. Everything about her had me in a chokehold. Her spellbinding eyes, her playful smile, her flawless skin, so soft and sensitive under my touch, and her energy—kind and so fiery, it warmed you like the heat of a hundred suns.

The memories of her haunted me until I felt half moon mad with anger and longing, tossing, and turning in my bed at night. Wanting her. Hating her. Loving her. Wishing I'd never laid eyes on her.

I tried for three months to rip apart my fixation with her like a limb in dire need of amputation. It was impossible. I couldn't eradicate her from my mind, my body, or my goddamned soul.

Her ghost was here to stay.

And I'd gladly give it a place in my bruised heart.

Stepping out of my en suite with a towel wrapped around my waist, I trudged out into my room, another towel hanging around my neck. I used it to rub the wetness out of my hair and pat the tattooed skin of my chest, now freshly healed after four weeks.

Tattoos were sacred to me. They were etched on my right arm and my torso, a web of defining memories serving as a reminder of the things that shaped me into the person I was today.

I also learned during the past summer that tattoos were the perfect coping mechanism to drown out your thoughts. When I sat in the chair and heard the gun's buzzing and felt the grind of the needle against my skin, my mind paused.

As a result, my body was covered in various ink and I had no intention of stopping anytime soon.

With thirty minutes left to get ready, I walked over to my dresser and yanked out a pair of black briefs and jeans. I pulled open the top drawer and froze, my eyes spotting my thin gold chain, threaded with *the* promise ring, nestled between my folded black hoodies.

I wore it every day like a pathetic lovesick fool. I didn't know how to be without it.

Fastening it around my neck, I breathed better once it settled between my inked pecs.

Without a knock, my door twisted open and Josh sauntered inside like he owned the place. My pet peeve was people entering without my permission and Josh had no concept of personal space. He parked his ass on the edge of my unmade bed like a lazy king lounging before his subject. "Hey."

"Hey," I returned, throwing on my black hoodie.

When I faced him, he was frowning, his eyes locked near my right rib. I ground my jaw. He saw *that* particular tattoo and chose not to comment on it.

Clearing his throat, he asked, "Where are you going?"

"Out. I'm meeting Shaun and some of the boys from the team." I didn't tell him about Initiation Night because he'd know I was only going for Ella. The last thing I wanted was pity from my family. "What about you?"

Josh cleared his throat again. A trait that emphasized his nervousness. "Layla is coming over tonight, but...nobody knows."

One thing about us Remington men?

We loved hard and forever.

If Ella was my obsession, then Layla was my brother's. For all intents and purposes, she was his best friend, but he had it bad for her with a capital B. One night, we stole a bottle of whiskey from Uncle Vance's stash, got drunk on the mansion's rooftop, and Josh finally confessed he was in love with Layla.

"I want to marry her," he'd slurred, halfway drunk. "I want to give her a big home and lots of babies."

I'd laughed and taken a swig of the whiskey. "Does she know all of this?"

Josh had stared at the moon with awe, his mouth hanging half-open like an idiot. "N-No. But I'll tell her one day." He'd rubbed the left side of his chest like he was soothing his heart. "T-There's only one thing I want in this whole world and...that's to be her husband."

I hoped Josh got his wish and that Layla too realized she was head over heels for him. Preferably in this decade.

"Good luck getting her past Julia and Vance." I smirked, snapping on my watch and donning my silver rings. "If they catch you both, you're getting the birds and the bees monologue."

Uncle Vance actually gave me the talk when I started dating Ella. He also said there would be hell to pay if I made him a grandfather before I graduated university.

Josh scowled. "Yeah, no, thank you. I'd rather stab myself with a knife than hear Mom and Dad talk to me about sex and contraceptives."

"If you need to sneak her in, do it using the east garden doors. No one will see you."

To be frank, Layla often came over during the day so she and Josh could study and play videogames. Aunt Julia and Uncle Vance really liked her but assumed she was just their son's 'friend.' If they found out Josh and Layla actually *liked* each other, Aunt Julia would throw a tea party and Uncle Vance would throw a box of condoms at Josh. Both equally embarrassing scenarios for the two.

"I shouldn't have a problem sneaking her in." Josh combed his fingers through his hair and joined his hands at the nape of his neck, glancing ceilingward as he exhaled slowly. "I hate to admit this, but I'm feeling nervous."

I arched an eyebrow. "Why?"

"We've kissed before, but I don't know if she'll want to go all the way tonight."

"Well, if she does, make sure you give her plenty of foreplay. Girls like that."

"I've also never done it," Josh admitted then groaned. "What if I screw up this entire thing?"

I crossed my arms over my chest and perched against my dresser. "You won't, Josh. Sex isn't a competition. It's about communication and doing what feels right for both of you. Make sure you ask her how she's feeling with everything you do, and don't forget to tell her what you like as well. The rest will come naturally."

"You're right." He cracked his knuckles and stood up. "Thanks for this."

"Anytime, man."

"Before I get going, I need to ask…Are you okay?"

"Why wouldn't I be?"

His eyes searched mine. "There's something different about you for quite some time. I'd like to say it's the stress from all the jobs we've been doing for Dad lately, but I have a feeling it has something to do with Ella."

I stiffened.

He didn't have to say it out loud. We both knew the truth.

I never got over my ex-girlfriend.

I was a fully functioning wreck without her.

When I remained silent, Josh grimaced. "Sorry. I don't mean to overstep by assuming. I'm just worried about you."

I forced a smile. "I'm fine, Josh. I just have a lot on my mind. Freshman year of university and midterms are already kicking my ass."

Josh knew I was bullshitting. "Okay, if you say so." He clapped my shoulder in a brotherly gesture. "Just remember I'm always here for you, all right?"

I truly hit the jackpot when I got adopted by the Remingtons. I gained great parents, a stable home, and an amazing brother who was nothing but loyal and supportive. Two things I always reciprocated.

Besides both being nineteen, Josh and I were identical in many ways. Dark hair, signature Remington chiseled jawline, tall heights, and athletic builds. When we were high schoolers, Josh had attended Westwood High for its exceptional football program, while I attended St. Victoria—located closer to our home in South Side—for its renowned hockey team. Since I played the sport until I was fifteen, Uncle Vance insisted I get back into it when I started living with them.

But that's where our similarities ended.

Josh hadn't been completely tarnished by the violence of our world. I, on the other hand, entered this world having already tasted its flavour. Life had forced me to grow up faster and tougher from a young age.

If there's one language I was well-accustomed to, it was brutality.

I'd been on the receiving end and I knew how to fucking dish it.

Which made me a perfect soldier in Vance Remington's eyes.

My uncle made it clear that our destiny was tied with being the successors of the Remington criminal empire. A role that Josh and me both embraced wholeheartedly.

"Thanks, J," I told him. "I appreciate it."

Josh left shortly afterwards.

I rummaged through my drawers for my wallet. I kept my space clean, but I wasn't always the tidiest. Sometimes I misplaced my belongings. Cursing, I opened each one until I got to the bottom drawer.

An old baseball bat lay within, one I thought I effectively hid months ago.

The sight of it, with the letters *E + C* carved on the surface, sent a wave of pain through my chest. Longing. It burned my insides like acid.

I took a deep, shaky inhale, closing my eyes.

Everything in my space was a constant reminder of her.

The baseball bat. The promise ring around my neck. The tats on my body. The imprint she left on me.

In this lifetime, I was cursed with loving her and only her.

Once I found my wallet, I grabbed my keys, leather jacket, riding helmet, and my De la Croix gun before I took the elevator down to the underground garage, where my Ducati was parked.

Uncle Vance would not allow his little princes to leave his kingdom without security or weapons. Since I wasn't exactly a stickler for rules, I omitted the former. But I'd be plain stupid to leave without a gun, especially when Montardor was brimming with filthy rats who had a vendetta against my family.

It was only when I got on my motorcycle and blazed out of the premise, that the longing quickly morphed into simmering excitement at the prospect of seeing the object of my affection once more.

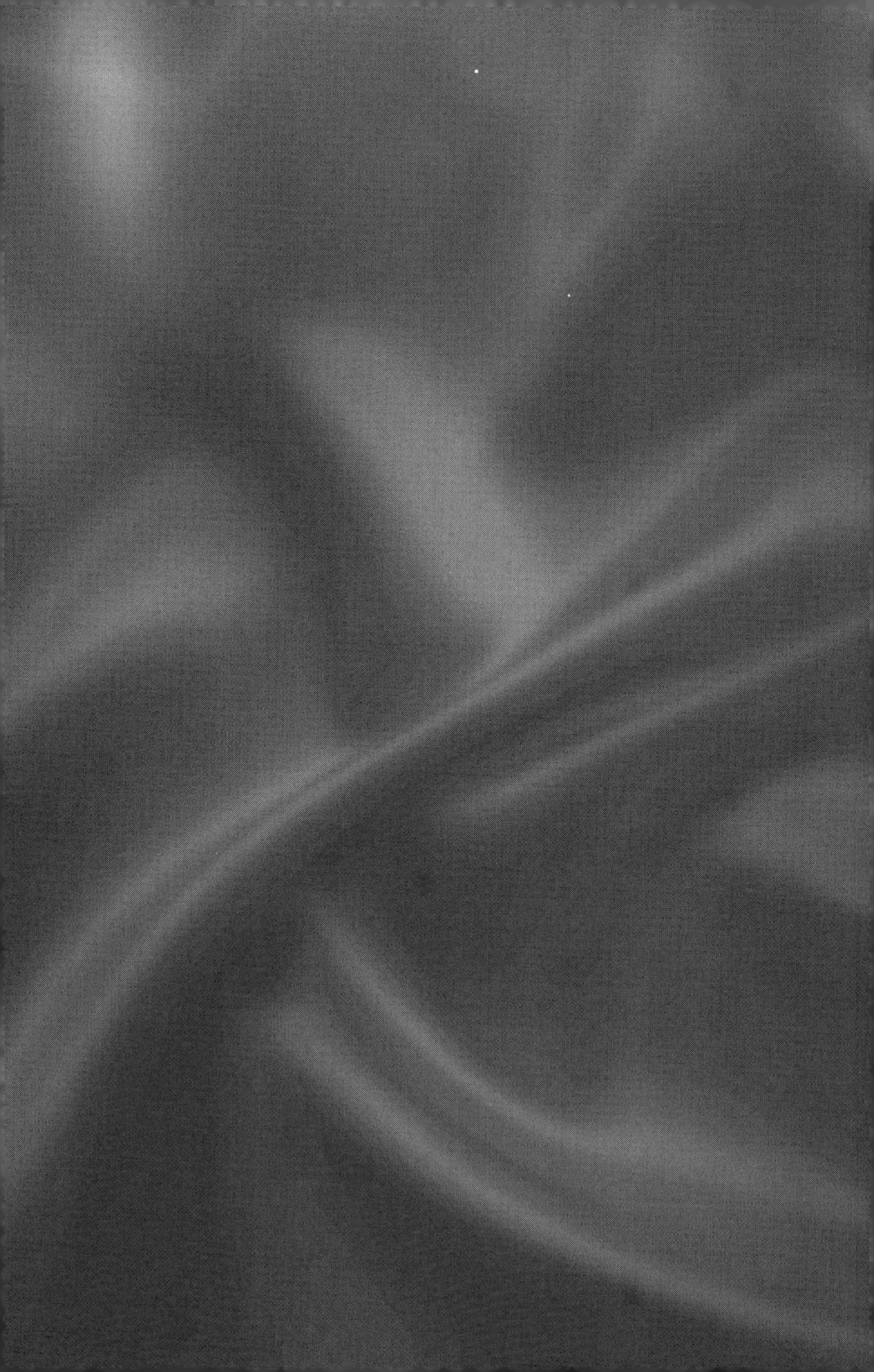

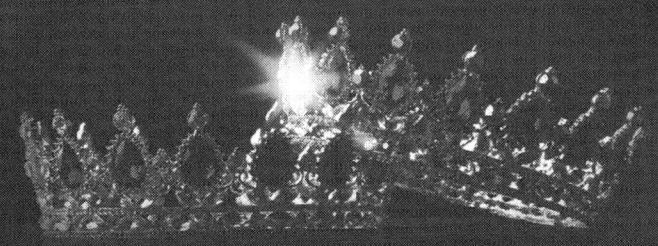

CHAPTER 2

Reminders of You

Ella

The Present

My gaze was fixed on the grandfather clock in the dining room. I was waiting for it to strike 10:00 p.m. so I could plan my escape from this party.

Currently, the Cordova household was buzzing with guests as my parents hosted their annual fall soirée with all their close associates. I was born and bred in Montardor, which was as beautiful as it was corrupted. Living within the high society of this city, I was well-accustomed to its key players—the rich, depraved men and their bored trophy wives.

We Cordovas weren't criminals per se, but we did socialize with the kind of people who were. As a result, we found ourselves in these circles.

I swirled my glass of pinot noir and took a tentative sip while the chatter rose in decibels. Butlers walked around the perimeter of the room, offering more wine and flirting with the socialites.

Across the candlelit dining table, I met Julia Remington's eyes, which were soft and kind as she sat in front of me. My body tensed up, but I forced myself to return her smile. It was awkward in nature, despite my best efforts.

Vance Remington sat next to his wife. Tall, muscular, dark hair, ice blue eyes, beautiful jawline, and in his mid-forties, he looked like an older version of my ex-boyfriend. From the looks and down to his mobster demeanor.

A pang of yearning travelled through my chest when I saw him reach for his wife's hand and bring it to his lips for a kiss. The way he gazed at her with quiet adoration reminded me of the way his son used to stare at me.

Before he fucking ruined us.

I'd seen Cade's adoptive parents multiple times since our breakup. It didn't get easier with time. Especially when I remembered how I once thought the Remingtons would be my future in-laws.

Truly, I'd loved them like my own family.

Noting my pensive state, my *papá*, sitting to my right at the head of the table, said with a prickly undertone, "What's on your mind, *mija*?"

Francisco Cordova was nothing if not perceptive. Outward appearances meant everything to my family. My little brother Emilio and I were expected to conduct ourselves in a manner that brought honour to our name. For me, that meant playing the role of the classic good girl daughter in front of the world.

He didn't like that I sat aloof, not participating in the conversation or giving a single shit about the latest gossip. Really, I was just here to eat and then quickly take my leave.

After all, I had big plans for tonight.

"Oh, I'm just wondering what's for dessert," I replied peachily.

Tres Leches cake, my favourite, but I already knew that.

Papá picked up on my lie and his eyes narrowed. "How's school going?"

"Great." I swirled my glass and gulped the wine in an unladylike fashion. "Loving my classes."

Surprisingly, I was actually enjoying university. I was a freshman at Vesta University's business school, double majoring in management and marketing. My true calling was art, but *papá* demanded that I take over the family business. An idea that I found abhorrent when I was a kid, even though it was my birthright as the firstborn.

Now I looked forward to inheriting my legacy and being the first female figurehead in our business.

Women were the future leaders of tomorrow.

And I was ecstatic at all the ways I could transform our company and elevate it to a whole new level with my ideas and leadership.

"You're an intelligent girl, Ella, with a good head on your shoulders." *Papá* cut through his steak and cast me a pointed look. "I'm assuming you're acing all your assignments and exams."

I didn't know why, but the '*good head on my shoulders*' felt a bit barb-like. A compliment and an insult. While I'd always worked hard in my academic life, I'd been known to make some bad decisions in my personal one. At least, that's what my parents believed.

"Mhm. You know me. I'm a smart cookie." I rarely used sarcasm because I was raised to respect my elders, but I was on edge tonight and a bit irritated. "I get it from you, *papá*."

He shot me a timely glare.

I didn't back down either.

He ran his tongue over his teeth then nodded slowly, as if telling me two could play this game. "Tell me, *mija*, have you seen Josh around campus? He's attending Vesta University, too, yes?"

The temperature on our end of the dining table chilled.

My smile was wiped off my face.

Vance's and Julia's heads swivelled our way at the mention of their son.

My *mamá* sat next to me and she too perked up at the mention of Josh, abandoning her conversation with the young socialite to her left.

The fingers holding the stem of my wine glass clenched. I almost shattered it under my strength. By a miracle, I held it together, counting to five in my mind as I breathed through my nose.

Uno, dos, tres, cuatro, cinco.

I could not believe he'd thrown Josh in my face right now.

My *papá* and Vance were long-time friends. I knew Josh since we were babies. He was a great guy—funny, charming, respectful, and cute. My parents adored him and wanted me to date him since the dawn of time. It would be a great way to merge our families, yet Josh and I had never seen each other *that* way. Ever.

He was in love with Layla.

And me?

I'd fallen in love with Cade Killian Remington three years ago.

My parents hated that I dated the adoptive son who was nothing short of bad news.

After our messy breakup, they basically said, 'I told you so,' with haughty voices.

"No, I haven't seen Josh around," I whispered, my voice frail despite the fire burning under my skin.

Mamá put a comforting hand on my shoulder, inching *papá* a frown. And for a second, I saw guilt flash across his face when he realized he'd hit a nerve.

I'd needed weeks to glue my broken pieces once I broke up with Cade. Our separation took a physical toll on me. My parents were first-hand witnesses to it. I was a shell of a girl after the whole thing happened. Even now, I barely felt healed.

"Ella—" *Papá* started with an apologetic tone.

Frustrated, I threw my napkin on my plate like a white flag, signalling the end of dinner for me. Scraping my chair back, I got up and ignored the guests' curious looks. "Excuse me, but I think I'll retire for the night. I've had a long day and I'm exhausted."

"Dessert will be served soon, *mija*," *mamá* said in an attempt to keep me at the table.

"No, thank you." I adjusted the silk skirt of my rust-coloured gown and grabbed my wine glass. "Hope you all enjoy the rest of your evening."

Nobody bothered to stop me afterwards.

I was an adult who could make my own decisions.

Even if they weren't always the best ones.

Head held high and shoulders squared back, I sauntered out of the dining room with all the grace of a young *princesa*. My invisible crown in place, my heels clicking against the marble flooring, and a cloud of fury looming above me.

Once I entered the empty hallway, the fast beats of my heart were magnified and my left hand's fingers flexed before forming into a clenched fist.

I had the irresistible urge to hit something.

The only thing in my vicinity was a crystal vase resting on a demilune table. A recent purchase made by *papá* during his last trip to France.

On my way past it, I slammed the antique item onto the floor in retaliation.

Crystal bits shattered everywhere. The sound was so loud and jarring, it caused the party in the dining room to fall silent for a minute.

I smirked and walked away.

I used to believe heartbreak pain was ephemeral.

Never had I anticipated it to feel like a residual pulse that expanded through your system. Akin to a plant growing vines and wrapping itself around your heart, squeezing in steady intervals to remind you of its presence. Letting you know that it was here to stay unless you built the courage to rip it out of its roots.

It had been so many weeks that I no longer remembered where my hurt began and where it ended.

My bedroom was on the second story, a slow journey from the dining hall on the ground floor. Before I reached the grand staircase, a piano melody resonated in the foyer.

My parents liked to hire a professional pianist for events like these. I followed the sound until I found an old gentleman playing Céline Dion's ballad, "The Power of Love", on a Yamaha.

It felt extremely ironic to be hearing this song when my heart was in shambles, having been wrecked by the very sentiment of love itself.

Maybe it was the wine. Maybe it was the music.

Or maybe it was the reminder of *him*.

But suddenly, a fresh tear trekked down my face.

I used to love this song. Now I couldn't hear it without wanting to burst into tears.

Pivoting on my heels, I climbed the grand staircase in my six-inch stilettos, sipping my wine as the train of my gown trailed up the steps.

I needed fresh air, a pint of ice cream, and reruns of old '90s sitcoms.

The minute I landed on the second floor, a soft breeze drifted into the atmosphere.

I walked towards the open French doors that led to a limestone balcony.

The moonlit night fueled my melancholy.

As did the sight of the orange begonias cascading around the balustrade in abundance. With a scent I adored, they were my favourites. In the warmer months, a pair of hummingbirds often drank from the nectar whenever Cade and I stood together on the balcony, watching the scenery, whispering sweet nothings, sharing soft kisses.

After downing the remainder of my wine, I rested the glass on the stone banister. Then I closed my eyes, letting the fall wind nip at my skin and rustle the strands of my black hair.

I recently cut it straight and shoulder length, wanting a change from my usual long, wavy mane. That's what girls were supposed to do after a life-altering event, right? Chop their hair and start all over again? Unfortunately, it hadn't done anything to make me feel better.

If I could curse Cade Killian Remington to hell, I would.

I'd always been a strong, independent girl. One blow to the heart and I was reduced to a weak, pathetic version of myself. I didn't want to be the kind of girl who moped over her lost love—especially when *he* hadn't handled my heart with the care he promised.

Perhaps what gutted me the most was I lost more than a boyfriend that one fateful night three months ago. I lost my best friend, my soulmate, and an important piece of me.

My favourite person in the entire world became my biggest lesson.

Time heals all wounds, as the saying went, and I had faith that eventually I too would be fine. I would fully heal, I would move on, and I would find love again.

I firmly believed that the universe threw your way only what it knew you could handle. Every obstacle was meant to strengthen and help you grow into a better version of yourself.

The strongest ones were those who'd sipped the wine of pain and not regurgitated any of it.

I hoped I'd proven my strength to the universe and that it would finally give me a reprieve.

Lost in my reverie, I startled when my cell phone blared in the quiet, dark night.

It was my best friend, Callie Mackowski, calling. I quickly answered and brought it to my ear. "Hello?"

"Hey, girl!" Callie exclaimed. "Are you ready for tonight?"

"What?" I cleared my throat to rid myself of the thick quality in my voice.

"Hello? Did you forget? It's Initiation Night."

Ah, yes. My so-called big plans for tonight. I'd received the invitation for Initiation Night over a month ago and RSVPed as soon as possible.

The wheels in my mind were just churning a little slower than usual after my moment of weakness.

"No, I didn't forget." I tucked my hair behind my ear. "I just need to change and I'm ready in twenty. Will you come pick me up?"

"I'm already on my way, babe."

"Thanks, Cal. See you soon."

We hung up and then I got ready at record speed.

When I'd been in high school, Initiation Night at St. Victoria was something I looked forward to every single year in October.

And I knew a night of debauchery would be the perfect distraction from the chaos brimming in my life.

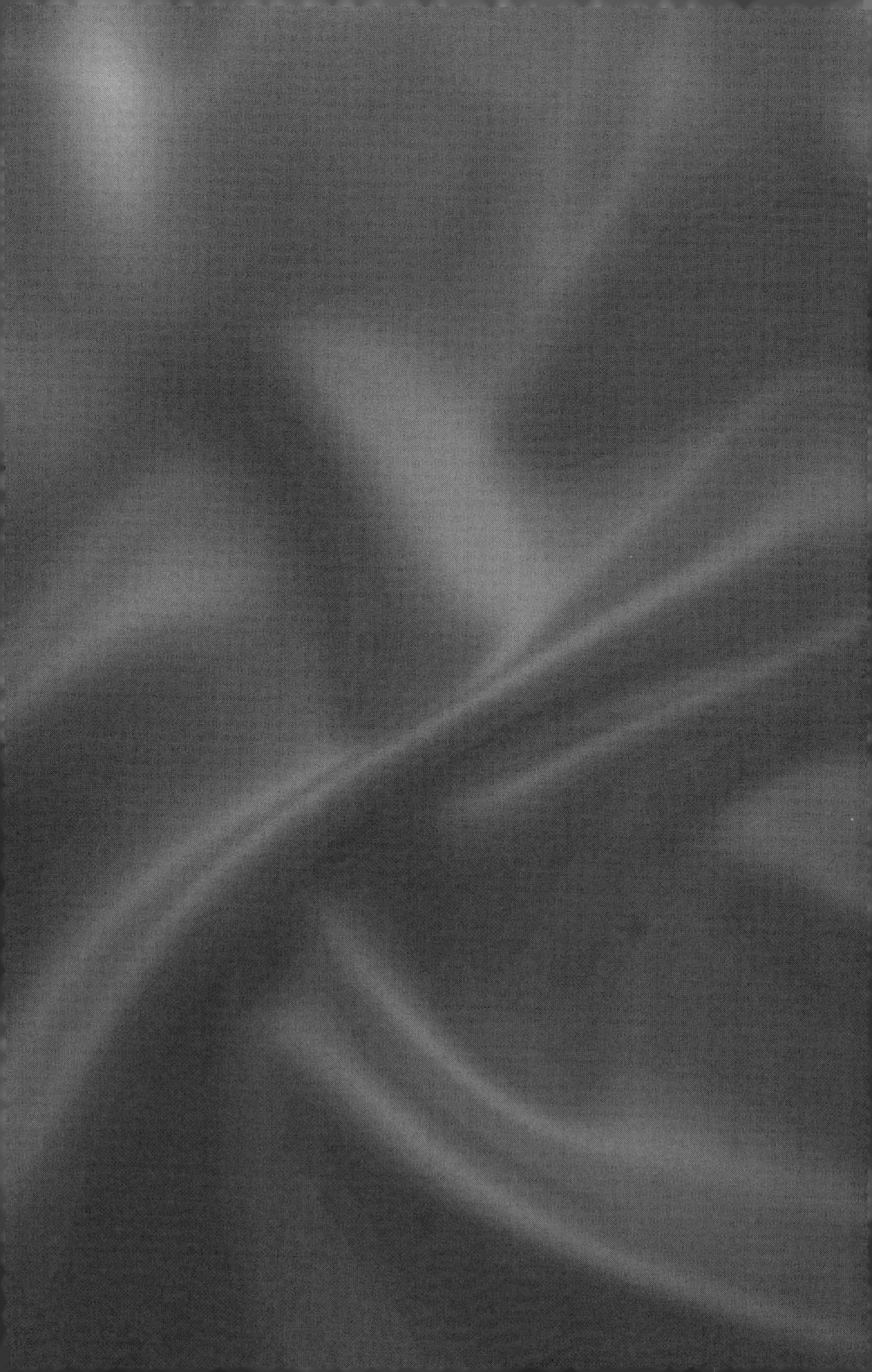

CHAPTER 3
The Witching Hour

CADE

The Present

The wind howled as I rode up St. Victoria's hill.

My motorcycle's light guided me through the tenebrous night, my leather-gloved hands tightening on the handlebars as shadows, scattered amongst the maple trees lining the pathway, played in my peripheral vision like wraiths. This ancient motherhouse—now converted into an educational institute for the elite's offspring—was rumoured to be brimming with phantoms. *If* you believed in that sort of thing. Although the series of macabre deaths revolving this place was quick to prove that there was something diabolic in nature deeply rooted at its core.

Over the years, many students claimed they'd seen things, heard things, felt things. Things that were intangible and challenged their grasp on reality.

I wasn't a believer in the paranormal, therefore my experience at St. Victoria remained untainted by these speculations. In my book, the only demons that existed were the sick humans who walked this earth, sinners in all shapes and forms.

Perched like an old relic in a contemporary world, St. Victoria's edifice unravelled at the top of the hill as I neared the gates. Centuries-old architecture laden with dark turrets, grey stones, and discreetly hidden gargoyles on the roof, the school was a sculpture straight out of gothic literature.

Despite the eerie ambiance, one could still appreciate its beauty.

When I parked my motorcycle near St. Victoria's woods, a myriad of memories flooded my mind. Ella and me riding together to school, her arms wrapped around my middle and her vivacious laugh in my ear as she enjoyed the wind in her hair. Ella and me crossing the hallways together, my hand braided with hers and the other one holding her purse because she'd gotten tired of hauling it. Ella and me seated by the fountain in the courtyard, stealing kisses between classes and making plans for a future that would no longer come to fruition.

Everywhere I looked, I saw Ella.

She was my favourite memory and my mind loved revisiting her.

It gutted me that I lost the privilege of so many things that made me feel like her protector, but most importantly…it gutted me that I lost *her*.

Ultimately, there were two prominent reasons I was here tonight.

To see Ella and to win her back, once and for all.

Far in the distance, I heard low ruckus and knew the boys were already here.

These woods were reminiscent of the ones at Remington estate, but ours were more tamed and serene. St. Victoria's forest was unruly and high enough to block out the night stars. It even hosted a small cemetery for the graves of the children who'd perished when this institute was still a motherhouse back in the early 1900s.

Colourful leaves crunched beneath my black boots as I trudged into the woods. Back in the days, after home games, the boys would hang out here with alcohol and locker room talk.

Less than four minutes of walking and I entered a clearing where everyone—the current hockey team and my old teammates—sat around a small fire. It was near pitch black save for the light emanating from the flames, allowing me to see everyone's faces. The air was laced with the smell of weed, as well as boisterous chatter and a rap song playing on somebody's phone.

Shaun Jacobsen the III, previous captain of St. Victoria's Rangers, was the first to spot me. "Bro, you made it!"

Greetings echoed in unison. I saluted the boys and headed towards Shaun. He sat on an old tree trunk with a bottle of Sam Adams. I shook his hand and clapped his back. "How's it going?"

"We're making bets on who's going to win tonight." Shaun chuckled around the rim of his bottleneck before taking a small swig. "Of course, none of us think it's the freshmen."

Freshmen never won Initiation Night. They were too new and too nervous to play this game. It took a seasoned player who'd been around the block at least once to win.

"Let me guess: You think it's one of us."

"Yup. I'm betting on one of the alumni." Shaun scratched his blond beard. "Besides Darla and me, since we'll be monitoring the competition."

I noticed belatedly that Shaun actually came dressed for the event—as most people did, since it was close to Halloween—and the first genuine laugh in weeks escaped me. "Dude, what the fuck are you wearing?"

"Oh, I'm a plague doctor," he said merrily, garbed in a black cape, a plague doctor mask over his head, and holding a cane topped with a winged hourglass. It was ridiculous and very much on-brand for Shaun. He wiggled his eyebrows. "Do you like my costume?"

Shaun was nothing short of a jester and that's one of the things I liked most about him. Even though he came from the kind of money that would make most weep, he was funny, selfless, and humble. Unlike the rich, snobby kids of St. Victoria. The best word to describe him was *kind*. Shaun had taken one look at me in sophomore math class—the new, quiet kid—and decided we'd be friends. He made sure I met everyone in his circle and that I never sat alone during lunch.

Essentially, Shaun was one of the best people I knew. He'd been there for me through thick and thin. If anybody ever messed with him, I'd make them regret ever existing.

"It's great." I shoved my hands into my pockets. "You look like an overgrown garden gnome."

We both laughed at that.

I sat down next to Shaun and a guy from the team offered me a beer.

I shook my head in response.

For three months, I didn't drink a drop of alcohol. I wasn't planning on starting now.

I sensed Shaun watching me with a quizzical expression as I pulled out a cigarette and tucked it in the seam of my mouth, searching the inside pocket of my leather jacket for my Zippo. The same one Ella gifted me two years ago with my initials—**CKR**—engraved and an orange lollipop painted on the metal surface.

We had many love languages. Words of affirmation and gift giving remained at the top. Ella and I always gave each other small, meaningful things. It wasn't about materialism, rather about showing the other person that you were always thinking of them.

Running my thumb over the flint wheel, a bright flame flickered and I lit my cigarette. Bad habit, I knew, but in my defence, I'd stopped for nearly three years. This was a recent development.

"I'm going to do you a favour tonight," Shaun murmured so low, I had to strain to hear him.

My cheeks hollowed as I took a drag. Releasing the smoke from the side of my lips, I asked him, "What kind of favour—"

A booming voice interrupted the rest of my sentence. "Yo, Shaun!"

My head snapped up to find Gavino Ricci, another alumni, heading our way.

Truth be told, I was cordial with the boys on the team, but Shaun was the only one I was close to—the only one I cared about.

Ella used to tease me about being a lone wolf. She wasn't wrong. I liked to keep to myself and rarely opened up to others. Outside of St. Victoria, I had a small, loyal group of friends and that's how I liked it.

"Hey," Shaun replied. "Everything okay?"

"Just wondering if we're going to start Initiation Night soon," Gavino asked, then grinned at me like he just noticed my presence. "Oh hey, how's it going, Cade?"

"Good, you?" I chin-nodded, shaking his outstretched hand.

"I'm doing good too." He leaned against a nearby tree. "Haven't seen you around lately. Where have you been?"

Stalking my ex-girlfriend. Running through the city doing errands for Uncle Vance. Trying not to fall into a depressive pit with all the shit marathoning in my head. "Here and there. Mostly occupied with my studies."

"Nice. I heard you got into business school."

I hated small talk. "Yeah, majoring in accounting. You?"

"Nah. University isn't on my radar until next year." There was a bit of a self-deprecating edge in his tone. "I got other things on my plate right now."

Gavino was a nice guy. Not very tall and blond like goldilocks. We'd both been defencemen on the team, though I was the alternate captain and he was on the second line.

Despite all the surface level stuff, I respected Gavino's hustle. He was born on the rough side of South Side, Montardor—just like me—and had attended St. Victoria courtesy of a scholarship. He was smart and worked many odd jobs to sustain himself from what I remembered. I found that quite admirable.

We turned our attention to Shaun when he cleared his throat, fiddling with his phone. "Darla just texted. She's at the front doors. We need to head out." Then louder for the rest of the guys, he yelled, "Almost quarter to midnight, boys! Let's fucking go!"

The crowd roared in excitement, Shaun's shout galvanizing them into action.

We were leaving the woods when I grasped Shaun's shoulder and pulled him back. "What favour were you talking about?"

Shaun gave me a smirk laced with dark amusement. "You'll see soon enough."

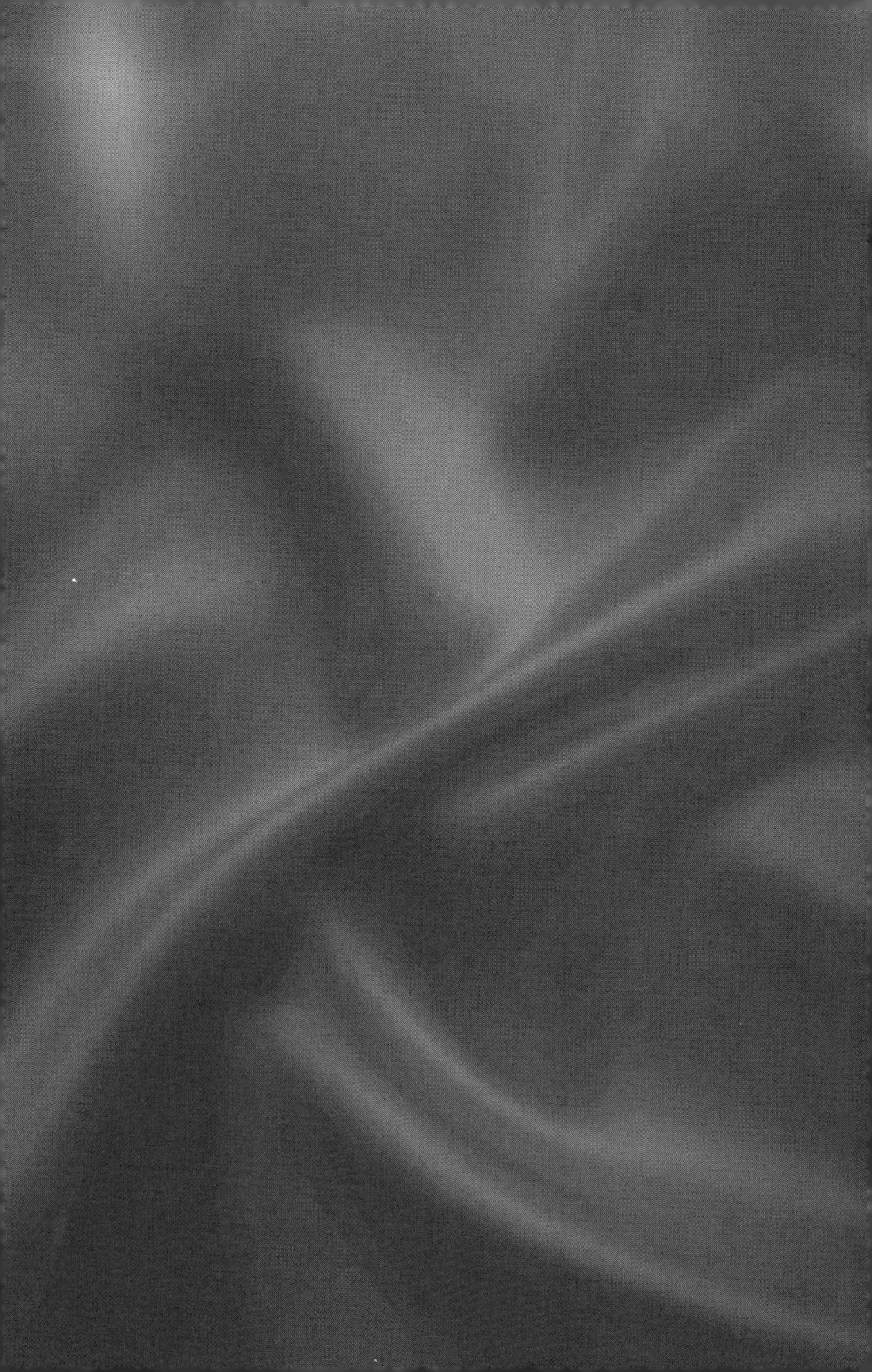

CHAPTER 4

Let the Games Begin

Ella

The Present

When Callie and I crossed through the doors of St. Victoria high school, the dark aura surrounding the gothic-style building and the thick fragrance of incense, wood, and blood orange hugged my frame like an old inamorato.

Four months since I graduated, yet it felt like just yesterday I was sauntering down these arched hallways in my cheerleading uniform with my ex-boyfriend by my side.

Cade and I had been *that* couple. Inseparable and indestructible. I was the co-captain of the cheerleading team and he was the alternate captain for the Rangers. We weren't oblivious to the gossip that followed our trail. People were either jealous of us or wanted to *be* us. No matter what or where we went, we incited envy and revered glances.

South Side's resident good girl and bad boy was a goddamn headline.

For three years, we'd been the center of attention, sitting on our high horses.

Now we were nothing.

Funny how lovers who were tighter than a nun's vow could be reduced to ashes.

Walking further into the dark foyer illuminated by our flashlights and lined with mosaic windows, brass-accents, and wooden floors, memories of our relationship played in my mind like a film.

From our first meeting to our last sighting. From our first kiss to our last fight. From the first moment we said *I love you* to the very moment he shattered my heart with a sledgehammer.

Even with all my pain, it was impossible to erase his memory.

He'd built himself a home in my heart and he never, *ever* left.

Being in St. Victoria magnified all the feelings I'd tried to avoid for three months. They clawed to the surface like ghouls and I desperately tried to kick them back below the surface, in the graveyard of all the things I once held dear to me.

Callie wasn't oblivious to my inner turmoil. She kept shooting me worried glances as we leaned against a row of lockers, watching Initiators entering the building after us. They chatted in low voices, their excitement palpable in the air.

My best friend's gaze burned a hole into my side. She finally bit the bullet and asked, "Are you okay, Ella?"

I knew what she actually meant to ask. *Are you okay being back here after everything that happened with you and Cade?*

Masking my emotions, I pasted a fake smile because I was in public. And as per my parents' rules, you never let your guard slip in front of the world—never wore your emotions on your sleeve for others to witness. "Yeah, just waiting for the game to begin."

"I can't believe this will be our last one," Callie whispered sadly. "I'm going to miss Initiation Night."

Initiation Night was for the current St. Victoria students, but every year, former graduates—namely first year alumni—were granted the privilege to come play the game one last time.

My smile wavered when the hockey team entered at the end, cutting my gaze elsewhere so I didn't start counting bodies and searching faces. "Me too, Cal."

For decades, Initiation Night was a rite of passage—a coveted ceremony—taking place on the grounds of St. Victoria, where individuals from the cheerleading and hockey team broke into the school for a night filled with debauchery and mischief. In the afterhours, like a fever dream, it was a nail-biting and thrilling experience. It was a night that gave students the excuse to behave immorally and get away with it.

Restless anticipation thrummed through the throng of people gathered in the foyer, waiting for further instructions. We were breaking several laws by being here, but that's what made it fun.

St. Victoria used to be a motherhouse—a convent, if you will. Less than a hundred years ago, it was converted into a high school. It'd been renovated through the years, but an eerie atmosphere was forever associated with the establishment.

In daylight, it was bearable. At nightfall, it was a beast. Like the walls lived and breathed old wives' tales.

"Who do you think you'll get paired with tonight?" Callie asked, adjusting the hem of her white minidress and her red cape. With her pixie blond hair and blue doe eyes, she resembled an angel instead of a slutty Red Riding Hood.

"Hopefully you." A lot of the people in our senior class had been fake and gossip-hungry. I was big on protecting my peace and keeping only a few close people by my side.

I only trusted Callie now.

She smiled. "Yes, hopefully."

"I'm going to win this year," I manifested. "Watch it happen."

I had a big competitive streak and Callie knew it too.

Last year, Darla Ivy Hill—my teammate, cheerleading co-captain, and now *ex*-best friend—and I were the reigning Queens of Initiation Night.

It was an epic competition. The level of exhilaration when we'd been crowned the winners was indescribable. I wanted to feel that rush again and break a record. No one in the history of Initiation Night had ever won twice.

"Well, here's to you winning the game." Callie raised her flashlight to mine in a toast. "You got this—"

"What are you ladies talking about?"

Cursing in unison, we both startled at the unexpected voice filled with amusement, resonating from our left.

"Oh my God!" Callie shone her flashlight at the intruder.

Gavino Ricci crossed his arms and leaned against a locker beside

Callie, a devious grin sketched on his lips, showcasing a pair of fake fangs. His shoulder-length blond hair was mussed and he wore faded blue jeans with his old hockey jersey. I guess he was dressed as a hockey-playing vampire or something of the sorts. "Did I scare you?"

Callie swatted his bicep and jokingly glared at him. "Yeah, you did, asshole! A little warning next time, eh?"

"My bad." Gavino appraised her like he wanted to devour her whole. "You look cute."

Callie blushed under his perusal.

Not wanting to slice the sexual tension but also wanting to help escalate this, I inserted in a sly manner, "We were just talking about who we'll get paired with tonight."

Although Callie and I would make a wonderful team, I sincerely wished, like any good bestie, that she and Gavino got paired together. They were definitely into each other, but neither of them had the courage to make the first move. Perhaps tonight they'd get some action. It wasn't uncommon for Initiators to abandon the competition and hook up with their teammate, especially if it was someone they'd been crushing on for the longest time.

Pressing his forearm on the locker above Callie's head, Gavino closed into her personal space and said suggestively, "Is that so? Maybe you and I will end up together."

My eyes widened, shocked at his forwardness and double meaning. But also applauding him for it because *fina-fucking-lly.*

"Y-Yeah," Callie stammered, blushing harder than ever. "Maybe."

Biting my proud mama smile, I angled away from them to give them privacy to flirt.

Meanwhile, my eyes swept over the darkness in the foyer, broken up by the wedges of light emanating from our torches, the caliginous sky visible from decades-old windows, and shadowy figures housing the familiar faces of those I had not spoken to since the summer.

I'd been so wrapped up in my world of hurt that once university started, I lost touch with a lot of my so-called friends. I didn't mourn those lost connections. Not when I had more important matters to tend to.

I waved at a few of them with borderline ersatz smiles. Sometimes it was tedious maintaining a perfect, happy façade before others.

But a real smile split my lips when I saw a group of young cheerleaders dressed like The Hex Girls, taking selfies, as a handful of boys from the hockey team whistled and showered them with compliments.

Despite my love for Halloween, I didn't wear a costume tonight. Instead, I opted for an all-black outfit. Ankle high-heeled boots, high-waisted skinny jeans, cropped leather jacket with a white painted skull on the back, small crossbody bag with necessities, and an orange knit bralette—my sole pop of colour.

Just to be safe, I pocketed my signature black ski mask.

If Initiation Night went south, there was no way in hell I was risking getting caught, much less recognized. My parents would punish me by revoking my car rights, taking away my credit cards, and turning me into an example for my little brother Emilio. Basically, my life would become hell.

It didn't matter that I was nineteen.

In my parents' eyes, I remained a little girl forever.

Hearing a familiar girlish laugh, my attention drew to Darla, who tossed her long raven hair behind her shoulders with a beauty queen smile while a freshman cheerleader spoke to her in an animated fashion.

Darla looked tired, but similar to me, she was trained from a young age to always be sweet and attentive in public. Never allowing the outside world to really see how you're feeling. Never allowing anyone to see the real *you*. It was one of the many woes of being a high society daughter.

Knowing Darla, right this moment, she probably wanted to be curled up in bed with a romance novel and a sugary treat, reading about Prince Charming and happily ever afters.

Without breaking her conversation, Darla's head tilted my way, feeling my gaze on her. Giving me a once-over, she quickly dismissed me as though I was a mere fly on the wall. An inconvenience. Absolutely irrelevant.

It stung more than I'd like to admit. I lost Cade and Darla—two of my pillars—during the summer. Him, for obvious reasons and her, for reasons I still couldn't fathom.

Due to our mothers running in the same circle, Darla and I met when we were three years old, bonded over Fruit Fantasy Barbies, and instantly became best friends. All my prominent childhood and teenagehood memories were tied with this girl, who'd been like the sister I never had.

Somewhere in the last few months, Darla decided she hated me.

She now treated me like her enemy. It was heartbreaking to see such an amazing friendship crumble to nothing. We knew each other before Callie became part of our group in fourth grade. I once asked the latter if she knew why Darla was acting the way she was, but Callie claimed that Darla no longer spoke to her either…

I never figured out what went wrong between Darla and me, and my ex-best friend refused to speak up.

I tried to mend our bond in the beginning until I realized you couldn't fix something you never broke. I was sad such a wholesome friendship ended like this, but I was done extending an olive branch.

Shaun wrapped an arm around Darla's shoulders and whispered something in her ear. She nodded in return. They were getting ready to make their announcement.

This year, Darla and Shaun were the ringleaders. Tradition called for both alumni captains on either teams to lead the night. Since I wanted to actively participate in tonight's game, I let her run the show with Shaun.

Finally, Darla faced the crowd and cupped her hands around her mouth like a makeshift speakerphone and yelled, "Welcome to St. Victoria's thirty-fifth annual Initiation Night!"

The foyer rang with loud cheers and boisterous claps.

"We are ecstatic to have everyone here tonight!" Darla said loudly over the crowd's noise. "As most of you know, Initiation Night was formed decades ago by our predecessors and every year this tradition serves to initiate the newest members of our team into the roster. To belong here, you must embody trust and loyalty. Initiation Night is a test of your character. You will demonstrate *trust* by working with your teammate to accomplish every dare and you will exemplify *loyalty* by never speaking to an outsider about this night. Each and every single one of you was chosen for a specific reason: you were deemed worthy. Now it's up to you to prove that you deserve to be one of *us*."

Shaun picked up where Darla left off, his booming voice carrying through the horde. Newcomers listened with rapt attention while people like Callie and me, who'd done this many times, impatiently waited for the game to begin. "Now for the rules. They are simple. One, no phones permitted. Nothing about this night can be documented. Two, no fighting. This is self-explanatory. Three, you are not allowed to break anything on campus. Everything must be left how you found it: in complete fucking pristine condition. The last thing we want is outsiders to piece together what happened tonight. Those who've failed to comply with our rules in the past have been penalized and punished in various ways. Don't force us to make an example out of you.

"As for pranks, anything that isn't physical or involves breaking shit on campus is fair game." Shaun's blue eyes met mine knowingly.

Shaun was what you'd classify as a class clown with a heart of gold. We had a love and hate relationship, but I truly adored him. The last few years of high school were packed with us pulling pranks on each other.

I shook my head at him and mouthed, "Don't even think about it."

If he messed around with my chances of winning Initiation Night, I'd smash the windows of his brand-new Rolls Royce.

Shaun gave me a teasing wink in reply and Darla continued their rehearsed speech.

"Tickets to Montardor's Ravens' hockey game, two crowns, and your name forever immortalized in the Black Book of Initiation," she bellowed. "Those are what await our winners. Once the initiation starts, you must see it through. The first ones to finish all their dares win. If you decide to forfeit in the middle of the game, you get kicked off your respective teams. We have no place for quitters here."

Shocked gasps and murmurs rose around us.

I always thought kicking people off the cheerleading and hockey teams was a bit extreme. But Darla and Shaun insisted we stick with the rules set by our predecessors. In the past, the hockey players had easily influenced Coach Ryan to remove someone off the team. Pure talent wouldn't keep you on the roster. Not when you didn't obey St. Victoria's elites.

Essentially, Initiation Night was sacred to us, the same way enchiladas were sacred to my *mamá*.

"One last thing. Although this has never happened in the history of Initiation Night, if, for whatever reason, the cops show up...run like hell. Try not to get caught. And should you get caught, you will not breathe a word about what transpired tonight or say the names of those involved," Shaun added sternly. "Have I made myself clear?"

Low echoes of *yeses* rang in our circle.

I glanced around and instantly froze, spotting a familiar figure amongst the group of hockey players huddled close to Shaun.

Was it really *him*?

My eyes must be playing tricks.

Cade would never show up willingly to Initiation Night.

And it wouldn't be the first time my traitorous mind conjured up the image of the boy who broke my heart. The one who still held its tattered pieces in his rough palms.

Excitement and fear bubbled in the pit of my stomach. Conflicting feelings were the norm when it came to thoughts of my ex-boyfriend.

I wanted nothing to do with him...yet a small masochistic part of me *did* want to see him in the flesh.

I forced myself to listen to the rest of the instructions, but all my mind kept chanting was *Cade, Cade, Cade.*

"Remember, this isn't just a competition." Shaun gazed around the circle conspiratorially, his flashlight flickering. "This is a chance to prove yourself worthy of your team and to have a fucking good time!"

Students roared their glee to the rafters, the noise parallel to a crowd in the coliseum.

Initiators pounded their fists against the row of lockers, creating a beat that mimicked the loud bass at a club. It skyrocketed my own excitement.

I loved Initiation Night. Something about it appealed to the adrenaline junkie inside of me. Other high schools were notorious for taking hazing way too far, but we toed between the line of safe and completely insane.

One thing I could do without was the tenebrosity looming over the campus. The lights out at St. Victoria would freak out even the seasoned horror movie loving fiend. It felt like Sister Victoria's ghost would make an appearance any second.

There was a rumour that Cassidy Johansson, a sophomore in the chess club, fainted last year when she stayed back to clean the crypt during detention. Apparently, she saw Sister Victoria glaring at her from her resting place.

Not a lot scared me, but a one-hundred-plus-year-old ghost roaming the halls of the institute in her habit did. It was said that Sister Victoria and twelve other nuns died in an unforeseen fire, their skeletons buried in the crypt below us.

Apparently, if you paid close attention, you could hear their screams till this day.

Darla asked all the Initiators to leave their phones with Shaun, who held out a brown tote. Everyone lined up to deposit their devices, including Callie, Gavino, and me.

My eyes chased one person after another to confirm if what I'd seen before was a mirage or really Cade. There were many hockey players present…though none of them were him.

Standing behind me, Callie murmured in my ear, "Don't look now, but Darla's glaring at you."

My hackles rose. I waited a few seconds before my eyes flicked over to Darla.

True enough, my ex-best friend glared in my direction.

Seriously, what's her problem? Won't speak to me anymore, yet still shoots me daggers with her eyes…

Once all the phones were deposited in the bag, Darla walked around with a chalice filled with red paint. She dipped in her fingers and smeared them along the back of our hands, branding us with the customary mark of the hellhound—the Devil's very own print. It was something we'd always done since the dawn of Initiation Night, but no one knew the exact reason for it.

When she got to me, I extended my fist with an apathetic look.

"Do you pledge your allegiance?" she demanded blankly.

My jaw tightened. "Yes."

Cold, brown gaze fixed on me, she scraped the back of my hand with three fingernails. Luckily, she didn't break any skin. Didn't mean I was going to let her get away with it.

I snagged her own hand and smeared my mark over the back of hers. "Oopsies."

She bristled but didn't say anything, moving on to the next person.

Then Shaun and another player brought forth last season's hockey championship trophy like it was the Holy Grail. The golden cup brimmed with folded pieces of paper housing the first round of dares and our team numbers.

I plucked one when it was my turn, and Shaun canted his head to get a better look. "What did you get?"

I unfolded the piece of paper and read it.

Team number: 6
The key resides in the land of fiction.

"Huh. That's quite interesting," Shaun mumbled cryptically.

I frowned. "What's that supposed to mean?"

Shaun quickly moved on to the next person without replying.

The low whir of conversation started once again as people matched with their partners. Callie and Gavino let loose surprised chuckles. By some twist of fate, they actually got paired together.

I walked around the foyer aimlessly, trying to find my partner without avail. So far everyone said *no* when I asked them, "Are you team number six?"

"You have three hours to complete the game," Darla hollered. "Shaun and I will be waiting right here for the winners."

Every year, we got away with Initiation Night because Darla's mom—Diane Hill—was the principal and St. Victoria was the legacy of the Hill women. They practically ruled and owned this establishment since its conversion from motherhouse to high school. Principal Hill willingly chose to turn a blind eye every year during the weekend of Initiation Night. As far as I knew, she had also participated in this tradition during her younger days.

By 3:00 a.m., Initiation Night would be complete. Everything would resume as normal once the weekend was over. No traces of the shenanigans that went on tonight come Monday morning.

Shaun blew a whistle with his fingers. "Good luck!"

Bodies scampered around, jostling my frame until I was pushed against the lockers. The pitter-patter of footsteps echoed as people broke away to start their dares.

Everyone was in pairs, except for me.

"Um, I don't have a partner," I drawled, confused.

Gavino and Callie blinked at me. My best friend rubbed my shoulder in comfort and glanced at Darla and Shaun. "How is it possible that Ella has no one?"

Darla ignored us and pretended to busy herself with her phone.

Shaun folded his palms over his cane, shrugging his shoulders almost comically under that ridiculous plague doctor costume. Even in the dark, I felt as though he were watching me with a calculating look. "All forty-two of you were paired. Twenty-one teams. Maybe your partner got a head start?"

"Without me?" I hedged, surprised at my teammate's audacity if that were really the case.

The ex-captain of the Rangers said slyly, "You never know. Maybe they saw your face, got scared, and ran away."

I narrowed my eyes at his shitty sense of humour. "Wow. Thanks, Shaun."

"You're welcome."

"We're going to get started." Callie added sympathetically, "You'll be fine, Ella. Don't worry."

I was a little peeved to be in this predicament, but at this rate, I'd just have to get started alone.

I gave them what I hoped was an encouraging smile. "All right. Good luck, guys."

Not that they'd need it since I'd be winning Initiation Night.

With or without my partner.

Callie and Gavino ran away with quick waves, murmuring about their dare, while Shaun's eyes drilled into mine. "You got this, Ella."

Sighing, I headed down the hallway and shone my flashlight over my first dare again.

The key resides in the land of fiction.

I only had to ponder for a few more seconds before it clicked in my mind.

Then I ran headlong for the library on the second floor.

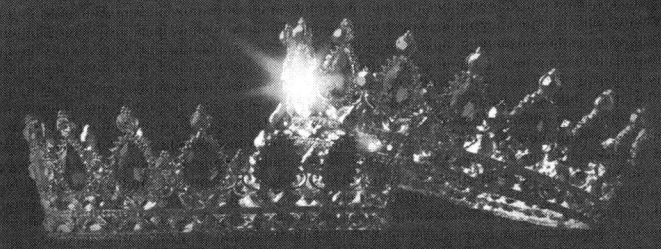

CHAPTER 5

Just You And I In This Hellhole

CADE

The Present
12:02 a.m.

I got paired with my ex-girlfriend for Initiation Night.

As it so happened, the universe was finally working in my favour.

Or, at the very least, Shaun was. When the first round of dares was being distributed, he peeked at mine, ripped it from my hands, and swapped it with Jamie Callahan, a junior on the hockey team, who was team number six.

"Thank me later," Shaun had said.

This was the *favour* he was talking about.

And I was not complaining one bit.

When I snuck into St. Victoria with all the boys from the hockey team, I made sure to stay in the shadows. I was afraid if Ella spotted me, she'd get out of dodge before I had the chance to be near her, speak with her, fucking breathe the same air as her.

My chest tightened with a twinge when I traced her silhouette by the row of lockers. Excitement slowly veined over her visage as she perused the crowd with the confidence of a girl who'd only ever stood on a pedestal.

God, she was beautiful as ever.

My memories didn't do her justice.

That modelesque body was poured in tight, high-waisted, black jeans that looked painted on her skin, a cropped black leather jacket that emphasized her badass allure, and her palm-sized tits were covered in a triangular-shaped orange bralette that was sexy and indecent. Even standing from afar, she got me so fucking hot. Not to mention, Ella's black mane was now chopped into a straight line just above her shoulders, showcasing that slender neck that used to be layered with my love bites and teeth marks.

During our three-year relationship, Ella usually wore her luscious waves down to her waist. I'd been obsessed with her hair. Running my fingers through it when she lay her head on my stomach. Washing it thoroughly when we showered together. Fisting it as I fucked her from behind like a dirty little princess.

But I didn't mourn the length of it. Not when she looked *that* good with her new cut. I was already fantasizing running my fingers over her nape and testing the short strands against my strength.

When everyone broke off to find their partners and Ella said she was looking for number six, I bowed out before she could find me. It might seem like a cowardly move, but I needed to buy some time to mentally prepare myself for the storm that was my ex-girlfriend.

She wouldn't be happy with our pairing. I was banking on her throwing a fit. Anger meant emotions and anything was better than the indifferent front she'd assumed whenever we ran into each other. Montardor was a big city, but the elite society ran in the same circles, including our families. I saw Ella a handful of times throughout the summer because of galas, family dinners, Olivia and Emilio's playdates, and so on.

Glimpsing her usually came with a mixture of joy and hurt.

But I didn't care as long as I saw *her*.

Now I waited for the little heartbreaker inside the library, leaning against the wall beside the ancient double doors, my arms folded across my chest.

On cue, I heard the familiar click-clack of her high-heeled boots entering the hallway of the north wing. The sound caused my blood to pump faster.

Ella's pace slowed as she reached the doors—which I purposely left ajar to catch her off-guard—and after a few seconds, she shoved them open and sauntered into the dark library like she owned the place.

The doors swung back and clicked shut.

Ella was a few steps inside when I snagged her wrist from behind, pulled her back into my front, and swiftly turned us around until we were pressed against the wall.

She screamed bloody murder. "Holy—"

I covered her mouth with my palm to muffle the sound, letting the warm metal of my silver rings graze her glossy lips.

Her scent—orange blossoms and jasmines—shot through my system like an aphrodisiac. Ella was my very own walking, talking drug. One inhale and the addict prancing inside me felt satisfied after weeks of need.

My lips journeyed to her right ear, brushing the gold hoops. "Guess who, princess?"

I relished the shiver cascading down her back as realization sank into her bones. She straightened with awareness in my hold and I barely contained my smirk. When I knew for certain she wouldn't scream again, I dropped my hand to her neck, my body keeping hers plastered to the hard surface.

A flash of disappointment hit me. She wasn't wearing the necklace I gave her. Knowing Ella's temper, she probably incinerated it with a flamethrower.

"*Cade*," she spat my name like a curse.

I nearly groaned from how perfect it sounded on her tongue.

"Surprise, surprise," I taunted, brushing two fingers over her pulse to feel it *thump, thump, thump*. "Missed me, baby?"

Ella shoved her elbow into my rib with vicious strength. I stumbled back with a breathless, "Fuck."

Pain—because shit, that hurt—and pride—because I'd taught her how to fight—unfurled within me. I would have praised her if the circumstances were different.

Ella whirled around, thrust me against the wall, and dug her forearm into my throat.

In a silent threat, she pressed her limb harder against my jugular. Just enough to drive her point across: she didn't appreciate me sneaking up on her.

"You asshole." She seethed, eyes burning with intensity. "What are you doing here?"

Starved, my eyes desperately ate up the sight of her. It wasn't enough. It would never be enough. My hands flexed by my sides. Wanting so badly to grab her. Wanting so badly to crush her to my chest and beg her, once and for all, to never let me go.

Instead, I grinned smugly and chucked her under the chin. "Don't you know?" My voice was strained. "Initiation Night is my favourite holiday of the year."

"Liar," she fumed, her elbow creating a divot in my skin. "Answer me. What. Are. You. Doing. Here?"

I decided to go with the truth, lest risk suffering asphyxiation. Although dying by the hands of the love of my life may not be the worst way to go. "I wanted to see you, Ellie."

You'd think the nickname drove into her like a stake with the way she dropped her arm and staggered back in shock.

Ella composed herself within seconds. "Well, you wasted a trip," she sneered. "I don't want to see your face ever again. I thought I made myself abundantly clear the first time."

The searing insult burned, no less hurtful than all the jabs she'd hurled my way in the span of three months. But I expected it. Accepted it. I would take this version of her over the insouciant one any day.

"Tough shit. You'll be seeing my face a lot for the next three hours, so better get used to it."

She barked a humourless chuckle and retreated another two steps. "Yeah, that's not happening. I'd rather stab myself in the eye with a pencil than be in your presence."

"You always wished we'd get paired for Initiation Night." I smirked despite the ache spreading through me like poison. I couldn't stand the look of revulsion on her face as she glared at me. "Now's our chance, Ella."

"That was before I found out you had a community dick, you piece of shit."

My nostrils flared and my smirk fell, her words lashing my insides like a whip.

Ella thought I cheated on her during Josh's nineteenth birthday party this summer.

I never fucking did.

I'd sooner drive my erection through a meat grinder than ever betray her.

When I tried to explain to Ella what happened, she didn't listen to me. In lieu, she barred the gates of her heart, banished me to the purgatory, and doled out her retributions via cruel insults.

For something that was completely out of my control months ago.

"Still obsessed with my dick, I see," I mocked. "Let me guess, you want another ride, sweetheart?"

"I wouldn't fuck you if you were the last guy on earth."

If given the opportunity, my ex-girlfriend would probably gouge my balls with her witchy claws and feed them to Francisco Cordova's guard dogs.

Since it was her broken heart speaking, I let her statement slide. "Keep telling yourself that, Ella."

"God, you're so arrogant. I really fucking hate you."

That one hurt the most.

No matter how much pain she inflicted upon me, I didn't hate her.

Even now, with all the bad blood between us, I loved this girl more than my own life.

Our love had been like a two-sided coin. Dark and thorned. Beautiful and transcending. We'd been young, all-consumed, and everything to one another. There were no secrets, no judgements, no qualms in our bond. Without a shadow's doubt, in my next life, I would find her until our destinies intertwined once again.

She was mine for all lifetimes to come and I was irrevocably hers.

We were fated.

Though there were times where I cursed the day I laid eyes on her. By falling in love with Ella, I unknowingly gave her power over my being.

In front of the world, I was indestructible. But in her palms, I was malleable—she could mold me, break me, mend me all in one stroke.

I was clay and she was the creator with the ability to breathe life into me.

The first two weeks after our breakup, I felt like a shell of a man. I could barely eat, sleep, or function. My body was in a state of utter numbness. As though I'd physically lost a part of me and was just learning how to cope without it. Nothing compared to the torment of heartbreak.

It took me a very long time to put my pieces back in a semblance of my once whole.

I was bruised but patched up and ready for another chance to explain my truth…If she would let me.

"Who's the liar now, Ella?" I threw back, wanting her to fucking eat her words.

She may not admit it now, but our feelings ran deep. Ella, regardless of her spiteful words, still felt something for me. Even if it throbbed faintly in her heart.

It was still there.

In the way she watched me, with a mixture of forlorn and determined wrath, whenever we chanced upon each other. In the way her pulse sped up whenever I was near. In the way her eyes drew to my mouth, helplessly, like a moth to a flame.

On the outside, she could pretend to hate me.

But on the inside, I knew some part of her still wanted me.

Ella marched over to the closed library doors. "I can't do this with you right now." She held her flashlight with her left hand, while her right hand struggled with the olden handles. "*Joder mi vida.* C'mon, c'mon. Open up!"

Sick perversion rolled through me at the thought of us being stuck together. I had an inkling that the library doors were locked, unless we found the key to get us out. This was all part of the game.

"It's no use," I said, crossing over to her.

Ella started pounding her fists against the doors, hoping someone would hear the commotion. "Goddammit, this can't be happening right now!"

"You're trapped with me, Ella." I closed the distance between us until my front and her back were a hairsbreadth away. Bringing my mouth to her ear, I whispered darkly, "Looks like it's just you and I in this hellhole, sweetheart."

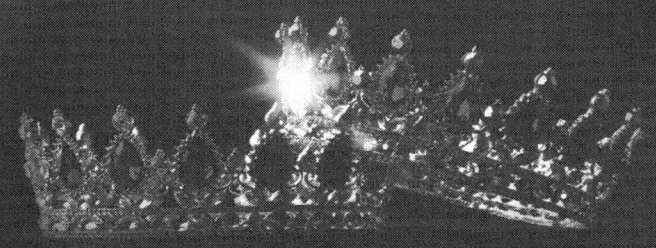

CHAPTER 6

Kill For You

Ella

The Present
12:07 a.m.

The universe was goading me, rubbing salt in my wounds and refusing to give me the reprieve I'd begged for—the one I, respectfully, *earned*.

Of all the possible outcomes, this one I had not anticipated. Getting paired with my ex-boyfriend for Initiation Night? Plot fucking twist. And not the good kind.

It suddenly made sense why I couldn't find my teammate in the foyer. Cade must have heard me calling for team six and decided to get a head start. He knew if I realized we were partnered, I would have run from St. Victoria like a bat out of hell.

"We are not trapped. This is all part of the game," I said through gritted teeth, feeling Cade's breath stir the short strands of my hair, warming the flesh of my collarbone in a manner far too intimate for exes who were broken beyond repair.

"Mm. You don't say." That deep voice, laced with unmistakable hunger, had another involuntary shiver running through my spine. "Do you want to play with me, Ella?"

Goddamn him.

51

Cade was fighting dirty.

Since our breakup, it was clear he wanted me back and would do everything in his power to achieve that goal. Including throwing our past in my face to remind me of how good we once had it.

Do you want to play with me, Ella?

There was nothing innocent about the request. It was a sentence he'd used many times in the past when we were acting out our filthiest fantasies, right before he brought us to sweet oblivion.

I hated what those words did to my body. The goosebumps on my skin. The tingles running from the top of my head to the tips of my toes. The heat simmering in my core.

And I hated the way Cade crowded me with his close proximity. I used to love it when he overpowered me with his strength when we fucked. There was nothing like being gagged, handcuffed, and clutched by him as I rode him like a rodeo.

Obviously, he remembered this and was using it to his advantage. *Asshole.*

"No, I don't want to play with you," I snarled and spun around in his caging hold to face him. "Get that through your thick skull."

"You afraid of being alone with me, princess?" he egged on, the bravado in his tone feeling false and…forced. "I thought you'd do anything to be Queen of Initiation Night, especially if it meant making history."

Fuck.

Cade knew I was hell-bent on breaking the record since last year.

Now he really had me cornered. If I backed out now, I'd be perceived as pathetic because I wasn't able to suffer through three hours for the sake of winning my prize.

And I never backed down from a challenge.

My Cordova pride—the Leo in me—would not allow it.

"I'm not afraid of anything, Cade," I retorted with a scoff. "Least of all you."

His lips curved into a half-smirk. "Prove it, Ella."

Beyond the walls of St. Victoria, a torrential downpour began, crashing against the windowpanes with a ferocity that mimicked my inner turmoil. I jolted when lightning and thunder joined the cacophony.

The fulminating moment illuminated the inside of the library for a mere second and it was enough for me to *finally* glimpse Cade.

With a muscular body carved from the finest chisel, a handsome face housing sky blue eyes, an aristocratic nose, a jawline that could cut, sensuous lips harbouring an arrogant tilt, and dark brown hair that was longer on the top and cropped shorter on the sides, he resembled a young god descendant from the heavens. Divine, in a way mere mortals could not comprehend. Magnificent, in a way only an artist's gaze could appreciate.

As a lover of arts, I used to wish I'd been blessed with the ability to paint visages so I could capture his splendour on a canvas.

Cade Killian Remington, my dark prince, was perfection personified.

From the moment I first laid eyes on him, he'd taken my breath away. Three years later, my foolish heart still bloomed in the presence of its beloved.

Tonight, he wore all-black like me. Black boots, black jeans, black hoodie, black leather jacket. Also like me, I knew his black ski mask was somewhere on his person.

For a fleeting minute, I forgot about all the hurt he caused. All I could think about was how my emotive yearning, despite my pain, was finally sated after weeks of not seeing him.

I wished I didn't feel this way, but the heart wanted what it wanted.

"Fine," I snapped. "Let's get this over with as fast as we can so I don't have to see your face again."

Fat chance of that happening when we attended the same university. For the most part, I managed to successfully avoid him on campus. Unfortunately, it was only a matter of time before we crossed paths once more.

My statement had the desired effect on Cade. His smirk dropped and I internally cheered. Since he chose to stay, I assumed he was willing to put up with all the venom I'd spew his way.

Truth be told, I didn't always have a fiery temper and Cade wasn't necessarily a glutton for punishment. But our breakup fundamentally changed us in ways that twisted our dynamics into something ugly and a little fatal.

"Did you decipher the riddle?" he asked in a cavalier manner, but the anger in his undertone apprised that my words hurt him.

"*The key resides in the land of fiction,*" I repeated like he was daft. "The land of fiction meaning the library, which we are currently standing inside. Obviously, you and I both figured that out, otherwise we would not be here. And, since there were no other clues, the key, which we are looking for, could be just about anywhere at this rate."

"I could do without your smart mouth, Ella." His eyes narrowed. "Since you're running it anyways, tell me, where should we start searching?"

I almost made an inappropriate comment like '*Didn't hear you complaining about my mouth when I was screaming your name the last time we fucked,*' but stopped myself from letting that slip. Anything regarding our sex life and past was better left unsaid.

"I'll work my way through the book aisles. Why don't you check the common area? Maybe there's a key hidden by the study tables."

Not waiting for his response, I side-stepped him and walked deeper into the library so I could finally inhale air that wasn't tainted by his cologne. His scent was my kryptonite. Cedarwood, musk, leather, and something utterly masculine that drove me crazy.

I used to love burying my face in his neck when we lay together just to get a whiff. And when we made love, there was nothing like the taste of his fragrant skin on my tongue.

"*You're insatiable, sweetheart,*" he'd murmur while thrusting savagely inside of my pussy, my legs wrapped around his waist, my mouth latched onto his neck. Sucking. Licking. Nibbling. Begging for more, more, more.

The cadence of my breathing increased as I failed to eradicate memories of Cade from my mind. This was not the time or place to be reminiscing. Nor could I afford to get horny around Cade when he'd been the only guy to slake my hearty sexual appetite.

There were days where I felt haunted by a relationship I feared I'd never get over.

Would the pain ever lessen? Would I ever heal? Would I ever get over him?

Don't think about the past until you're finished with Initiation Night, Ella. You don't have the strength to revisit it right now.

In an attempt to distract myself, I veered straight into the book aisles to begin my search for the key, as far away as possible from Cade.

St. Victoria's library was an uncanny wonder. Once monastic, its style was a mix between gothic and baroque, featuring dark walls and bookshelves, gold ornate molding, deep alcoves, crystal chandeliers, stained glass windows depicting roses and faith, and a restored painting on the high ceiling, displaying renaissance-inspired art. It was breathtaking, one of the oldest structures in the institute, and there was something holy about it, despite the blasphemous rumours haunting this place.

I began perusing the mystery aisle. I had a hunch the key was wedged between a book—yes, that's why I sent Cade to the common area because the petty side of me wanted to be the one to find the key—so I used my flashlight to illuminate the weathered spines, while ignoring the way my ex-boyfriend cursed in the background as he overturned tables and chairs in his search.

Minutes later, when I sieved through the romance aisle and made a mental note of the books I wanted to add to my to-be-read list, Cade's voice intoned behind me, "There's no key in the common area."

"*Fuck!*" Caught off guard, I whirled around and my body collided into him. Cade steadied me with hands on my hips. "You trying to scare me or something?"

He smiled darkly. "Wouldn't dream of it, Ella."

Bastard. He was teasing me since I enjoyed role-playing those kinds of scenarios. The ones where he pretended to scare me and then fuck my pussy seven ways to Sunday while praising me for being his dirty little princess. *With* his ski mask on. And yes, it was hot as hell and orgasm inducing. I had a kink and wasn't ashamed of it.

I was about to reply with a sassy retort when my hip brushed against his stomach and I felt something poking me. *You've got to be kidding me.* "Uh, want to explain to me why you're hard right now?"

He arched an eyebrow when I aimed my flashlight at his face. "I'm not hard, sweetheart. That's my gun."

"You brought a fucking gun to Initiation Night?" I deadpanned.

He chuckled. "Have you forgotten who my dad is?"

Touché.

Vance Remington was a renowned mobster in the underworld, ruling South Side, Montardor for the last two decades. The Remingtons had a long history of being criminals, their pockets fueled from their art and drug empire…as well as other shady dealings. I used to teasingly call Cade my gangster, but as far as the public was concerned, the Remingtons were strait-laced 'businessmen.'

Vance insisted Cade always carry a weapon whenever we stepped out. However, I hadn't expected him to bring one tonight. There was no danger here, unless you counted the Initiators who liked to occasionally pull pranks.

"Fair enough." I palmed my forehead. "Just don't accidentally shoot anything, okay?" He gave me a blank look and I almost cracked a smile. For all his flaws, he wasn't irrational. Meaning he wouldn't engage in a shootout just 'cause some Initiator decided to fuck with him. "Keep looking. It's got to be here somewhere."

I turned around and continued sifting through rows of books.

Shuffling footsteps indicated that Cade crossed over to the shelves opposite mine.

The crashing rain acted as a background orchestra as we searched relentlessly. Darla was big on reading and writing romance. Therefore, I was ninety-nine percent sure the key would be hidden somewhere between *Pride & Prejudice* or *Twilight*.

But alas, it wasn't there.

"This is impossible," I muttered. We were in the library for almost twenty minutes and I was getting nervous about the other dares awaiting us. We should have found the next one already. Especially if we wanted to stay on track.

Last year, I crushed the first dare in ten minutes flat.

If we didn't find the key fast, we'd be here forever. And that was not an option. You couldn't win this competition by being stuck on the same dare all night long.

Another worrisome thought skipped in. *What if we never make it past this level?*

"Say the word and I'll shoot the locks to get us out of here."

"That's not going to help us find the second dare. And as per the rules, we are not allowed to damage anything on school property."

Cade crossed his arms and rested back against the shelves. "Since when have you cared for the rules, princess?"

I paused, my jaw clenching.

Nobody suspected that underneath my good girl façade was a hellraiser. I'd always been a bit rebellious behind closed doors and dating Cade amplified that side of mine.

He was the calm to my storm, the smoke to my fire, and the other half of my soul.

His comment was a prominent reminder that he was the only one to have known me in that way. I hated it. And sometimes, I wished I could truly hate him too.

"Since *now*. A lot has changed after we broke up. I'm not the same girl you once knew." Shaking my head, I cast him a meaningful look and sauntered down the aisle. "I've grown. Met new people. Expanded my horizons."

Footsteps followed after me. "What did you say?"

"You heard me."

"*Who* did you meet, Ella?" he demanded, his deep voice desperate and rough.

The tormented quality of his words had me turning around, brows knitted in confusion. "What—"

Bright lightning and a clap of thunder interrupted me.

The jarring stroke of Mother Nature's wrath lit up the inside of the library and in that small fraction of time, I caught Cade's face twisting with anguish. "Who else...after me?"

I was rendered speechless by the realization that his hurt stemmed from the fact that he thought I was talking about *other* men.

Clearly, Cade was recounting that summer night a few weeks ago where we ran into each other at the bar. I'd put on a great show for him.

I should let him believe that's what changed. The number of men I've taken to my bed. But the truth was I couldn't bear the touch of anyone except for Cade. And I despised myself for it.

Healing happened in stages. Parts of me were patched up enough to go about my day-to-day, though I was nowhere near ready to take on another lover. My soul still lived in the plane where *we* once thrived—a place where Cade and I spent years decorating a future that would no longer see fruition.

And it was all his fucking fault.

I couldn't believe he had the audacity to appear heartbroken at me moving on.

"I don't owe you any answers, Cade. Not after you ruined us and betrayed me."

He flinched.

My statement struck a chord.

I'd never convey this to Cade, but what had actually changed were the scars on my heart. They morphed me into this new version, forcing me to face the music and grow up in the span of three months from the teenager who put trivial things on a pedestal to a young adult who understood the consequences and weight of her actions.

Taking advantage of Cade's momentary silence, I darted out of the romance section and into the horror aisle.

Behind me, Cade's angry strides echoed as he asked raggedly, "Did you fuck that bastard from the bar to spite me after I beat his ass?"

My finger skimming over the hardbound copy of *Dracula*, I glanced at him over my shoulder. Acting blasé while visceral agony cascaded over his features. He was getting all verklempt over the thought of me sleeping with another guy. Like the thought of it was so excruciating, he couldn't withstand it.

Good. Feel pain. Feel what you fucking put me through when I caught you with that other girl.

"What if I did fuck him?" I returned wickedly. "What are you going to do about it, gangster?"

I hadn't fucked the guy from the bar, but he didn't need to know that.

A cold, lethal smirk carved over Cade's face.

He closed the distance between us in three steps, backing my body into the shelf. His hand reached out to cup my jaw and his thumb stroked my cheek in a loving manner.

"I'm going to track him down and chop him to pieces," he rasped so softly, it barely sounded like a threat. "Then I'll deliver his head to you on a silver platter, Ella. You'd like that, wouldn't you? My little bloodthirsty princess."

My breath hitched from the admission. It appeased my darker side. The one that loved it when Cade got revenge on people who mistreated me.

There was something exhilarating about a morally grey man who protected you and worshipped the ground you walked on.

White knights did not hold a candle to my dark prince.

Cade Killian Remington was the only one I had ever wanted. My dangerous addiction. My favourite sin. And *mi alma gemela*. I feared, in this lifetime, I was wretchedly cursed to always long for him.

Before I could throw an insulting remark, my gaze drifted over to a faint glimmer at the base of his throat.

A heady buzz rushed through my veins—part euphoria, part swivet—at the unexpected sight of a gold band threaded through a thin chain, looped around his neck like an inseparable keepsake.

It was the promise ring I gifted to him on his eighteenth birthday.

The one that marked him infinitely as mine.

He still wore it.

I nearly swayed, my knees feeling weak.

Cade dragged his knuckles under my chin, tipping it up to meet his inquisitive gaze. "Ella?"

The cuff of his black hoodie caught my eyes.

My heart twisted inside my rib cage.

EXC was stitched in gold threading like a mark of ownership.

It was no secret that I'd been a territorial girlfriend during our relationship. To the point where I sewed my initials on all of Cade's clothes. And he, in return, loved it, watching me warmly as I went about branding him as mine.

Why has he not gotten rid of all the hoodies etched with my print? Why is he still wearing my ring? Why, why, why…

My mind spun as conflicting emotions waged a war inside of me. Hurt from his betrayal. Indignation, from the casual way he carried the emblems of my love after ripping me apart. Satisfaction, from the fact that after all this time, I never stopped owning him.

Cade made a mistake and he still wanted, still cared, still felt *everything* for me.

The evidence was right before my eyes.

And he saw first-hand what it did to me, if the glimmer of hope flaring in his blue eyes was any indication.

Mustering the strength to replace my cracked armour, I steeled myself and slapped his hand away. "Get over yourself. I can fuck whoever I want without you threatening bodily harm. Mind your fucking business, Cade."

"You are my business," he grated, snatching my hand when I tried to walk away. "You'll *always* be my business. No one—no *fucking* one—will ever lay their hands on you in disrespect. I'll put a bullet through the skull of anyone who hurts you, Ella."

Cade promising to keep me safe and defend my honour, despite us not being together, messed with my head while simultaneously causing my heart to soar like a thousand doves taking flight. I was a strong, independent woman, but there was something gratifying about a man who swore to protect you from all harm.

One thing was for certain.

This devastatingly beautiful man, who broke my heart, was still crazily obsessed with me.

"Do you hear me?" he repeated softly, squeezing my wrist, his thumb circling over my fast-beating pulse. "I would kill for you, baby."

The darkness of the room, the sound of our breathing, and the sonorous weather laced with romanticism heightened every feeling of love and angst.

I searched his eyes for lies, finding only a mixture of longing, vexation, and adoration.

I would kill for you, baby.

God, that statement was akin to an act of worship to me and I loved it.

My own gaze never wavered from Cade's as I leaned closer, like I was getting ready to kiss him. His Adam's apple coasted up and down in his neck with anticipation.

Then I went for the kill. "I bet you said that to every girl you cheated on me with, huh?"

Cade fell back a step, stunned. I basked in his ache. It satisfied a sadistic facet of my nature that was previously dormant.

I jerked my wrist out of his hold and pivoted away. At the end of the aisle, there was a magazine stand next to the librarian's main desk. My flashlight shone over it and I caught something completely out of place.

Oh, you've got to be kidding me. That's where they hid the key?

I marched over to the stand. It had a selection of tame business and journalism magazines. Sometimes there was the occasional Architectural Digest.

But never had there been a *Hustler* issue sitting smackdab in the middle amongst the rest. It was Shaun's favourite reading material. The pornographic kind.

I plucked it out of the stand and a bronze key fell to the ground. A piece of paper—the second dare—was threaded through the hole in the bow.

Cade materialized out of thin air and grabbed it. Not having seen or heard him move across the aisle, a bolt of surprise struck me, followed by unmissable heat when he stood to his full six-foot-two frame. He uncurled the fingers of my right hand and deposited the key in my palm.

The pads of his fingers grazed over my heart and life lines.

My breath caught in my throat at the softness of the caress.

The walls of the library juddered with the next claps of thunder. Cade's gaze gleamed with an unnamed emotion as it bore into mine. "What does it say?"

I opened the scrunched-up paper to reveal the next dare. Wordlessly, we bent our heads together to stare at it.

East Wing
Balthazar Building

X – XIII – XXI
Sixth Floor
A picture is worth a thousand words...

"Balthazar Building—the dormitories?"

"Yeah, I think so," Cade said quietly. "The roman numerals must be the combination to get inside the building."

Balthazar Building harboured the abandoned dormitories and was linked to the old bell tower, located in the east wing. The building was off-limits and I'd never seen the inside of it. According to rumours, it was the most haunted place in all of St. Victoria.

"How do you know that?"

"I have a hunch. Shaun once mentioned that you need a code to get inside the building."

"Ah." I clicked my tongue. "Makes sense."

"I don't understand the '*A picture is worth a thousand words...*' but we can figure it out once we get there."

"Okay." I tightened my fist around the key. "Let's do this."

Cade swept his hand in front of us almost in a condescending manner. "Ladies first."

Hah. Now he chose to show his ire and not when I made the cheating comment.

I sashayed to the library doors. Inserting the key, I twisted slowly and the lock unlatched with a soft click.

Gracias a Dios, it worked.

I shoved the doors open and gave Cade a condescending smirk of my own. "Gents first."

Without sparing me a glance, he walked ahead with the swagger of a young kingpin, his broad shoulders stiff and his posture on high alert as he scanned the dark hallway for any threats.

And unceremoniously, my eyes caught the back of his black leather jacket.

Where I once painted *Property of Ximena* in stark white.

An old memory flitted into my mind. The day we sat together on a bench in St. Victoria's courtyard. I decided then and there that he would be mine.

That I'd paint, stitch, and brand my name on every inch of his possessions. So everyone who looked at this boy knew he belonged to me.

Back then, we were so young and naive to the future that awaited us.

My throat dried up and my feet stayed rooted on the ground, unable to move as another rush of turbulent emotions slashed me.

I only had one question for him, but no will to utter it.

Why did you ruin us, Cade?

My ex-boyfriend cheated on me.

He broke my heart.

Yet he still wore all the reminders of our relationship…like he still loved me.

CHAPTER 7

Mine

Ella

The Past – 3 years ago

A warm breeze caressed my legs when I stepped out the doors of St. Victoria. The mid-September sky was painted in beautiful hues of gold, pink, and blue as evening fell upon Montardor. I tugged the strap of my purse higher up my shoulder and glanced down at my wristwatch. Seven minutes past six.

I cut cheerleading practice early because there was someone I wanted to see.

Cade Remington.

The boy I met a few weeks ago. The one I couldn't stop thinking about.

I texted him that I wanted to buy more weed, but it was a cheap excuse to see him.

Since the moment I laid eyes on him, a tender feeling ignited in my chest, striking the strings of my heart until my insides reverberated with an elation that had me short of breath.

I was unaccustomed to this feeling—unaccustomed to closing my eyes and seeing blue eyes and dark hair. Tall stature and busted knuckles. Quiet expression and *don't-fuck-with-me* demeanor.

Part of me already knew the truth: I had a crush on Cade.

The other part of me was in denial. I tried to play it cool whenever we crossed paths in the hallways. I did my utmost best not to turn around in my seat during math class and ogle him. I failed, of course.

He fascinated me.

There were so many things about him that I didn't know yet.

So many things I suddenly *needed* to know.

Our first meeting happened in the middle of summer.

Darla, Callie, and I wanted to try smoking weed during our sleepover that weekend, and I heard from an acquaintance that there was a boy who could help. They gave me his number and I texted him.

He replied instantly and suggested a place to meet. I knew nothing about him except that his name was Cade.

According to the rumour mill, he was a young, ambitious gangster working with a local gang to sell illicit substances to the teenagers of South Side.

When we linked up in MacGregor's empty alleyway, a popular Irish pub in Montardor, it was nearing evening. Bathed in the warm sunset glow, he stood against the brick wall, a raised hood partially obscuring his face.

When I approached closer and *really* saw him…I halted in my steps.

Tall, blue eyes, dark brown hair, and regal aura with a lick of danger.

He was handsome in the way of dark fairy tales. Enchanting and mysterious, a prince with an ensnaring, quiet charm. His armour consisted of black clothing from head to toe, but I noticed silver rings sitting at the base of his knuckles in adornment.

My God, I'd never seen someone like him.

I was mesmerized.

Cade spotted me and froze too.

The way he drank in my appearance with parted lips and a blush smattering across his cheeks, he clearly liked what he saw.

A few drops of rain began to drizzle as our gazes twined with one another. The air immediately charged with an invigorating energy. It transformed the lump in my throat to a hundred little butterflies in my stomach.

Why was I feeling this way? What was happening to me—us?

The atmosphere shifted and the wind wrapped around our bodies like an invisible tie holding us together, spellbound in the moment.

Cade was the first to speak, his voice low and a hint raspy, like a gritty sounding lullaby. "It's Ella, right?"

I liked how he enunciated each syllable in my name, caressing it on his tongue as though learning its flavour.

I blushed too. "U-Uh, yes. H-Hi." I was stuttering, tongue-tied. Rarely did I react this way with boys. I was an extrovert, bubbling with confidence and endless chatter. "That's me."

Cade cleared his throat, still staring at me in awe. "How are you?"

"I'm good. You?" When he gazed at me longer than expected, I realized he was probably waiting for me to pay him first. I fumbled with the zipper of my purse, reaching for the cash. "Um, this is for you."

I extended the bills towards him. He eyed them confusedly for two seconds before his lips set in a grim line.

"Right." He reached inside his hoodie pocket for a baggie of weed. "This is yours."

Electricity zinged between us when our palms touched.

I sucked in a sharp breath, feeling off-kilter.

Words ceased to escape us both. I would have given anything to know what was going through his mind. My heart sped up in beats the longer we stared at one another. He looked like he wanted to say something, his gaze warm and curious.

My goodness. He had such precious blue eyes. A girl could gaze into them forever.

I didn't have forever, though. My friends were waiting for me at Marnie's Shack, the retro-themed dessert spot right across the street. I felt my phone vibrating with their incoming text messages.

"Thank you," I finally said with a faint smile. "I should go. I'll text you again when I need more, if that's okay?"

His eyes fell to my lips like he couldn't help himself. "Yeah. Sounds good."

Neither of us moved from our positions. Not even when the rain started pounding harder against the ground, soaking us to the bone.

Was it wishful thinking to assume he didn't want me to leave?

My phone blared with the familiar ringtone of Darla calling. Cade and I both flinched at the sound. I declined and retreated a few steps. "All right, well, see you around."

Stop me. Say something. Give me a reason to stay.

Cade chin-nodded and whispered in what I'd like to believe was a reluctant manner, "See you."

After our goodbyes, I walked away, though I couldn't help but glance over my shoulder. He was watching me, making sure I reached my destination safely.

Later when I was with my friends, I realized I hadn't seen Cade smile. It bothered me more than I'd like.

After that encounter, Cade stayed on my mind for days. I wanted to see him again.

And then it happened. Our second meeting. The one that altered my brain chemistry.

In August, I saw him sitting in my garden while I stood on my balcony, an awestruck expression on his face as he gazed in my direction.

He looked at me like I was the answer to every question he'd ever asked the universe.

The confidence that had been previously missing on our first meeting returned to me tenfold and I winked at him.

Seeing his face morph with a hint of embarrassment at being caught checking me out was extremely cute.

He was cute.

It's like we shared a secret no one else knew. The moment in my garden felt sacred, something solely for us to treasure.

God, I couldn't wait to see Cade now. Couldn't wait to properly exchange words and not just stolen glances across a dining table, across the hallway, across the classroom.

This time I'd use all my charm to coax a smile from him.

Like he'd been summoned by my thoughts, his text arrived within seconds.

I'm sitting on the bench in the courtyard. —Guy who doesn't smile

I'll be there soon  —Ella

I practically ran to where he waited for me.

St. Victoria's courtyards were an arresting sight laid against the old gothic-style institute, possessing gardens filled with roses and towering trees. Students usually sat amongst the lush greenery during recess, but after school, I found the place to be even more soothing. There was no one roaming the grounds.

Except for one person, who sat alone on a bench under the shade of a century old tree. My favourite spot. I liked to come here to knit my latest creation, if I wasn't preoccupied with my friends.

Did Cade see me sitting here often? Was that why he chose this place, knowing I was fond of it?

All these questions ran through my mind as I neared him.

Locked in a pensive state, his head hung low, his elbows rested on his knees, and his joined hands lay suspended between the V of his spread legs. He looked like a prince sitting on his throne, pondering over life's woes.

From the very beginning, Cade never gave the impression of being a young teenager. The frown on his face, the downturn tilt of his lips, and the heaviness in his posture made him seem wiser and older beyond his years. As though he'd seen the darker side of life and never recovered.

If you paid close attention, you'd noticed the haunted quality in his eyes that spoke of a story that was far too complicated for others to understand.

But I wanted to understand.

I wanted to unravel every layer of Cade Remington and learn the things that made him...*him.*

Without warning, I fell into the seat next to him and chirped loudly, "Hi!"

Cade flinched, muttering a curse under his breath, his body tightening until his head snapped my way and our eyes met. I witnessed the exact moment relief sank into his muscles and he relaxed, reclining back against the bench. "Oh, hey. It's you."

My lips twitched. I loved that I got a reaction out of him. "Were you expecting someone else?"

"No." He shook his head bashfully. "How...How are you?"

I crossed my legs and stared at him, batting my lashes. "I'm great now that I'm here. You?"

"I'm good." Cade's gaze fell to my bare legs and slowly trekked up my torso. "Do you just hang around in your cheerleading uniform?"

"No, but would you like me too, *querido*?"

I was being bold and flirtatious.

I think he liked it.

A slow blush crept up his cheeks. "What does *querido* mean?"

"*Querido* is a term of endearment in my language." I smiled and angled my body his way so we were more face-to-face. "Now answer my question."

His gaze rose to mine, pinning me with that blue that evoked a maelstrom of feelings in my chest. Three heartbeats travelled between us, suffusing the air with the kind of tension that forced you to bite your lip in anticipation. "What if I said yes?"

"Then I'd say you're flirting with me." My smile grew. "Are you?"

"I'm obviously doing a bad job if you have to ask me."

I chuckled softly. Tenderness feathered over his face. I didn't want to get ahead of myself, but it felt like there was a strong possibility that Cade might have a crush on me, too.

At our joint family dinner a couple of weeks ago, I noticed him shooting me curious glances while everyone at the table conversed, completely oblivious to the tension between us. I figured he was a man of few words. Or perhaps he was shy and didn't know how to talk to me in front of so many people.

"For your information, I don't hang around in my cheerleading uniform. I had practice after school. It's my second year on the team and Miss Nova—our cheer coach—wants us to start preparing for the upcoming hockey season." I inched him a sly look and curled a strand of my black hair around my pointer finger. "Speaking of hockey, I heard through the grapevine that you're officially a Ranger."

At St. Victoria, I made it a point to know anything and everything about Cade. Did that mean I was on my way to becoming obsessed with him? Most likely.

Cade combed his fingers through his dark brown hair. My own fingers itched to run through it. "You keeping tabs on me, Ella?"

I couldn't make my interest in him more obvious. "What if I said yes?"

Cade's voice dropped low with a hint of mischievousness. "Then I'd say you're flirting with me."

Okay, I was obsessed. It happened. Right there and then. The way he perused my body once more with a scorching look and playfully bantered with me? I was done for. I never stood a chance.

"Caught me," I teased, propping my elbow against the back of the bench and turning my face into my palm. "So what position are you playing?"

"Defenceman. I've played hockey my whole life, but I had to stop a year ago," he said, his tone a hint…dejected. "Uncle Vance insisted I continue playing once I moved in with them. Since St. Victoria is known for its reputable hockey team, he enrolled me here."

I was going to give Vance Remington the biggest hug the next time I saw him. "Well, I'm really glad you're here. I can't wait to see you play. I'll be cheering for you from the bleachers."

"Yeah?"

"Yeah. Isn't that what friends do? Cheer each other on?"

"So you want to be friends, pretty girl?"

Pretty girl.

Oh my God. Don't let him see how much you love that, Ella. Be cool.

Although, the blush on my face probably told him just how affected I was by those two words.

"I do." For now, I'd settle for being friends.

I didn't think there was a possibility in the universe where Cade and I existed in the same realm and didn't end up together. And once I set my mind on something, there was no stopping me.

I was going to make this boy mine.

"Then friends it is."

He reached inside his black leather jacket's pocket for a cigarette and lighter, and I had the strong urge to bedazzle his personal belongings with my touch. Maybe paint an orange lollipop—my favourite candy—on the surface of his Zippo. Or go full-on crazy and print my name on the back of his jacket.

"Do you mind if I smoke?" he asked, pulling me out of my reverie.

I wasn't a big smoker—the occasional weed, yes—and I knew it wasn't good for your health, but I didn't want to come off as rude and tell him that. Everyone had their vices. Cade was allowed to have his.

"No, it's okay."

Then I watched in fascination as he rolled the cig across his lips before tucking it in the seam of his mouth. He tilted his head and flicked the Zippo with a deft thumb. Once a small flame ignited, he lit his cigarette while his gaze, burning with intensity, clashed with mine.

Why did I find that so hot?

He was the personification of a timeless, quintessential bad boy.

Cade took a drag, his cheeks hollowing.

The only thing I could focus on was how handsome he looked with the tall trees and lowering sunset behind him, painting a beautiful canvas that was almost ethereal.

Gazing at him, I realized I was caught in something far greater than mere infatuation. It grew inside of me with the promise of *more*. The pull of that same magnetic force from the alleyway in MacGregor beckoned me. This guy…he had me entangled. The need to know him inside and out, to see how his mind worked, to learn what made him *smile*, ruled me ever since we collided.

Based on the way Cade watched me, I was convinced he felt this too.

This connection was not one-sided.

"Am I your first friend here at St. Victoria?" I asked him.

Cade craned his head in the opposite direction and blew out his smoke, ensuring none of it landed on me. How chivalrous. "You and this guy named Shaun that I met in math class."

72

I perked up. "Shaun Jacobsen?" He nodded slowly. "Oh, he's the best. And funniest. You two are going to get along super well."

Cade took another drag of his cigarette but not before mumbling, "Do you like him?"

At first, I didn't get it. Then I saw his half curious, half sullen expression. Was he jealous? And was it bad that I enjoyed it?

"Sure, I like him." I toyed with Cade, grinning when his shoulders sagged with disappointment. "As a friend. Shaun and I have known each other since our elementary days. We're platonic."

Cade's posture straightened. "Oh. Okay."

I couldn't keep the goofy smile off my face. "Now that you and I are friends, we should get to know each other better."

"What do you want to know, Ella?"

My name, it sounded so good on his lips.

I wanted to hear it, again, and again, and again.

"What's your favourite colour? Mine is blue." It was orange actually, but the colour of his eyes was definitely changing my choice.

Cade gazed at me pointedly and murmured, "Mine is brown."

Like the colour of my eyes. Oh my God. My heart squeezed inside my chest. "That's a pretty colour."

"The prettiest."

Tension ballooned between us.

"Do you have a middle name?" My pulse pounded fast. "Mine is Ximena."

"Killian," Cade rasped, French inhaling his smoke and continuing to gaze at me with hooded eyes.

God, he's so hot.

"Cade Killian Remington." Tasting his full name on my tongue, I found that I loved its flavour. "I like it."

"You've been asking all the questions. It's my turn now."

I gave him the reins. "Ask away."

"I see you sitting on this bench often during lunchtime. You always seem to be…weaving something. What is it?"

Ah, so he was keeping tabs on me too. "I'm currently knitting socks

73

for my little brother Emilio," I answered, pleased that he noticed what I was doing. I never saw him in the courtyard taking peeks at me, but I wouldn't be surprised if he watched me from the shadowed corners. "My *abuela* taught me how to crochet and knit when I was little. Over the years, it's become a hobby to help relieve stress. Whenever I get overwhelmed, I come here to work on my latest project."

My *papá* made it really clear that when I grew up, our family business was mine. My responsibility. My legacy. But I had an artistic soul and I thrived the most when I was creating something. I spent a big chunk of the summer designing various knit bralettes because I had plans of opening an online store in the upcoming months. A few girls in my cheer team expressed their interest in my creations. While my parents provided me with a monthly allowance and access to their credit cards, I wanted to step on my own two feet and try my hand at a bit of independence. I imagined there was a different sense of satisfaction in receiving money you worked hard to earn.

"That's really amazing, Ella," Cade praised. "I'd love to see your projects one day."

"Thank you. I'd love to show you one day," I replied. "Tell me, do you have any interests outside of hockey?"

While he pondered over this, I stole the cigarette from his fingers, surprising him.

His eyes widened when I brought it to my lips and took a drag. When I released the smoke, Cade was riveted by the lip-gloss stain on the tip.

I grinned and handed it back to him. "So?"

Gauging my reaction, he brought the cigarette to his mouth. Seeing the shine of my gloss transfer over to his lips made my toes curl.

Cade gave me a knowing look as he exhaled the smoke. "I love books."

Interesting. I did notice that every time I saw Cade, he held a new book. I just assumed it was for a class reading. Not leisure. "Oh, that's so cool. I don't read much, though I have completed the entire *Twilight* series because my best friend Darla gifted me the paperbacks."

Cade nodded, looking wistfully at the ground for a moment. "I love reading. I read at least thirty books a year. Literature is the best form of escapism. I've turned towards fictional worlds whenever I've had the shittiest of days. It's the best coping mechanism for me."

His words tugged at my heartstrings.

If you spent more than a few minutes holding a deep conversation with him, it was clear he had lots of underlying pain. And no one to listen or help with it.

I wished I could be the person Cade trusted with his secrets.

I would safeguard them—*him*—to the ends of the earth if given the chance.

"It doesn't surprise me that you're an avid reader. You're very smart and eloquent. I was taken aback by your essay on *The Scarlet Letter* in English class last week when Mrs. Richards paired us for team work."

"Thank you." He seemed happy but uncomfortable under my praise…like he wasn't used to people complimenting him. It made me a bit sad. I always empowered my loved ones. Moving forward, I'd remember to compliment him whenever the chance presented itself.

Cade deserved to be reminded how special he was.

For the next ten minutes, we continued playing twenty-one questions. Cade clearly wasn't someone who opened up easily, but I adored that he lowered his guard with me.

We lost track of time during our game and completely forgot the main reason for us meeting up today. Though the weed was just an excuse to see him. Cade obviously saw through my pretense.

He knew I was here simply for him.

And he too was simply here for me.

I still had so many questions for him. About his past. About his family. About how he came to be adopted by the Remingtons. Yet all of those could wait for another day.

Eventually, my phone buzzed with a text from my driver.

My *papá* sent a town car every day like clockwork.

"I have to go," I informed regretfully since I wanted to spend more time with him. "My ride's here. But it was nice seeing you, Cade. I'm really glad you're at St. Victoria. I think you're going to enjoy it here."

"I think I will too," he said softly.

"I'll see you tomorrow?"

"Yes."

But I couldn't leave yet.

Not until I saw his smile.

I didn't know why I was so fixated by the lack of it. Just knew that I had to see it.

One thing I learned in life? When you wanted something, you should flat out ask for it. No use beating around the bush. "Cade, do you ever smile?"

He blinked, confused by how the conversation did a one-eighty. "What?"

"I've never seen you smile. I'm wondering if you know how or if I should teach you," I said cheekily.

Cade eyed me like I was an enigma. "Ella…"

"Since the moment I first saw you, I've been wondering what your smile looks like." I gazed at him tenderly. "I bet it's really nice."

And slowly, just like magic, it happened.

Cade huffed, shook his head like he couldn't believe me, and the corners of his lips tipped up the slightest. I beamed victoriously. And perhaps it was seeing my joy at something so small that caused a full-blown grin to blossom over his face.

¡Dios mío! He had dimples.

And his smile?

It wasn't just nice.

It was so beautiful, I was floored.

Suddenly, I was addicted to the sight.

"You're so…handsome," I murmured. "It's official. I'm going to need you to smile like that for me every day. I won't accept anything less than that."

Cade chuckled and I melted.

Our gazes clashed and time slowed.

"You're a little crazy, Ella."

"I think you like my type of crazy, *querido*."

A touch of wickedness entered his smile, filled with the kind of danger and zeal that could get me in trouble.

I had a weakness for bad boys and Cade Killian Remington just did it for me.

Taking another drag of his cigarette, Cade tilted his head back and his lips parted, smoke pluming into the air. "You should really get going before you show me any more of your true colours, pretty girl," he tutted darkly. "I think I'm beginning to see through you."

He might just be my brand of crazy too.

"What makes you say that?"

Cade gently tucked a flyaway strand behind my ear. "I see you watching me every day, following me around campus, then shooting me little waves and flirty smiles whenever I catch you. You can pretend that every time we've crossed paths is a coincidence, but I know better... You're not sly, Ella," he whispered, his thumb grazing my jaw. "And something tells me that South Side's princess isn't such a good girl after all." He fingered the amethyst crystal necklace resting in the hollow of my throat. I shivered at his touch. "I'm willing to bet you've got a bad streak underneath that sweet exterior."

I leaned close enough to whisper in his ear, "I wasn't trying to be sly."

Cade sucked in a sharp breath and I smiled, the air around us swarming with electrifying energy.

"And you're right"—I stole his cigarette and took another drag, blowing the smoke in the space between us, letting it linger over his lips like an intimate caress—"I'm not always a good girl, Cade."

His eyes narrowed, breathing uneven. "Say it like it is, Ella. Tell me what you want."

"I want to be your friend." Until I could attach the word *girl* in front of it. "Remember?"

I passed him the cigarette, making sure our fingers touched during the exchange.

His jaw tightened and he nodded once. "Okay."

"I should really get going." I stood up and smoothed my hands over my cheerleading skirt. "If you text me tomorrow morning when you get to school, we can walk to English Lit together."

"I got a better idea: I'll pick you up for school starting tomorrow."

"My, my. Someone is eager to be my *friend*."

I could tell 'friend' was beginning to grate him, and I was willing to bet Cade was just as hell-bent on attaching the word *boy* in front of it.

"Would you rather Peter pick you up instead of me?"

I adored his jealous tone.

Peter was a sleazy little shit. He was caught a few days ago peeping into the girls' locker room after cheerleading practice. He ran away when the girls shrieked. A few minutes later, when I exited the locker room after changing…I found Cade roughing him up in the dark hallway.

Biting the inside of my cheek, I stepped between his legs. "I don't want anyone but you to pick me up, Cade."

He reclined, his arms spanning out like wings along the back of the bench. The expression on his face as he peered up at me with half-lidded eyes could only be described as arrogance and pure, molten heat. "Is that so, princess?"

Cade looked every bit the son of a notorious kingpin.

A dark prince holding the keys of a kingdom filled with bloodshed, riches, and rousing temptation.

One taste of his presence and I was lured into his world.

There was no escaping for me.

I never wanted to leave.

The nickname *princepin* flitted into my mind. He called me princess. It was only fitting for me to address him with a word that described him as a young ruler of a corrupted empire.

"Mhm. Only you, princepin." I ran the tip of my nail down the front lapel of his leather jacket suggestively. In just a matter of weeks, I'd be painting *Property of Ximena* on the back of it. Mark my words. "You know what's funny? You accuse me of not being sly, but you aren't either. What's your excuse for hurting Peter?"

His chin jutted stubbornly. "You know why."

"Say it like it is, Cade," I threw his own words back at him.

"He stared at you, without your consent," he said through gritted teeth. "I...I wanted to gouge his eyes out. It was the first time in my life that I felt the urge to do something like that."

Oh, my. I liked how protective he was of me already and how he wasn't afraid of teaching stupid fuckers who behaved badly with his...girl.

I lowered my head until our eyes met.

A strong gust of wind blew the strands of my hair into his face.

He caught them in his fist and yanked me even closer.

I gasped under my breath.

"How does that make you feel, Ella?" he rasped with a dark edge. "That I had those thoughts."

"Like I see right through you too, Cade."

An understanding passed between us. This was going to happen. Him and me. Two people at the mercy of a conspiring universe who wanted us in each other's orbits.

Who were we to deny fate?

"Seven a.m. tomorrow." His gaze ran over me like he was committing every detail to memory. "Be ready for me."

The double entendre of that statement filled me with verve.

I was so ready. He had no idea.

"All right." I grabbed his wrist, my thumb running over his veins to feel his pulse racing. For me. I unwound his fingers from my hair with a coy smile before I winked at him. "See you tomorrow, Cade."

As I whirled around and walked away, I felt his eyes on me the entire time.

Once I got in my car and the driver pulled away from St. Victoria's gates, I changed Cade's name in my phone to *Mine*.

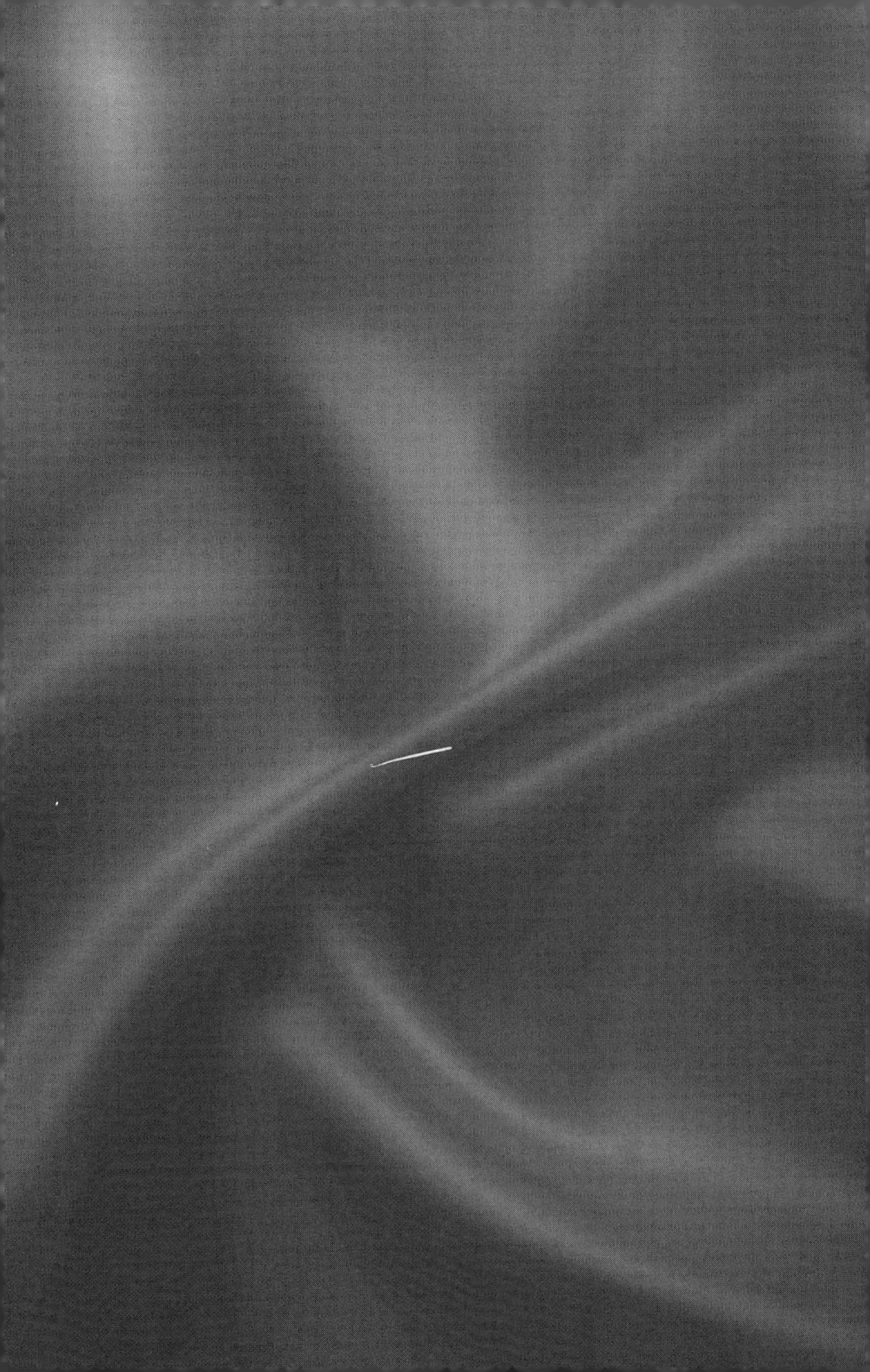

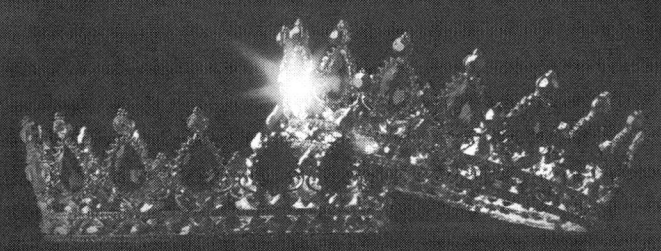

CHAPTER 8

Dreaming of You

CADE

The Present
12:32 a.m.

"**W**hat if I did fuck him?"

I was livid with my ex-girlfriend.

Her words played like a broken record in my mind, torturing me with every loop. She threw that axed jab in hopes of watching me drown in misery and it worked.

If Ella screwed him, he was a dead man walking. Once Initiation Night was over, I'd hunt down the fucker and teach him a lesson. The kind that involved my knife and his balls.

The thought of her giving to him what she gave to me was so soul crushing, I could barely breathe past the fumes of my despair.

We were each other's first. We swore to be each other's last.

Since our breakup, I'd been celibate. My heart and my body only wanted Ella. Shit, the *only* way I could even get hard was by thinking of her. Her smile. Her moans. Her tight pussy, squeezing me so good.

I never slept with another woman because there was only her for me.

And she'd fucked other men?

For both our sakes, I hoped she was bluffing. Otherwise, dead bodies would start piling up in the streets of Montardor.

"I bet you said that to every girl you cheated on me with, huh?"

Ella actually believed I cheated on her with multiple girls. Not just that one time she 'caught me' at Josh's party. Goddammit, I never fucking cheated. But she wouldn't listen to me even if I tried to tell her what really happened. She was stubborn and still too blinded by her pain.

It had permanently painted her vision red.

Hearts were broken that wretched summer night. I would unbreak hers if she just heard my truth. I would rid her of all her fears, all her tears, all her aches, if she just gave me the chance.

I came tonight with the sole purpose of winning her back.

I wasn't leaving until we mended what was broken.

Ella Ximena Cordova was meant to be my fucking soulmate.

I'd fight tooth and nail to get back what was meant to be mine forever.

The storm outside—visible through the windows lining the darkened hallway—seemed to have simmered down from roaring to absolute tranquil. I paused a foot away, noticing the bench in the courtyard where I had one of my earlier exchanges with Ella.

Back then, I was a lonely sixteen-year-old boy falling in love with a beautiful girl who reminded him what it was like to smile again after so long.

Who knew this was where we'd wind up three years later?

Casting a glance over my shoulder, I saw Ella planted at the library threshold. Eyes wary and mouth downturned. There was a chink in her armour, but she remained stoic.

My girl was spectacular at masking her emotions in public. No one ever saw the real her. I had the privilege, once upon a time, to see what lay behind her good girl exterior. And as her beholder, Ella was nothing short of stunning. With me, she'd always been stripped bare to her core. Artistic. Carefree. Funny. Naughty. Rebellious. And so much more. I held all those layers on a pedestal. I could fill a notebook with poetry to describe my love for her.

It was an honour to witness her in her rawest form.

I wanted to see her like that again.

Without the trace of sorrow surrounding her flesh and bones.

"You coming?" I prompted.

Ella snapped out of her trance and her gaze cut to mine. "Nice jacket. I thought you'd have thrown it by now."

Ah, she spotted her name scrawled across the back of my leather jacket.

"I'd never throw away anything you gave to me, pretty girl."

She froze mid-step, another fissure cracking her armour. The sincereness in my voice unbalanced her. Good. I'd kill with kindness if I had to.

It was obvious to everyone but Ella that I never stopped loving her.

She scoffed. "Can't say the same thing about all the stuff you gave me."

I wasn't offended because one, I was choosing to believe that was a lie and two, I knew her bitchiness was a defence mechanism.

Together, we walked down the hallway. Our flashlights guided us as our strides ate the distance towards the underground tunnels that would lead to the abandoned dormitories.

"What about the Ducati I bought you for your birthday?" I kept my tone playful. "Did you throw that away too?"

Ella glared at me as we increased our pace.

"That's what I thought." I tsked.

Three years ago, I started learning how to ride a motorcycle. Not wanting to be left out, Ella took up lessons with me. One of our favourite things was riding together late at night. Daddy Cordova wasn't impressed with his little girl riding a crotch rocket, but I liked to indulge all of Ella's desires. I loved spoiling her.

As a result, I bought her a slick black motorcycle to match mine.

Tense silence brewed as we descended the stairwell at the end of the hallway.

The comfort I always associated with St. Victoria during the day evaporated at night. There was nothing sacred about these grounds in the afterhours. Allegedly, the school was built on one of the gates of hell.

While I found that rumour to be laughable, it didn't seem so far-fetched right now. On our way to the ground floor, I swore, when I blinked, the angels carved high in the ceiling moldings resembled ghouls instead. And as our thumping footsteps echoed against the floor, my mind imagined the rumbly chuckle of demons and the rough crackling of hell fire.

Just half an hour into the competition and I was beginning to lose my mind.

We passed by a lot of Initiators. They shot us scandalized expressions, gossiping right in front of our faces with no decorum.

"Omigod. I can't believe they got paired together."

"I heard he cheated on her. Yikes."

"Damn, that sucks."

We pretended to hear nothing.

Unfortunately, our breakup was publicized in front of a big chunk of St. Victoria's populace. By the end of the competition, news that we were teammates would make the rounds in our circle. People would have a field day with this tidbit.

On our way to the tunnels, we spotted Shaun and Darla by the foyer. My best friend gave us a salute. "Good luck, lovebirds!"

Ella threw him a middle finger.

I rolled my lips into my mouth to tame my grin. When Ella wasn't looking, I mouthed to him, "You're the best."

Shaun shot me an air kiss like a jackass and mouthed back, "I know."

It didn't go unnoticed by me how the temperature rose to icy when both girls' gazes met. It was odd how their sixteen years of friendship ended abruptly. Some months ago, Ella mentioned Darla stopped responding to her texts and calls.

Whether it was Vesta University's campus or one of the many parties hosted within the society, Darla still remained cordial with me whenever we ran into each other.

Finally, we entered the dimly lit tunnels, the beige cobblestone walls reminiscent of ancient catacombs. Built in the late 1800s, they were used as passages for the nuns and residents to travel underground through the motherhouse. The only way to get to the dormitories from the inside was through here. Even when I was a student, I seldom walked by this path. The musty smell and the eerie atmosphere of the tunnels didn't mesh well with me.

Nor did the way our flashlights bounced against the walls, giving the illusion of shadowy figures following our every step.

There were many myths surrounding St. Victoria. The walls of the tunnels hiding the bones of the dead convent inhabitants was a popular one.

My favourite, though, was that Sister Victoria made an appearance every time you went downstairs to the crypt, where she and her fellow sisters rested. She'd stand by her grave and stare at you in her habit until you lost your mind or ran away. It was obviously a load of bullshit. I'd been to the crypt twice—once to drink with the boys after a Rangers' win and another time to fuck Ella in the confessional booth—and never once saw her.

I checked my watch as we fell into a half walk, half jog. "We have about two hours and twenty-four minutes left."

Ella grimaced. "I want to finish this dare in fifteen minutes flat. Otherwise, we'll be pressed for time with the other ones."

Otherwise, we wouldn't win. That's what she wanted to say.

"We'll get you your crown soon. Don't worry, princess."

"Don't call me that," she hissed and hurried ahead, her shapely ass tempting as hell in those tight jeans.

A shot of pure lust travelled through me. I wanted to lick, bite, and suck my mark onto her ass cheek. The same one where I almost tattooed *Property of Cade* after a night of hard-core fucking on ecstasy.

I missed Ella so much—her jokes, her laugh, her ability to always set me at ease—but damn me if I didn't miss that tall model body. She was so easy to handle. I could throw and flip her around like a ragdoll. And she loved it, moaning wantonly when I fucked her in every filthy position. No one could have known that South Side's resident princess enjoyed being praised, degraded, and treated cruelly in bed.

Fuck, remembering all our wild nights sent blood rushing to my cock.

"Call you what?" I feigned ignorance as we took a left hook in the tunnels. "Princess?"

"Yes." She seethed. "And if you don't stop, I won't be responsible for what I do."

"What will you do, hm?" A wise man wouldn't poke the bear. But I loved riling her up.

"Knee you so hard in the balls, you'll wish you never opened your mouth to speak."

Grinning, I pushed Ella against the tunnel walls and covered her body with mine.

The way her breath hitched. The way her long orange nails curled into my shoulders. The way her chest rose and fell against my own. The way she bristled at my audacity but wasn't able to shove me away because she craved *this* as bad as I did.

I loved it all.

My palms smoothed over her waist, the skin-to-skin contact nearly searing me. I bit back a groan, staring at the pebbled nipples poking through her orange bralette. My mouth watered. I wanted so badly to flick the strings of her top so it came undone and lick her pretty little tits like a starved man devouring his first meal after days.

"Do your worst, Ella," I rasped. "You know I like it rough."

"Cade…" she warned. "Your gun's poking me again."

I brought my lips close to hers so she could feel my whisper. "That's not my gun, baby."

"Ah." Ella tilted her head, arching a brow. Her glossed lips curled in a pompous smirk. Oh, yeah. She liked knowing she still had that effect on me.

God, she was sexy.

Temperamental, confident, and a whole lot bad.

Feeling emboldened, my hands snaked down to grab chunks of her generous ass, giving it an affectionate squeeze. Just the way she liked it. "Fuck, the things I want to do to you, Ella."

"In your dreams, *querido*."

Querido. Hearing that term of endearment made my heart clench with happiness.

"I always dream of you, sweetheart. Ever since the first moment I saw you."

Ella's lips parted and her eyes searched my face for lies, finding nothing but my truth. No matter our history, my feelings for her never waned. Didn't she realize how much I still loved her? How all I wanted was to be with her again?

I thought the numerous text messages and voicemails I left her like a pathetic beggar the first two weeks after our breakup were an obvious indicator. Not to mention all the times we saw each other since then and how I tried, in vain, to talk to her.

Shadows played on her face from the faint light emanating from the tunnel torches. Her features hardened into a brief scowl. Though she wasn't ready to face our past now, she would be by the end of the night. I was sure of it.

She dug her claws deeper into my shoulders like a feral cat. "Do you, huh?"

My hand roved over the valley between her breasts, past the hollow at the base of her throat, till my fingers wrapped around her slender neck. "You want to hear what I dream about?"

"Tell me." She was losing the cocky edge, her voice a hint shaky.

Her gold hoop earrings grazed over my knuckles and my thumb settled right under her chin, tipping her face back so she met my gaze.

I licked my bottom lip.

Her eyes followed the movement like a moth drawn to a flame.

When she absentmindedly licked her own in return, I tightened my hold on her neck.

"*You*, Ella. Every. Single. Night," I rasped. "Your body writhing beneath me, taking every inch of my cock so perfectly. Your voice in my ears, begging for more. Your eyes filled with lust, crying pretty tears." Ella's breathing quickened when my arm curved around her bare waist and dragged her body deeper into mine. "I dream of how much you loved it when I fucked you like I hated your guts. How gorgeous you looked with your black ski mask on, while I took you from behind like my dirty little princess. And how you'd split on my dick and bounce that cheer pussy like a bad girl working hard to please her princepin." I let our lips brush in the hottest almost-kiss of my life. "You're on my mind twenty-four seven and

I still can't get enough of you."

Ella absorbed it all, her expression morphing from curiosity to straight up hot, carnal desire. The sensual glint in her eyes cinched my own rapacious need. She knew how much I always desired her, but my words fortified it.

I was so hungry for this girl.

I wanted to devour her sweet cunt while her fingers knotted in my hair and her heels dug into my back. I wanted to kiss her delectable mouth and pound into her while she left scratch marks all over my shoulders. And I wanted to love her now and forever. Until she forgot all the past hurt and made room for the paradise I would bring to her world if she just gave me one more chance to make it right.

"Dream on, Cade," Ella drawled, acting unaffected by my confession. "You and I will never happen again."

"What will it take for you to change your mind?"

Ella's fingers crawled down the front of my leather jacket and slipped underneath the material of my black hoodie, lightly scoring my abs. I shivered when her lips poised at my ear and she whispered seductively, "It'll cost you."

"Name your price, baby."

"I'm priceless, *mi corazón*. Remember?" She bit my earlobe and I moaned. "You'll have to gift me something really grand for me to even consider giving you the opportunity to lick my pussy." She sucked the sting she left behind like a wicked maneater. "And I know just how much you loved tasting me."

Keeping my gaze on her, I reached for my wallet and pulled out my black card.

My girl liked to spend money and I liked to watch her do it. Good thing I had enough zeros in my bank account to sustain her shopping habits.

"Every cent to my name is yours, Ella." I fisted the hair at the nape of her neck and tugged hard until her body arched. She watched me with a mixture of hate and lust. The fire in her eyes fueled my own. "It always has been."

In a move that left her astonished, I shoved the black card in her bralette.

Right under the strap between her tits.

Ella's eyes widened in surprise.

My fingers skated down to the button of her high-waisted jeans. I flicked it open and stopped at the zipper, gauging her reaction. Ella's silence felt like a challenge. She was testing me. Seeing how far I was willing to take it.

Grabbing her hips, I dropped down to my knees like a sinner seeking reparation. My atonement could only come if she bestowed it upon me. "Change your mind yet, sweetheart?"

In a move that left *me* astonished and even more aroused, Ella stole my gun and cocked it against my jaw. "Every cent?"

Fucking hell, she was going to be my end.

"Every. Single. Cent." Impatient hands molded down her thighs, urging her to spread her legs. Or call off this bluff. My cock couldn't handle this much teasing. It was straining in the confinements of my briefs.

I *felt* her sinful smile down to my balls. "What's the pin?"

"Eight, nine, nine, six."

Ella couldn't hide her shock. When we were together, I had a different pin.

Now it was her birthday.

"Mm." Digging my gun's barrel into my jaw, Ella's nails grazed my cheek before her thumb snagged over my bottom lip, pulling gently. "Is that so—"

The sentence hung in the air.

Her eyes flared at my new tattoo. My favourite one yet.

ELLA was inked in the inside skin of my bottom lip.

The love of my life stared at my tattoo with a speechlessness that had my heart drumming a fast rhythm against my ribcage.

"What else do you want?" I urged now that she had my gun and access to my riches. "My Ferrari? My book collection? Maybe another bouquet of orange lollipops?"

At the mention of orange lollipops, the hand holding my gun faltered.

Ella had an affinity for orange. The colour, the taste, the scent. Every month, I'd make her a bouquet of orange lollipops because they were her favourites and gift them to her with a handwritten letter. It was a small offering but perhaps the most meaningful one to her.

I wondered how she'd react to knowing I still carried orange lollipops in my pocket whenever I left the house. Sometimes it was for myself—a treat for whenever I missed her. Other times it was on the off-chance that I ran into her and…I didn't even want to finish that thought. It birthed too much hope and I had to thread carefully for the sake of my own heart.

Ella removed her thumb from my lip and tried to compose herself. It was too late. I saw all the repressed emotions bubbling beneath her surface. Anger. Desire. Fear…of falling for me again.

"Oh, Cade," Ella started with a saccharine sweet tone—the total opposite of her deviant nature—and cocked the gun at my jaw once more. For a second, I thought she'd actually pull the trigger. "While you look great on your knees, you should know that no amount of money or grovelling can make me change my mind. Once I throw trash out the door, I never look back." She patted my cheek condescendingly. "Hold onto your dreams because that's the only time you'll ever be with me again."

Trash. Out the door. Never look back.

My hands fell away from her thighs like I'd been burned. Goddamn, that hurt like a motherfucker. So much so that it robbed me of breath.

Ella used my stillness to push away from the wall and dart towards the dormitories.

It took me a few seconds to cool off before I got to my feet and ran after her. I wouldn't be deterred by her rudeness. I prepared myself for this version of her tonight.

Ella was a fast runner.

But I was faster.

The predator in me thrived on the chase. It caused the blood running through my veins to pump vigorously.

And Ella was well aware that I'd chase her until the ends of the Earth. Come high or hell water. I made a promise ages ago that I would never let her go.

When I caught up to her, I grabbed her waist and hauled her over my shoulder fireman style, ignoring her squeals. "Where do you think you're going, huh?" I growled.

"Away from you!" she growled back, kicking her legs out like a brat throwing a tantrum. "I'm going to win this game without your help. I don't fucking need you!"

I carried her the short distance towards Balthazar Building's indoor entrance. "Yeah, right. Without me, you'll be stuck here till dawn trying to solve the riddles. You need me. Whether you like it or not."

"Fuck you!"

"Ask me like a good girl and I might consider giving *you* the opportunity to suck my dick," I goaded. "I remember how much you loved getting your face fucked, Ella."

Feeble fists pounded at my back. "Let me down, asshole! Or I really will knee you in the balls! I'm not kidding! *Cade!*"

"Careful, *princess.*" I spanked her ass in two successive swats that echoed in the tunnels. "Once I redden your ass into my favourite shade of red, I'll fuck the disrespectfulness out of you in no time."

"You're insufferable." She squirmed in my hold. "Are you forgetting I literally have a gun in my hand?"

Dark amusement curved my lips. "Hard to forget since you currently have it poised at my head."

We reached the door leading to Balthazar Building and I dropped Ella to her feet. She swayed with a curse and I rapidly retrieved my gun, tucking it back in the waistband of my pants. Then I backed Ella against the hard surface, pressing my hands on either side of her head.

Her chest heaved up and down with her inhales and exhales. She glared at me with a daring expression.

In the dead quietness of the tunnels, every breath and heartbeat felt magnified.

It was the chase. It always exhilarated both of us. The excitement mixed with fear released a rush of adrenaline that roused our pulses like no other.

"Would you have done it?" I asked gently.

"Done what?" she spat.

"Shoot me."

Ella's shoulders deflated and she closed her eyes on a sigh. "No. Even if I hate you, I don't wish you dead."

"What will it take for you to forgive me?"

Silence stretched between us for a few seconds. When Ella answered, her voice was thick with emotions. "A miracle, Cade."

I flinched, hearing what she really wanted to say. *For you to not have broken my heart. For the last three months to have been a fever dream. For us to go back in time and erase all the wrongness that overshadowed our perfect start.*

"Ella—"

"Don't," she said vehemently. "Don't look at me like that."

"Like what?" My tone was inexplicably hoarse.

"Like you want to kiss me," she whispered. "And never stop."

"I always want to kiss you, Ella," I whispered back. "That's what I dream about most. Kissing you and never, ever coming up for air."

My words punctured another layer of her thinly composed mask.

I stepped back to give her space and focused on the electronic lock.

While I entered the combination, Ella stared straight ahead. Unblinking. Frozen like a goddess Nemesis statue. Trying to make sense of what I just said.

With a small buzz, the door unlocked.

Ella didn't budge. Neither did I.

Maybe I underestimated the depth of her hurt. Maybe I was a fool to believe that a handful of hours would be enough to convince Ella to give me another chance. The way she stood now with an unyielding quality, I feared our three-month separation had cemented her walls to a point where breaking them would be nearly impossible.

Though I would not stop trying.

"Clock's ticking, Ella," I told her.

She snapped back from whatever place her mind had wandered off too and marched past my body, but not before uttering words that sliced me. "There was a time when I dreamed of you too, Cade. But you broke us and there's no coming back from that."

CHAPTER 9

I'm Yours

Ella

The Past - 3 years ago

Cade was sneaking over tonight.

And for the first time, we'd actually be alone in my place.

Previously, we were always surrounded by others, whether it be joint family dinners or the spontaneous times his uncle dropped in with him and Josh to discuss 'business' with *papá*. It was hard to converse under their watchful eyes…especially when this thing between us felt so new.

We were now *best* friends, but it was obvious we wanted more.

Cade didn't make any moves on me. I didn't make any moves on him. We were carefully threading the waters, while strengthening the unexpected bond we struck two months ago since he started attending St. Victoria.

Constantly in each others orbits, we became inseparable. When he wasn't near me, I craved his presence. When he left, I kept time based on when I'd see him next.

Obsession had curled deep inside of me, its roots caging my heart and climbing around my bones like the beautiful vines encasing St. Victoria's castle.

Before I knew it, Cade became vital to my existence. I needed him. Could not imagine this version of me without him.

My pulse leapt when my phone lit up with Cade's text. I recently changed his contact name to 'Princepin' since mine was 'Princess' in his, and I thought it was cute to have matching nicknames.

Be there in an hour, pretty girl. I need to do something with Josh for my uncle first. —Princepin

Okay. Text me when you get here. I can't wait to see you. <3 —Princess

<3 —Princepin

The simple heart emoji made me weak in the knees. There wasn't a single doubt in my mind that he liked me more than a friend.

I'd confess my feelings tonight, I decided.

My three-year-old brother, Emilio, watched me curiously as he sat on the kitchen counter, licking the last spoonful of ice cream from his bowl. He probably wondered why his big sister was grinning at her cell phone with giddiness.

"Ella, I done," he said sweetly, depositing the spoon in the bowl with his cute, chubby hands.

"Good boy. Let's do some dishes, and then I'll read you a bedtime story."

Because I was a strong advocate for equality, I started teaching Emilio how to do the dishes, a feat that caused most of the maids in our household to stare at me with horror. Some of them were quite old-fashioned and thought this was a chore for women. Which, of course, was bullshit.

Thankfully, the maids had the night off, so we were safe from prying eyes.

I washed Emilio's bowl and set it before him, handing him a clean washcloth. He dried his bowl with diligence, working his fist in a circular motion with all the might in his little body.

"This is fun, eh?" I crooned.

He gave me a toothy grin, nodding enthusiastically.

"Boys clean up after themselves when they finish eating." I dried off my hands on a spare towel. "Do you understand, *manito*?"

96

"*Sí*, Ella." He nodded, blinking those big brown eyes at me. "Boys clean."

"There you go, Emi!" I gushed, yanking him into my arms and pecking all over his face. He cackled, loving it when I showered him with kisses. Emilio's arms went around my shoulders as he muffled his boyish laugh in my neck. I turned off the kitchen lights and carried him up the grand staircase. "Are you tired?"

He was playing with the strands of my hair, his head on my shoulder. "Mhm. Sleepy."

Both my parents were away for the weekend. Sometimes *papá* liked to plan romantic getaways for *mamá* and whenever they were gone, it was my responsibility to put Emilio to bed.

Once we went through his night routine and I finished reading him a bedtime story, Emilio started dozing off, his hand fisting the material of my T-shirt like he didn't want me to go. "Wove you, Ella…"

"I love you, too," I said tenderly, kissing his forehead.

Once my little brother fell asleep, my phone pinged with Cade's text just as I was leaving Emilio's room.

I'm there in twenty. —Princepin

Sounds good 😊 —Princess

My parents would lose their shit if they knew Cade was coming over. *Alone.* He had to sneak in because I didn't trust any of the guards not to snitch on us.

Mamá and *papá* adored Josh but remained wary of Cade. I noticed the fake smiles and suspicious glances they shot him whenever we were all in the same room. They found it odd how Cade and Olivia plopped into the picture, and even odder how the Remingtons remained tight-lipped on the subject of their newest children.

People in our society were speculating. Vance and Julia remained unbothered, much to everyone's chagrin.

I wished my parents could see Cade through my eyes. On the outside, he may seem cold and reserved, but on the inside, he was sweet with a lone wolf spirit. If they tried to get to know him, they'd realize how intelligent and kind he was. And how he had the best smile with the cutest dimples.

Cade trusted me and it filled me with so much pride that I got to learn this amazing, complex guy in a way the rest of the world did not. We talked a lot. In class. In between classes. After classes. We often studied together. He helped me with my math homework and I helped him with his art class projects. The banter and chemistry between us unfolded with ease. His energy balanced mine. He was the quiet, observant, to my feisty, energetic self.

We fit together so well, like two halves of one perfect whole.

After that shared moment on the bench in St. Victoria's courtyard, Cade, true to his words, started picking me up for school every day at 7:00 a.m. We were seen roaming the hallways and walking to classes together, while ignoring all the inquisitive looks people threw our way. I got asked many times if we were an item. So did he. But we never confirmed or denied the rumours.

Last week during a hockey game, I was cheering from the bleachers after he scored a slapshot goal, when I noticed the girls from my team fanning themselves and talking about how hot number 6—Cade—was.

Red hot jealousy bubbled in the pit of my stomach.

Therefore, I took it upon myself to stake my claim.

Now all the cheerleaders knew he was *my* boy best friend. If you wanted to flirt with him, you'd have to get through me first.

And I was one territorial bitch.

Cade was mine.

All. Fucking. Mine.

Back in my room, I dimmed the lights to create an ambiance, lit some candles to have my room smelling like warm vanilla, and changed into a matching baby blue ensemble: high-waisted miniskirt with a flare, knit bralette, and a small cardigan to ward off any chill.

We were supposed to watch a movie after he helped me with our latest math assignment. While this wasn't a date per se, I still wanted to dress to impress.

In the middle of adding another coat of my lip gloss, I flinched when I heard a rattle against the doors leading into my Juliet-style balcony.

I peered over my shoulder and saw a dark silhouette.

The scream died in my throat when I realized it was Cade.

His fist rapped against the glass surface with impatience.

Oh my God.

He was supposed to text me when he arrived. What in the world was he thinking climbing up to my balcony?

I hurried towards him and wrenched open the doors.

"Are you insane?" I whisper-shouted, dragging him into the safety of my room. "How did you get up here?"

Cade inched off his motorcycle helmet and grinned down at me with the most heart-melting smile, his dimples making an appearance. He ran a leather-gloved hand through his dark brown strands to fix them back into their usual style. "Hello to you too, princess."

The moonlight peering through the open balcony doors illuminated the space between us. It gave his masculine features an ethereal glow and made those beautiful eyes of his appear almost silver. My goodness, he was so handsome, gazing down at me with an expression filled with pure joy.

My heart twisted painfully in its cage.

I wanted to hold him in my arms and never, ever let go.

"How did you get up here, Cade?" I repeated, failing to tame the fear in my voice. Didn't he realize how precious he was to me? How I couldn't risk anything happening to him?

"I used the ladder I found in your garden to climb up to you."

Horror scalded my insides. That old ladder was on the verge of breaking apart. My parents were supposed to replace it weeks ago. The fact that Cade climbed it and reached me in one piece was a wonder.

Grabbing fistfuls of his leather jacket, I shook some sense into him. "What if you fell? You could have died! Or, at the very least, gotten badly injured! Don't do something like that again!"

"*Ella.*" Cade grasped my hands and gave them an affectionate squeeze. "Don't worry. I'm fine. I only wanted to surprise you."

"That's some surprise!" I wailed before lowering my voice. Usually, I was a thrill junkie, but not where his safety was concerned. What if his foot or hand had slipped? "That was very reckless of you."

"I thought you liked reckless behaviour," he teased.

"Not when it means losing you…when I've just found you."

Cade's expression fell and he exhaled softly.

I closed my eyes, having revealed too much.

Suddenly, he urged me into his chest for a crushing hug. I wrapped my arms around his waist and inhaled his familiar, comforting scent.

It was the first time we touched in a manner beyond platonic. The air around us floated with a newfound feeling I could not decipher yet but felt deep in my soul.

"I'm sorry, Ella." He laid his cheek on top of my head. "I didn't mean to scare you."

Cocooned in his warm embrace, I could forgive anything. The feeling I could not decipher finally translated in a faint echo of *home*.

Clutching him tight, my forehead mashed against the place where his heart beat gently, willing my own vital organ to march to the same rhythm. "You're forgiven, princepin."

His smile brushed against my middle part. Cade loved when I called him that.

When I pulled away, he gingerly framed my face. "Ella, your eyes," he remarked breathlessly.

Oh, I forgot to wear my contacts tonight. "Um, about that…"

"You have brown eyes, but your right one is tinged with blue." He continued staring at me in amazement. "How is that possible?"

No choice but to tell him the truth, I mumbled with a bit of shame, "I was born with sectoral heterochromia and was bullied in elementary school because of it. As a result, I've been wearing brown contacts since high school to avoid being called a freak. If you think I'm one too, just say it now so we can get it out of the way. I know my eyes are imperfect and tend to make people uncomfortable."

"Sweetheart, you don't look like a freak and you don't make me uncomfortable. I love your eyes. They're so unique."

I swallowed with difficulty. "Do you truly mean it?"

"Your right eye reminds me of the earth," he murmured. "The bottom half of your iris is brown—filled with riches—and the top half is blue—filled with spirit. Your eyes, even with your so-called imperfection, are exquisite and anyone who says otherwise is just fucking jealous."

I wanted to cry. No one in my life had said such inspiring, poetic words to me.

Cade took my insecurity and Molotov cocktailed it far into the distance, letting it burn to ashes.

"You're so beautiful, Ella," he husked, thumbing my cheeks softly. "Please believe me."

I couldn't take it anymore. The intense connection between us rose like a tidal wave and submerged us in its glory. Words of fondness concocted on my tongue, begging to be voiced aloud. He needed to know that I spent every night dreaming of him since the day I met him. He needed to know that out of every thought circling through my head, *he* was the most prominent one. He needed to know so many things, yet the only one I could vocalize was...

"I want to kiss you," I finally admitted. "I've wanted to kiss you from the first moment I saw you. Will you let me?"

Cade's eyes flared and he dropped a rough, "Yes."

He was so tall and while I wasn't a short girl, I still had to rise on my tippy-toes to reach his mouth.

Tiling my head, I gently pecked his mouth.

It was my first kiss.

A bolt of electricity crackled in the space between us at the soft brush of our lips.

I opened my eyes.

Cade watched me, observing how our first kiss completely shifted my world.

When my breath escaped my lips in a slow glide and mingled with his own, his chest bowed as he inhaled, his expression darkening with the same hunger on mine.

Slowly, my fingers trickled over the material of his leather jacket until they interlocked behind his neck, pulling him down to me. "I've never kissed anyone before."

"Neither have I."

Knowing that I was his first filled me with euphoria. "I want to do it again, *querido*."

"No one's stopping you, Ella," he whispered, using two fingers to tip my chin up. "Do it."

Encouraged by his response, I pressed my mouth to his again. Desperate. Hard. Longer than the last time. Until my lungs needed air.

Cade's hand slithered to the nape of my neck. He suddenly fisted my hair and yanked.

I broke away with a gasp.

He gazed at me, enthralled and a little vexed. "Don't play with me," he warned. "Kiss me like you mean it, Ella. Kiss me like the possessive girl who told her whole squad they couldn't make a pass at me."

My eyes widened. How did he know?

"Did you think I wouldn't find out?" He chuckled darkly. "You want me all to yourself, hm, princess?"

I nodded. "Yes, I'm greedy. They can't have you."

The smile curving the corners of his lips was filled with bad boy mischief.

Cade grazed his mouth against my jaw before coming at my ear. "Want to know a secret?"

"Y-Yes."

"I don't want any of them. Only you."

This time when our lips joined, it was tantalizing.

A branding, *no-going-back-from-here* kind of kiss that made my toes curl from the sheer gratification of finally having him as mine.

Our kiss expressed what our words could not.

We'd been longing for one another since the moment we met. Now that the longing was fulfilled, it gave hope to a future I never dreamt of until him.

"*Cade*," I whispered as we withdrew for oxygen, barely getting a lungful before his mouth was back on mine with a broken, groaned, "*Ella.*"

Our lips moved in unison, sipping from one another vigorously, falling into a thrilling dance where we learned each other's flavour. His tongue swept over my seam and I shivered, instinctively giving him access.

A burst of stars lit up behind my closed eyelids as our tongues met languidly and I tasted mint, smoke, and a hint of sweetness. My room was soon filled with the sounds of our kisses and the howling wind coming through the ajar balcony doors.

Cade's hands tightened around my waist, pulling me deeper into him.

My own hands delved into his hair, anchoring him to me.

I was floating on cloud nine, dizzy with the feel of him, me, and *us*.

Every sense of mine was permeated with my princepin. I could only hear the desperate way he uttered my name, could only smell his heady cologne, could only taste his essence, could only feel the contours of his strong body as my hands roamed. And when we pulled away from one another with mutual gasps, only to join our foreheads together, I could only see *him*.

He was a vision to behold.

Tousled hair, flushed cheeks, gleaming eyes, and the sweetest grin tugging at his mouth, showing me those dimples I loved.

I squeezed his jaw with one hand and playfully growled, "God, you're so cute. I adore these dimples."

Unable to resist, I kissed them. One by one. Over and over again.

Loving my enthusiasm, Cade laughed softly. "Are you done?"

"For now." I gave him another peck.

He laid his forehead to mine again and simply breathed me in. "I've wanted to kiss you from the first moment I saw you too, Ella."

"Yeah?"

He nodded and kissed each one of my eyelids. "Never seen a more breathtaking girl in my life. I wanted you. I *needed* to have you."

A gold-tipped arrow struck my heart with his admission. "You have me, Cade."

"You have me too, Ella," he confessed. "I'm yours."

Did he realize what that statement did to me?

I'm yours.

He said it with such conviction, my insides rearranged until the shape of my heart had enough space to create a forever home for him.

"I'm yours, too."

Cade kissed me again.

Now that we'd kissed, I never wanted to stop.

I didn't have to ask Cade where this left us. We'd still remain best friends, but now I was his girlfriend and he was my boyfriend…which had always been my end game.

My victorious smile carved against his lips and Cade pulled back, arching an eyebrow. "What are you thinking?"

"I'm going to kiss the shit out of you at school come Monday morning."

"Sounds good." He winked, knowing I'd want to stamp my ownership all over him in front of everyone.

"We should probably get started on that math assignment." My fingers laced with his and I began veering him out of my room. "The faster we finish, the faster we can watch that new horror movie."

"Wait a second." He tugged my hand back. "I have a surprise for you."

He shrugged off his hard-shell motorcycle backpack, and laid it on the floor next to his helmet. Cade crouched down, unzipped the bag, and plucked out a black fabric.

It was his Rangers hockey jersey. *Remington* was written across the back, right above the number *6*.

"Catch." He tossed it my way.

I caught it. "You didn't!"

"You asked for one." His eyes twinkled in the moonlight as he peered up at me. "So I brought you one."

I barely suppressed a squeal as I whirled around to face the full-length mirror resting against my wall. Straightening the jersey, I held it against my body and admired the sight.

"Are you going to wear it when you attend my away games?" Cade came to stand behind me, hooking an arm around my neck and drawing me back into his chest. "You promised me, Ellie."

I smoothed my hands over the hockey jersey. It smelled like him, and I was going to sleep in it tonight. "Ellie, hm?"

"It's my new nickname for you."

I loved it when he gave me cute nicknames. "I like it."

"I like *you*." He pressed a kiss against my cheek, watching me through the mirror with stark craving. "And I like this little outfit you have on."

His fingers trailed over my collarbone, teasingly snagging the shoulder strap of my bralette. The way his gaze caressed the short hemline of my skirt, I could tell just how much he liked it.

"Yeah?" I shot him a kittenish expression. "I can knit you one too if you'd like. I'm sure all the girls at St. Victoria will go gaga if they see you in one of my creations."

He burst out laughing. "Fuck, you're a brat."

Cade didn't laugh often, but when he did, it was infectious. I giggled too. "I know."

Once our laughter faded and we sobered up, I said softly, "I like you too, Cade."

He rested his chin on top of my head, gazing at me with reverence. "I have another surprise for you."

"You're spoiling me tonight."

"I'll always spoil you from here on out."

Be still, my heart.

Cade drew out something he'd been holding behind his back and inched it my way. "For you, princess."

"Oh, this is so lovely, Cade." I clasped the small bouquet. It was made with orange lollipops and tied together with a blue ribbon.

He suddenly looked shy. "I always see you enjoying orange lollipops at school."

It was so thoughtful of him to gift me an entire bouquet of them. "You've been watching me this whole time, eh? From the beginning, you've kept tabs on me too."

He nodded. "Yes."

I spun around and wound my arms around his neck. "Thank you for the jersey and lollipops. Very sweet of you. We've been official for less than ten minutes and you're already the best boyfriend ever."

Pride glimmered on his face. "Anything you desire, Ella, is yours. You tell me what you want and I'll get it for you."

"What if I tell you I want to ride the Ferris wheel at the carnival next week and kiss you when we reach the top?"

He tightened his hold on me like he was afraid of letting go. "Then we'll ride the Ferris wheel to the top and I'll kiss you."

"What if I tell you I want to steal your leather jacket so I can paint *Property of Ximena* all over the back of it?"

Cade shrugged off his leather jacket and draped it over my shoulders. "Then I'll say go for it."

He wasn't kidding when he said I could have anything I wanted. "What if I tell you that I want the whole world to know you're mine?"

He pondered over this, brows furrowed. "Then I'll go get your name tattooed on my skin so everybody knows I'm yours."

I pretended to swoon and faint in his arms. Cade laughed and burrowed me deeper into his warmth. "You like that, huh, pretty girl?"

"Yes," I said shamelessly. "But you're sixteen. A tattoo isn't legal until you're eighteen."

He tucked the strands of my hair behind my ears. "Sometimes, rules are meant to be broken, Ella. You want me to get a tattoo, I'll get a tattoo. I have my ways."

Spoken like a true mob prince. "If you get one, then I get one."

He smiled. "Deal."

Rising on my toes, I pressed our foreheads together and murmured one last thing, "What if I tell you that I want *this*—you and me—to last forever?"

Cade Killian Remington gazed at me like I created the entire universe. "Then I'll promise you that *this* will last past our dying breaths until I inevitably find you again in the next lifetime, Ella."

CHAPTER 10

You for me

CADE

The Past - 3 years ago

It was strange being in the Cordova mansion late at night, without Ella's or my family watching over us like hawks. Waiting for us to slip up and give them an indication that we were more than *friends*. Aunt Julia and Uncle Vance would be delighted if they knew we were together. Francisco and Silvia, who pretended to like me in front of my adoptive parents, might pop a fuse if they found out their goodie two-shoes daughter was now my girlfriend.

Ella Ximena Cordova was the most beautiful thing to have graced this Earth and she was finally mine.

All. Goddamn. Mine.

I didn't give a shit if her parents didn't think I was good enough. I'd prove them wrong. I'd prove to the world that I deserved this incredible girl. I'd become the man she needed, treat her with the respect, care, and affection fitting for a princess.

For a long time, my bleak life was filled with a never-ending series of hardships. Following my parents' deaths, I was certain I'd never see the light at the end of the tunnel.

Then I met Ella.

She was akin to a rainbow entering my grey skies after the longest storm.

One look from her and I was bewitched.

After our first meeting, I kept thinking of her.

How pretty she looked getting soaked in the rain while staring at me with unabashed wonderment.

After our second meeting, I started dreaming of her.

How prophetic she looked standing in her balcony wearing that white dress, as though she was the living embodiment of a blessing I'd spent years praying for to the universe.

Wherever I looked, I saw Ella. Even if she wasn't there, my mind conjured her image. Like a shadow, she followed me everywhere. Like a beacon, she guided me towards her.

I never had such a visceral reaction to another human being. I wanted to own and possess this girl. I wanted to shield her from all harm and keep her safe in my arms. I wanted to dote on all facets of her personality and cater to all her whims. I wanted to…love and help her flourish while standing by her side through thick and thin.

Mere weeks of knowing Ella and I was madly obsessed.

Could you blame me?

This girl was straight out of my fantasies. She was placed in my path, hand-picked and delivered straight from the heavens.

The void in my heart mended when she was in my orbit and I craved her presence like an addict craved its choice of drug. Mine just happened to be a five-foot-seven girl with luscious black hair, slim curves, and an extraordinary gaze.

Speaking of my girlfriend, she was currently making us *champurrados*—Mexican hot chocolate with a dash of spice—by the stovetop while I leaned against the kitchen counter beside her, eating the enchiladas she reheated for me.

I skipped dinner since I had a long night tending to business with Josh and Uncle Vance. So Ella took it upon herself to feed me after we finished the math assignment.

"Is it good?" Ella asked after I demolished half of my plate.

I waited until I swallowed my forkful of enchiladas to speak. "Delicious. Did you make it?"

"Yes," she said proudly, stirring the pot with a wooden whisk called a *molinillo*. The aroma of chocolate, cinnamon, and chilli wafted in the air. "I enjoy cooking and this is my speciality."

Was there anything this girl couldn't do? "This is my new favourite meal."

"And why is that?"

She was going to make me spell it out. As she should. I'd cherish anything she gave me. "Because you made it."

Ella smiled smugly. "Well, I'm glad you're loving it. Do you want more?"

I finished everything on my plate and patted my stomach. "I'm good, Ellie. Thank you for feeding me."

A soft gleam entered her eyes when she reached forth to cup my jaw. "You don't have to thank me for that. It makes me happy to provide for you in any way I can."

I turned my head to kiss her palm. Ella didn't know about my past. I could feel her wanting to ask, but remaining patient until I was ready to talk. I appreciated it. I didn't know how to start explaining to her that I was malnourished for months in the last year.

Food was a sacred resource to me. So was the girl in front of me.

"I enjoyed this meal." I pulled her into my arms. "Will you make it for me again someday?"

"Of course I will, *querido*."

My heart warmed. "What's something you like that I can do for you?"

She shook her head. "I'm not expecting anything in return for making you a warm meal, Cade."

"I know, but I want to provide for you, too." I wanted to fulfil all her materialistic and non-materialistic wishes. "Tell me, what would you like?"

Ella gave it some thought, tapping her chin with a finger. "Maybe you can give me a bouquet of lollipops every month?"

That was easy. "Done. What else?"

"There's not much else I want besides you." She kissed my cheek and my whole body melted under that singular touch.

"C'mon, humour me, Ellie." I tightened my hold on her waist. "I know you like purses and shoes." She always wore new ones and colour coordinated her outfits. "Maybe I can take you shopping some time?"

"Careful what you wish for, Cade," Ella teased, grazing my cheek with her knuckles lovingly. "I have a bad spending habit and I'm known for doing damage whenever I go to the mall."

"I'm good for it, baby."

Ella hummed. "You weren't kidding about spoiling me, huh?"

"What my princess wants, my princess gets." I dotted fervent little kisses all over her face. She giggled, a lilting sound marrying with the music playing from the radio on the counter, where a woman sang about dreaming of her lover.

We drank our *champurrados* and then I did my dishes. Ella sat on the kitchen counter, sifting the tips of her orange-painted nails through my hair. The gesture caused emotions to well in my chest. I couldn't remember the last time someone touched me with this much tenderness. I wondered if she could see on my face how much it meant to me.

"Will you tell me what you were doing tonight?"

I frowned. "With Uncle Vance and Josh?"

"Yes. Though it may not be the norm to discuss business with the women in the household, I'd like to know."

Actually, Uncle Vance shared everything with Aunt Julia, besides the gory details. I wouldn't be surprised if she cooked his books, too. "I'll only ever give you honesty, Ella."

She chewed her thumbnail. "So what were you doing tonight?"

I dried my hands using a clean tea towel. "Uncle Vance took us to the art gallery because we received new paintings…and a few pounds of cocaine."

Ella blinked. "Oh. Wow."

Folding my arms over my chest, I gave her a chance to digest the news. It was well known in our society and the underworld that Vance Remington ruled South Side, Montardor. The Remington wealth rooted from the various art galleries, strip clubs, bars, and illicit substances that travelled through our territory.

When the time came, Uncle Vance made it clear that Josh and I were to follow in his footsteps. It was our birthright. Our legacy.

For now, Uncle Vance put his sons—he refused to refer to me as anything else—on his company's payroll. Alongside Josh, the last two months were spent doing odd jobs for him. Helping his debt collectors. Touring the establishment where he grew cannabis. Hanging art pieces in his galleries. Keeping track of his various inventories. And the list went on.

I wasn't kidding when I told Ella I was good for it. Uncle Vance compensated us generously for every task. He even rewarded Olivia for watering the flower pots in our garden. My little sister noticed the gardener slacking one day and decided to steal his watering can and complete the job herself. Now Uncle Vance gave her chocolates and all the loose change in his wallet whenever she did her little 'chore.'

After my parents died, I had lived a hand-to-mouth existence, therefore it was shocking to step into the kind of wealth people only imagined in their wildest dreams.

"Do you have a lot of nights like these?" Ella hedged.

"I've had several in the past few weeks," I said. "Uncle Vance's business continues to grow and he thinks it's a great opportunity to show Josh and me the ropes. After all, this is our future."

Most of our businesses were legal entities, despite the money running through their veins being filthy. No one in the world was perfect. Everyone had to make a living. Running an empire of sin may be frowned upon by the general population, but most of the elites in Montardor were crooked.

You didn't make your way to the top by playing fair.

Learning about the inner workings of our operations was thrilling. Uncle Vance was pleased with my genuine interest in our affairs. Since I was good with numbers, he promised to give me the chance to manage our finances one day if I was serious about my studies.

"Ah, I suppose it's important for Vance to start integrating you in his...*dealings*," she said with a sinister calm that set me on edge.

A sinking feeling settled in the pit of my stomach.

Would this deter our relationship?

Ella was a high society daughter whose family mingled with

criminals, including mine. Hell, not too long ago, her parents were pushing her onto Josh—something that irked me even though my adoptive brother had zero interest in Ella—so it's not like our family business would be a roadblock for us, right?

The thought of Ella ending us before we even began had me sweating.

"Are you okay?" Ella eyed me curiously. "You look like you've seen a ghost."

Ghost? No. I'm actually imagining what my future might look like without you and I'm panicking. Actually, I can't breathe right now. Maybe I'm close to dying. Or fuck, having indigestion.

"From my enchiladas?" she asked, bewildered.

I must have said the last bit out loud.

Before I could tell her the truth, she slapped a hand over her mouth and released a strangled noise. "Oh my God! Are you lactose intolerant? Shit, Cade! You should have said something! I think I put an entire pound of cheese in there! The bathroom is down the hallway in case you need to—"

"I'm not lactose intolerant," I barked, my cheeks flushing. "And I'm not having indigestion. I'm just…I'm just…"

"You're what?" She placed a comforting hand on my shoulder. "What is it?"

I gulped. "I don't want to lose you because of what my family does."

Her face softened. She grabbed a fistful of my black sweater and dragged me closer between her legs, locking her ankles around my back so I was trapped. "My family aren't saints either, Cade," she hushed. "I'm not blind to what yours does, and I don't condemn you for it. I know that deep down, you have a heart of gold. You're sweet, protective, and respectful. You make me happier than I've ever been. That's all that matters to me. As long as you never stop treating me well, you'll never lose me."

Relief suckered punch through my sternum like a bullet.

I clasped her face, gazing into those captivating eyes. "You'll never lose me either, Ella."

We kissed on it, sealing both of our fates.

I was hers. She was mine.

There was no undoing it.

I'd fight any force that dared to mess with our happily ever after.

"You keep kissing me like that and I promise you, I'm not going anywhere," she mumbled in the space between our mouths.

"Challenge accepted."

Before I could kiss her again, she ran a finger over my bottom lip. "You know what else I like about you, princepin?"

"What?"

"On the surface, you appear calm, reserved, unbothered, solitary. A true lone wolf. But you've got a bad side, don't you?" She smiled wickedly. "One that comes out to play when someone messes with you."

I wasn't violent by nature, but my past had shaped my strong sense of justice. I wasn't above teaching sinners a lesson they'd never forget. That side of me was sharpened now that I was living with the Remingtons.

"Or you," I said vehemently. "I'll hurt any motherfucker who touches you or looks at you the wrong way."

She smiled. "And why is that?"

"Because you're mine, Ella." There was no going back from here. "And if there are any guys from your past that I need to be aware of, tell me now."

"What are you going to do?"

Make them disappear. "Have a nice chat with them to make sure they stay away from you."

"Someone's possessive."

"You're one to talk, Miss *I-want-to-stamp-my-name-on-all-your-belongings*."

"Touché," she said. "You have nothing to worry about, though. You're my first boyfriend...and you'll be my first everything."

The satisfaction on my face had her giggling playfully. Fuck, I liked that too much. The sound of her laugh and the fact that I'd be her first everything.

"What about you?" Her eyes narrowed. "Are there any girls before me that I should be aware of?"

Sheathe your claws, princess. There's no one but you. I pretended to ponder over her question, just to watch her morph into a green-eyed monster.

"Who are they?" she demanded through clenched teeth.

"Why, are you jealous?"

"*Yes.*"

A smile broke over my lips. She held my face, thumbs digging into my dimples. Half warning, half adoration. She'd make me sorry if the answer was anything but what she wanted. My territorial little princess.

"You shouldn't be, Ellie. There's never been anyone before you. Other girls don't matter to me. Not when *you* exist. You make me smile. You make me laugh. You make me happy. Because of you, I look forward to every sunrise and every sunset," I confessed. "Ella, my chest fills with so much warmth when I see you cheering for me by the bleachers at every hockey game. Do you realize what kind of effect you have on me? You've lowered my guard and pulled me out of my safely built walls. I've never had someone treat me the way you do. You're my best friend. You're my girl. And from now on, you're my first and last everything. There will only ever be you for me."

Ella's jaw slackened by the end of my monologue.

"Good." Her voice trembled. "There will only ever be you for me, too. And if there were other girls, I'd paint the town red."

I chuckled. "I knew you were a little crazy."

"You've seen nothing yet, Cade."

"Show me all your colours," I rasped. "I'll embrace them all, Ella."

"Oh, *querido.* You're stuck with me. I'm never letting you go."

"I don't want you to ever let me go."

When our lips touched in another searing kiss, I knew this was forever.

I was going to marry Ella Ximena Cordova one day.

Mark my words.

CHAPTER 11

Unwanted Memories of a Lone Wolf

CADE

The Past - 3 years ago

There was a feeling of bliss moving through my chest as Ella grabbed my hand and led us downstairs to the basement after we finished eating. Though she kept taking pit stops to kiss me in between and playfully demand I show her my dimples.

It's like someone took a knife and permanently carved a smile on my face. My cheeks hurt from grinning so much. I couldn't remember the last time I was this content.

Maybe when my parents were still alive. Or maybe the first time I saw baby Olivia and knew I was going to be her big brother.

I went so long without experiencing true happiness. Now that I was getting my first dose after years, the hardened layer of ice caging my heart thawed in my girlfriend's presence.

Ella Ximena Cordova was the sun of my galaxy.

The universe finally gave me my reward for all my suffering. I was clutching Ella with all my might. I'd never let her go.

Holding hands, we walked down a massive hallway in the basement, encased with many family photos of the Cordovas. I barely glanced at Ella's baby pictures before she tugged me in a room to our right.

"Welcome to my secret lair." She cackled like a villain, Mr. Burns style.

She was crazy. *My* kind of crazy.

Walking ahead, Ella toyed with some switches until the fancy bulbs hanging from the ceiling were dimmed to create a cozy ambiance. Then she hummed while lighting up some candles resting on a coffee table.

"Is this where you are when we have our late-night calls?" The room was spacious. Quotes and symbols related to feminism and girl power were painted in various shades on an accent brick wall in graffito manner. There was a work desk with half-finished knitwear, tall shelves with cubbies housing colourful rolls of yarn, a velvet couch, a wall-mounted TV, and other knick-knacks that were part of Ella's personality.

"Mhm. Do you like my place?"

"It's really nice, Ellie." I walked towards a table sitting under the basement window. There were lots of colourful rocks laid out in a mishmash. "What are these?"

Ella sauntered towards me. "Those are my crystals. I charge them whenever there's a new moon."

My brows furrowed. I was extremely confused. "What?"

She stifled a chuckle and threw her arms around my neck. I grabbed her waist, pulling her closer. "Many ancient cultures believed that crystals contained healing properties that helped our mind, body, and soul. Each crystal is different and they are meant to boost good energy and rid you of the negative kind. I've been collecting them since I was a little girl. I like to carry a few crystals with me and even wear them as jewellery." Ella showed me her wrist, adorned with a friendship bracelet from Darla and a pink beaded bracelet. She touched the latter for emphasis. "This is rose quartz. It's said to emit strong vibrations of love."

The way she smiled up at me had my chest tightening. "I love how passionate you are about this. Where do you get your crystals from?"

So I can buy you more.

"There's a crystal shop in downtown that I really like." She arched a brow. "Why, you want to take me there?"

I nodded.

She grinned. "Do you want a crystal too?"

"Only if you want to give me one."

Ella gazed inquisitively at the table. She picked up a black crystal and handed it to me. "You can have this one. It's an obsidian. It'll help with any stress you're feeling and block off any negative energy. It also has protective properties. Promise to keep it with you at all times?"

I touched the opaque crystal, its shiny black surface gleaming. It was the size of a knuckle. I shoved it in my pocket. "Thank you, Ella. I promise I'll always have it with me." I laid a gentle peck on her cheek. "Is this your way of making sure I'm kept out of harm's way?"

I meant to use a teasing tone. Instead, my voice came out gravelly.

"Yes." Ella caressed her thumb over my jaw in a soothing stroke. "I know you've had a rough past, even though you don't talk about it. Though I can't do anything about what's happened before, I want to protect you in any way I can moving forward. If anything or anyone hurts you, I'll fight them tooth and nail. No one hurts my *querido* and gets away with it."

A myriad of feelings rushed through me. Emotions I never experienced until this moment bubbled to the surface and threatened to spill over. A slave to the pull between us, I drew her into my arms quickly.

She was my match made in heaven.

Mine in every sense of the word.

Ella hugged me back and rested her head over my wildly beating heart.

She understood everything I wished I could say but was unable to utter.

After Ella tossed my leather jacket around a sewing mannequin with a wink, my girlfriend swore to bedazzle it with her mark. Then she led us towards the couch in the middle of the room and put on a scary movie.

Most people tended to watch movies in silence. Not Ella. A total chatterbox, she kept giving her commentary. I didn't mind, though. For so long, my life was filled with silence. Ella's talkative nature was welcomed. I liked hearing everything that was on her mind.

It all mattered to me.

We watched the movie while Ella knitted something with black yarn, completely unafraid of the horror setting.

I remembered her telling me she had an affinity for spooky things. Ghost stories. Mystery movies. Halloween. Etc.

There was a bad girl hiding underneath that good girl façade.

And I was thrilled at the thought of unravelling her layers and beholding them in a way no man had *or* ever would.

"Are you excited for Initiation Night?" Ella asked sweetly, while the demon ate away at the priest in the background, shrilling noises echoing through the surround sound system in the room.

I was fascinated with how quick her fingers moved over her creation. "Yeah. Shaun gave me a quick rundown. It sounds like fun."

Her eyes sparkled with joy and I was once again hypnotized by her beautiful gaze. God, how was she so perfect? "Oh, it's fun all right. I played last year and came in second place. I'm hoping to win this year now that I have a better grasp on how the game works."

I liked her competitive spirit. "I hope we get paired together, Ellie."

"Me too. We'd make the best team ever and kick ass!"

Her happiness was infectious. Smiling, I leaned forward to kiss her, tasting a combination of chocolate and the orange lollipop she'd been suckling.

"That reminds me," she whispered against my lips. "I'm knitting a sweater for you."

I blinked. "Is that what you've been doing this whole time?"

"Yup." She pointedly lifted the black fabric attached to her knitting needles. "You always wear crewneck style sweaters under your jackets and I…wanted to make you one."

She's so sweet. "Thank you. I can't wait to wear it."

"Can I get your exact measurements?" Ella asked sheepishly.

"Yes, that's no problem."

"Take your shirt off, Cade."

A wave of ice washed over me when I really processed her request.

Take your shirt off, Cade.

Fuck.

I couldn't do that.

Sensing the tension coiling in my muscles, Ella searched my eyes. "What's wrong?"

You're together now, Cade. There should be no secrets between you two. Ella deserves to know the truth. Despite it being fucking ugly.

I decided to show her instead of saying it.

Holding my breath, I grabbed the hemline of my sweater and lifted it off my torso in one swoop.

Ella didn't see it right away.

But three seconds later, when she did, her gasp was loud. "Oh my God. What…What happened to you, Cade?"

Shame pelted me like rocks from every angle.

"Now's your chance to call me a freak." I glanced away, not wanting to see disgust—or worse, pity—in her eyes.

The raised angry pink lines started at the left side of my collarbone and criss-crossed over to my shoulder in a disarray pattern before travelling down my arm until they reached my wrist. It was everything horrendous, grotesque, and then some more.

I never felt embarrassed about the damage hiding beneath my skin. But the scars visible to the naked eye were the ones that made me wish, for a small moment in time, that I wasn't alive.

I avoided looking at them every day when I got dressed. The mirror was not my friend. I hated seeing what *he* turned me into. A beast of sorts.

Ella grabbed my face, urging me to meet her eyes. "How did this…I don't understand…" Horror laced her trembling voice. "Please, tell me."

My gut instinct always told me that I could trust this girl, be vulnerable with her, and eventually, when the time came, divulge all my secrets.

Now was that time.

"My uncle did this to me."

Her ashen face flared with anger. "Vance—"

"No," I swiftly corrected. "Not Uncle Vance. This was my dad's brother. The one I lived with after my parents passed away. Julius…Olivia's father."

"Start at the beginning," Ella pleaded. "I want to know everything."

When I pondered over how to best explain my story, she grabbed my left wrist and squeezed gently. "I'll never repeat a single word of what you say tonight to another person. All your secrets are safe with me, Cade. I promise you."

The fierce protectiveness in her tone did it for me.

I started talking and Ella listened intently and patiently, hanging on every sentence with a dedicated intensity that filled me with even more affection for her.

I told her about my parents—how Vera and Ronan said fuck-you to every rule in Montardor's high society when they fell in love and eloped. My mom was the only daughter of the Remingtons. By falling in love with a man not up to par with my grandfather's standards, she brought shame to their name and was disowned.

Then one night, when I was fifteen years old, I slept over at a friend's house, unassuming of how my life would change in the span of mere hours.

My parents' home was set on fire. Nobody survived, not even my pregnant mother, whose body was found burned to a crisp.

In the snap of a finger, everything changed.

They died and I was shuffled over to Julius's house. Uncle Vance and Aunt Julia probably thought they were doing me a favour by allowing my dad's brother to take me in and keep me away from their dark world. The same one responsible for my parents' death. Little did they know that the months I lived with Julius were the worst imaginable nightmare.

Ella inched closer to me on the couch. Her body buzzed with an untamed energy, like an earthquake waiting to unleash. She braided her fingers with mine and skimmed my knuckles over her soft cheek before pressing a kiss to them. As if trying to ground herself. "What happened when you started living with him?"

It was difficult to discuss the next part of the story. Especially when I was in the presence of the girl who meant so much to me. I hoped she saw me as nothing but strong after this.

Not a weak, pathetic boy who'd succumbed to his demons.

"Julius was an angry fucker. Unhinged and with a bad drinking problem. From the minute I stepped into his house, I was his verbal punching bag. I never talked back because what was the point? I was stuck there with nowhere to go. The faster I got used to my new reality, the better." I chuckled without humour, rage pouring through my bloodstream when I remembered Julius's craggy face. "The social worker said I was 'lucky' to be alive—that I should count my blessings for not being in my home when it burned to smithereens."

Was it really luck when you were breathing, yet everything you loved was dead?

"Oh, Cade." Ella battled with the need to say more. But she gave me the floor to share my piece.

"I lived in that shithole for months, Ella. My only solace came in the form of Olivia. Her mother unfortunately died during childbirth. She was a one-night stand and Julius had no attachments to her or his baby girl," I said hoarsely. "When I first met Olivia, she was a tiny little thing, sitting in her bed with a calm stillness. She stared up at me with big brown eyes filled with relief and reached out a chubby fist, wanting me to take her hand. My mom was pregnant with a girl before she died. In a way, fate cruelly ripped away my parents from my life but gave me the little sister I was meant to have. It was the only silver lining in my fucked-up situation."

"I'm happy to know you had each other," Ella whispered. "That means Olivia is technically your cousin, right?"

"Yes." But now that the Remingtons had officially adopted us, she was legally considered my sister. "Aunt Julia and Uncle Vance have been quiet on the subject of our adoption because it's nobody's business. That's why no one knows the truth."

"My parents thought you were Vance's bastard child." Ella winced. "You two look so much alike."

"Yeah, I get that a lot." Uncle Vance would never cheat. He was one hundred percent devoted and obsessed with his wife. "My aunt and uncle never bothered to deny any of the rumours, even though Montardor's elites are gossip-hungry vultures. If they found out I was the late Vera Remington's son, it would cause a huge upheaval and put me in the limelight…and not in a good way, Ella."

My mom, when she was still part of Montardor's high society, was beloved. I heard over the years that she broke a lot of hearts and caused a big stir when she eloped with my dad, Vegas style.

Not to mention…my grandfather had promised her hand in marriage to a rival family in the neighbouring city. Obviously, that business transaction went sour and caused a lot of bloodshed.

Uncle Vance and Aunt Julia said it was best to stay silent regarding my origins.

"Are you okay, Cade?" Ella gingerly pressed her palm to my jaw. "I mean, to continue talking about this. I want to know more, but I don't want to jog up too many bad memories."

I swallowed the tightness forming in my throat. "Yes, I want to tell you this." Remembering hurt but relaying this story to Ella felt therapeutic. "If you'll still listen."

"I'm listening." She rubbed my cheeks in a nurturing manner. "I'll always listen to you. I'm here now. Let me shoulder some of your burdens. You'll never have to fight your demons on your own. *Ahora me tienes, querido.*"

My pulse sped up. "What does that mean?"

"You have me now," she murmured. "I'll never leave you."

"Promise?" I murmured back, my voice cracking.

She wove our pinkies together and tugged me closer with a mischievous expression, planting a peck where our fingers were joined in a vow. "Promise."

A smile touched my lips. Ella kissed the grooves on either side of my cheeks. I chuckled. "You're obsessed with my dimples."

"I'm obsessed with all of *you*," she corrected. "But I do have a soft spot for these." *Kiss.* "Cute." *Kiss.* "Little." *Kiss.* "Dimples!"

I laughed harder and Ella grinned wide.

Once the small bout of happiness subsided, she mumbled, "Please, go on."

While I collected old memories, Ella curled into my side, pressing her cheek against my mauled shoulder. She slung an arm around my waist and squeezed encouragingly.

"As I was saying, Julius had lots of issues, on top of being bitter about having two mouths to feed. Day and night, he would cuss at Olivia and me for simply existing. He forced me to work around the house like a dog, telling me I had to do chores to earn my keep. Julius would threaten to put me on the streets if I didn't comply with his rules." I cleared my throat and clutched the obsidian stone in my pocket. "A handful of times, he'd make me sleep in the shed outside during the coldest nights. I always got sick, and the sadistic bastard would laugh and assign me more tasks. Going to social services wouldn't have worked. They'd split up Olivia and me and shuffle us to new homes. It wasn't an option. Not when we formed a bond and grew extremely attached to one another."

"This is so awful, Cade. He had no right to treat you like that." Ella's voice shook as it rose an octave higher. "No one has the right to treat you like that. *Ever.*"

I clenched her tighter against me, appreciating her words more than I could convey. "In the first few weeks of living in that shithole, it became obvious that Julius wouldn't take care of us when he couldn't even take care of himself. Therefore, *I* had to take care of us. My job opportunities were limited and desperate times called for desperate measures, so I got in touch with a guy who could help me put food on the table. That's how I started dealing. It may have been unethical, but drug money was good money. I was able to buy Olivia all her necessities and to finally have something decent to eat besides stale cereal for breakfast, lunch, and dinner.

"Julius hated seeing how quickly I took on responsibility while his worthless ass was rotting away. It bruised his ego to see a kid thrice his junior be the man of the house. Therefore, he started punishing me in his own sick way." I rubbed my hand against Ella's arm to bring some heat to my cold fingers. "The abuse went from verbal to…physical."

Ella froze.

Humiliation prickled my skin until my breathing turned ragged. "Julius's insults morphed into shoves and punches very quickly. I was strong enough to fight him off, but I never did, afraid of the consequences. I thought to myself, '*if he takes his anger out on me, Olivia is safe.*'" My features twisted with torment and Ella sat up, eyes filling with moisture. "Y-You have to understand that everything I-I did was to protect Olivia. I couldn't risk him hurting her. I just couldn't, Ella. It was me or her. It didn't mean that I was weak. I-I was never weak—"

"Shh…" Ella caressed my face soothingly, halting my frantic words. Tears freely streamed down the slopes of her cheeks. "You survived a horrible situation as best as you could. You're not weak. You never were. Please don't think otherwise."

I wasn't weak. I knew it, though I didn't realize until now how badly I needed to hear it aloud. From *her*. Ella's words began to slowly heal the parts of me that felt broken.

"Julius gave me these scars two weeks before I moved in with the Remingtons." I gestured to my scarred arm. Ella sucked in a sharp breath. "I had just finished tucking Olivia in bed when Julius stumbled into the house minutes later, completely drunk and with a bottle of Jack. He spotted me on the staircase and started throwing insults. As always, I took his verbal assault. I was used to it. I didn't care. But when he raised his voice, I got worried it would wake up Olivia, who'd been sick all day. So I…I finally talked back for the first time. I told him to 'shut the fuck up' and he lost it. He walked up to where I stood, smashed the bottle against the banister, knocked me until I fell flat on the stairs and then…"

"No, no, no," Ella chanted on a tortured whisper.

I inhaled a shuddering breath. "Then he carved me, Ella. He pinned me under his weight and scraped the broken ends of the bottle against my skin like it was a chisel and I was an inanimate object for him to inject his brutality in. He relished my agony and laughed like a lunatic while I screamed and begged for him to stop."

Suddenly, my mind was transported back to that night where he altered me forever. I felt as though I was right there, under the mercy of that devil as he cut me up like a fucked-up piece of art.

It was Ella's sob that drew me back to reality. I watched as she clamped a hand over her mouth, barely stopping her cry of pain. "Oh, God."

"Olivia woke up from my screams and started wailing. Eventually, the neighbours heard the commotion and called the cops. I thought I was going to die on that staircase."

"Cade…"

"By the time the ambulance and cops arrived, I had fainted from blood loss. The next day in the hospital, I was informed that Julius was behind bars and social services had contacted the Remingtons about me and Olivia. They immediately took us in and the rest is history. Finally, the universe gave me a miracle. My life changed in the blink of an eye and here I am today. Healing, not so broken, and confessing all my secrets to the prettiest girl I've ever seen."

The last bit was meant to uplift the mood.

Ella only cried harder. I wiped her tears with my thumbs. My girlfriend was clearly an empath. When her cries wouldn't cease, I hugged her tight and laid my chin over her head. "Please don't cry, Ella. It hurts me to see you like this."

In this moment, she was my lifeline.

I wasn't capable of letting her go.

Not now.

Not ever.

There was a time when I wished I'd died with my parents in that fire. It was morbid, but it was true. Back then, it felt like my life was over.

Thinking back to those dark days and where I was now, I was grateful life gave me a second chance and new circumstances with an amazing family who cherished me infinitely.

And I reminded myself that every hardship and obstacle changed the course of my fate and led me to this incredible girl right here, weeping in my arms and looking up at me with so much love that it undid me.

"I can't help it." She buried her face in my neck. "The thought of you in pain breaks my heart. I'm sorry, Cade. So sorry you had to go through that. I wish I could pay Julius a visit in jail and hurt him for hurting you."

When she laid her palm against my beating heart, as if ensuring it was there and alive, all the toxins from my past ebbed away. "Thank you for hearing me out, *mo chuisle*."

Her glassy eyes blinked up at me with softness. "What does that mean?"

"My pulse," I murmured, bestowing a tender kiss to her lips.

She sighed. "That's so romantic."

I smiled and pressed my forehead to hers. "You gave me a nickname in your language. It was only fitting that I give you one in mine."

My parents were of Irish roots. Mom thought it was important for me to learn a bit of our language at the very least. Before she died, she'd spent an hour every weekend giving me lessons.

"Say it again."

"*Mo chuisle.*"

"Again."

"*Mo chuisle.*"

"I love it, *querido.*"

Hearing her say *querido* and *love* together stirred something deep in the depths of my heart.

My tongue felt heavy with one monumental sentence. It was three words, eight letters, and demanded to be voiced out loud. She needed to know just how much she meant to me.

I was enamoured with Ella Ximena Cordova.

We were cut from the same cloth, halves of the same whole, flames from the same fire.

She was created for me.

My very own destiny.

Taking advantage of my speechlessness, Ella climbed into my lap, sitting on top of me like a queen on her throne.

God, she was so damn pretty.

I wondered what she'd look like ten years, twenty years, fuck, even fifty years from now—stunning, no doubt—and how I wanted to be around to see her gracefully age. Laugh lines. Crow's feet. Grey hair. And those radiant blue-brown eyes, still incomparable as ever.

"Cade?"

"Yes, baby?"

"Let me look at your arm, please."

I extended my left arm for her to inspect. The pads of her fingertips glided up the jagged lines. With a single touch, Ella breathed an exuberant amount of healing into me. I shivered, my skin sensitive under her caresses.

Since the incident, it was the first time I was letting anyone this close to my scars. Allowing yourself to be vulnerable and open for judgement was a scary feat. Though I stayed at ease knowing Ella wouldn't pity me.

She'd heard the worse and was still here.

"You're not a freak," she stated once she finished touching my arm. "Your scars tell a story, but they don't define you. This does—Your heart." Her hand pressed over to my left pec for emphasis. "You're a survivor, Cade, and that's incredibly beautiful to me."

I was astounded by her.

No force in the universe could have stopped me from echoing the next confession.

"I love you, Ella," I rasped and gently cupped her face. "I think I fell for you when I saw you standing in the rain, gazing at me like I was the best thing you'd ever seen. Every moment since, I've kept falling deeper. I don't know how to stop. You've bewitched me. I love you so much that I cannot think beyond that sentiment. During the day, my mind is filled with thoughts of you. And at night, I dream of you incessantly. My world revolves around you, *mo chuisle*."

Ella vined her arms around my neck and stamped her mouth to mine with an eagerness that made me gasp. My hands chased down her back and grabbed her waist, clutching her small body to my bigger one like she was unbreakable under my strength.

We kissed with desperation and yearning. I tasted the saltiness of her tears and the sweetness of her tongue. She tasted the bite of my teeth on her lips and the very essence of my admission.

"I love you too, Cade," she confessed, raw and truthfully. "You've been mine and I've been yours from the moment we met." She laid an abundance of kisses all over my face. "There's no stopping this, *querido*. You've got me addicted, hooked, obsessed. You're trapped with me and I'm keeping you. Forever."

Don't let me go, Ella. "Promise?"

"Promise." She smiled beautifully. "From here on out, it'll always be you and me."

CHAPTER 12

Ride or Die

Ella

The Present

12:48 a.m.

The atmosphere was pure frost by the time we reached the sixth floor of Balthazar Building, yet the tension brewing between my ex-boyfriend and me kept my insides hot like an inferno.

Having been a cheerleader throughout my high school tenure, I was in good shape and still active now that I was in university. But goddamn, my leg muscles were starting to ache from climbing six flights of stairs in heeled boots.

Meanwhile, Cade barely broke a sweat. Playing hockey and his gangster side hustle kept him plenty fit.

Vance Remington had two heirs—two mob princes—who weren't afraid to get their hands dirty in the streets of Montardor. Over the last three years, Cade earned himself a reputation for being a *fixer*. Roughing patrons, collecting debts, and thoroughly helping run his adoptive father's underworld dealings. He walked around with a lethal edge and no one dared to mess with him.

Except for me, of course. I was the only one allowed to tease Cade and he'd loved it.

I padded further into the dormitories, feeling Cade's presence lurking not too far behind. He was ruminating. And I too was still digesting everything he'd said in the tunnels.

"I always dream of you, sweetheart. Ever since the first moment I saw you."

"I always want to kiss you, Ella. That's what I dream about most. Kissing you and never, ever coming up for air."

Those words lowered a little bit of my resolve to stay away from him…Not to mention, Cade's dirty talk.

Good Lord, have mercy on me.

I was a woman who got off on praise and degradation. He knew it very well. Never failed to give me what I wanted.

"Careful, princess. *Once I redden your ass into my favourite shade of red, I'll fuck the disrespectfulness out of you in no time."*

"Ask me like a good girl and I might consider giving you *the opportunity to suck my dick. I remember how much you loved getting your face fucked, Ella."*

To top it off? The crazy motherfucker actually got my name inked on the inside of his bottom lip. It was the sexiest thing ever. After my initial shock wore off, my thong dampened at the thought of his inked lips, wrapped around my clit, sucking me to orgasm.

Dammit. It was getting increasingly difficult to ignore the attraction between us. It had never left since the moment we met.

And now my suspicions were confirmed. Cade only came to Initiation Night with one sole purpose: to win me back. He wasn't a fan of this tradition, but he'd do just about anything—including partaking in a trivial competition—if it meant being close to me once more.

I wouldn't be surprised if Cade planned for us to get paired together.

"Based on the riddle, we're looking for a picture." Cade's deep voice yanked me out of my thoughts.

On the bright side, we were laying the elephant in the room—the conversation from the tunnels—to rest. "Yeah. Maybe the next dare is hidden behind an old photo frame."

Decades ago, Balthazar Building housed dormitories for students who lived on campus. There were rumours that ghosts lingered in the dominion. Some students claimed to hear voices, eventually making them go mad, climb up the bell tower to reach the belfry...

And jump to their inevitable demise.

Too many dead students. Too much scandal. It forced St. Victoria to shut down this area. Since then, no student had stayed here. Though Principal Hill did say that the building was now strictly used for private faculty meetings.

The sixth floor had a musty smell. There was obviously a lack of proper ventilation.

Cade and I stood in the middle of a hallway, flanked by various doors on either side that led to separate lodgings.

"The picture is probably in one of these rooms." I walked to a closed door. When I tested the doorknob, it wouldn't budge.

I shook it with frustration.

"Easy, tiger. You're going to break it if you keep doing that."

"What do you suggest we do, huh?" I snarled, stressed because we'd wasted enough time in the tunnels.

"'As per the rules, we are not allowed to damage anything on school property'," he parroted my own words, his smirk growing at my sour expression. "And I suggest we use the bobby pin strategically hanging from the elastic band tied around the doorknob."

"Oh." That's the first thing I should have noticed. Snatching the bobby pin, I thrust my flashlight at him. "Hold this while I open the lock."

Cade taught me how to pick a lock in record time one night when we were out raising teenage hell around the city. My ex-boyfriend taught me a lot of things actually—how to shoot a gun, how to drive a motorcycle, how to sixty-nine, how to love and be loved in return—and this was just another reminder of how utterly perfect we'd once been.

Cade shone light over my hands as I opened the bobby pin at a ninety-degree angle. Then I inserted the pin meticulously, managing to disengage the lock on the first try.

Twisting the knob, the door opened with a creaky sound.

Our flashlights chased across the walls of the dorm room. There were two single beds, a small dresser, and a window covered with old, tattered curtains. It lacked personality, considering how long the building had remained vacant.

"I'll search one side of the room and you take the other. It'll go faster," I said.

Cade wordlessly agreed. He went to the right and I darted to the left. With the constant drone of the rainstorm as a backdrop, we searched through the drawers, the space under the beds, and the closet.

"There's nothing," Cade concluded after a few minutes of rummaging.

My shoulders slumped. "I don't see anything remotely similar to a photo either."

"We have exactly two hours left."

"Shit." I drummed my fingers against my thigh. "Okay, let's split up. That way we'll stay on track with the timer. I have another bobby pin here somewhere." I opened the zip of my crossbody purse and fished in the tiny compartment where I kept my pins and lip gloss. "Aha, here! Use this to unlock the other dorm rooms. I'll take the ones on the left side of the hall, and you take the ones on the right."

Cade killed the distance between us in two strides. Instead of grabbing the pin, he closed his fingers around my wrist like a manacle.

A shot of electricity pulsed from the touch.

Again.

His face dipped close to mine. "Is this your way of avoiding me— avoiding *us*?"

My expression fell. "There's nothing to avoid, Cade. There's just nothing *left*. For the sake of tonight, let's call it a truce. I don't—" I paused to inhale sharply. "I don't have it in me to rehash the past. Please, just drop it."

It was the honest to God truth. Regardless of our previous teasing and flirtation, I truly didn't have the energy to go over our history. There was too much of it.

Opening old wounds would not be wise.

"Before we go our separate ways, tell me something," he rasped. "In all these months, did you never once miss me…even for a second?"

I should lie to him. It's what he deserved. Yet in the dark room, the sliver of vulnerability in his tone was amplified and resonated with my softer side, the one that was completely weak for him.

It forced me to say the truth. "Just for a second."

Hope flared in the air like a tangible thing and I instantly regretted it. "Ella—"

"Please, Cade," I cut him off, not offering him the chance to build up on that hope. I made my stance clear on our past: I didn't want to talk about it. "If you find the next dare before me, just call out my name."

I couldn't see his eyes, but I felt them all the same, hugging every inch of my silhouette the way they'd done many times in the past. I used to love the way he watched me with quiet intensity, like he was marvelling at my existence.

It was euphoric to know there was someone out there who viewed you in the same light reserved for celestial beings.

But it was also painful when that so-called someone hurt you in unimaginable ways…and you knew you'd never be together again.

"Do you hear me, Cade?" I whispered.

His voice rumbled like low thunder. "Yeah, I hear you, sweetheart."

Sweetheart, in that revered tone, chipped away another layer of ice surrounding my heart. If I spent more time in his presence, he'd rip away my entire armour and I'd be left with my core—half-healed, half-hurting.

Mustering all my strength, I walked away from him and towards the next door, feeling his gaze burning a hole into my back.

Applying the same technique as before, I unlocked the room and slipped inside, shutting the door with a decisive thud. The sound ricocheted like the final nail pounding in a coffin.

Resting my back against the wooden surface, my heartbeat picked up in rhythm.

I couldn't believe I confessed to missing him.

How odd that the admission made me feel weak and powerful at the same time. Weak, for he had betrayed me and stripped me of my pride. Powerful, for I finally had the courage to say the truth aloud. Not just to him, but to myself.

Cade Killian Remington had been like oxygen to me. Necessary and vital to my being.

I never thought in a million years I'd have to exist without my sustenance.

My ear strained to hear noise on the other end. Cade's resounding footsteps indicated that he successfully opened a dorm room and entered.

The following moments were spent searching one room after another, irritation skyrocketing in the hallway every time we crossed paths because we hadn't found the next dare. There was no picture anywhere and with every room I explored, I was getting closer to reaching my breaking point.

Eight minutes later, Cade and I regrouped.

"I found nothing." He folded his arms over his chest and leaned back against the hallway wall.

I mimicked his stance against the opposite wall. "I don't understand. We cracked the code. We reached the sixth floor. We unlocked every door. And yet not a single picture in sight. How is that possible?"

I angled my flashlight upwards to get a glimpse of his face.

Only to find his eyes fixated on something to my left.

"Are you listening to me?" I asked, twisting my neck to follow his line of sight. "What are you looking at?"

"I think I found our next dare. I can't believe we didn't see it sooner." He came to stand next to me, touching the framed corner of a painting. It was a portrait of an old man with a beard. "This must be Balthazar."

"And he's apparently worth a thousand words?" I scoffed.

"Don't speak ill of the dead, Ella. This place is crawling with ghosts. You don't want to piss off the wrong ones."

"I thought you viewed the paranormal with a hearty dose of skepticism?"

"I do, but even I can't seem to shake off the strong sense of foreboding in this building." Cade's mouth pinched in a grim line. "All the cases of students jumping to their death from the belfry...It doesn't sit right with me."

"Yeah," I agreed solemnly then added, "Well, guess we better find the next dare quickly before a spirit starts to whisper all sorts of demonic shit in our ears."

"Or worse." Cade played along, shuddering. "Possesses us."

"Just imagine Shaun in his plague doctor costume, smacking us with a Bible and chanting, *I rebuke the devil in the name of Jesus!*"

"He'd happily take on the role of the priest." Cade snorted. "And douse us with holy water."

"Welcome to the exorcism of Cade and Ella," I teased. "Brought to you by the ghosts of Balthazar Building and St. Victoria's thirty-fifth annual Initiation Night."

"Oh no," Cade said with mock-horror. "I think I heard a whisper."

"Oh, God." I gasped. "It's starting."

We broke into a chuckle-cackle combo.

It soon faded away like the storm outside, leaving in its place a bittersweetness that only emphasized the length of time we'd gone by without laughing together. Something so simple but significant in our relationship. We had shared many jokes and smiles over three years.

Cade, to my surprise, didn't comment on the fact that this was our first shared laugh in three months. Instead, he ran his fingers around the edges of the painting. "This is the only picture on this floor, so we're obviously on the right path."

"Maybe if we lift the painting, there will be something hidden behind."

Cade wrapped his fingers around the ornate frame and tried to lift, his expression morphing with exertion. "Fuck, I think it's bolted to the wall."

"Let me try."

"It's heavy, baby, and I don't want you to hurt yourself," he said softly, not being patronizing at all. "And I don't want you to break your pretty nails either."

The sincere display of concern melted my heart into a puddle. This man, he incited the most hot and cold reactions from me. One minute I was happy. Another minute I was angry. And afterwards I was torn.

Despite knowing I was strong, Cade never let me open my own doors or lift anything too hefty. Princess treatment only for me. From him holding my designer bags during shopping sprees to him massaging my feet at the end of them. I was a goddess in his presence and he, my humblest, dearest devotee.

"I'm made of sterner stuff, Cade."

"Don't I know it." A crestfallen smile flashed on his lips, but it was gone as quick as it came. "If you insist, though, have at it—oh, fuck."

We both flinched at the gravelly noise that erupted in the hallway. Loud like the yawn of an angry monster being forced to rise from his slumber.

"What is that?" I hissed.

Still bolted to the wall, the painting was tilted at an awkward, sideways angle.

At the end of the hallway, there was a door disguised as a grey brick wall that creaked open like the gate to a demon's cave.

For the first time tonight, a frisson of fear skated down my spine.

"I think there was a lever hidden behind the painting. That's why I couldn't yank it off. It was hiding"—Cade chin-nodded towards the end of the hallway—"whatever lies beyond there."

"That's where the next dare is." *How wonderful.* "I really hope that doesn't lead us to the belfry."

The bell tower was connected to this building. I wouldn't be surprised if the opening was a passageway that led straight to the belfry. And the last thing I wanted was for us to climb all the way to the top and get pushed down to our deaths by some vengeful entity.

Sure, I was a thrill junkie, but I'd like to stay alive.

Protectiveness poured into Cade's frame. "Stay here. I'll go check it out. You don't have to come with me."

"I'm coming with you."

"It could be dangerous, Ella." He grabbed my wrist to halt me, his thumb roving over my veins in an endearing manner. "I can't risk it."

I glanced down at his hand, basking in the heat emanating from the touch. Before showing up to Initiation Night, I was still on the *I-hate-Cade* bandwagon. Now my feelings were a mess. Nothing was black or white. It was all grey and murky.

I wanted to continue hating him. Yet with every second spent in his presence, it was getting harder to remember how he'd betrayed, humiliated, and shattered me in one strike.

It was just the magic of the night and the close proximity that had us momentarily acting like our old selves.

The Ella and Cade before tragedy struck us.

That's what I kept telling myself.

There was no other reason because there was no hope of reconciliation. Ever.

I wiggled my hand out of his hold and lifted a haughty eyebrow in his direction. "I've ridden on the back of your motorcycle while you shot a grenade at mafiosos following us. I can handle danger, Cade."

Dating the son of a kingpin, danger naturally came with the territory. I'd spent many nights with Cade while he punished dirty rats and further solidified the Remington reign.

There had been some close calls, but I never worried for my safety when I was with Cade. I knew he'd always protect me come hell or high water.

"*Fine.*" He started walking ahead. "But stay behind me. I don't trust whatever is on the other side."

"You think it's the bogeyman?" I joked, falling into step *beside* him. "The proverbial monster hiding in the abandoned tower, waiting to feast upon the flesh of young students."

Cade chuckled. "You watch too many scary movies, Ella."

I wasn't going to deny it. I had an affinity for mystery, gothic, and horror movies. I'd made my ex-boyfriend watch at least one with me every other weekend.

Sometimes, I wondered if those were the reason for my interest in fear play and primal kink. A few months ago, I finally admitted to Cade my fantasy of being chased in the woods with his mask on. However, we never got around to fulfilling it.

We reached the end of the hallway. The only thing visible from here was a pair of hidden stairs leading up to an unknown destination.

All right, that was creepy.

Realistically speaking, it couldn't be a mythical creature like a three-headed dog. Perhaps it was a secret lair? St. Victoria was known for having many hideaways from its time as a motherhouse. Though most of them had been sealed over the decades.

"I think it's one of the bell tower entrances," Cade said flatly. "And it'll definitely bring us to the belfry."

My shoulders sagged. *Well, fuck.* "You're probably right."

Cade touched my waist, sensing my unease. "My offer still stands. I can go alone and you can wait for me down here."

Scared or not, I never backed down from a challenge. "I'm not letting you go alone, Cade."

"Always so ride or die." He smiled. "Fine. Let's go, Ellie."

A light inkling of pain pulsed through me.

Ride or die.

He knew what those words meant to us.

Once again, he threw the past right in our faces. I was doing my best to remain civil. But he was doing everything in his power to unbalance my emotions so I could react and give him the version of me I was keeping under lock.

The one that wasn't indifferent and wore her heart on her sleeve for him.

Ire swelled inside my body, running from the roots of my hair to the tips of my pedicured toes. Until I was vibrating with the urge to lash out and tell him to just fucking *stop*.

Instead, I calmed myself by sucking in a deep breath.

And then I entered the abyss with the man who'd once been my anchor in all of this maddening darkness.

CHAPTER 13

Bats in the Belfry

Ella

The Present

1:13 a.m.

An endless series of stone steps welcomed us. Cade walked ahead of me, his broad shoulders nearly spanning the length of the narrow stairwell as we ascended. It was a good thing we weren't claustrophobic. Otherwise, the competition would end right here for us.

"Are you okay?" Cade asked, his voice echoing in the tight enclosure.

A few spiders scurried out of the brick walls. I shuddered. "Yeah, just peachy."

I could practically hear his smile. "Don't tell me you're thinking of giving up."

"Not a chance, *querido.*"

I cursed at myself for calling him by his nickname. Even in the dark, I could see Cade's posture straighten with contentment. Bastard. He probably thought I was *this close* to forgiving him.

Hah.

I could forgive a lot, but cheating was a hard no.

In my humble opinion, once a cheater, always a cheater.

The last three months, I often lay in my room replaying the moment I caught him red-handed. Dazed and confused and in his bed with the other girl. My anger would flare up, my heart would break all over again, and I'd cry myself to sleep, despite swearing to never shed another tear over my ex-boyfriend.

Cade apologized many times through texts and voicemails. Once, he even climbed up to my balcony Romeo style and tried to give me his bullshit excuses.

I shut the doors in his face.

After that, he slinked away to his own kingdom.

Though his yearning was palpable. It followed me like a shadow whenever we were in the same surroundings. Sometimes he tried to talk to me, and I ignored him. Cade was remorseful, but I didn't care. Taking him back after what he did would have been a slap in the face to my self-respect.

After reflecting on our broken relationship for weeks, I concluded that most of my hurt stemmed from the fact that Cade, of all people, shouldn't have betrayed me. He was supposed to be the other half of me— my ride or die. He'd always been so crazy in love with me that I didn't understand *how* or *why* he'd cheat.

Had I not showered him with all the love and affection in my cup?

Had I not given him the world too?

Had I not…been enough?

The night of Josh's nineteenth birthday party, when I caught Cade cheating, I thought the whole scene was a figment of my fucked-up imagination. It was so out-of-character for him to do something like that.

Cade was loyal to me.

He said there would only ever be me for him.

He called me *mo chuisle*. His pulse. His heartbeat. His fucking lifeline.

So how was it possible that my *querido* would hurt me like that? How was it possible that he'd throw away everything we had and ruin us as if we were nothing?

I would have loved for the whole thing to be a lie. But there was no denying it. The evidence was right there.

My ex-boyfriend had cheated on me.

And there was no undoing that.

"Ella?" Fingers snapped in front of my face. "Hello?"

I jerked, veered out of my musings and back to reality.

The first thing I noticed was Cade's handsome face, twisted in concern and bathed in the moonlight.

I momentarily lost sense of where we were, but the slight pain in my foot was a stark reminder that we'd ascended a long flight of stairs. "Y-Yeah?"

"We're here."

I glanced around, realizing we reached the top of the bell tower.

We were inside the belfry.

And it was freezing cold, courtesy of the blustery wind whipping against our bodies.

The chamber was composed of a turret roof, brick walls pierced with arched openings, an ancient church bell hanging from the rafters, and a wooden railing protectively surrounding the hollow drop under the bell.

Nothing about this claustral closure felt sacred.

I peered over the railing and saw the rope attached to the bell fall endlessly down the tower. It looked ominous and reminded me of St. Victoria's most infamous rumour…that the establishment sat upon one of the gates of hell. Over the years, people speculated that its location was right under the bell tower.

Cade also surveyed down the tower's shaft. He flashed his light into the dark hole. "The rope probably ends at the bottom of the tower."

"When do you think this bell was last rung?"

"Decades ago, perhaps," Cade said. "Although Shaun swears hearing it once during detention last year. He said it was the ghosts of the dead nuns ringing it, trying to scare Mr. Crowley so he could give Shaun an early leave."

I shook my head with a smile. "Classic Shaun."

"Maybe the next dare is attached to the rope," Cade mumbled pensively. "Can you hold my flashlight while I try to see?"

I held both our flashlights while Cade leaned over to grab the rope. The wooden railing wobbled a little. Fear zapped through my body. "Careful. It's not stable."

"You worried for me, princess?"

"Call me princess again and I'll push you down the tower myself. Then you can ring the bell with the rest of the dead nuns."

He chuckled. "You wound me, Ella."

"You'll live."

Cade's fist latched onto the rope. My next inhale was packed with relief as he moved a step away from the railing and began to pull the rope up, one tug at a time.

The motion caused the bell to sway, ringing with a noise that sounded like a harbinger of doom. Goosebumps erupted over my skin. I wished Cade would hurry along. The belfry was giving me the creeps. There was one arched opening to my left whose louvers were halfway shattered. I was certain that's where all those students jumped to their deaths.

If I started hearing voices and seeing the deceased, we were getting out of dodge. Competition be damned.

While Cade continued to tug up the rope, I walked around the belfry, searching to see if there was any other hidden clue.

Lo and behold, I found a shovel propped against a brick wall. Upon closer inspection, I noticed the next dare was looped around the handle with a red thread. "Hey! I found the next—oh my God!"

Cade suddenly materialized behind me and my back collided into his muscular front.

"You scared me," I hissed.

"I'm sorry." He blinked bashfully. "I thought you were into that."

A blush warmed my cheeks. This was so not the time to talk about my kinks. "Shut the fuck up, Cade."

A devilish grin speared over his face. "I love it when you talk dirty to me."

Oh, I missed this. Our easy-going camaraderie and banter. Fighting the smile twitching my lips, I rolled my eyes and shoved his flashlight against his chest. "Can you get your mind out of the gutter for once?"

Cade pinned my hand, still holding the flashlight, against his chest. "With you in my vicinity? Impossible."

"You're such a horndog."

"Never heard you complaining about my sexual appetite when we were together." A cocky smirk flitted across his lips and he leaned forward, crowding me against the wall. "In fact, I recall you being an eager participant in our trysts. Remember that night I made you come three times in a row like a dirty little princess?"

Holy hell did I ever. My toes curled recalling the night he fucked me on his motorcycle under the moonlight. "No, actually. I have amnesia where you're concerned. Also, calling me princess again? That's three strikes."

"What are you going to do about it?" His hand shot out to cup my jaw and his minty breath fanned over my mouth.

"Well, since the threats of kneeing you in the balls and pushing you down the bell tower haven't worked, I'll have to resort to even more drastic measures." I sighed mockingly. "I'm going to set your beloved Ferrari on fire."

Cade played along, mock-gasping. "You wouldn't dare."

"You've got three options. Pick one. I'm being generous."

"Not the Ferrari." He gave me a suggestive once-over. "We have too many fond memories in it."

Ah, yes. Like bending me over the hood of it after a night of debauchery. "I guess I'm pushing you down the bell tower. Any last words?"

"If I die tonight, I'm haunting you for the rest of your life," Cade promised in a deliciously dark tone. "Until I can have you with me again, *mo chuisle*."

It was so twisted, yet a part of me loved it. "You're so predictable. That's exactly the kind of behaviour I expect from your possessive ass."

"Is that so?"

I pushed his hand away from my jaw. "We all know you have stalkerish tendencies. Since our breakup, you've followed me around the city." I threw him a glare and turned around to grab the shovel. "You're not sly, Cade."

He hushed in my ear, "I wasn't trying to be."

They were the same words I told him three years ago at the start of my obsession.

I inhaled shakily, concentrating on anything but the sexual tension brewing between us. "Look at the time. We've already wasted five minutes going back and forth over your funeral."

"Flirting with you is never wasted time, pretty girl."

I was a strong woman. Or I was trying to be. But if this man didn't stop, I was going to lose my sanity. "Enough chit-chatting. We have a competition to win."

Cade removed the dare from the shovel and read it. "Dig your own..."

There was only one thing you dug with a shovel on an occasion like this.

We caught on at the same time.

His eyes rose to mine with a knowing glint.

"Grave," I finished for us. "Dig your own grave."

As I completed the sentence, a cold breeze sailed through the belfry like a bad omen.

"We'll have to go into the woods."

Wordlessly, we both peered out an arched opening. St. Victoria's woodlands spanned a large chunk of its territory, safe-keeping an abandoned chapel, a decrepit resting place for those who burned in the fire decades ago, and several otherworldly secrets.

"The next dare is in the cemetery," I said and Cade nodded, watching the moon shine beyond the veil of murky clouds. "I hope we're not digging up a real grave because that's fucked-up even by Initiation Night standards."

In all my years of playing this game, I never received such a morbid dare.

Darla and Shaun didn't create the blueprint for tonight. There was an entire rulebook on Initiation Night that was passed down from one pair of alumni captains to the next. A lot of these dares had been in existence for decades and got recycled every few years.

"Are you going to give up if that's what it comes down to?"

I respected the dead and didn't want to disturb anyone's resting place. But at the same time... "I've never been a quitter, Cade."

The next gust of wind had my short strands sticking to my glossy lips. A mischievous twinkle sparked in Cade's blue eyes as he tucked them back behind my ear. I shivered, remembering the way Cade loved to play with my hair when we cuddled or made love.

"Mhm." He made a deep, satisfied noise in the back of his throat. "That's a good girl. We're going to get you that crown, aren't we?"

The feeling that throbbed through my flesh could only be described as unwanted desire. I wished—God, I *fucking* wished—this man didn't affect me the way he did. His voice. His words. His demeanor. His everything. I despised the way I trembled under his heady praise.

I had to strengthen my defences—had to adopt that stoicism that allowed me to escape in my head and far away from Cade.

I hated him for having so much power over my being.

My mind, my body, my soul.

It was still under Cade Killian Remington's control.

Rolling my shoulders back, I thrust the shovel at him and snatched the dare from his hand. "Let's get going. It's a long walk through the woods and digging a grave will no doubt take a lot of time."

I whirled around to leave, but Cade's hand on my shoulder halted me. His fingers feathered over my collarbone, the base of my throat—as though tracing his missing necklace—and up my neck until he cradled my cheek in his warm, calloused hand.

I once heard that eyes were the windows to the soul. And Cade had a way of staring at me with possessive warmth that made me feel so revered.

Like right now.

"Your eyes," he whispered as if seeing me for the first time under the glow of the moonlight. "You're wearing contacts."

He always told me my eyes were unique and didn't deserve to be covered up with contacts.

After our breakup, I'd made many changes, including reverting back to my old ways. I didn't want people to see my bare gaze when I started university. Having sectoral heterochromia made me feel vulnerable, a woe briefly tamed during my time with Cade, and now I felt insecure about it again.

With his remark, Cade threw our past in my face again, reminding me of how deeply we used to be embedded in each other's lives.

I couldn't forgive him for causing all these emotive feelings to whir in my chest.

"Yeah, I am. Do you have a problem with that?" I challenged. "Are you going to tell me next that you have a problem with the length of my hair? Perhaps you've gotten tired of the colour?"

"Don't," he warned, eyes flashing menacingly. "Don't do this, Ella."

A cold smile stamped over my lips and I batted my lashes. "Do you think I should dye my hair blond? Maybe I'll look more like the girl I caught you cheating on me with. That's your type, eh? *Blondes—*"

"Shut up, Ella," he growled, dropping his hand from my cheek like it caught fire. Going as far as retreating back a step. "You have no idea what you're talking about."

"No?" I chuckled humourlessly. "Because I could have sworn I caught you in bed with a blond girl, while you were in a committed relationship with me, you asshole."

I harboured resentment towards Cade for what he did, but I had no ill wishes for the other girl. After all, she didn't have any loyalty to me. But this motherfucker was supposed to.

Cade ran his fingers through his dark brown hair frustratedly. A muscle jumped in his jaw. He looked like he wanted to desperately say something.

Or throttle me.

Maybe a combination of both.

Cade's silence only fueled my wrath.

I wanted to hurt him the way he'd hurt me.

Taking another step his way so we were chest-to-chest, eye-to-eye, and heart-to-heart, I trailed my finger down his front, pulling the string of his hoodie in a provocative manner. "You know what I've learned about myself since breaking up with you?" I brought my lips to his ear, letting my breath fondle his skin in anticipation. "I've got a new type…And it's not you."

He flinched, my words ripping into him.

"I like brunets with *brown* eyes." I fingered the chain around his neck housing the promise ring I gave him. "Like the guy I fucked over the summer…and Josh."

Cade's tormented gaze clashed with mine as he absorbed my ugly lie, completely frozen under the weight of my deceit.

My expression conveyed my gratification. "Maybe I should have listened to my parents and dated your brother instead of wasting three years of my life on you."

I tore the promise ring from the chain and threw it out the window, right into the darkness of the night.

Then I whirled around and walked away from a shocked Cade.

My pride intact.

My invisible crown in place.

And my broken heart, leaving a trail of blood in my wake.

CHAPTER 14

Jealous Primepin

CADE

The Past – 2 months ago

The love of my life broke up with me twenty-eight days, two hours, and eight minutes ago. And since then, there's been a constant ache in my chest that wouldn't assuage no matter what I did. It festered in my core like a painful, pus-filled wound.

I couldn't eat, sleep, or breathe without thoughts of Ella consuming me. Day and night, whenever I closed my eyes, it was her face in my mind, tear-stricken and so heartbroken as she 'caught' me in the 'act.'

But I never cheated. I never had. I never would.

I tried to explain to her the truth, but she wasn't having any of it.

I called her. I texted her. I even climbed up to her balcony and tried to explain what really happened. She didn't want to hear me out.

Ella had moved on with her life. But I hadn't.

I was still here, pinning away like a lovesick fool.

Now I was at a crowded bar on a Friday night because Nico—one of my friends—texted me that my ex-girlfriend was here, playing pool and talking with a couple of preppy frat boys.

At first, I refused to believe it. Therefore, after completing business with Uncle Vance and Josh, I gunned it here to witness the sight myself.

Red mist coated my vision as I sat on a stool by the bar, not too far away from where Ella was flirting with a guy—tall, athletic-looking, and wearing an ugly red sweater. My stomach churned when she flipped her long hair over her shoulder and batted her lashes in that teasing manner that always did me in. And the fucker on the receiving end was eating up the attention like ice cream on a hot summer day.

Ella and I both turned nineteen a few days ago, and I bet this was her way of 'celebrating' her birthday. By spending her Friday night at one of the city's most popular bars, scouting the scene for fresh meat.

She didn't open my birthday messages and ignored all the gifts I sent to her home. A thousand orange begonias, a bouquet of orange lollipops, a basket filled with rolls of colourful yarn, and a key to something that couldn't be delivered to her—only *shown*.

Which was impossible to do if she refused to talk to me.

My knuckles tightened around my glass as I drowned my woes in a non-alcoholic drink, watching her flirt with another like I wasn't right here…bruised, bleeding, and in so much fucking pain.

"You need something stronger than that?" Nico asked, sensing my anger.

I glanced away from my ex-girlfriend and *fuckface*—that's what I was calling the dude with her—to address him. "I'm planning on being sober when I gut his insides, Nico."

Not to mention, I hadn't drunk a drop of alcohol since Josh's party. Couldn't bring myself to do it yet.

Nico chuckled and went on to pour a series of shots for a group of girls. They were eyeing him suggestively. This was the norm whenever he worked bartender duty, but he never paid attention to any of them, keeping his brown eyes downcast and running his fingers through his black inky curls.

Out of all the boys in our crew, he was the shier, reserved one.

Two more of my friends—Nate and Sam—suddenly joined us, flanking the bar on either side of me in a barricading manner. They'd been playing billiards, but Nico probably signalled them to come over, knowing I was about to carve a permanent smile on fuckface with my knife any minute now.

"What are you both talking about?" Nate inquired, slapping a twenty on the bar when Nico handed him his usual drink.

"Murder," I said conversationally and downed the contents in my glass.

"Slow down, Cade," Samuel drawled, green eyes sparking with mischief. "There are too many witnesses. Your uncle will have your head if you start shit now."

"Will be worth it. I'm itching for a fight."

"If it's a fight you want, I can jump in the ring with you." Nate grinned.

"Or me," Sam added.

I met these guys three years ago when I started going to the underground fighting gym in the city. We instantly formed a bond that was akin to brotherhood. After my breakup with Ella, I spent most of my evenings and weekends with them. I welcomed the pain of a gruelling match as it helped shift my focus away from the hole in my heart left by yours truly.

"Let me rephrase: I want to spill blood." I nodded to where my worst nightmare was being formed. "*His* blood, in particular."

"Tonight's not the night." Sam shook his head, running a hand over the dirty-blond stubble on his jaw. "If you're serious about this, wait until we can create a diversion and you have proper alibis."

I knew they were right. I was being irrational. But goddamn it, I couldn't stand to see Ella with someone else. It was one thing to imagine it and a whole other to see it in the flesh. If he started putting his hands on her? It would be his last night on Earth.

I never claimed to be a saint and they didn't call me a fixer for no reason.

"Fine," I gritted out. "I'll wait."

Likely not.

While the guys chatted around me, I revelled in my fury and observed Ella, letting the way she giggled and trailed a finger down fuckface's body burn in my retinas. When we got back together—and we would because we were fated—I wanted to remember this very moment so I could turn her over my lap and give her the ass-reddening spanking she deserved.

Was she playing with him to piss me off?

Had she even seen me yet?

"She definitely saw you," Nico answered, refilling my glass. "I think she's testing you, but don't—and I can't stress this enough—fall for it."

Too late.

I had carnage on my mind.

And the way she came dressed tonight?

Ella looked like sin and revenge wrapped in a pretty silk bow.

Her hair was straightened to perfection and her modelesque body was poured in stiletto black heels, a short black leather skirt on the scandalous side, and a matching top that barely contained her little tits. I had the animalistic urge to snap the straps with my teeth, suck her beaded nipples, chase my way down the valley between her breasts with my tongue, yank off her skirt, and graze my teeth over her hip bone, where *my* tattoo rested like a brand.

Fuck, I wanted to unravel her until she was a writhing mess of a dirty little princess. Her lipstick smeared, her mascara ruined, her nails scratching my back, and her pussy stretched around my girth as I pounded into her mercilessly.

My God, I craved this girl. She was everything to me.

The match to my fire.

The ying to my yang.

The storm to my calm.

The only one created for me.

Ella's face was flushed from the heat in the bar and the vodka sunrise she nursed, giving her the prettiest glow. Her lips were glossy and inviting. Fuckface couldn't stop staring at them.

The thing that hurt the most? My necklace was missing from her neck.

Meanwhile, I still wore the promise ring she gave me.

Sheer misery stroked my insides from seeing her throw her head back with laughter because of him. He smiled at her. She bit her lip. He moved in closer and lowered his head to whisper in her ear. She laughed some more.

I was tired of feeling like this. Heartsick, exhausted, and so fucking desperate for her touch. I'd give anything to see one smile, one glance, one inch of acknowledgment from my ex-girlfriend at this very moment.

Look at me. I'm right here. I need you so bad.

She didn't look at me. She didn't see me. She didn't need me the way I needed her.

Today was nothing short of a shitshow. Firstly, Uncle Vance, Josh, and I went over to the De la Croixes—another crime family in Montardor—whom we had a truce with to discuss business. Secondly, on our way back home, a group of bandits Uncle Vance once pissed off ambushed us. Thirdly, we had to dispose of the corpses and burn our clothes, and nothing irked me more than ruining a new suit with blood.

And now *this*...watching the person you love most in the world ignore your very existence as though you were invisible and insignificant.

I turned my focus back to my friends to help alleviate the pang reverberating in my chest.

Nico was busy blushing under the perusal of a few sorority girls. Nate was casually flirting with the woman sitting next to him. And Sam was scanning the crowd for a certain blond bombshell as he took a pull of his Jack and Coke.

"Have you found her?" I teased, but my voice lacked its usual enthusiasm.

Sam released a groan. "Yes, and she looks so fucking perfect."

I smirked. "Are you finally going to make a move?"

"If she stays put in one place long enough for me to make a move, I will," he rasped. "She's always slipping through my fingers."

I chuckled and followed his line of sight.

Tucked in the corner of the bar near a billiard table, Anna—the beauty queen Sam was obsessed with—was talking to Gabby. I knew them both because they were friends with Layla, who wasn't here tonight because Josh texted her that he was sneaking over to her place. He had a little scrape on his cheek, but he liked to dramatize everything in Layla's presence. That way, she'd give him all her affection and attention as she tended to his injuries. And I was actually jealous of them.

If things were different, I'd be with Ella right now, and she'd be fussing over my wounds and giving me sweet kisses.

Apparently, I could only go three minutes without thinking of her.

My gaze automatically jerked to where she stood by the wall.

And caught the exact moment when fuckface's hand slipped up Ella's thigh and into her skirt.

My nostrils flared.

Ella glared, slapped his hand away, and shoved him back. He didn't budge, getting closer with a sloppy laugh. She launched into a tirade, her orange claws digging into his chest in warning.

My mind buzzed like a hornet's nest, one murderous thought after the other bouncing in my skull. The black mood pervading my being exploded until the only option was ending the fucker.

The boys sensed the shift in my demeanor and noticed the scene before us.

"Fuck." Nico cursed and dropped one warning, "*Cade.*"

Sam slammed me back on the bar stool when I tried to get up. "Don't do it. Not here."

"I'm going to kill him," I murmured with an eerie calmness. "I have to."

The image of his blood on my hands, his broken limbs, and his eyes devoid of life flashed through my head. It pleased the envious beast inside of me who wanted his pound of flesh.

Nico pinched the bridge of his nose, Sam sighed defeatedly, and Nate said something intelligible to the woman he was talking to and she left before he fixed his attention on me.

"Listen to us for once, you stubborn ass," he grated. "This is not the time or place. I'll go have words with him so he backs off. But you'll have to wait for another opportunity to behead him."

They were all right. I just couldn't reason with my anger.

"Make sure you get his name," I gritted out.

Josh could run fuckface's details in his system to get me his address… so I could pay him a friendly visit with my gun.

Nate nodded and went over. He reached them and started having

160

words with the soon-to-be-dead guy.

Satisfaction coursed through my veins seeing the tipsy fucker scurry away like a mouse with his tail between his legs. Ella's expression went sour and she exchanged heated words with Nate. He crossed his arms over his chest and let her have at it.

Knowing my ex-girlfriend, she was probably shouting at him that she had the situation under control.

Nate said something to her.

Ella's back stiffened straight, the colour leaching from her face.

Then her head snapped in the direction of the bar.

And she finally acknowledged me but didn't smile at me.

Without seeing her eyes up close, I knew they'd be burning with that fire I loved.

Her gaze narrowed and she flicked her chin in a haughty, dismissive manner before shouldering past Nate.

Nate smoothed a hand through his black hair, tired. Ella had been really tight with my crew, and I knew our breakup fucked up the dynamics of their friendship. She barely spoke to the guys anymore and when she did, the mood was hostile. They missed her and were always nice to her. But Ella had a hard time being around anything or anyone that reminded her of me.

Knocking back the rest of my drink, I stood up and adjusted my diamond cufflinks. "I'm calling it a night. I'll see you boys tomorrow?"

Nico and Sam eyed me suspiciously.

Revulsion continued to build in the pit of my stomach. Whether Ella was talking to other guys just to piss me off or actually trying to fuck someone to get over me, I couldn't stand here and watch her slink off to another target.

"If you see her flirting with another guy, I trust you know what to do."

They both nodded.

I bid them good night and tossed a salute to Nate before leaving through the back exit.

Crickets chirped in the summer night when I stepped out.

The warm air chafed at my skin and I reached up to loosen my tie, only to remember I ditched it in my car before entering the bar. A feeling of suffocation thrummed in my throat.

My footsteps ate the short distance to my black Ferrari, parked in the alleyway next to the bar. Every step away from Ella yanked at the invisible pull connecting us together. To the point where I physically hurt, swept under a current of torment that gave leeway to harsh cravings.

I wanted her so bad; I couldn't think past the shameless hunger.

Fuck. I needed a smoke to take the edge off.

Reaching into my suit jacket, I pulled out a cigarette and the Zippo she got me two years ago for my seventeenth birthday. One side of the surface was engraved with my initials and on the other side she'd hand-painted an orange lollipop.

Depressed, I lit my vice and leaned against a brick wall, drawing smoke into my lungs in a vain attempt to calm my racing mind.

I couldn't elude thoughts of Ella.

Not when I was carrying tokens filled with her reminder. The Zippo in my suit jacket. The obsidian crystal in my pocket. The promise ring around my neck. The initials stitched in the cuff of my dress shirt. And the tattoos inked into my skin.

She was everywhere around me like the wind, ribboning my form in her balmy embrace. Without her, I was lonely like a starless summer sky.

When I finished my cigarette, a miracle happened.

Fuckface, now drunk as a skunk, stumbled out of the bar. *Alone.* There was a lack of lighting in the parking lot, except for a run-down lamppost that pulsed every few seconds, but I recognized his chin-length hair and ugly red sweater.

And his car was parked right behind mine.

It's like the universe was giving me the greenlight to teach him the most important lesson: *don't touch my girl unless you want a new face and your spleen ripped out.*

He hadn't seen me yet as he swayed to the driver's door. I took that as my cue. Not only did he deserve a beating for touching Ella, but the moron was about to drive drunk.

I pushed off the brick wall, put out my cigarette, and asked him, "What do you think you're doing?"

His head snapped up and he swivelled around. It was amusing watching him search for the source of my voice in the darkness. "W-Who's there?"

Your grim reaper. "I asked you a question, asshole."

I stepped out of the shadows and his eyebrows comically rose to his hairline. "Who the fuck are you?"

"If you don't answer my question in the next five seconds, I'm the man who's about to drive his fist through your face."

Fuckface's expression morphed from shock, horror, and then to pure disbelief. Despite his obvious drunkenness, he had gall, throwing his hands up in a fighting stance like he actually had the skills to take me on. "You don't want to mess with me, bro. My daddy is a lawyer."

I grinned savagely. "And *my* daddy is a murderer."

Then I punched his jaw, sending him flying backwards on his ass. His body hit the ground with a sickening crunch. I yanked him up by his collar and planted a few more hits.

Every time my fist connected against his face, my bloodthirst ramped up. Hearing his loud whimpers go mute and seeing his skin split into a crimson mess was instant gratification.

No one touched my girl without permission and walked away as a free man.

No. Fucking. One.

My reputation preceded me and after tonight, he and his so-called lawyer daddy would know to never mess with a goddamn Remington. We liked to hold vendettas and we were not afraid of getting revenge on those who wronged us.

Wrapped up in my task, I heard Ella's familiar gasp.

The red haze surrounding me slowly evaporated.

I glanced over my shoulder and saw her standing to my right.

Expression blank. Eyes unreadable. Stunning as ever.

Fuckface's body went limp in my hands and I dropped him like a sack of potatoes. Touching two fingers to his pulse confirmed he was still alive. Just unconscious. Good enough for now.

I straightened and dusted my hands over my suit jacket to remove any wrinkles. "Ah, princess." I smiled. "Fancy seeing you here."

There was nobody outside except for us. Our steady breaths broke the dead of the night.

"What are you doing?" Ella enunciated, trying her utmost best to hide her emotions from me.

It was futile when I was so attuned to her. I knew what made her sad, what made her laugh, what made her cry, and every little thing in between.

And right now? She was practically vibrating with rage despite her mask. The tightening of her knuckles was a telltale sign.

"We were practicing our fighting skills." I gestured to the idiot's unconscious body. "Naturally, I won."

Ella grabbed my arm and pushed me aside, wedging herself between me and fuckface to inspect the damage.

"Have you lost your mind?" she bit out. "What were you thinking beating the shit out of him, Cade?"

The only thing I could concentrate on, in this split second, was that my ex-girlfriend was touching me. Willingly. And how my heart pumped faster with joy.

"He put his hands on you, so I taught him a lesson."

"You can't go around killing every guy I talk to or touch," she argued.

"If the hands are *unwanted*—" I crowded her against the brick wall of the alleyway. "Watch me."

I dipped my face and she tipped hers up, erasing the distance between us.

Her exhales were now my inhales.

My senses were permeated with her decadent scent.

And just like that, the edge I tried to take off with my cigarette returned tenfold.

This was the first time in weeks that we'd been this close. A knot of yearning unfurled in my core.

With her maneater outfit, smoky makeup, and anger rolling off her body in waves, Ella was nothing short of devastatingly beautiful.

She looked like a dark angel ready to rip my heart out.

Heat and tension escalated in the minuscule space separating our bodies. Her eyes dropped down to my lips then back up to my eyes.

I licked my bottom lip.

We moved closer instinctively until our chests brushed.

I always believed that Ella was my reward for everything I'd been through. I wanted to marry this girl. She was my happily ever after. How could fate be so cruel as to give me the only thing I ever wanted and then rip her out of my arms like it was nothing?

"Who said they were unwanted?" She cocked an eyebrow.

Goading me? Fuck, it was working. "I saw you slap his hand away and cuss him out, Ella," I spat.

"Hm, so you decided to send Nate to do your dirty work?"

"Would you rather I have come over to stab him myself?"

It wasn't the first time I killed someone for her. I'd do it again in a heartbeat.

She knew it too.

Her eyes darkened, the blue in her right eye vivid as ever. "No. I would prefer you leave me alone. We're over. For good." Then she chin-nodded in the direction of fuckface. "And I don't need you to defend my honour, yet you still went ahead with your caveman tendencies. If anyone catches you, you're fucked, Cade."

"Spending the night in the slammer would be worth it, pretty girl." I pushed a lone strand behind her ear, resisting the urge to kiss those pouty lips.

"I'm being serious." She glared at me. "You've done enough damage for one night. Leave before you get caught."

Witnesses be damned. I wasn't afraid of spending the night in a cell. Plus, Uncle Vance or Josh would bail me out. It wasn't a big deal.

"Careful, Ella," I tutted. "For someone who claims to be done with me, you sound an awful lot like you still care." The way her body relaxed into mine with muscle memory spoke volumes. She was still as possessive of me as I was of her. "Now the truth: why did you come outside?"

Did she follow me out of the bar because she was desperate to get another glimpse of me? The same way I was desperate for a glimpse of her?

Suddenly, a mean smile curled over her mouth. "Certainly not for you, Cade. I hate you, remember?"

Pain pricked through my chest like a thousand little needles.

If she really came out for fuckface, I was going to paint the town red with his blood and drown his dead body in the Atlantic Ocean.

"Then why?" I growled.

"Maybe, I came outside…" Her voice was fused with wickedness as she ran the edge of her sharp claw over my jaw like a blade. "To *fuck* him."

I'd been beaten and tortured in the past.

But nothing came close to the wound she just dealt me.

I couldn't speak. I couldn't think. I couldn't breathe.

My trembling hand grasped the ends of her hair, twisted them twice around my fist like a leash, and tugged her head back with ardour, forcing her to acknowledge the havoc she wrecked within me with her words. "Tell me you're lying, *mo chuisle.*"

A whimper—part pain, part pleasure—escaped her parted lips. "*No.*"

Under the glittering stars, cratered moon, and inky night sky, she met my anguished gaze.

The heavens opened and unleashed their wrath in the form of rushing droplets that soaked us to the bones. They did nothing to cleanse us of our sins or the sensation of defeat barrelling through my frame.

Ella was my poison and remedy wrapped into one. My damnation and my salvation. My ruin and my triumph.

I loved her more than my own life.

I would die for her, kill for her, live for her.

But she was softly destroying me, twisting her knife deeper into my chest.

"Did you enjoy that?" I rasped, skimming my nose against the slender column of her throat, inhaling that tantalizing fragrance that morphed me from level-headed to a hot-blooded brute with a voracious need for her. I resisted the urge to bite her pulse. "Flirting with him to make me jealous? Touching him to rip me to shreds?"

"*Yes.*" Pretty venom laced her voice as she raked her claws down my chest like she wanted to slice me open. "You deserved it."

"Is this how it's going to be between us?" I kissed the skin under her chin. "You'll taunt me with other boys?"

Her hands fisted the lapels of my suit. "If that's what it takes for you to understand that we're over, then yes."

"Break my heart a thousand times, Ella. It's always been yours to do with as you please," I confessed and licked the raindrops lingering on her bottom lip. "But make no mistake…You and I? We're meant to be. Forever."

It was our promise.

"That was before you broke us." She retaliated by wresting my bottom lip with her teeth until she drew blood. "Fuck you and all your promises. Go to hell, Cade."

"I'm already there," I snarled, panting against her mouth and tugging her hair until her whole body arched under my strength. "You fucking put me there, sweetheart."

"Good. I hope you rot in your misery." Over the sound of the pounding rain, Ella's wretched words were like arrows tipped in poison, driving straight into my sternum. "Our undoing is on *you*. Therefore, you don't have a right to dictate who I speak to or fuck, you bastard. We're over. Get it through your thick skull."

"Please, Ella, just—"

"*No*. I'm done with you and your deceit." She pressed her palms to my shoulders and shoved me away. "I wish I never met you. God, I wish I *never* laid eyes on you."

Her words carried over the rain and wind, coiling deep in my muscles with a chilling quality.

Never met you. Never laid eyes on you.

I'd relive the moment where I first saw her a million times if given the chance. It was one of the happiest days of my life.

Ella was the best thing to have happened to me. I lost her and I was frantic to have her back, but she refused to hear me out. I stopped myself from falling to my knees and begging her to take back what she said.

The nerve endings in my body throbbed with grief. I hated that this amazing girl, who'd once loved me with her entire soul, was looking at me like I was scum beneath her stiletto heels.

It made me feel like the neglected, broken boy who'd arrived at the Remingtons' doorstep three years ago. The one who felt lost and inadequate. The one who was constantly fighting his demons and trying to prove to the world that he had worth.

"You don't mean that. Please, don't say that," I whispered vulnerably, trying to get through to her with the only words I had left in me. "I love you, Ellie."

A nasty gleam flared in her eyes. "Wish I could say the same to you, Cade."

Her strike left me raw, bleeding, and stunned.

I watched through a blurry veil as Ella sidestepped me and slipped back into the bar.

Dismissing me like I was a mere toy she'd gotten bored with. Leaving me alone in my solitude. Pretending like we never vowed that this—*us*—would last until our dying breaths.

I stood outside in the dark night, frozen in time. When the sound of the rain was louder than the deafening crack splitting my heart in two, I finally left, utterly numb and miserable as ever.

And still pining away for her.

CHAPTER 15

Broken Souls

Ella

The Present

1:28 a.m.

I journeyed down the secret staircase that connected the bell tower to the dormitories in Balthazar Building. When I landed on the sixth floor, my ears strained to hear if Cade was following.

He wasn't.

Based on the stark silence that welcomed me.

I should be happy that my jab dug into Cade like a bullet wound—that it hurt him as much as it hurt me to witness him with that other girl.

A cocktail of regret and resentment swirled on my palate. I wished I could let go of this grudge. Not because he deserved it. Because *I* did. I deserved to feel at peace without all of these unfettered emotions constantly warring inside of me. Not only was it painful, it was beyond exhausting.

Knowing Cade would recover from the burn of my insults and come after me, I descended the stairs of the dormitories. I knew from past experience of wandering the school grounds that the woods had a pathway connected directly to Balthazar Building, meaning there must be a door in the foyer that would lead us straight outside.

Every clack of my booted heels against the stairs echoed like a cacophonous beat reaching crescendo. The light of my torch ate away at some of the tenebrosity in the building, but an inkling of trepidation wrapped around my body, causing my flesh to pebble, as if warning me that *something* lurked in the vicinity.

The foyer opened before me as I reached the last flight of stairs. With two last steps remaining, my hand reached out for the gargoyle carved newel post…when the air suddenly rippled with a sinister aura.

In a flash, the ancient church bell started ringing.

I practically jumped out of my body at the horrifying sound tunnelling through the building in banging strokes, growing louder, louder, and *louder*. I lost my grip around my flashlight and it rolled down the staircase.

Out of nowhere, a hard shove came from the side.

I shrieked, tumbling down the last steps and landing painfully on my hands and knees.

I panted, a mixture of fear and fury.

Holy shit. What just happened?

The bell kept ringing, but the chimes were receding.

I crawled forward for my flashlight, my heart pounding, sweat perspiring my skin. When I grasped a hold of it with shaky hands, I lifted my head and let loose a strangled scream.

A man wearing a Guy Fawkes mask lowered to his haunches in front of me.

"I've been looking everywhere for you." The stranger grazed his knuckles over my cheek and leaned close until millimeters separated our faces. "You stupid little bitch."

What. The. Fuck.

His hand shot out to grab me. I dodged it in time and clocked a solid punch to his throat, causing him to grunt and land sideways.

In a trice, he came for me again with renewed vigour.

But I quickly stood up despite the protesting ache in my body. I was going to nail this motherfucker in the nuts. Some lowlife Initiator playing a shitty prank didn't scare me.

"You asshole!" I grabbed his shoulders and kneed him in the groin area, narrowly missing his bulge. Lucky bastard still stumbled away from me, winded by my hit. "Who are you—what's your fucking problem?"

"You," he seethed, coming forth once more to rip the dare from my hand. "This isn't over, you spoiled cunt."

The stranger ran away, towards the entrance leading into the tunnels.

But not before I caught sight of a very *familiar* skull tattoo on his hand and a platinum watch with a sapphire encrusted bezel.

I froze, an odd sensation crawling over me like a hundred tiny ants.

I had seen that exact tattoo and watch twice in my life.

I would never forget it.

A memory of a man with sandy brown hair, soulless eyes, demanding attitude, clammy hands, and those same markers pitched from the deep recesses of my mind. It was months old but now felt fresh and palpable like a noose around my throat.

He's dead, Ella.

Cade made sure of it.

You were there.

Was I hallucinating?

The soreness radiating through my body from that fall was all the confirmation I needed. This was reality and I most certainly saw what I saw.

Too distracted and disoriented, I noticed belatedly that Cade was descending the stairs, shovel in one hand and flashlight in the other.

A quick glance at him and it was clear that he was still basking in the fury of my parting shot. He looked far from my soft-hearted *querido* and more like Montardor's fixer. Stiff broad shoulders, inscrutable mien, and gangster gait as he advanced my way.

"I heard you screaming the house down," he said dryly. "Just like old times."

No flicker of worry was sketched in the lines of his face. I'd truly pissed him off if he was acting this unaffected. For a split second, I wondered how he'd feel if he knew a man wearing a Guy Fawkes mask attacked me.

Though I squandered that thought as fast as it came.

I didn't want him to show his care for me. I wanted impassiveness so we could power through Initiation Night and finally go our separate ways.

"Unfortunately for you, you'll never hear me screaming again," I piped up with a sickeningly sweet tone. *"Just like old times."*

"I wouldn't be so sure, baby."

My mouth gaped, my viper tongue ready with a riposte. But I swallowed it down along with the feeling of agitation surging in my person. Cade wouldn't get a single fiery reaction out of me. It's what he wanted. I refused to give in.

Instead, I spun around and winced at the throb in my ankle. "Whatever. Let's get out of here. There should be a door in the foyer that leads outside."

My ex-boyfriend and I often visited St. Victoria's woodlands, mostly when we were high and wanted to stargaze at night. Not our finest moments, but at least we knew the territory like the back of our hands. Getting to the cemetery would be a breeze.

Cade didn't reply, choosing to marinate in the strained silence as we walked to the main door. It just so happened to be left ajar and propped open by a wooden doorstopper. Probably due to other students having dares in Balthazar Building.

I instantly thought back to the encounter I had with the angry, insulting Initiator and my aggravation returned tenfold. It was so disturbing and unexpected. Sabotaging other teams was quite common during Initiation Night. But we were never supposed to take it to a physically-harming level. That was grounds for punishment.

I fine-combed through all the hockey players—current and alumni— and yet couldn't decipher who the stranger was. Nor did I recall seeing anyone with *that* specific mask.

I never had a problem with any of the boys on the team when I was a cheerleader at St. Victoria. In fact, I was on good terms with everyone, considering my boyfriend at that time was the alternate captain of the Rangers.

No one would have dared to insult or put their hands on me.

More so if they'd known that beneath my nice exterior was a cutthroat bitch who loved teaching a lesson to assholes that had the audacity to fuck with me.

The masked man sounded furious…like this was a personal vendetta. And goddammit, that tattoo and watch caused a flurry of vexing thoughts to race through my brain. *Who was that? Why would they attack me? What could inspire so much spite in them?* I wanted to connect the puzzles pieces, except I was missing the entire picture.

But when I got my answers?

That masked fucker will have wished he never crossed me.

Cade grimaced as he peered out the entrance door and observed the rainy night, fragrant with the sweet-musky scent of autumn leaves. "Shit, it's still raining."

I was about to ask him why he stated the obvious when he surprised me by shrugging out of his leather jacket and tossing it around me, making sure it covered my head and shoulders.

My kryptonite—the smell of him—engulfed my senses. I associated his cologne to pure comfort and inhaling it made me feel like I was stepping through the threshold of my home.

Off-kilter, I could only gawk at him in confusion. "What are you doing?"

Cade rubbed the back of his neck, unable to meet my stare. He lifted the hood of his black sweater to cover his head. "Your hair will get wet… and you've always been prone to catching a cold this time of the year."

My expression fell, hands clenching fistfuls of his leather jacket. "Cade…Just stop."

Stop messing with my mind and my heart. I'm not strong enough for this again. You. Me. Us. I can't do it.

He replied back, his tone ragged and desperate, "I *can't*, Ella."

CADE

1:51 a.m.

I'd dug enough graves to last me a lifetime, and here I was…digging up another.

Mind you, this was a fake one with a Halloween prop-style tombstone.

It wasn't difficult to spot in the cemetery, when the other graves had rudimentary markers like simple cross signs with no embellishments. Most of these belonged to the children who'd died in the fire nearly a hundred years ago.

When we were still students at St. Victoria, Ella used to drag me here every now and then so we could clean the graves and leave little flowers for the deceased.

As I dug, my traitorous mind replayed her words from the belfry and my jaw clenched. I couldn't believe she had the effrontery to spit those words. They ripped open old wounds, pouring salt inside of them.

"I've got a new type...And it's not you."

"I like brunets with brown *eyes. Like the guy I fucked over the summer... and Josh."*

"Maybe I should have listened to my parents and dated your brother instead of wasting three years of my life on you."

They were all lies designed to hurt me and it worked. She'd left me stunned inside the bell tower, counting my breaths to calm myself before I lost it.

The fact that she actually threw my promise ring out the window was just the cherry on top of this fucked-up cake. I wanted to snap at her, but I knew this was Ella's way of rebelling against what she *still* felt for me. I wasn't a delusional prick; I just knew her better than anyone in the world.

Ella's actions were proof that she hadn't moved on. Neither had I. And we probably never would until we talked about what happened. Even then, I knew for me...there was no moving on from her.

She was my beginning, my middle, my end.

If we were each other's venom, then we were each other's antidotes too.

Ella refused to acknowledge it, but the only way we'd heal was if we laid all our cards, all our feelings, all our fucking pain on the table.

And when I heard her scream on my way down the stairs of Balthazar Building, my heart stopped with fear. I thought someone was hurting her. I thought I heard another voice.

Yet when I arrived in the foyer, she was the only one standing. Composed and aloof, she didn't say anything. My guess was an Initiator

176

pranked her.

She'd trudged through the woods with a slower stride. Her booted heels kept sinking into the wet forest ground, holding back her pace. For a second, I thought she was limping.

The need to princess-carry Ella beat at my chest like a gong. I resisted the urge to grab her, lest risking her thwacking me across the head with the shovel.

Speaking of Ella, she now silently leaned against a tree, absentmindedly gazing into the distance. My jacket sheltered her while she held up both of our torches, giving me enough light to complete the enervating task of shovelling aside wet soil.

Ella's stillness unsettled me. I wanted to know what was going through her mind. Plus, I needed a distraction. Otherwise, I'd never get to the bottom of this fake grave. My muscles were starting to ache from tonight's exertion.

"Why'd you cut your hair?"

Her attention snapped my way. I liked having her eyes on me. Craved it, really. "Why, you don't like it?" she asked insolently.

Ah, finally. Some more emotions.

I chuckled, but it was strained as I heaved another pile of dirt. "You look good, pretty girl. It suits you."

She could wear a garbage bag and still look gorgeous.

"Thanks." Perhaps it was my imagination, but I believed the compliment thawed her a bit.

Our dares were long and with every second trickling by in the fictitious hourglass, I was uncertain that Ella would get her crown. We started this night with her determined to win this competition and me determined to win *her* back.

Both things seemed so far out of reach now.

There was so much I wanted to say, so much she needed to hear.

Yet the only thing that escaped my lips in this instance was, "I got a Doberman."

Ella perked up. "What?"

"His name is Knight. You'd love him. I found him at the shelter two weeks ago. He's a puppy."

Actually, Ella was his mommy…though she didn't know it. I showed Knight a picture of her and it was currently in his playpen. I caught him snuggling with it a few times.

In the beginning stages of our relationship, we made a bucket list. Adopting a dog together was one of Ella's wishes. We never got the chance. Though two weeks ago when I went to the animal shelter with Olivia…I saw Knight. At first glance, I knew he was coming home with us.

When Ella stayed silent, I added, "I'll show you a picture of him at the end of the competition once we get our phones back. He's adorable."

"You named him Knight." Her tone was almost accusing.

"Yeah." Avoiding her gaze, I heaved another shovelful of dirt and noticed a small treasure chest nestled in the ground. With my gloved hands, I yanked it out. "Found our next dare."

"*Why* did you name him Knight, Cade?"

The rain came down harder than before, but my voice was still unwavering and audible as it carried over to her. "It's the name you picked. It was on our list."

I saw the shift inside of her just as a flash of lightning struck above us.

Once more, I threw our past in her face and unbalanced the little composure she managed to uphold.

Ella instantly went from the vengeful, icy princess perusing the world from her balcony to the fiery Ella who went toe-to-toe with me. I hated the one who kept everyone, including me, at arm's length, so we could never see the wreckage brimming inside of her.

Let me see all your hurt.

Let me help heal your broken parts, sweetheart.

With a scoff, Ella marched towards me, throwing my leather jacket to the ground with an exaggerated flourish. She snatched the treasure chest from my hands, flipped open the lid, took out the next dare—another key with a paper threaded through the bow—and threw the empty box, along with my flashlight, into the grave.

Then she gave me the full force of her anger and finally yelled, "Fuck the list and fuck you too! Sometimes I look at you and all I see is a mistake!

My biggest fucking mistake!"

My biggest fucking mistake.

The cruel words had the devil on my left shoulder throwing his head back in laughter, causing the pressure in my sternum to explode and shrapnel to travel through my body with a painful ricochet.

When I looked at Ella, all I saw was my biggest blessing.

And she saw a mistake?

How did you tell the girl you loved that she still held your heart in the palm of her hands…while she looked at you with hatred?

How did you convince her to trust you one more time and hear your truth…when she remained blinded from her rage?

"I just want to erase your presence from my life," Ella rasped, chest heaving up and down as the rain battered harshly against our frames. "Your memory, your touch, your kiss—"

"Fuck a hundred men if you want, Ella," I threw back angrily, clutching her throat and drawing her deeper into my body. "But it will never erase me. None of them will give you what I did."

Feeble fists smacked against my chest in a vain attempt to free herself. "And what's that, huh?"

"The freedom to drop your guard and be whatever you choose— good, bad, fucking dirty—without an ounce of judgement." My panting breaths fanned against her parted lips. "No one can give you the feeling of euphoria like I did. And that's what kills you. You search for me in all those men, don't you, baby? You want to feel the way I used to make you feel— like a fucking goddess—when I worshipped the ground you walked on."

"You're wrong!" Teeth chattering, she shook her head, whipping the wet strands of her hair back and forth. Lightning sparked in the sky above us, illuminated her lovely, frustrated expression. Clapping thunder followed, like Zeus himself was laughing at our predicament. "All you're capable of giving me now is heartbreak. You ruined us with your cheating ways!"

"Why would I cheat on you when you were all I ever wanted?" I growled, desperate to lick the rain streaming down her face like tears, kiss the pain from her lips, and bleed absolution into us.

Ella grabbed my neck, her long nails sinking into my skin like a snake bite. "You tell me." She grazed the heated words so close to my parched lips, barely quenching my thirst. "I gave you everything. Every. Fucking. Thing. And it wasn't enough. *You* threw us into the flames!" Pocketing the dare in her cropped leather jacket, she spun around. "I'm done with you and this conversation. I should have known this truce wouldn't last. You can't even respect my one wish."

Goddammit.

I was sick and tired of staring at her back as she walked away from me.

I snarled, "Fuck, just listen to me—"

"Ow!" Ella only took two steps before she winced and nearly fell. I caught her on time, wrapping my arm around her waist to hoist her up.

All my anger disappeared at seeing her visage fragment with pain. I knew something was wrong the minute I reached Balthazar Building's foyer. "What happened to you?" I barked. "You've been limping since we left for the woods."

Ella tried to dislodge herself from me. It was futile. I was stronger than her. And now that I knew she was hurt, I wasn't letting her walk back to school in this weather, wearing booted heels and barely dressed to ward off the chill.

After plucking up my discarded items, I swung her into my arms princess-style, finally giving in to my earlier urge. Ella protested, attempting to squirm out of my hold. "Put me down! I don't want to be carried!"

I silenced her with a glare and started walking, giving her no choice but to put her stubborn pride aside. "What. Happened. Ella?"

The rainstorm's pitter-patter decorated the silence between us. Ella collected her thoughts before muttering, "I got pushed when I was coming down the stairs."

I abruptly stopped, my anger returning. "Who hurt you?"

"Keep walking, we're on a timer," she hissed in her usual bossy manner. When I wouldn't budge, she sighed. "By another Initiator. He was wearing a mask."

"Did he excuse himself?"

Otherwise, after Initiation Night, I'd hunt down the motherfucker and punish him. Nobody hurt my girl and walked God's green earth unscathed.

Ella hesitated. "No, but he said some unsettling things and…put his hands on me."

He was a dead man walking. "Elaborate."

"He said, 'I've been looking everywhere for you, you stupid little bitch.'"

I nodded, running my tongue over my teeth. "I'm going to kill him."

Uncle Vance had an amazing stash of knives in his mancave. Maybe he'd let me borrow one so I could cut off this prick's dick.

As my long strides carried us out of the woods, Ella relaxed in my hold, our fight momentarily forgotten. The vulnerable expression on her face as she stared ahead filled me with tenderness. I missed holding her like this—missed being so close to her that I could smell her perfume and feel her pulse against mine.

St. Victoria's gothic structure came into view through the canopy of trees. A minute later, we reached an entrance door.

"There's something else, Cade," Ella said once I lowered her to her feet. "He had a skull tattoo on his hand and he was wearing a platinum watch with sapphires encrusted in the bezel…Just like Kian Wilson."

Every line in my body tightened with alert. "He's dead, Ella."

"I know."

"I killed him. You saw it with your own eyes. It couldn't have been him, sweetheart."

"Maybe it was someone that looked like him." Her shoulders stiffened and she walked ahead of me in a trance, murmuring, "Or maybe this place is fucking getting to me and I'm seeing his ghost."

A sliver of foreboding crept down my spine.

The last thing we needed was the ghosts of our past resurfacing.

As I followed Ella into the school, my mind drifted back to the summer night when we extinguished Kian Wilson's lights for good.

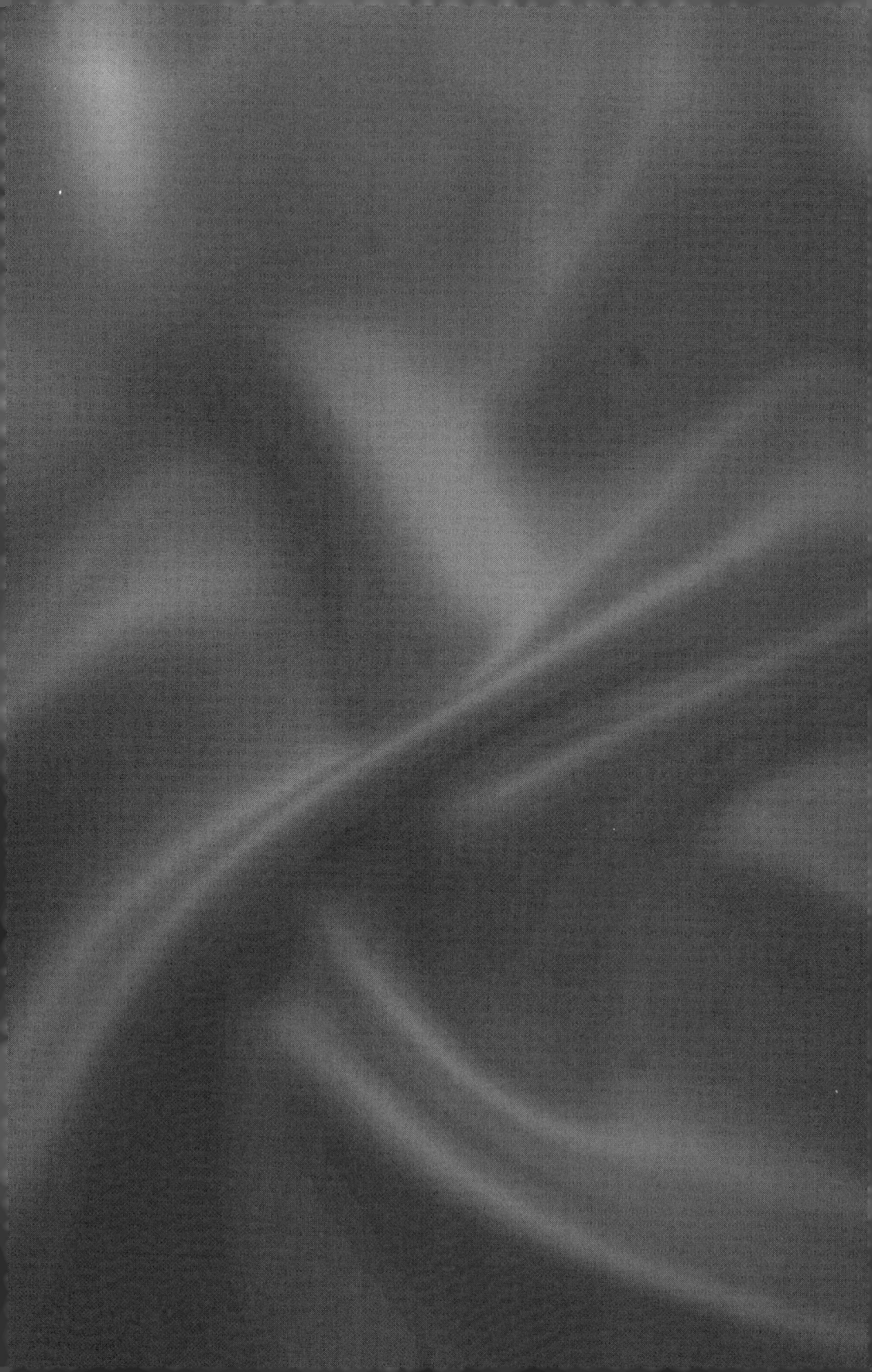

CHAPTER 16

Bonnie and Clyde

CADE

The Past – 3 months ago

An undertone of anarchy wafted in the air as I pulled up to Cordova mansion in the afterhours. The guards let me through without a fuss, though one still managed to inch me a scowl. I was tempted to pull out my gun and shoot his pissy-looking face, but I wasn't in the mood to deal with a bitching Francisco Cordova. You had to pick and choose your battles.

Nearly three years of dating Ella and her *papá* was nowhere near close to accepting me. He went as far as begging his daughter to ditch my ass and date Josh instead, but I was like a pesky fly, refusing to leave. Here to fucking stay.

The faster he got it through his thick skull that I was his future son-in-law, the better. At least Silvia Cordova, Ella's mother, excelled at hiding her contempt. She even offered me a *champurrado* with a grimacing smile the last time I visited.

Point was, I didn't give a shit what anyone thought of me. Ella's opinion was the only one that mattered.

I parked my motorcycle on the perimeters of the driveway, furthest from the prying eyes of the other guards. Pulling up the visor of my black helmet, I plucked out my phone from my leather jacket and shot my girlfriend a text.

183

Come out, baby. —Princepin

Ask me nicely. —Princess

I chuckled, hearing her spoiled voice in my head.

Dearest princess, I hope this finds you well. Will you
do me the honour of gracing me with your wonderful
presence? Otherwise, I'm leaving and doing this mission
on my own <3 —Princepin

Nice enough for you? —Princepin

Add a 'please' and it's perfect ☺ —Princess

Ella… —Princepin

I'm cominggg. —Princess

You will be. Before the night is over. —Princepin

Promise, querido? —Princess

My little opportunist. She never missed a chance to seek her pleasure.

Promise. Now come out. Please. —Princepin

Starved for the sight of her, my eyes devoured Ella's silhouette as she
darted out of the gardens and headed towards me. She was stunning as
ever, her long hair billowing wildly in the wind like a black flag.

A smile broke across my lips as she threw herself at me, knowing I'd
catch her without fail.

Immediately, I was slammed with her mouth-watering scent.
Jasmines. Orange blossoms. An unrivalled tonic that triggered a sense of
aliveness through my being.

I spun her around just to hear that sweet laugh ringing in my ears.
It was my favourite melody in the world. After the sound of her heartbeat.

Placing her back on her feet, I stole a kiss when Ella jerked off my
helmet.

"Hi, *querido*."

"Hi, pretty girl." I grabbed her jaw with one hand, squeezed her cheeks until her lips puckered, and planted aggressive kisses packed with zeal all over her mouth.

It made my girl giggle in the cutest manner.

She was irresistible. I always thought of kissing Ella. And when I was kissing her, I was thinking about when I could kiss her next. I was just that obsessed with her.

"Long time no see," she teased.

I arched a brow, running my thumb over her glossy lips. We saw each other this morning for brunch before I left to go help Uncle Vance and Josh with new shipments at the art gallery. But if I could have it my way, I'd stay glued to Ella's side forever. "Right? How dare you disappear from my sight for longer than a minute?"

"Needy boy," she tutted, wrapping her arms around my neck. "We were only apart for a few hours."

"Which translates to eternity in my book, sweetheart." Grabbing the back of her thighs, I lifted her onto my motorcycle. "So now I'm kidnapping you and taking you to my secret lair."

"Mm. Kinky." Ella automatically locked her feet around my waist and drew me into her body. "What are we going to do in this secret lair of yours?"

I nipped her bottom lip and whispered, "Bad, bad things, baby."

The wicked gleam in her eyes matched mine. Crazy, just like me, and down for anything.

Including tonight's carnage.

She was dressed in all black to impress—or *kill*, more accurately. A cropped leather jacket and knit bralette adorned her chest. Her ass and shapely thighs were barely contained in her high-waisted miniskirt. And stiletto high heels gave her enough height to reach my chin. I was salivating like one of Pavlov's dogs.

Before I could make us late to our destination by suggesting a quick romp on my motorcycle, Ella dragged her fingers down my cheek. "Are you hungry? I brought you a cookie."

Grinning wolfishly, I tightened my hold on her waist. "Oh, baby. I'm always down to eat *your* cookie."

She wheezed out a laugh, batting my chest playfully. "No, you horny devil. I actually baked some sugar cookies." Reaching into her small crossbody purse, she pulled out a Ziploc bag with a giant, blue frosting cookie. "I was worried you didn't have enough time to eat."

I was overcome by gratitude.

Three years ago, when Ella found out I'd been malnourished in the past, she took it upon herself to pack extra snacks in her bags. I no longer suffered from hunger since living with the Remingtons, but it was adorable how she made sure I was constantly fed throughout the day.

And I had a sweet tooth that she catered to so well.

Best. Girlfriend. Ever.

Ella handed me the cookie and I broke it in two, offering her a piece. She shook her head and touched my cheek again. "I already had one. You eat."

I scarfed it down in five bites.

"Do you like it?" She unscrewed a water bottle for me and I took a sip. "I tried a new recipe."

"It's delicious. You did a great job." I patted my abs, satisfied, and kissed her. "*Gracias, querida.*"

Ella beamed with joy. I was learning her language and she loved it. "*De nada, querido.*"

I got on my motorcycle after placing a helmet on Ella. Usually, we rode alongside each other in separate vehicles. Hot summer nights, cruising down the street, side by side, was one of our favourite things.

Tonight was a special occasion, though. We were breaking many rules and needed to ride together for a fast, secure escape.

Arms wrapped around my waist, she plastered her body behind mine. The note of anarchy swirling in the air shifted to include a hint of dark excitement.

"You ready, princess?" I revved the engine.

Without seeing her face, I imagined the corrupt smile blooming on her face. "Ready, princepin."

The secret lair in question was an abandoned warehouse off the highway. A common spot for our associates to conduct business.

Tonight's culprit was Kian Wilson, one of our dealers.

He started working for us as a bartender in one of our joints and was eventually offered a job with a better ranking. The few times I dealt with Kian, he came off as a strait-laced dude with the ability to use his fists as required. Both important qualities when working in our line of business.

Then Kian made the fucking mistake of touching Ella last weekend at Jared Roy's party on the East Side, where we were celebrating graduating from St. Victoria.

She was tipsy and dancing with her friends when Kian had the audacity to grope her on the dance floor. He whispered his plans to her in explicit details. Meaning he wanted to fuck her. Without consent. In front of everyone. Ella slapped his hands away and threatened to kill him.

By the time my girlfriend found me and told me what happened, Kian had skedaddled out of the party like a fucking rat. I regretted leaving her for the two minutes it took me to get our drinks.

Otherwise, I'd have shot him on the spot.

Nobody touched Ella without permission.

Nobody threatened to assault her.

And no-fucking-body walked away without suffering the consequences.

Without a doubt, he had no idea who she was or her connection to me. If he'd known, Kian wouldn't have touched my girl with a ten-foot pole.

Every man under Vance Remington's reign knew you did not bite the hand that fed you.

That's exactly what Kian did. And for that, the vermin had to be terminated.

Revenge was a dish best served cold. I took my time digging into the stupid fucker to learn his habits and vices. Imagine my surprise when I found out he not only put his hands on my girl but had a record for being pushy with other women, too.

Oh, and I learned that he'd been stealing from us. For months.

Amateurly covering his tracks and filling his pockets with the extra cash.

It was dirty, bloody, drug money. But Remington money regardless.

Thievery was high on our shit list. No one robbed us and lived to speak about it. Any soldier who dared to mess with the boss and his sons would have a bullet lodged between his eyes faster than you could say *please*.

Kian Wilson walked around like a pathetic male peacock desperate to mate. Soon, I would pluck the fucker's feathers and teach him an unforgettable lesson: don't touch my girl and don't touch my money.

By the end of the night, he'd know why they called me a fixer.

Uncle Vance gave me the greenlight to slaughter Kian like a pig. Josh offered to help with the cleanup job. And Aunt Julia said she'd leave my favourite slice of cake on the kitchen counter for when I got back home. My family was insane, but I loved them.

I also loved the girl sitting behind me, who decided she wanted in on the action.

There were two things that heated my blood with passion. Ella and getting justice.

Last night's memory drifted to the surface as I drove us to our destination.

"Are you sure you want to come tomorrow?" I'd asked her. "I'll be fine on my own."

"No way." She shook her head. "We're a team. We do everything together. Ride or die, remember?"

Kissing her forehead, I relented. "Ride or die, Ellie."

"Plus, this is my *graduation gift."*

Of course she'd see a torturing session as an acceptable graduation gift. "I mean, I was going to give you a Birkin..."

Ella looped her arms around my waist. "What colour?"

"Orange, obviously."

"I'll take the Birkin," she quipped. "But I also want to teach him a lesson."

I grinned. "You're absolutely crazy."

"You love my type of crazy, querido.*"*

That I did.

The summer wind cut through our frames as I finally eased off the highway and neared the abandoned warehouse. It was protected by CCTV—which Josh and Uncle Vance already disabled—and a guard employed twenty-four hours to ensure no one trespassed.

I parked my motorcycle near the edge of the property, camouflaged by unruly trees. Only three people knew what we were doing tonight, and that's how I intended to keep it.

Ella hopped off first and removed her helmet. I did the same. "How are we doing on time?"

She checked her watch. "We have thirty-five minutes before he arrives."

"Perfect." I kissed her cheek. "Stay here while I talk to the guard."

"Okay."

Gravel crunched beneath my combat boots as I rounded the warehouse and spotted our old guard Johnny working the graveyard shift.

He wasn't the least bit surprised to see me, having already been expecting us.

Nodding, he said, "Hey, kid."

"Hey, Johnny." I extended my hand for a shake. "How's it going?"

"Good." His fingers felt the wadded cash in my palm. "Do you need anything else from me?"

"No, just this." He thought I was paying him to give Ella and me privacy to indulge in some kinky activities in the warehouse. There was some truth there, I supposed. "Thanks again for your discretion."

I watched Johnny get into his car and drive off the property.

I slipped on my black ski mask and returned to Ella.

My girlfriend was texting on her phone, leaning against a tree. I snuck up from behind and fortressed her body in my arms, whispering in her ear, "What are you doing, baby?"

She gasped but relaxed into my chest when she realized it was me. "Texting the girls. They're asking when we're arriving at the party…"

Her sentence trailed off when she noted my covered face.

I smirked. "See something you like?"

She licked her lips and eyed me like I was a piece of candy. One she couldn't wait to lick, suck, and fuck. "You already know, Killian."

Killian.

I was always Killian when the mask came on.

Not too long ago, Ella confessed her many fantasies to me. Primal kink. Fear play. Mask kink. She loved it when we roleplayed, saying it got her hot and excited. I nearly orgasmed when she asked to be chased, pinned, tied, and fucked like a slut in the woods. Since I lived to please this girl, I swore I was going to make that scenario a reality very soon.

"Tell me what you want tonight, Ximena."

We effortlessly slid into another dark game. Her airy inhale at the sound of *Ximena*—used whenever we were like *this*—chained around my core and clenched.

Immersed under the luster of the stars, sheltered in the warmth of my embrace, and her undisguised desires on display, she reminded me of the first time I saw her standing on the balcony. Bewitching like a goddess and ethereal like the orange begonias she loved so much.

Whenever I gazed at her, the personification of my heartbeat, I felt abundantly blessed for being alive in a time where our existences collided. My world was no longer dark, now completely lit with her iridescent presence.

I wouldn't have it any other way.

I loved her with every fiber of my being. I would until my dying breath.

And as God was my witness, I'd do everything in my power to ensure she stayed happy, protected, and smothered with all the love in my cup.

"Revenge...and you, Kill." She bit her lip and gently grazed her fingertips over my jaw. "Always *you.*"

Without breaking eye contact, I dragged my palms to her inner thighs, putting pressure with intention. Instinctively, her stance widened and I glided my fingers under her miniskirt, stroking her thong. It clung to her like a second skin.

Fuck, she was soaking wet.

A few hours ago, she sent me the most erotic shot. Two fingers stuffed in her sticky pussy while she pleasured herself. I was in a meeting with some associates and nearly lost my mind.

"Did you think you could send me a dirty picture and get away with it?" I growled, my fingers cupping her possessively.

When she remained speechless, I slapped her pussy. "Answer me."

She moaned throatily, back arching. "N-No, I didn't want to get away with it."

Of course she didn't. She wanted to be punished. Forced into submission. Her ass rubbed against my growing cock and I ground back, giving her a small teaser of what was coming later.

"Good, because you won't." I slapped her pussy—once, twice, thrice—and the sound, meshed with her slutty moans, chimed in the night like a beautiful hymn.

"Oh my God!"

"He's not the one spanking this cunt. Fucking say *my* name, Ximena."

"*Killian.*"

"Good girl." I rewarded her by thrusting a finger inside of her slick heat. Fast, quick, and so unexpected, she shot to her tippy-toes. I thrust a second finger and curled against the spot that made her see stars. She sobbed in pleasure. "Goddamn, you like that, eh?"

"*Yes!*"

I roughly pushed the flimsy material of her bralette over her tits, baring her pebbled nipples. I squeezed one and twisted it. Hard. Just the way she liked. "Beg me for more."

Ella groaned, body squirming in my hold, her hips writhing, trying to fuck my fingers. I slapped her tits and rasped, "I said beg, Ximena."

"I want to come!" she whined. All the blood rushed south and my cock soared to full-mast at the plaintive sound. "*Pleasepleaseplease.* Make me come, Killian!"

"That's what I'm talking about." I chuckled darkly and started fingering her pretty pussy, my thumb polishing her clit rhythmically. "I love it when you beg. *Eres hermosa, mi amor.*"

Ella threw her head back against my shoulder, sweet moans escaping her parted lips, her eyes glittering with veneration. She caressed my cheek over my mask. "*Te quiero,* Kill."

"*Te amo.*" I pressed the heated words of romance against her skin. "So much, *mo chuisle.*"

The smell of desire, heat, and Ella's unique scent permeated the dark atmosphere like a delicious philter. There was something about being out in the open, where anyone could chance upon us, that got her extremely aroused.

My girl had a budding sex drive and I was a devoted servant, here to fulfil her needs. I wanted to fuck her so bad, but we didn't have the time for that. Therefore, I settled for rubbing her tight pussy to orgasm.

"You know what the hottest thing about you is?" I thrust faster, enjoying the squelching sounds of her cunt. I added a third finger. "You appear prim and proper on the outside. The perfect little heiress with a shiny crown." I crooked my fingers against her upper wall, making her scream blasphemously. "But on the inside, you're nothing but a filthy, needy brat." I pinched her clit. "*My* filthy, needy brat. Isn't that right, baby?"

She didn't answer me, trembling and lost in the sensation of her pussy being stretched and stroked. Ella's cries were growing too loud.

"Shh. Be quiet, pretty girl." I slammed a hand over her mouth and watched her eyes roll back into her skull with my next thrust. "We can't risk getting caught. Unless…" I teased. "You want everyone to know you go from being South Side's princess to Killian's fuckdoll the minute I get my hands on you."

Ella lived for my dominance, my dirty talk, my fingers wrecking her cunt, and my hand muffling her porn-worthy noises. She was so close. I could feel her tightening and her juices trailing down to my knuckles. One hand clamped over my wrist, she held my hand between her thighs, making sure I wouldn't withdraw at the last second and leave her on edge. With her other one, she played with her nipples. Squeezing, twisting, pulling to the point of pain.

"I should rip this little outfit off your body and bend you over my motorcycle before fucking you like the bad girl you are," I rasped, my taunt having the desired effect. She went wild, moving her hips in beat with my thrusting fingers, moaning against my palm. "You'd like that, huh?" *Thrust.* "You'd like it so much, you're dripping all over my hand like a slut."

Thrust. Thrust. "All it takes is something filling you up and your bratty side is tamed." *Thrust. Thrust. Thrust.* "Look at you, panting and crying pretty tears like a world-class sinner, baby." With another thrust, I vowed, "Don't worry, Ximena. Before the night is over, I'll have fucked every inch this tight cunt has to offer. Now come so I can lick you clean, you dirty little princess."

Ella was beautiful when she let go with a scream, her body contorting in my hold. I kept strumming her pussy while her cum flowed all over my hand.

She went limp, resting back against my chest, while I gently withdrew my fingers from her. Expression swimming in euphoria, she watched as I sucked those same fingers, humming at the delectable taste of her nectar. A little tart. A little sweet. My favourite treat.

"Can I taste myself?"

Ella knew she could. I liked to make her fuck herself and lick her fingers clean. "Do you think you deserve it?"

She nodded, eyes glimmering with mischief. "Yes."

I squeezed her jaw. "Open your mouth."

She obeyed and I kissed her hard, drinking in her gasp. My tongue darted inside her mouth, twining with hers before I dribbled a bit of spit. My nasty girl moaned, loving it. "Mm. *More*, Kill."

I manacled Ella's throat with my hand as our mouths consumed each other with an uncontrollable need. The kind where you longed to sink inside their skin, fuse with their bones, become one with the breath travelling through their lungs, and match your heartbeat with theirs until it felt like you were one whole being.

As we pulled away, Ella panted against my wet lips, "It's your turn."

"For what?"

She spun around and pushed my chest lightly. I retreated until my back pressed against a tree. Ella dropped to her knees with a saucy smile, her hands going to my belt buckle. "We have a few minutes and I want to reciprocate."

She's going to kill me.

I threaded my fingers through her hair and she pulled my dick out of

193

my pants, immediately sucking the head through her pouty lips. I watched one inch, two inches, three inches, four inches—Holy God, more than half of me—disappear in her mouth. "Fuckkkk."

With a groan, I threw my head back as she took me to a whole new heaven.

Ella

Kian Wilson was arriving soon. He texted me that he was two minutes away.

The idiot thought I was buying coke from him.

For two thousand and five hundred dollars. Hah.

If Kian knew I was dating his boss's son, he'd understand that I had no reason to contact him for drugs when my boyfriend could supply me with any substance for recreational use.

And if he'd known who *I* was, then he never, *ever* would have touched me.

Now he was going to pay the price for his mistake.

"You good?"

I smiled and turned to Cade, finding his tall figure huddled against the side of the warehouse. His mask was back in place and he held a baseball bat, the one with *E + C* carved on the barrel.

"I'm good." I was practically vibrating with reckless energy. "Is everything set?"

After the mind-numbing orgasms, Cade cleaned us up and kissed me before going into the warehouse to check out all the equipment. Guns, knives, and enough petrol to light the whole place on fire.

"Yeah, baby." He threw a glance over his shoulder towards the empty road, most likely gauging Kian's arrival. "You have the ammo on you?"

I opened my cropped leather jacket and flashed him the hidden gun and the wad of cash. "Yes."

"Good girl." His eyes twinkled with pride and that look melted me.

"Now stay on the lookout. If there's someone else with him, signal to me. I'm going to shoot."

I nodded.

Kian mentioned that he was coming alone, but you could never be too sure.

Speaking of the devil, two headlights emerged from the road leading to the warehouse. Tires screeched as the car hooked right and haphazardly pulled into the parking lot.

I shielded my eyes against the brightness and cringed at the loud bass emanating from the Chevy. It was painted an ugly yellow.

Now or never, Ella.

With a deep inhale, I stepped forth from the shadows.

My heels echoed against the ground before I slowed to a stop in front of his car, highlighted by the headlights. I pasted a fake, seductive smile. It usually worked like a charm on single-minded bastards like Kian.

He rolled his window down and stuck out his head, whistling. "Good Lord. Did it hurt when you fell from heaven?"

Ew.

He dropped the lamest pick-up line and I struggled to keep my smile in place.

I think I heard Cade gagging in the background.

Tossing my hair over my shoulders, I leaned forward, bracing my palms on the hood of his car. I cocked my head and hollered over his loud music, "Why don't you come out and I'll tell you?"

He turned off the ignition and slid out.

Once ensuring that he was alone, I turned around to sit on the hood of his car, flirtatiously twirling a strand of my hair around my finger.

Kian came to stand in front of me while running his fingers through his slicked back sandy brown hair. I hated the cheap cologne emanating from him and the way he licked his lips like a creep as he leered at my body. It made me want to skin him alive. All in good time, though.

He winked. "All right, cutie. Tell me."

Cutie? I was going to barf.

"It didn't hurt a single bit," I said teasingly and trailed a finger down his shirt. "Falling from heaven."

But you know what will hurt? Your face once it's broken, motherfucker.

"You're adorable." He chuckled then narrowed his eyes. "And you look quite familiar."

"We met last weekend at Jared Roy's party."

'Met' was putting it lightly. This sleezy fuck put his nasty hands on my body, trying to take something from me without my permission.

"Ah, yes." A mean grin tugged at his lips. "Though I last remember you pushing me away and calling me an asshole."

"People can change their minds." I shrugged. "Plus, you have something I want."

He closed in on my personal space and raised his brows. "Oh, yeah? And what's that?"

Now that he was fully focused on me, I saw Cade, from my peripheral vision, sliding closer to us.

"We'll start with the goods, then *maybe* you can take me for a spin in your sweet ride."

"Maybe I will." Kian perked up like a kid on Christmas. "How'd you get my number?"

"A mutual acquaintance. We run in the same circles."

"Yeah, I doubt it." He snorted arrogantly. "No offence, but you don't seem like the kind of girl who gets her hands dirty."

Oh, you don't know what kind of girl I am, Kian. "Appearances can be deceiving."

"You can spend the night convincing me otherwise." He wiggled his brows. "What did you say your name was?"

I had him eating out of my hands like a sucker. "*Nemesis.*"

His forehead scrunched and he reached into his pockets, pulling out a bag of cocaine. Once again, I noticed a skull tattoo on the back of his hand and an expensive sapphire encrusted watch. I knew he couldn't afford the latter on his salary. "Weird name. But that's not my concern. Anyways, pay up, cutie. This shit isn't free."

I reached into my jacket for the wad of cash. My eyes connected with Cade's over Kian's shoulder and excitement zinged through my bloodstream.

Fanning out the twenties, I threw them sharply at Kian's face with a hiss, "Count this, asshole."

His eyes widened when the bills slapped his face and flew in the air.

And my boyfriend chose that exact moment to attack.

Cade smacked Kian with the baseball bat. The satisfying sound of it hitting his skin broke the cricket filled melody of the night.

Kian cried out as his useless body folded on top of mine. Before he could reach for his weapon, I shoved him off me. Cade's baseball bat came around his throat, choking him and sandwiching his body between us.

"Surprise, motherfucker," Cade spat with a sinister edge.

Kian panted, clutching weakly at the baseball bat cutting into his throat suffocatingly. He was turning blue and his flailing hands tried to claw their way out of this predicament. "What's…going…on?" he garbled with a strained voice.

I whipped out my gun and cocked it under his chin. "Stay put or I'll blow out your brains."

Kian halted, eyes popping out of his skull like a squeeze-toy. I relished the way fear wrapped around him. It almost drowned out the stench of his pathetic cologne. "W-Who are you?"

His ashen face fed my bloodthirst in a way I couldn't explain.

"I told you," I said in a mock innocent voice. "My name is Nemesis."

"Y-You're f-fucking crazy, bitch!"

I smiled like it too. "Oh, you have no idea how crazy I am, Kian. But you'll know by the end of the night."

"Are you ready to play, baby?" Cade chimed in with a dark laugh.

"You know I am."

With a wink in my direction, Cade dragged Kian's body backwards into the recesses of his new hell, while the culprit screamed for mercy with gurgling noises.

I skipped after the two of them with a Cheshire cat grin.

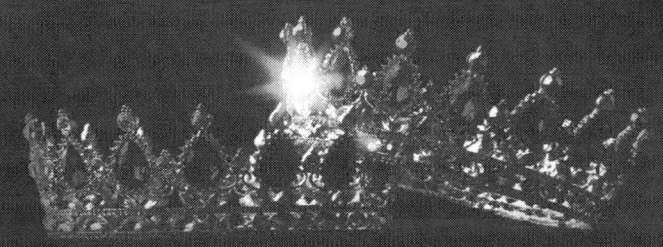

CHAPTER 17

Nemesis and Her Dark Prince

CADE

The Past - 3 months ago

Justice was supposed to be blind, but in my court, it was purely poetic.

If karma didn't deliver fast enough, I liked to take matters into my own hands and bring it forth, making sure that the perpetrator walked away with the lesson entrenched deep in their bones.

Or didn't walk away at all, in this case.

I busted Kian Wilson's legs to a point where he would never walk again. The only way he was leaving this warehouse was in a body bag.

"Please, please, please," he whimpered. "Just stop!"

Spending the last three years in the city's underworld, I became immune to traitors' tears and begging.

Kian's face was a cracked map of blood, salt water, and mucous. His left eye was swollen shut, his voice had gone hoarse from all the screaming, and his weak body was shackled with chains hanging from the ceiling, his stance a pathetic genuflect before me.

As though I were the very God from whom he sought penance.

Unfortunately, there was no mercy in my court either.

Kian signed his death warrant the minute he stole from us and touched my girl.

And as the fixer, it was only fair that I teach him one final lesson before sending him off to Hell.

"What's that, Kian?" I tapped the shell of my ear with a condescending expression. "I don't think I heard you."

Ella cackled, an evil laugh that incited my own malicious smile.

I loved when we were like this—relentless and vicious until we reached our end goal.

She was my Nemesis for tonight, holding scales of justice that slowly rebalanced as we settled the score, and I, her favourite dark prince, reigning over our dominion.

"I'm sorry! Please!" he cried like a beggar down on his luck. "Let me go! I'll do anything!"

"Louder, Kian."

He kept alternating between pleas and apologies.

The sound was grating, but slightly entertaining. Though if Kian thought there was an option where he walked out of here alive, I wasn't doing my job properly.

Well…If you observed the white canvas I laid out on the floor, decorated with splashes of his blood in a symphony of violence and vengeance, I might just give Picasso a run for his money.

Just kidding. But Uncle Vance would be proud of my work. Enough to maybe display this canvas in one of his art galleries for the next showing.

Too bad Kian wouldn't be alive to see it. He was a few blows away from having his light snuffed out permanently.

"Do you think I should spare him, princess?" I asked the love of my life.

Ella circled Kian like he was a sculpture at an auction and she debated placing a bid. A sensual, dark aura accompanied every roll of her hips as she tapped her lips in thought. "Hm. Very good question."

My smile stretched to a grin. Dropping my baseball bat, I assessed the small table to my right, housing a plethora of torture tools. Usually a gun did the trick, but I was feeling fancy tonight. I picked up a butcher knife and juggled it between my gloved fingertips. "What's the verdict, Ximena?"

She skipped over to me, wrapping her arms around my torso from behind, while resting her cheek against my shoulder. The front of my white T-shirt was coated in Kian's blood, yet Ella stared at me with stars in her eyes.

Like I wasn't the villain, but the knight in shining armour in her story.

I loved it.

I loved *her*.

My goddess Nemesis, the Bonnie to my Clyde, the gun moll to my gangster.

She never had to doubt my devotion. No matter the time or day, I'd always deliver on my promise to protect and fight for her.

"I think," Ella whispered in my ear. "That you should show him why no one messes with you, Killian."

Translation: she wanted me to kill him. Good. I would have done it regardless, but I liked knowing she was on board with the idea.

All notions that she may not fit into my life after learning about my family business were smashed to smithereens years ago. This girl truly was the other half of me.

Anarchy, dark excitement, and now sweet revenge joined the mixture of tonight's concoction. It swirled in the air, feeding the sanguinary fires raging in my soul.

"Your wish is my command." We shared a grin and she kissed me openly in front of Kian, making sure to flick her tongue against mine in a bold display.

Kian, having now understood that death was the only outcome, started screaming for mercy with renewed energy.

I sighed, annoyed with him. "All right, sweetheart, which hand did he use to touch you?"

"The left one."

"Then that's the one I'll start with."

Kyan was squirming like a fish out of water, bellowing as I neared him, knife in hand. "No, no, nooooooooo!"

"Aww, poor little Kian." Ella pouted, cocking her head. "Are you scared?"

"Shut the fuck up, you psychotic bitch!"

My nostrils flared. No one was allowed to call her a bitch.

Before I could shove my knife in his jugular and end the torture session early, Ella grinned deviously and picked up the discarded baseball bat.

I watched in fascination as she swung it high and thwacked Kian across the face.

The chains holding his body ratted loudly as he was whipped to the ground in a heap of groans. Blood arched out of his mouth and sploshed across the white canvas, adding another stroke to the unholy masterpiece.

"Talk dirty to me, Kian," Ella growled playfully, fisting his hair and jerking up his head. "I fucking like it."

His lips slackened, a mixture of incoherent threats and curses coming out of him.

"What's that, Kian? You want another hit?" She introduced her six-inch stilettos against his jaw with a feisty kick. "My fucking pleasure, *cutie*."

More blood. More cries. More begging as his body recoiled back from being smacked like a whack-a-mole game.

"That's my girl," I praised warmly. "Give him hell."

Ella struck him a few more times. I let her get it off her chest. She earned it, after all. My only regret was not having a glass of whiskey to accompany the show. Pride and joy coalesced in my system at witnessing her in her avenging glory. What a fucking stunner.

I was clearly the luckiest man on earth.

With a huff, Ella dropped the baseball bat and stared down at Kian's limp body, fighting for his breaths.

It was a fitting end for a thief and assaulter.

"My body is a temple." She pressed her foot against his throat, holding him to the ground while he whined like a battered dog. "You do not lay your hands on me without permission, let alone shove your fingers in places they don't belong." The heel of her stiletto pierced his skin as she dug deeper. "Women are not puppets for you to use as you please, you nasty bastard. Let this be your final lesson, Kian: hell hath no fury…like a wrathful queen."

In that moment, she was the embodiment of the goddess of revenge, looming above her slain offender. Black hair tousled from battle, expression wild with gratification, chest heaving with satisfactory breaths, and a victorious smile blossoming over her glossy lips.

Glimmering eyes met mine and I smiled back in encouragement.

A vigorous heat pulsated in the connection that bound us. She felt it too, based on the way her lids lowered and her lips parted, sucking in a slow inhale. Ella had never looked sexier to me. I cherished her in all her forms but when she was like this—angry, ruthless, and powerful?

She was a goddamn force to be reckoned with.

I adored it.

The energy escalating between us demanded to be purged.

Once we finished this job, I was stealing my princess away so we could celebrate with dirty words and hard lovemaking under the stars.

"Did you get it out of your system, baby?" The thick quality of my voice was laced with so much *want* for her.

Ella shook her head and grinned. "Not even close."

I advanced towards her. Grabbing the nape of her neck, I planted a rough kiss on her lips. "You will, before the night is over."

She liked hearing the reminder of my promise. Smiling, she said, "Your turn, Kill."

I nipped her bottom lip and withdrew to crouch down next to Kian. He still made noises. Still refused to give up. "Hold him down, sweetheart."

Ella stepped on his neck again.

I dragged the tip of my knife over his forearm, slicing him open slowly before arriving at his wrist. "I bet you never would have touched her if you knew she was my girl, huh, Kian?"

He didn't say anything, watching me with a glassy, half-dead look in his eyes.

"Guess we'll never know." I smirked and brought down the knife, chopping his left hand.

Kian cried out again, a horror-stricken yell.

I plucked up his severed hand and dragged off the silver watch. Under the light, sapphires encrusted into the bevel gleamed impressively.

It must have cost a pretty penny. I whistled. "Sweet watch. Is this what you bought after stealing from us?"

His response was more tortured yells.

In the background, Ella casually popped a gum bubble and stared at her nails as if this was just a casual Friday and she was at the salon, deciding on a new colour.

"Tell you what," I hollered louder than him to ensure he heard me. "I'm a man who values equality—just ask my girlfriend—so as a result, I'll chop off your other hand too."

Not waiting for his reply, I held his right hand down and chopped it with my knife.

His screams of agony faded into the distance as I watched a spray of blood hit Ella's ankle.

"Oops. I'm sorry, baby."

"Killian," Ella chastised like a spoiled diva. "Be careful. You dirtied my new heels."

"It's okay, sweetheart. I'll buy you another pair."

"Promise?"

I winked. "Promise."

Grabbing my loaded gun, I rose over Kian's frame.

Ella sidled up to me, wrapping her hands around my arm.

I aimed my gun at his crotch and fired. "That's for my girl."

His body jolted, a muted sob escaping him.

Now I aimed for the area between his eyes. "You were a mere pawn, Kian. Not a king. You forgot who runs this side of the city, and it certainly isn't you. So let me remind you one final time."

My bullet pierced through his skin with a sound that echoed in the warehouse like the final nail in a coffin.

We both watched him bleed out like an animal in a slaughterhouse.

I felt no remorse for him. He made a grave mistake and he paid the price.

Uncle Vance always taught me that a good boss did his own dirty work. That's why he trusted me to see this through. If he were here, he'd slow-clap and ask me where he should frame my artwork.

Now that Kian was dead, I took a deep breath, finally feeling relief.

Ella pressed a kiss to my shoulder. "Wanna clean up and get out of here?"

I nodded, tucking a strand of her hair behind her ear. "We have a party to attend, remember?"

One organized by my friends to give us an alibi for tonight. My crew was good like that. Always supportive without asking all the *whys, whos, whats, wheres,* and *whens.*

"Do we have time to stop by Marnie's Shack? I want a chocolate milkshake."

I almost laughed at the absurdity of the situation. Kian's dead body was barely cold, but Ella had already moved on to food.

Hooking my arm around her neck, I drew her to me for a kiss. "I'll take you anywhere you want."

"Yeah?"

"Mhm."

She dotted little kisses all over my face. And dimples too, of course. "Hey, Cade?"

"Yes, Ella?"

"Thank you for my gift. I'm…I'm glad he's gone."

Pressing my forehead to hers, I whispered, "You don't have to thank me, Ella. All your battles, all your demons, all your pain. It's mine too, baby. You'll never have to fight on your own. You have me now."

I repeated the same words she once told me years ago.

She smiled and brushed the tip of her nose against mine. "You and me against the world, right?"

"You and me." I vowed. "Always."

Homicide complete, we cleaned up—I had no choice but to burn my clothes and switch into another pair of jeans and T-shirt—and then locked up the warehouse.

In the trunk of Kian's old Chevy, we found a torn-up duffel back with wads of cash. Remington money, one thousand percent. Since Ella had been such a good sport, I handed her a cut and Josh, who came over to help us dispose of Kian's dead body, took the rest home for Uncle Vance.

Now Ella coyishly fanned herself with a load of one-hundred-dollar bills, leaning against my motorcycle, while I doused Kian's car with petrol.

It had to be burned to ensure there was no evidence of tonight.

From my understanding, Kian was an orphan. Nobody's son, nobody's brother, nobody's father. He wouldn't be missed in our ranks or on this fucking planet. It was a clean job with no loose ends.

Once the car was dripping slick with oil, I pulled out my trusty Zippo and paused when something occurred to me.

I glanced over my shoulder. "Do you want to do the honours, pretty girl?"

She clicked her tongue. "I thought you'd never ask."

Slapping the bills against my chest, she murmured, "Hold onto that for me, will you? I'm going to need every cent for that new pair of heels."

I grinned and handed her the Zippo.

My girlfriend flicked the flint wheel and a small flame appeared, quickly catching onto the trail of petrol licking the ground. The flames exploded within seconds, engulfing the car in a picturesque display.

Ella threw Kian's watch into the fire.

I gave her the option of taking it to a jeweller to exchange it for something else, but she said it was a bad omen, just like Kian.

The summer night temperature skyrocketed with the rising heat.

I wiped my temples and slipped on my riding gloves...when Ella whirled around and sauntered my way, the blazing fire an arresting backdrop behind her.

Wicked eyes and seductive smirk. Wild hair and glistening skin.

My dark princess.

My goddess of revenge.

My fucking religion.

I wanted to bow down and kiss the very ground she walked on like a worshipper.

I also wanted to consume her whole and not leave a single crumb behind.

Ella Ximena Cordova was the living embodiment of all my fantasies. And she knew it too.

Wherever you go, sweetheart, I'll follow. No matter the journey, I'll always brave it with you. You're a part of me, you live *inside of me, and I would do anything for you. In this lifetime and all the ones to come, you'll always have all my love and twisted devotion.*

She stopped in front of me and trailed a finger over my lips, as though reading all my lustful thoughts and naked truth. "Tell me what's on your mind."

I kissed the side of her throat, feeling her pulse shaking madly. For me. Always for me. I swore I'd be six feet beneath the ground before she ever died.

I'd never live without Ella.

There was no *me* without *her*.

"That I made you a promise." I bit her jaw to warn her of what was to come. The beast raging inside of me demanded his due. "One I intend to fully keep."

The last thing I heard was her girlish laugh as I swung her over my shoulder and headed for my motorcycle.

She wasn't getting away from me.

The night had only just begun.

CHAPTER 18

Dirty Little Princess

Ella

The Past - 3 months ago

The pulsing energy rocking between us all night long came to a pinnacle as we arrived at our next destination. Cade parked his motorcycle in an empty, secluded alleyway just adjacent to the building where the glow-in-the-dark rave was being held.

The summer air was muggy, causing a bead of sweat to trail down my neck. My entire body felt like a live-crackling wire from the minute I saw my boyfriend waiting for me in my driveway, looking every bit like the beautiful dark prince of my fairy tale.

The second my feet hit the ground, Cade drew off my helmet after his, and grabbed the nape of my neck in a tight squeeze that had my breath whooshing out of my lungs in anticipation.

I never had to wait long.

His mouth crushed mine with a desperation that caused my core to throb. I responded back with equal fervour, my arms squaring around his shoulders. He hoisted me into his strong embrace and spun us around, depositing me sideways onto the seat of his motorcycle.

Sweltering desire flowed through my veins like ambrosia, my thirst for him increasing with every frantic kiss, every deep groan, and every desperate swipe of his hands on my skin.

209

I threw my head back on a moan as he planted hungry, open-mouthed pecks over my jaw and down my neck, stopping to lick the bead of sweat resting in the hollow of my throat. Before biting my skin in a brandishing manner.

The animalistic gesture made my pussy clench.

"C-Cade." I delved my fingers into his hair and tugged his head back to stare into his eyes. The blue was darker than ever, drenched with lust. "Anyone could walk by and see us."

A roguish smirk curled his lips. "But that's what excites you, pretty girl," he drawled shamelessly, his palms dragging my miniskirt higher until it bunched at my waist. "The rush of sneaking around…and almost getting caught."

Oh, God. Yes. It did.

My heart pumped in rhythm with the faint echo of the party's thumping bass as Cade drank in my shaky exhale with his inhale. "And you get fucking hot knowing that I'll shoot any motherfucker who has the audacity to gaze at your naked, sexy body, hm?" His fingers latched onto the ends of my hair and wrapped them around his fist. Thrice. He tugged at my scalp while his other hand came to cradle my jaw in a possessive hold. "It turns you on knowing I'm so goddamn crazy that I'd kill for you. Go as far as to fuck you in their blood if I feel like it." He bit my bottom lip until I mewled. "Admit it, Ella."

"*Yes.*" My fingers scored down his leather jacket, ripping it open hurriedly. I felt needy in a way I never had before. The aftermath of my bloodthirst being fed? I was ravenous all over again. But now for *him.* "I love that you're unhinged."

Satisfied with my admission, he dropped to his knees like a man in worship.

My breath hitched as I watched him lean forward to press kisses from my ankles all the way up to my thighs, his hands mapping along the surface of my hypersensitive skin. The silver of his rings glinted in the night like a beacon and glee racketed through my system at seeing the promise ring—the one I gifted him last year for his eighteenth birthday—sitting proudly at the base of his knuckle.

Cade's being was stitched with my essence. My name on his jacket. My initials on his cuffs. My art on his Zippo. My ring on his finger.

I loved that the whole world knew he belonged to me.

"Spread your thighs, sweetheart." He threw my legs over his brawny shoulders and used his teeth to tuck my thong to the side with a bad boy smirk. "I want to lick your pussy until you're dripping like a nasty slut before fucking you hard enough to have the whole city know you belong to your princepin."

I was going to come with just his words at this rate.

Doing as he ordered, I choked on a moan when his tongue flicked out and licked my slit in one demanding stroke, opening my pussy for his ministrations. I was already wet with arousal, my clit swollen and begging for his attention. "*Cade.*"

His fingers dug into my thighs and he peered up at me with a heated look. "Keep saying my name in that sultry voice and I'll give you anything you want, Ella."

Unintelligible sounds fell through my lips as he started eating my cunt like I was his last meal. One he planned to enjoy until the last lick.

My fingers knotted in his hair like reins, holding him to me, as I pushed my hips against his face for *more, more, more.* He was driving me wild with the way he parted my flesh with his tongue, searched my slit for my wetness, circled my clit with the tip of his tongue before battering it with quick flicks that had me whimpering, tears gathering in my eyes.

When he latched onto my clit and sucked, my body twisted on the seat and my pleading grew louder. "Please, please, please, Cade!"

He chuckled darkly, the sound reverberating against me. "You think you deserve the honour of coming all over my face, rich girl?"

"Yes." I cried out when he took away the suctioning of his lips. I was going to lose my sanity. "Please, I've been s-so good."

"Liar." He spat on my pussy and spanked it in two consecutive swats that resounded in the atmosphere. I squirmed, whining. "You're nothing short of a heathen." He pinched my clit with a cocky smile. "But that's what I love most about you, baby."

He thrust his tongue into my opening and started fucking my pussy with the dirtiest, sloppiest noises that rivaled every single X-rated video I ever watched. My boyfriend was my personal porn star, bringing me straight to the edge.

"Mm, it tastes so good, Ellie," Cade murmured mischievously, enjoying the way I unravelled for him. "Like heaven…and the sweetest sin."

No thoughts existed in my mind anymore. I was lost to the sensation of one finger, two fingers, three fingers moving in and out of my pussy while he showered my clit with all the attention. A constellation of stars formed behind my closed lids as I shook with the oncoming orgasm.

The nonsensical little *ohs* and *uhs* spilling past my lips spurred on Cade. He became even more determined in his quest to make me climax for the second time tonight.

"Good girl. That's my good fucking girl. You're right there, aren't you?" His depraved voice, his thrusting fingers, his lips around my clit. All of it did it for me. "Now come for me. Come all over my tongue so I can have your taste in my mouth when I fuck you on my ride like a dirty little princess, Ella."

The praise and degradation were the cherry on top of the cake.

My heels dug into his back and my body arched on a half scream, half sob as my orgasm rushed out of me. Cade went feral, lapping at my pussy with coarse, insatiable groans, swiping to collect every remnant of my flavour.

Reeling from that climax, I panted and watched him rise to his full six-foot-two height.

My cum glistened all over his chiseled jaw and lips. Keeping his intense gaze on me, he wiped his mouth with the back of his hand, silently letting me know this was far from over.

Good Lord. He's so sexy, so rugged, so mine.

"You made a mess, baby." Cade tutted, swirling his fingers over the seat. He brought them to my mouth for a taste and I obliged. "I should make you lick every drop clean."

Who knew the tender-hearted, almost shy, reserved boy I met three years ago would turn into this naughty and sexually deviant man over the course of our relationship? He was the most unexpected surprise in my life.

And I loved that he let his demons come out at night to play with mine.

"Fuck me instead, *querido*. I'm tired of waiting. You made me a promise."

"Impatient little brat." Cade crudely smashed his lips to mine before spitting in my mouth.

"Mm." I moaned. "But you love it."

Our mouths met in an erotic dance fueled by frenzied lust. He ripped off my thong and I worked on his belt buckle. I dragged off his shirt and leather jacket, then he helped me out of mine before hooking our clothing items on the handlebars of his motorcycle.

We never broke the kiss as our hands chased over each other's skins like the world was ending and every second needed to be savoured till the last breath.

"My God, Ella, there's no one like you," Cade mumbled as I laid kisses down his neck, my fingernails grazing over his muscular pecs, his taut abs, and his hip bone, where the **X** tattoo for my middle name rested. Right before I dived under his pants and briefs to grasp his weighty erection. "You're so—ah, *fuckkkkk*."

I grinned brazenly and swept my fist from root to tip, my thumb swiping over the pearly bead on his plump head. He was so long, so thick, so hard. I was salivating. "I don't think I heard you, Cade."

He groaned while I jerked him off, head tilted skywards and eyes screwed shut, fighting not to come too soon. I loved that look on his face.

I squeezed his length. "Tell me, Cade."

"You're so beautiful, Ella." He framed my face with shaky hands. "So goddamn beautiful."

Despite the darkness of the night, the moonlight and a faraway lamppost provided just enough illumination for us to see one another.

I kissed the left side of his chest, feeling his heartbeat flutter under my lips. The myriad of tattoos and scars on his canvas only magnified his beauty. He was a masterpiece, regardless of what he thought. I would always be there every step of the way to remind him. "I can say the same

213

thing about you. To me, you're the most beautiful man in existence, *mi corazón.*"

My boyfriend loved to praise me—outside and inside of the bedroom. Yet whenever I praised him back, his features softened in surprise like it was the first time he was hearing sweet words. It was extremely endearing.

He was so precious to me.

Instead of answering, he showed me how he felt with a soul-baring kiss. It was fused with all the unsaid sentiments churning inside of him.

While we made out, Cade rolled protection onto his dick and slowly guided himself between my thighs.

"You know I love you, right?" His words were casual, but the guttural state of his voice betrayed him.

"Yes." I gasped when he massaged his tip through my wet folds, teasing me for what was to come. The kind of rough lovemaking that set our bodies on fire.

"Keep that in mind." He seized my throat with one hand and nudged his cock into my entrance, slipping just the tip. "'Cause I'm going to fuck you like I hate you, baby."

He slammed all eight inches into my pussy in one unforgiving thrust.

I screamed at the intrusion, so brutal, so hard, so perfect. My arms went around his neck and my legs tightened around his waist. "Oh, God."

Cade tsked, pulling out all the way. "Told you he's not the one putting in the work." Squeezing my throat until I couldn't breathe, he snarled, "Say my fucking name, Ella."

"*Cade.*" My teeth coasted over his Adam's apple to take a bite. "Take me. Fuck me. Own me."

He started pounding into my body like I was his personal fuckdoll while I whimpered in pleasure and pain, clawing at his shoulders for purchase.

My cries, my pleas, and my submission fueled him.

Everything was for my dark prince's dirty enjoyment.

The way he shoved aside my bralette to lick my nipples and tug on the hardened tips. The way he grasped my ass and bounced me onto his cock with a bruising quality that would leave my pussy so deliciously used and sore. The way he kissed my mouth like a famished god devouring his sacrifice.

I relished his cruel treatment with wondrous abandonment.

There was something utterly erotic in watching the obscene sight of his glistening cock thrusting in and out of my pussy with our foreheads pressed together and breaths mingling. The air was suffused with the smell of our desires and the sound of our sexes slapping against one another as we ascended into crescendo.

"Fuck, I love watching this little cunt stretch so wide around my cock." *Thrust. Thrust. Thrust.* "It hurts in the best way, doesn't it, *mo chuisle*?"

I barely nodded, squealing when he threw one leg over his shoulder and jackhammered deep, the angle causing him to rub against my clit and G-spot simultaneously.

"And you take it so well." *Thrust.* "Every inch." *Thrust.* "Like your pussy was designed just for me."

Tears leaked out of my eyes. It was too much. It was not enough. My heart raced and my mind spun with the onslaught of feelings he invoked. "Harder, Cade. Fuck me till I can't breathe."

He licked the tears on my cheeks with a hum. "Look at you." His voice purred at my ear, soft and soothing, yet whispering the filthiest things. "You may have everybody fooled with your good girl act, but I know the truth. You're a bad girl, baby. One who comes alive when being fucked like a dirty slut. *My* dirty slut."

I moaned brokenly, taunting him. "A-Am I?"

"No one else's but *mine*, Ella. Don't you dare forget it." He kissed me with possessive fury while fucking me like he wanted to ruin me forever. I was already falling apart at the seams. "Or I'll fucking collar you, chain you, and paint your body with my cum until you get it through your thick skull that you belong to me."

His dominant threats coated my insides like warm honey. "Promise?"

"I never break one, pretty girl."

The next dozen thrusts had my eyes rolling back into my head. My nails scratched his back and drew blood. Cade fucked me harder in retaliation, grunting like a beast. He adored a dose of pain with his pleasure too.

Adrenaline and ecstasy swirled in the space between our colliding bodies.

I didn't care that we were loud and out in public, where anyone could walk by and see us. Cade would simply shoot them like a true mob prince and continue screwing me.

I was begging for more, wishing he'd continue to take from me until I was depleted and resting in his arms like a puppet with its strings cut, my light fully consumed by his enticing darkness.

"Goddamn, you're so gone for me, pretty girl." Cade slapped my tits and twisted my nipples, without easing his merciless pace. "Your pussy's strangling my cock like it never wants to let me go. Like you'll die without my touch."

The sick voice in my mind chanted that I would die without him.

Unable to vocalize it, my hips met his every vicious thrust and I goaded instead, "Y-You're imagining it."

"Oh." *Thrust.* "Am I?"

"Y-Yeah."

"You've officially lost the privilege of coming until I say so," he rasped. "Since you know, I'm 'imagining it.'"

He was going to kill me. Or edge me all night long. Both horrible options. "You're being an asshole."

"And yet your pussy is making a sloppy mess all over my cock, baby." He slowed down, but his upstrokes remained deep and punishing, hitting every spot that turned me into a passion-fueled madwoman. "If you don't lose that spoiled attitude, I'm going to bend you over my ride and spank your ass until it's red. I won't stop even if your voice is raw from yelling my name."

"I fucking dare you."

A dark smile spread over his lips. He dropped my leg from his shoulder and spun my body around with agile hands, never pulling out of me so we both felt every bit of *that*. I gasped at the sensation and Cade grated, "Challenge accepted."

The first slap hit my ass cheek with a jarring sound that echoed in the empty alleyway. I cried out, fingers digging into the seat as I lay bent over his motorcycle, skirt twisted at my waist, bralette undone, pussy dripping wet. The second slap arrived before I had time to recover.

Blistering heat burst over my skin. I loved it. "*More*, Cade."

Three consecutive slaps were my reward.

And then another three on my clit.

Fuck, yes.

"That mouth is going to get you in trouble." Fingers twisting in the hair at my crown, he jerked my head back and pulled out achingly slow before thrusting back with enough force to make my teeth chatter. "Then again, you love trouble."

That I did.

Now that I was ass up, face down, he resumed his dirty pace. Going even deeper in this position. Stroking every spot. Driving me to a new precipice with the promise of completion looming right at the horizon.

Thoughts escaped me once more as I choked out moans and screams. I could only focus on Cade's rough drives, his appreciative grunts as my ass bounced in his lap, and his voice like a wicked melody as he dragged hot kisses up my spine.

"Bad girls don't get to come."

"Mm, back that ass up, baby. I love watching your sinful body work hard to cram every last inch of my cock in your horny little pussy."

"Your punishment is far from over. I'm going to defile this cunt until it's so sore, you think of me and the pounding I gave you every time you sit down tomorrow."

"Goddamn, you're begging for it like the only thing keeping you sane is my filthy fuck. And you still have the audacity to say I'm 'imagining' it?"

Gone was my sweet boyfriend. This was Montardor's fixer, fucking me like I owed him a debt and he was here to collect.

"Scream for your salvation, you dirty little princess," he growled in my ear, hitting my pussy from behind like a ruthless monster. "I'm your God tonight."

His impious threat curling around my bones, I obeyed him. A myriad of sensations crawled through my body. All created by him. I mindlessly screamed and trembled with his name on my lips like an orison. "*Cade, Cade, Cade.*"

"Yes, Ella." Clasping a hand around my throat, he jerked me up until my back was plastered to his front. One hand molded over my tits, playing with my nipples, and another lowered to my clit, alternating between slaps and rubs, while he continued pistoning his hips and whispering to me, "*More.*"

We both edged closer.

If he didn't give me permission to come soon, I'd die.

"*Mi corazón*, please." My head resting in the crook of his neck, I combed my fingers in his dark brown strands, lavishing his jaw with gentle kisses to show him my surrender and that I could be a good girl, despite his remarks. "I'm right there."

"Sweet and docile when you want something from me, hm?"

"N-Not true." Only a little true.

"Come for me, Ella. Let go. I've got you."

My heart beat furiously. My toes curled in my heels. My pussy tightened around him.

A couple more strokes and I finally peaked, crying out into the dead of the night. My orgasm was so powerful, it flooded out of me, shaking my very roots. Every fiber of my being vibrated like the plucked strings of a guitar.

I had transcended to another realm.

Still hard as steel, Cade pulled out of my spasming core and turned me around to face him. Before I had time to regain my bearings, he picked me up and laid my back along the motorcycle's frame with my head resting between the handlebars, while his own body stood and straddled the vehicle, hands grasping my ass in a way where I knew I'd have finger-shaped bruises tomorrow.

"I gave you what you needed," he snarled above me, ramming back inside of my pussy. "Now it's my turn."

I was in my very own paradise, riding on a new high, howling in pure ecstasy. My heels dug into the passenger footpegs and my hands held on to his shoulders, meeting his pumping hips thrust for thrust. Cade's groans melded with my moans in a lush orchestra that increased in decibels with every passing second.

My dark prince had the most sensual gleam in his blue eyes, the strands of his hair were mussed by the summer wind, and sweat rivulets cascaded down his muscular, tattooed body. I wanted to lick him and taste the salt on my tongue. And under the pull of the bright moonlight, I wanted to hear him murmur how much he adored me in that gravelly voice as our bodies made love.

"You've got me wrapped around your finger." He sounded tortured and raptured all at once, pressing fervent kisses and love bites all over my skin. Every line in his body shook with his impending release. He looked like a beautiful wolf, fighting that place between half man and half animal, succumbing to his mate's need. "I'd do anything for you, *mo chuisle*. You're my beginning, my middle, my end."

My heart lurched in my chest.

Cade Killian Remington had branded himself so deep inside of me, we were one heart, one soul, one being.

He straightened me so I sat upright in his lap and wrapped his arms around my body like I was a treasure to be safeguarded, finishing inside of me with a few more thrusts. We came together in a choir of salacious sounds.

"I love you," I panted, our mouths alternating between kissing and simply breathing each other in. "So much."

"You're my world," Cade confessed, kissing my eyelids...and halting at the right one. "You're my favourite shade of brown and blue, Ella."

He was right with this earlier statement. A part of me would die without him.

Our existences were intertwined.

There was no Ella without Cade.

There was no him without me.

With our limbs intertwined, our hearts singing in unison, and the wind curling around our bodies, cooling our unwavering fire to a lulling, sated flame, Cade mumbled against my lips, "I bought you a little something."

I sifted my fingers through his hair, inciting a full-body shiver to course through him. I loved his reaction to my touch. "You've already given me so much tonight, *querido*."

"Then allow me to give you one more gift." Without letting go of me, he reached for his leather jacket, still hanging on the motorcycle's handlebars, and pulled out something from its pocket. Between us, he brought a small velvet box. "Here. Open it."

My throat tightened with emotions. "If it's an engagement ring, I hope you know I'm dragging you to Vegas."

He didn't know it yet, but I'd taken my favourite white leather jacket and bedazzled the back with pearls, gemstones, and the words *Mrs. Cade Killian Remington*. I was going to wear it when we inevitably exchanged wedding vows. Although we were young, our destiny was already written in the stars. This was the man I'd marry. Someday we'd start a family and grow old together. And even after death, he would still be mine.

"In a hurry to marry me, baby?" he teased.

"What if I am? I want every woman on this planet to know you belong to me."

"I like you possessive, pretty girl." He dragged a finger down the column of my neck, before placing a kiss in the hollow at the base of my throat. "But I've got the tattoos and the promise ring on my finger to prove I'm yours. We're a sure thing, Ella. You don't have to worry about anyone else."

Hearing the reassurance turned my insides to mush.

Holding my breath, my fingers gingerly open the velvet box.

A small heart-shaped blue aquamarine sat nestled in a gold chain, the gemstone winking under the moonlit night. It was of the most beautiful things—besides the man holding me in his arms—that I'd ever seen. I was at a loss for words.

"Do you like it?" Cade hedged, sensing my silence for something else entirely.

Awestruck, I murmured, "It's stunning, Cade."

He smiled. "I had it made for you. It reminded me of the blue in your right eye."

"Oh." I nearly sobbed, overcome by a multitude of feelings, all of them stitched from the love this man harboured for me. Unable to fully express myself, I kissed him instead. "Please, put it on me."

He fastened the clasp around my neck. The gold chain and gemstone felt cold and foreign for a few seconds before my flesh warmed up to the jewelry. Becoming one with it. As though it had always belonged there.

I already possessed his heart, but now he'd gifted me the tangible depiction of it, asking me, in his own vulnerable way, to protect it forever in the depths of my soul.

"You have my heart, Ella. It's yours." His eyes gleamed with reverence as he swept his thumb over the pulse in my neck. "Don't ever take it off."

"I won't," I swore. "I'll never part ways with it."

Cade kissed me for all he was worth before we called it an end to a thrilling night.

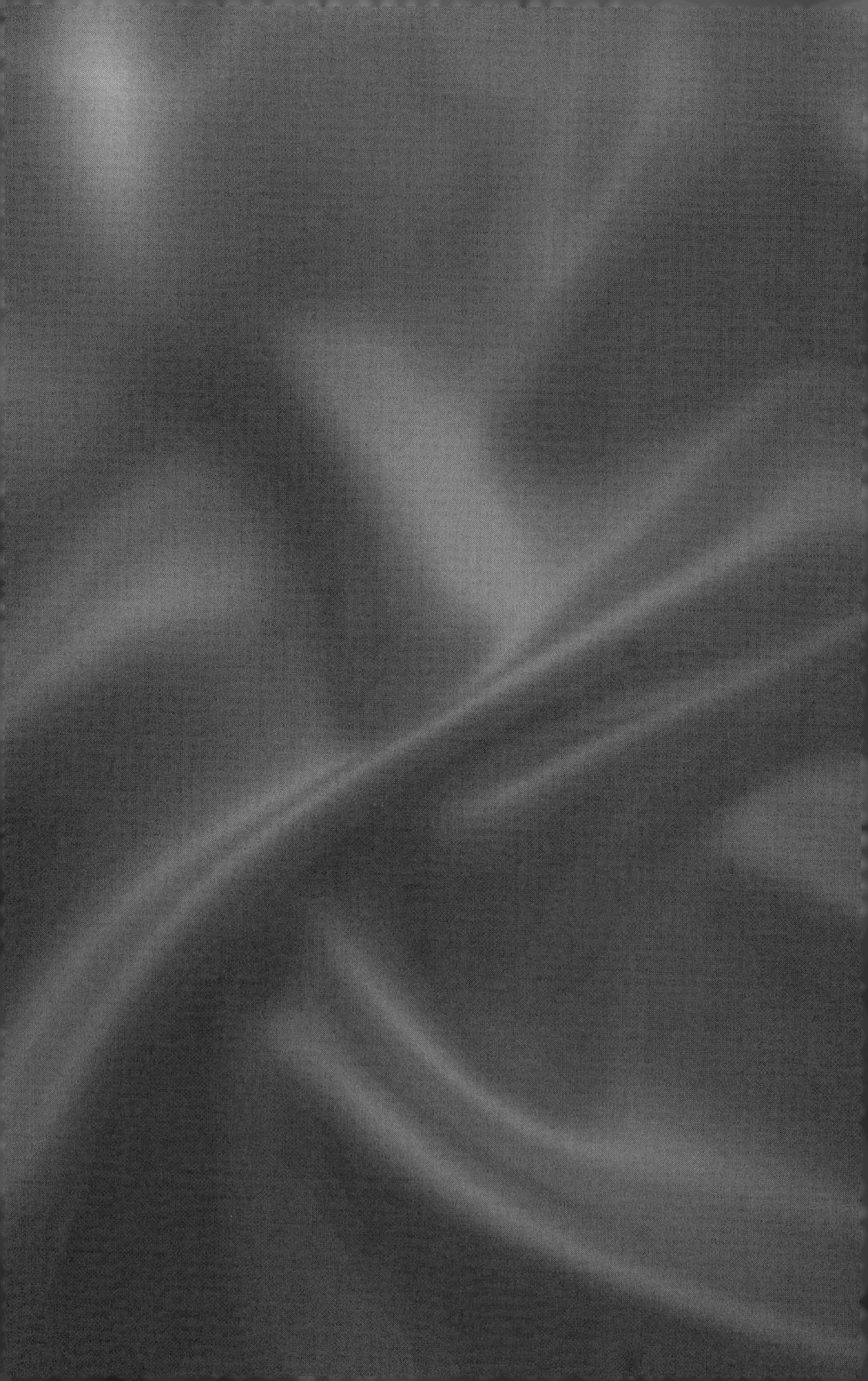

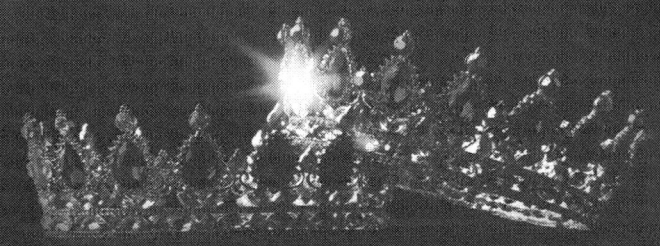

CHAPTER 19

Cold Hard Truth

Ella

The Present

2:02 a.m.

I was reaching the end of my rope.

Cold and bleeding anguish from every orifice, I walked back into the school with my very own grim reaper trailing behind me. A constant stalking shadow that never, *ever* left me alone.

Dark energy swirled around Cade. He seemed perturbed by his thoughts. I didn't ask him what was on his mind. Not when my own was a graveyard filled with ghouls feeding off memories that were best left forgotten.

I increased my pace, but my whole body protested, tired from tonight's events and turbulent emotions.

I shouldn't have come to Initiation Night, making history be damned. I was safer in the perimeters of my home, drinking wine at that stupid dinner party and playing the good girl high society daughter. Anything was better than being here.

All my scars were ripped open again. Cade left me unbalanced; my armour fully shattered. The only thing keeping me held together were the strings of my pride. The universe was having an enormous laugh playing the puppeteer to my puppet.

I felt like a queen on a chessboard forced to retreat from the opposing king's pressure. Halfway through conquering my desires—my healing and freedom—yet now I receded back to square one. Scared and bone-weary.

The bronze key in my hand, akin to the one we found in the library, weighed me down. Keeping me hostage. Telling me to finish what I started and not run away like a coward. Regrets would eat me alive later and I wasn't about to submit to anymore *maybes* and *what-ifs*.

To avoid looking at the presence behind me, I read the paper threaded through the key's bow with the next dare again.

Blind as a bat, but the truth lies in front of you…
SW-3-208

South wing, third floor, room 208. I deciphered the coordinates and Cade followed me wordlessly like a lost puppy. Still desperate. Still obsessed. Still lovesick.

The moment in the woods replayed in my mind on an endless loop, his despair-fused voice resounding in the chamber of my heart like a lonely echo.

"No one can give you the feeling of euphoria like I did. And that's what kills you. You search for me in all those men, don't you, baby? You want to feel the way I used to make you feel—like a fucking goddess—when I worshipped the ground you walked on."

Yes. I searched for him in every single guy I encountered since our breakup. I tried to find his dimples, his warm smirks, his serene blue eyes, his protective streak, his *devotion*. The tarred edges of my heart curled on themselves, birthing a big hole in my chest the longer I searched…to no avail.

"Why would I cheat on you when you were all I ever wanted?"

I asked myself that question a million times. If Cade loved me the way he claimed, why did I catch him in the act with a random girl, his mouth, jaw, and neck lavished with red-stained kisses?

I meant it when I said I gave him everything and he threw us into the flames.

Room 208 on the third floor was strategically hidden behind a row of portable lockers. I knew every nook and cranny of this school. But weirdly enough, I'd never seen this room. We rolled aside the portable lockers and entered an old student lounge of sorts, the door already unlocked.

"What are we looking for?" Cade's voice lacked animation.

"'*Blind as a bat, but the truth lies in front of you,*'" I whispered without looking at him. "That's what the dare says. I think we're looking for a bat, or something with an imagery of it."

Or anything else, really. This particular one was very cryptic.

And truth be told, I was ready to get this night over with. I no longer felt optimistic about winning this competition.

The exchange from the woods had deflated us both.

Nail-biting silence ensued between Cade and me. He went over to one side of the room while I stayed planted in my corner, searching quietly. The room had three walls laden with floor-to-ceiling bookshelves, one grey brick wall with various frames, three sofas with a pattern reminiscent of the '70s surrounding a swanky coffee table, and work desks with frosted glass lamps. It was a pleasant, cozy room, harbouring the same musty smell that was prevalent in Balthazar Building.

Eleven minutes later, hopelessness spread in the chilly atmosphere. It was inching closer to 2:30 a.m., and there was a strong possibility that another team had finished before us. Last year, Darla and I completed the competition in under two hours.

Speaking of another team…Except for that Initiator who attacked me, I hadn't seen anyone else. It was a rare occurrence not to see others throughout the competition.

Unease bloomed in my chest. Something felt cataclysmically wrong. Nothing about this Initiation Night had gone according to plan.

I peeked over my shoulder and spotted Cade crouching near the brick wall…removing bricks? My lungs inflated, ready to give him the speech of how we're not supposed to destroy anything on campus, but immediately stopped short.

I marched towards him. "What are you doing?"

"My foot accidentally collided with one of these bricks. Then I realized they were protruding and loose. Got my suspicions going."

Cade continued removing a series of bricks, his flashlight resting on the ground.

I squatted beside him and angled my torch to offer more light. Cade reached his hand into the wall's crevice, brows furrowing in concentration.

I tried not to focus on the endearing way his wet hair was slowly drying with a hint of a wave, the way his tongue ran over the inside of his inked bottom lip, the way his eyes rose to meet mine and flared with wonderment at my nearness.

My God. It should be a sin to be this handsome.

It had been months since we were intimate. Would screwing him one final time get him out of my system and give me the closure I needed? Then again, wasn't there a saying that closure was a myth? And fucking him one final time would only be a slap in the face of my self-respect.

Cade yanked out an object and smirked at me. "Well, would you look at that? Just like old times, huh, Ellie?"

It was a baseball bat with the final dare tapped along the barrel's surface.

I blanched, convinced tonight was a long-awaited punishment for all my past sins.

The baseball bat was an eminent symbolism of our frenetic relationship. Cade and I both knew what it stated.

The will to continue this game suddenly left me. Why was I putting myself through this suffering? For a crown and title I had already won? It wasn't worth it.

Feeling defeated, I whispered, "Why do you keep bringing up the past?"

"Because I can't let go of it," Cade returned ardently. "I can't let go of you, Ella. You're the other half of me. Don't you get it? I'm stuck in the past because I can't move on from you, *mo chuisle*."

Mo chuisle.

It was beautiful, the way Cade caressed the term of endearment on his tongue. It had been so long, I almost wept at hearing it twice tonight.

If only his sweet nothings could fix everything broken between us.

Old memories resurfaced, reminding me of the physical pain I felt after catching Cade in the act. The helplessness echoing inside of me while I sat on the bathroom floor, tears streaming down my face as I accepted my loss.

"I don't want to do this anymore." I felt numb as I stood up, almost robotically. "I *can't*, Cade."

Perhaps running away was the cowardly route. But when the next stop ahead was a dead end, turning around was the best solution.

My ex-boyfriend dropped the baseball bat and it rattled loudly against the floor. Mimicking me, he stood up and chuckled without humour. "This isn't about the competition anymore, eh? This is personal."

I placed a hand over my stomach, feeling another old wound rip open. "It was *always* personal."

Cade ran a palm over his mouth and jaw, shaking his head like he was seeing something inside of me he wished he could unsee. "I don't know why I bother with you, Ella. You've got so much pride. I've been trying for goddamn weeks to get through to you, yet you refuse to give me an inch. I'm at a crossroad, baby, and I really need you to see beyond the pain of our past and hear me out."

Did he not understand? Hearing him rehash *that* night would transform me into the shell of a girl I was over the summer. I would never be that version of me again. I refused to.

"You have no right to talk about my pride, when you stripped me of mine. You're the very reason for my humiliation." Vehemently, I confessed, "You *broke* me, Cade."

I watched as he jerked back like I shot him.

Cade's face fell and he rolled his lips into his mouth, as though physically holding himself back from saying something he shouldn't.

He said it anyway.

"You saw what you saw at the party and branded me a cheater." Barely concealed fury plunged through his frame as he pinned me with harsh eyes. "There's always two sides to a story, but you played judge, jury, and executioner before hearing mine."

"The evidence was there." A bitter chuckle escaped me. "What was there to say?"

"What was there to say? We were together for *three* years! You were my best friend before my girlfriend! You were supposed to listen to me! You were supposed to give me the chance to fucking talk! I've always been there for you," he barked incredulously, voice cracking as he pointed an accusing finger at me. "Through thick and thin, I was your pillar. Any fucking thing you needed, I gave to you." In his rising anger, he knocked a glass world globe off a work desk. It shattered into little pieces on the floor. Neither of us flinched in the aftermath. It was no worse than what already lay broken between Cade and me. "So why couldn't you have given me the one thing I needed?"

To be heard.

That's all he wanted.

I silenced him and he hated me for it.

"You're out of your mind if you thought I'd give you the time of day after you cheated!" I shouted back. "Did you expect me to sit down, offer you tea and cookies, and listen to your explanation when I found you in bed with another girl, drunk and high as a kite? Be so fucking for real, you asshole! I don't give second chances! Especially to two-timing scums!"

Innumerable individuals watched me get humiliated at that party. They watched me get betrayed in the worst way possible and then filmed it for hundreds to see, laughing at my expense like I was a toy for their amusement.

I could never forgive him for the sheer desolation I experienced in that moment. I wanted to die. I wanted the earth to swallow me whole so I could disappear forever.

Next thing I knew, Cade flung aside the work desk and it crashed against a shelf with a jangling noise, causing a few books to fall.

The air rippled with weeks' worth of pent-up tension and the long-awaited confrontation. It was suffocating and I could taste its flavour on my palate like a foul substance I was forced to choke down.

"Fuck you, Ella!" Cade seethed and advanced towards me, a vein protruding in his neck. "You're so sure of what you saw, huh? You think you have it all figured out, but did you stop to think, for one second, how out of character it would be for me to cheat on the love of my life? Did it ever cross your mind that betraying you is the last thing I'd ever want or do?"

Glass crunched under the weight of our steps as he backed me against the brick wall.

Cade talked like he wasn't guilty and it didn't settle well with my gut. Doubt crept in my mind, making me question small details from that night.

"It may have been the last thing you wanted, but you still did." My hand reached up to clutch the necklace at the base of my throat…only to remember it wasn't there anymore. I took it off after we broke up. Now I missed it like a vital organ. "You hurt me, Cade. You hurt me so much."

"And you hurt me too, Ella." One final step and he was back in my orbit where I could not evade him. "You were supposed to trust me…love me. Instead, you cussed me out, slammed the doors in my face, and all but pushed me out of your life like I was trash."

Trust and love. I always thought those two words were synonymous.

While some part of me still loved Cade, I no longer trusted him.

And I could never be with someone I didn't trust.

The faster he got that tidbit through his head, the better.

It was finally time to rip off the bandage and tell him the truth of why his betrayal burned so deep.

Cade claimed he was there for me through thick and thin, but there was one instance where he wasn't—though he had no clue—and my irrational mind could not forgive him for it.

"I was in no condition to hear you out that night, Cade," I said. "Or the days and weeks that followed."

"Why?" He gritted his teeth.

"I came to Josh's party because I had something important to share with you."

"What?" Cade's blue eyes darkened as he sensed the change in my tone. "Spit it out already, Ella."

I snaked a hand between our bodies and pressed it to my stomach. "I was pregnant."

There are certain moments in your life where you feel like you're having an out-of-body experience. You're physically there, rooted in your spot, but your mind and spirit have drifted away and are watching the entire scene unfold from a different view.

That's what it felt like right now.

The wind knocked out of his sails, Cade faltered back a step. "*No.*"

"Yes," I confirmed, feeling bleak, fatigued, and way past done. "I was five weeks pregnant."

Cade was frozen, but the haunted quality veining over his features, twisting them into something utterly broken, spoke volumes. "*No.* Goddammit, *no*, Ella."

"I miscarried the night of the party."

I'd seen Cade tormented once when he recounted the story of his past. But it was nothing compared to my revelation, which seemed to physically crush him. His posture sagged and his hands twitched, reaching out for me until they decided against it. "Ella, I'm so sorry…"

I smiled wryly, tears stinging my eyes. "It doesn't matter anymore."

"But it does." He stepped up to me again, a light trembling taking over his body. Up close, his own eyes held a sheen of moisture. "I'm so sorry." His hands cupped my face and I let him. "I'm so fucking sorry you went through that, Ellie. You didn't deserve it."

I didn't realize how badly I needed to hear those words. My own self-destructive thoughts had chanted that I'd deserved it—that it was karma for all the shit I'd done.

In my book, there were only two things I wished for: a happy ending with my princepin and a family of our own. I always wanted to be a mother. Cade knew it too. Although nineteen was young, I'd already loved the little life growing inside of me and I was ready to protect and raise it. Despite knowing my parents would disapprove of a teenage pregnancy.

When I miscarried our baby, I was devastated.

"Who knows about this?" Cade urged.

"Only you," I whispered. "I couldn't tell anyone."

"Fuck, Ella, you were completely alone." His deep voice shook with pain. "You should have talked to me. I would have been there for you."

I knew he would have, but he was the last person I wanted to see.

"It's all right. I found ways to cope."

"Like what?"

My throat worked with a rough swallow and my fingers curled into the lapels of his leather jacket. "I knitted a onesie for our baby."

Raw ache splattered over his expression. Cade released a strangled noise and pressed his forehead to mine, tucking my hair behind my ears and holding on to the strands like an anchor. "God, Ella. I'm so sorry, baby.

I sucked in a choppy inhale and to my mortification, a tear swept down my face. I didn't cry often. It made me feel weak. But sometimes the strongest souls cried, not because they were weak, but because they'd been tough for too long, right?

Cade followed the trail with his lips, ending it by pressing a kiss to my right eyelid. My imperfectly, perfect eye. That singular gesture caused another tear. Until a small waterfall cascaded down the slopes of my cheeks.

My *querido* wrapped his arms around me and I melted into his embrace, needing his touch now more than ever. His uneven breaths matched mine as my tears soaked his collar.

For the first time in weeks, my heart calmed down in the presence of its companion, its erratic fluttering slowing until Cade's and my rhythm beat in unison. A lulling symphony that could only be heard by us.

"When did you realize you were pregnant?" he murmured.

"A few hours before the party. I took a pregnancy test to confirm. My periods were late and I was suspicious."

"Five weeks you said, right?"

I heard the question in his voice.

"Yes, we conceived in June…on prom night."

CHAPTER 20
Plot twist

CADE

The Present
2:31 a.m.

My world felt thrown off its axis from Ella's revelation.

Of all the things I expected her to say, *this* I did not see coming.

My girlfriend had been pregnant.

I replayed prom night and how we snuck out of the venue after getting crowned prom king and queen. We spent the next few hours locked in a state of bliss, making love in a hotel room. I forgot condoms and Ella wanted us to fuck bare.

I pulled out every single time, but apparently not well enough… because Ella actually got pregnant with our baby.

And although pulling out wasn't a foolproof method to prevent a pregnancy, I should have known better, despite both of us consenting to screw without protection.

I lost Ella weeks later, but she lost me *and* our baby. I knew we shouldn't compare sufferings, but her loss was grander than mine. Only now was I coming to terms with the amount of trauma Ella harboured from the summer.

My heart broke again. This time, for my Ellie.

The one who always fought and cared for her loved ones like a fierce lioness. The one who wanted to grow old with me and start a family.

She didn't deserve this.

Suddenly, I understood the pure dolor Ella felt when she found me with that other girl. Suddenly, I understood *why* she shut me out. Ella was unable to see my face or listen to my voice when she was dealing with the aftermath of a miscarriage. On top of a boyfriend whom she thought cheated on her.

I forgave her for all of it.

Fuck, I forgave her even before I came to Initiation Night.

I once told her that she could break my heart a thousand times. It was the truth. It was hers to break, hers to mend, hers to love. Now and forever.

I used to think heartbreak was the most hurtful thing I had experienced. Not even Julius's assault could compare to the pain of loving and losing my girlfriend. But as I pressed a hand against Ella's head and heard her sniffle, I knew it was the realization that she miscarried and I wasn't there to help her get through it.

That was the most hurtful thing.

Locked in an embrace, we lost sense of time and our surroundings. That's usually what happened when we were in the same vicinity. The edges of the world blurred around us until our visions tunneled and we only saw each other.

Ella—the strongest, bravest, wildest girl—was all I ever saw.

Despite holding her in my arms, we still felt lightyears away.

The only thing left to do now was tell her my side of the story.

"Ella?" I exhaled slowly.

She lifted her head from my shoulder.

We were so close, our breaths mingled. I wanted to kiss her so bad. I was dying too.

Her tongue peeked out, wiping over her bottom lip. Leaving it slick and inviting. Resisting Ella was damn near impossible. Though I pushed aside those thoughts and concentrated on what mattered most. Acknowledging her pain.

"Yes?"

"I'm truly so sorry," I said again. "I wish things could have been different."

"Me too." She stepped away and without her warmth, I was back to feeling cold. Empty. "We should probably head out. I'm sure we lost the competition and it's probably already three a.m."

I glanced down at my watch. "No, we still have time. We should finish this."

Ella heard the double entendre in my sentence. She stiffened and turned around, giving me her back. "I'm in no mood to continue this competition, Cade. I'm depleted. Mentally and emotionally." Bending down, she snatched the discarded baseball bat and flinched. "Ouch. Shit!"

I rushed to her. "What's wrong?"

"I cut myself on broken glass." Ella angled her hand towards her flashlight. A crimson slash in her palm had blood trickling over her skin.

Damn me for shattering that glass globe in anger. "Fuck, show me."

Blood didn't make me squeamish. But blood on Ella did.

I hissed through my teeth when she extended her hand. "You need to get that cleaned and bandaged right away. The nurse's office is right around the corner. I'll take you."

It wasn't deep enough to need stitches, but I didn't want her driving home with a bleeding hand.

Stubborn as ever, she shook her head. "I'm fine." Reaching into her little crossbody purse, she pulled out a few tissues and bundled them against her palm. They instantly turned scarlet. "This will do until I get home."

No, it wouldn't. "Ella, please. Let me take care of you."

For a second, I thought she would oppose.

But there was no spark left in her. None of that fire from when we started Initiation Night.

She sighed, resigned. "Okay."

I successfully broke down some of her walls, but I hated the dejected air surrounding her. This was still a win, though. And if I had to spend the rest of our time in this godforsaken place resurrecting the old Ella I loved, I'd gladly do so.

I inched my hand her way.

She stared at it.

I was giving her the choice to accept me for I had yearned to hold her hand for weeks.

And when her fingers hesitantly reached out for mine, I released a breath I didn't realize I was holding in. Tension coiled deep in my muscles evaporated like mist.

We wove our fingers together.

Calmness seeped through my pores.

"Let's go, sweetheart." I squeezed her hand the way I did every time I got off my motorcycle, every time I tugged her closer for a kiss, and every time I made love to her.

Then I veered us out of Room 208 and walked down the vacant hallway, towards the nurse's office.

I was holding the hand of the girl I loved and she gave it to me willingly.

Though I was elated this instant, I knew this feeling might be short-lived.

Because our next stop?

It was my personal hell.

<hr/>

Ella

Cade's fingers threaded with mine sparked a tendril of jubilance in my veins. I'd always loved the feel of his slight calluses against my softer skin.

The fondest memory I recalled of those hands was when they mapped the lines of my body like they were travelling on an endless road, leaving trails of goosebumps in their wake. Caressing me in the kind of places where the sun didn't shine but where the stars did…until I was love drunk, floating on a cloud of ecstasy with his name on my lips.

Cade tugged me along the third floor hallway. It fostered a spine-chilling ambiance that was straight out of my favourite gothic romance novels. The light emanating from his torch lit up our path, while mine hung uselessly by my side.

I was too caught up in the pain radiating from my bleeding palm and my earlier confrontation with Cade.

"You saw what you saw at the party and branded me a cheater. There are always two sides to a story, but you played judge, jury, and executioner before hearing mine."

Those words bounced inside my skull with startling lucidity. I didn't want to hear Cade's side before. Now uncertainty crawled in my mind. The sheer conviction in his voice had me thinking that perhaps I missed something...

And that was a scary thought because I was firm in my beliefs regarding what I saw. Him. Her. On the bed. Red-stained kisses.

"You're so sure of what you saw, huh?"

Did I see wrong? The high from my newfound pregnancy and then the plummeting heartbreak I experienced in the same night had my rationality crashing like a series of dominoes. I wasn't in the right mindset when I caught him, let alone when I ran away from the party.

"You think you have it all figured out, but did you stop to think, for one second, how out of character it would be for me to cheat on the love of my life?"

I did find it out of character for him, which was why his betrayal hurt the way it did.

"You were supposed to trust me...love me. Instead, you cussed me out, slammed the doors in my face, and all but pushed me out of your life like I was trash."

Whenever I stepped out on my balcony, that memory often replayed in my mind like a film. Now as we inched closer to the nurse's office, I remembered it again.

The whistling wind screeched as I flung open the doors, finding a wary Cade standing on my balcony. His hair was mussed by the summer wind and his gaze held a look that basically said, 'I'm lost without you.'

It cut me to the quick. I steeled myself and glared at him. "What the fuck are you doing here?"

It had been three nights since Josh's birthday party. Three nights since I caught him in his bedroom with another 'pretty girl.' Three nights since I miscarried our baby. He didn't know the last tidbit and he would never find out.

"Please, Ella," he pleaded. His hands gripped the balcony banister with knuckle-whitening strength, stopping himself from reaching out for me. "Give

me five minutes of your time. Let me explain."

Hadn't he done enough damage? Now the asshole actually had the gall to show up at my home. He was lucky I didn't tell my parents that we broke up. Otherwise, my papá would murder him for how he hurt me.

"Spare me your bullshit excuses. We're done, Cade. Get the fuck out, you cheater."

Cheater.

I never thought I'd associate Cade to that word in my entire life. He was faithful to me. Until he wasn't.

Pain splintered through my body. I choked on a gasp and the onslaught of tears. Was he here to beg for another chance? Or was this a sick ploy to torture me some more?

"It's not what you think—"

"I caught you red-handed in bed with her!" I lost the fight with my tears. They rivered down my cheeks. "You had her lipstick stains all over you! There's nothing to explain! I know what I saw!"

He finally tried to grab me. There were dark circles under his eyes and he looked extremely haggard. "Please, Ellie. I'm sorry—"

I raised a hand to his face, silencing him, and thundered on, "You're despicable! I gave you everything—my love, my trust, my loyalty—and you stomped all over it! You make me sick!" I yelled, voice breaking. I fisted the roots of my hair, shaking my head to erase the image of him standing before me. Looking apologetic. Looking weak. Looking like a fucking cheater. When that didn't work, I pushed at his chest to get him to leave. From my sight and from my life. "Don't think you can beg for a second chance because you're not getting it! If I ever see you here again, I'm calling the cops!"

He seemed shocked at my outburst.

"Please don't do this, Ella. Just hear me out. Five minutes," he said desperately, backing away reluctantly when I shoved at his chest again. He was almost at the edge of my balcony. Almost gone. "We made a promise. You and me. Ride or die. I love—"

I slammed the doors shut in his face.

But I still heard the muffled word he uttered. "You…"

Then I closed the curtains to block him out and ran for my en suite where I vomited in the toilet bowl.

I finished the night crying into my pillow.

Wishing I never laid eyes on Cade.

Wishing I never gave him my all.

Wishing I never, ever fell in love with him.

With Cade's monologue from Room 208 and the revisit to the moment in the balcony, which I saw in a new light, for the first time ever…I doubted my decision to shut him out.

Some people deserved a second chance.

But did you really need a second chance if you never truly lost your first one?

I was actually suspecting Cade hadn't, and that messed with my head more than anything. An odd sense of guilt settled in my stomach like cement.

"We're here." Cade's voice yanked me back to the situation at hand.

The broken glass. My bleeding palm. The nurse's office.

"The door's unlocked, so someone's been here already." Cade tugged me inside the room. "C'mon, Ellie."

Once inside, he closed the door. The nurse's office felt too small for both our presences and demons. Cade surveyed our surroundings with a critical look. Like an Initiator may be hiding, ready to pull another prank.

"There's no one else," I mumbled. "Just us." Speaking of… "Cade, don't you find it strange that we haven't seen a single person in over an hour? It's not normal."

St. Victoria was a ginormous campus, but we were a big team of Initiators every year. Crossing paths with other teams happened quite often.

Cade grimaced. "I know. I was thinking that too."

Fear dribbled into my system. "Do you think someone found out students were here after hours and reported it to the authorities?"

"I don't know, Ella." He shook his head. "And I don't care. The only thing that matters to me is getting your cut bandaged."

Cade directed me towards the single bed in the nurse's office and I sat down while he rummaged through drawers for medical supplies.

Staring out the bay windows, I watched the outside world. It was a murky blur with torrential rain decorating the stygian sky, the medley of thunderbolts and lightning breaking the inky canvas every few pulses. The sight and sound were a mirror reflection of my heart's inner turmoil, and the vagary of the weather was a depiction of Cade's and my relationship. Temperamental and persistent despite the odds.

Cade parked himself on a backless stool and wheeled closer to me, bringing with him antiseptic wipes and gauze. He already washed his hands at the sink and snapped on a pair of blue exam gloves. "How do you feel?"

Are you asking about my hand or my heart? Because both hurt tremendously.

"Exhausted," I answered truthfully. "I'd give anything to be in my bed right now."

During his rummaging, Cade found a spare candle, which he lit with his Zippo and placed on the table next to the bed. The candle provided a mellow glow that softened our little bubble. "I'll take you home after this so you can sleep. Did you drive here?"

"No, I hitched a ride with Callie."

With nimble fingers, Cade tore open the square package of antiseptic wipes and tended to me calmly.

Day or night, whenever I hurt myself, he was there to save the day.

Some things never changed.

I hissed in a breath from the burn when Cade wiped my cut. "I know, I know, babe. It hurts. I'm sorry."

The tenderness he displayed while dressing my wound nearly undid me. I focused on the gauze he wrapped around my palm instead of the endearing way his brows puckered and the way his lips parted in concentration, giving him a youthful boyishness that only presented itself when he was around me.

In front of the world, he was quiet, lethal, and every bit Montardor's merciless fixer. Behind closed doors, he was my smiling, gentle, mischievous princepin. The one who laughed with me, held my hand, championed all my ambitions and dreams, and promised to love me until our deaths and beyond.

That's what drew me to him like bees to honey. The duality of him. The ruthless mob prince and the playful bad boy. Two sides of one coin. Mine to treasure.

As Cade finished bandaging my wound and disposed of his gloves, two prominent thoughts struck me.

Though what if you were never betrayed, Ella?

What if there was more to the picture…and you failed to see it?

When Cade glanced in my direction, he saw the conflict on my face. I was battling with the need to walk out of this place and never look back, or stay right here forever, where the only people to exist were him and me.

"What is it, Ella?"

I debated asking the question weighing on my mind since the summer. Then I reminded myself no more *what-ifs*. "Why wasn't I enough for you, Cade?"

Why were you with that girl? Why did you need her when you had me?

It looked like he lost some one-sided battle with himself when his eyes closed and he whispered, "You were enough. You've always been, sweetheart."

I fisted his leather jacket and dragged him closer. "Then why did you cheat on me, Cade?" I spat, shaking him. "Why do you talk like you aren't guilty, dammit!"

"Because I didn't cheat!" Cade snapped, pure agony coating his vocal cords. "You were everything to me. I would never fucking cheat on you. I loved you!"

I loved you. I loved you. I loved you.

A broken sob escaped me.

Cade heaved out a shaky exhale and uttered words that shocked me to my core. "I was drugged the night of Josh's birthday party."

I flinched, rearing back as though I'd been slapped.

No, no, no.

Please, tell me I didn't just hear him say that. "W-What?"

Cade peered at me with so much vulnerability, my heart squeezed. "I never cheated on you. I would rather die than hurt you like that, Ella."

Stunned, I sat before him, struggling to digest the bomb he just dropped. "Tell me what happened. All of it."

Cade inhaled a deep breath and finally told me his version of the night that changed everything for us…

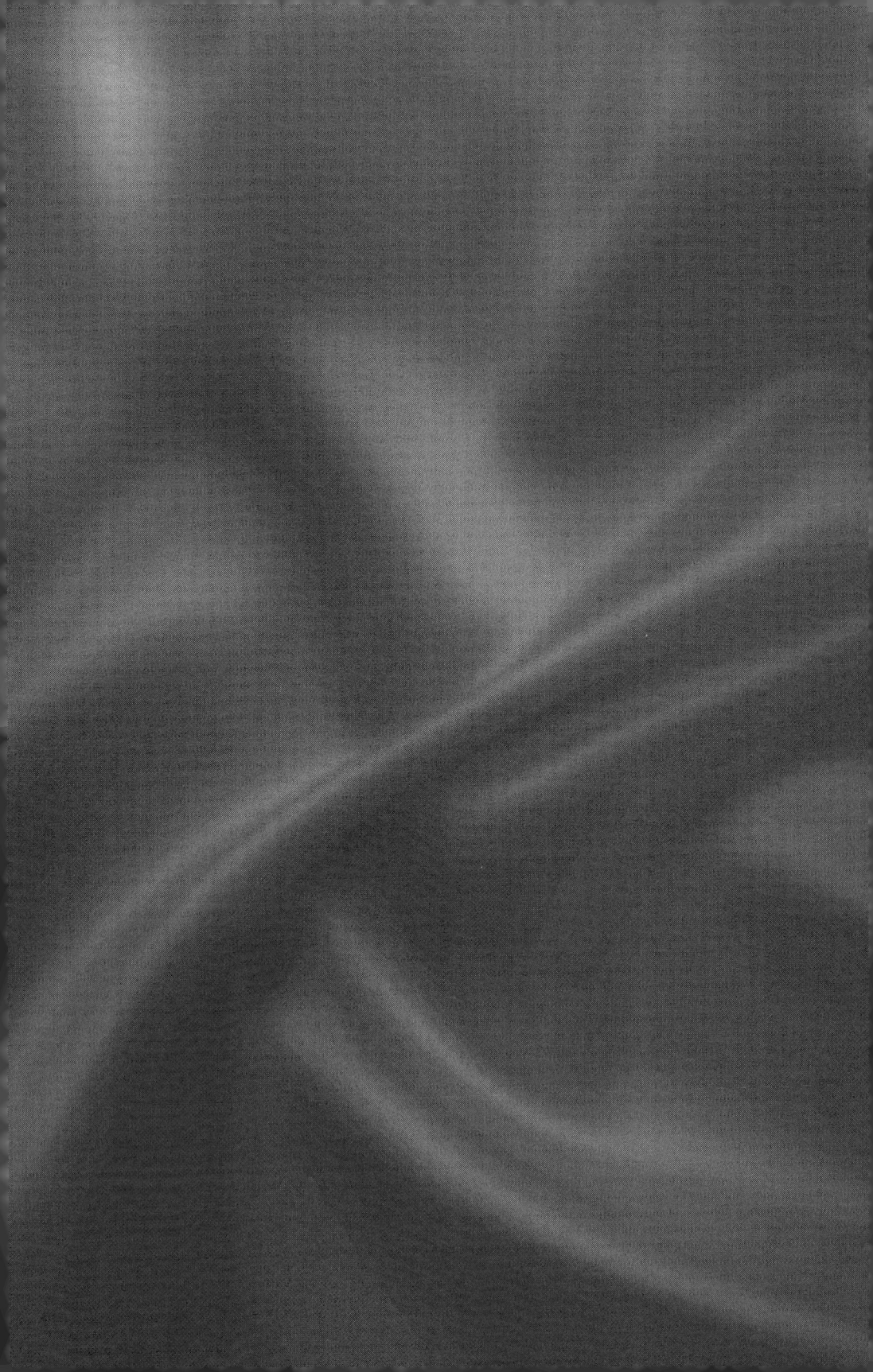

CHAPTER 21
The Deceit

CADE

The Past – 3 months ago

Ella left me on '*read*' three hours ago.

My last text message sat at the bottom of our conversation with no reply on her part.

When are you getting here, sweetheart? —Princepin

Granted, she called me this afternoon to let me know she'd be arriving after 9:00 p.m. It wasn't uncommon for Ella to take hours to get dolled up for a party, and usually I waited on her patiently.

But I was a needy man who liked having my girl by my side. Twenty-four seven, preferably. Sue me for being clingy.

I took a sip of my beer and glared at my phone. The rational part of my brain said to calm down. Everything was okay. The irrational part wanted to blow up her phone like the obsessed psycho she teased me of being.

The Remington residence was blasted in colourful neon lights and big garish décor for Josh's nineteenth birthday party. The mansion's first floor was converted into a makeshift nightclub with gyrating bodies, and the backyard was flanked with more partygoers drinking and playing beer pong. The smell of alcohol, drugs, sin, and teenage recklessness was thick in the air.

The whole affair was over-the-top but very on-brand for my cocky, confident, and boisterous brother. He loved to put on a good show.

And Uncle Vance and Aunt Julia loved to indulge their children. They asked me if I wanted a lavish birthday party like this for mine in two weeks and I replied, "over my dead body." I was lowkey and happier to celebrate with my tight-knit crew.

I hovered near the railing on the second floor, where I had an eagle's eye view of the front entrance. When Ella walked through, I'd see her right away.

Three minutes later, my beer was finished and Ella still hadn't arrived. I checked my phone and texted her again. She didn't open it. Maybe she was driving over and couldn't answer.

With a sigh, I left my position and walked down the grand staircase, pushing through the bustling crowd. People were drinking, laughing, hooking up, doing lines, and popping molly. Their cheeriness pissed me off—how dare they be happy while I sulked away waiting for my girlfriend?

My friends were exactly where I left them in the kitchen, huddled around the island counter littered with bottles of liquor, Solo red cups, and a dusting of fine powder that couldn't be anything but coke. The music was less deafening here.

Nico was dodging flirtatious attempts from a few girls. Nate was busy making out with one whose face I couldn't see. Sam was downing his drink while searching the scene for a certain beauty queen. Shaun was talking to Hunter, one of Josh's friend.

And the birthday boy was surrounded by his fan club, aka every jock and cheerleader from the west side who practically worshipped the ground he walked on.

Josh was dressed in his football jersey that had a flurry of black sharpie scrawls on the back—multiple *happy birthdays* and *xoxos*—as he chugged a bottle of Jack Daniel's, his admirers cheering him on. He spotted me quickly. "Yo! It's my twin!" he slurred, pointing the bottle in my direction. "Everybody, wish him a happy birthday, too!"

I grinned at the chorus of enthusiastic 'happy birthdays' and walked to him, throwing an arm around his shoulder. "Happy birthday, bro."

"I love you!" he hollered and pressed a kiss to my cheek. Josh was an affectionate drunk. "And I love my gift!"

I chuckled and clapped his back. "You're welcome, Josh."

Uncle Vance and I bought Josh a yellow McLaren for his special day. If anyone deserved a grandiose gift, it was him. He was truly the best cousin slash adoptive brother Olivia and I could have asked for. Even though he liked to jokingly tell everyone that we were fraternal twins, separated at birth, so it stopped people from questioning my sudden addition to the Remingtons' lives.

"Where's Ella?" he asked the million-dollar question. "I haven't seen her around."

"She's not here yet. Has she texted you?"

"Nah, except for the message she sent me a few hours ago. She said happy birthday and to expect a big surprise."

The surprise was a penis-shaped piñata filled with jolly ranchers. Ella sent me a picture yesterday when she picked it up from the store. "All right, well, if you see her, let me know."

Josh gave me a shit-eating grin. "Dude, you're whipped."

I shoved him away and flashed him the bird. "Says the guy who professes his undying love for Layla every day."

"I'm a romantic." He hiccupped. "I can't help it."

I laughed and shook my head.

Moments later, I started drinking again with the boys, taking shots and cheering for Josh. Someone passed around a joint and I inhaled a few puffs. The party around us buzzed with excitement. My friends were having the time of their lives and all I could think about was how incomplete I felt without Ella by my side.

Unable to hold back, I texted her again.

Where are you, princess? —Princepin

Are you almost here? —Princepin

I'm getting worried. —Princepin.

I miss you. —Princepin.

I was extremely attuned to Ella. Whenever something was wrong with her, my chest burned in a specific spot. Call it intuition, if you will. Despite the joyous occasion, I couldn't brush off the fact that something was off about tonight.

"You've been moping and staring at your phone for the last five minutes." Shaun leaned against the island counter next to me, crossing his arms. "What gives?"

"Ella," I said gruffly. "I haven't heard from her in a bit."

Shaun's mouth formed in a retort, but he paused his inevitable teasing when he saw the expression on my face. He squeezed my shoulder instead. "I'm sure she's okay. She said she was coming tonight, right?"

"Yeah." I ran a palm over my jaw. "She's probably driving over right now."

"Exactly. Don't sweat it. I'm sure she'll be here soon."

Shaun was right. I was overthinking it.

For the next hour, I immersed myself in drinking games with the boys. Beer pong, flip cup, and never have I ever until I was way past tipsy and close to hammered.

"Never have I ever had a threesome," Nico said.

We all watched Shaun take a shot. I wasn't surprised, since I knew my best friend had a bit of a playboy streak.

"No way!" Josh was wide-eyed. "Details. Now."

Shaun chuckled. "A gentleman doesn't kiss and tell."

Josh was about to rib him when Layla squeezed through the thick crowd of partygoers, two of her friends in tow, one redhead and one blonde. Gabby and Anna.

"There she is! There's my girl." Josh hooked an arm around her neck and drew her closer, kissing her cheek in a drunken fashion. "Hi, Lay."

Layla blushed. "Um, hi. Happy birthday."

They still toed the awkward line where they were more than friends but not exactly dating. Although Josh made it very clear to everyone that Layla was off-limits and completely his.

I noticed Hunter freeze and his lips part as he stared at Gabby, almost in an entranced manner, while she laughed and chatted with Shaun.

On the other hand, Anna, the object of Sam's desires, was busy perusing the island counter for something to drink.

My attention turned towards Sam just in time to watch him look like he got struck by Cupid. He gazed at Anna like she created his very universe.

When her hand closed over a can of Pepsi, Sam wrapped his fingers over hers reflexively. So not smooth. Nico, Nate, and I sighed in unison.

Her amused gaze rose to his and she spoke softly, "Do you mind?"

Sam opened his mouth to speak, but no sound emerged. She smiled like a pageant contestant and snatched her drink away with a polite 'thank you.' Then she and Gabby disappeared alongside Josh and Layla. Probably to go dance.

"You fucking blew it, man," I slurred to Sam.

"I did." Sam ran a hand over his face, mesmerized and still staring at the space Anna vacated. "She's so fucking beautiful that sometimes I just feel…speechless."

While the rest of them teased him about his crush, I reached for my phone and reopened my conversation with Ella.

Still nothing.

Worry and irritation coalesced in my stomach. With every second I was left unanswered, I grew more annoyed. Overwhelmed, too. There were too many sounds, too many neon lights, too many fragrances and BOs wafting in the kitchen.

I needed to leave for a bit and get some fresh air.

Filling my red Solo cup with more Jack and Coke, I saluted the boys. "I'll be back soon."

Muscling my way through the crowd, I entered a quiet hallway, devoid of people.

I dialed Ella's number and brought my cell phone to my ear. One ring. Two rings. Three rings. Four rings.

"Hey, you've reached Ella. Can't come to the phone right now. Please leave your name and number, and I'll give you a call back as soon as possible."

At the beep, I recorded, "Hey, Ellie. It's me. I'm getting worried. Give me a call as soon as you hear this, all right? I love—*what the fuck!*"

A guy wearing all-black with his hood up shouldered into me. I staggered against the wall. His hand moved over my cup before he grabbed my elbow to steady me.

"Sorry, bro," he mumbled and quickly darted down the hallway.

"Watch where you're going, fucker!" I slurred.

It was too dark to see, let alone decipher his features. I didn't know who it was, and I was way too plastered to even give a shit right now.

After a deep breath, I continued recording my message, only to realize the call ended. "Goddammit."

Throwing back the rest of my drink, I winced at the odd aftertaste.

Not quite like Jack. Not quite like Coke.

I swore that's what I poured into my cup, though.

Before I could ponder further, Ella finally texted.

I'm here. Meet me in your bedroom. —Princess

Don't turn on the lights. —Princess

I have a surprise <3 —Princess

Trepidation escaped through the cracks of my ribcage like feathered smoke and relief took its place instead.

This is why she didn't reply earlier. She was preparing a surprise. Everything is fine.

I strolled out of the hallway and headed for the grand staircase, dodging more people.

Perspiration started beading my temples. I tugged at the collar of my T-shirt.

It was too hot in here.

Too suffocating.

A nugget of anxiety crawled down my spine like a spider. My chest tightened and my throat grew thick. The chatter of the party faded into the background and my heartbeats were amplified in my ears.

As I climbed up the stairs, every step felt like I was walking in quicksand.

Fuck. Something doesn't feel right.

I paused halfway up to my room, feeling drained all of a sudden.

My skin prickled when I reached the second floor with the help of the banister. Bleary gaze and breathing unevenly. A wave of dizziness smacked me out of nowhere and I grabbed the wall for support, palming the sweat off my forehead.

I stumbled to my bedroom door, my hand-eye coordination messed up.

Why was I feeling so depleted?

Fuck, I shouldn't have drunk that much.

I'd have to apologize to Ella. My girlfriend had a surprise for me and I was arriving shit-faced.

Swaying into my room, I remembered not to turn on the lights like she instructed. Darkness welcomed me and the ground beneath my feet felt malleable.

"Sweetheart, I'm here," I announced, with a slow and guttural tone I barely recognized.

"You made it."

I squinted my eyes. The voice came from my bed. I could barely make out her silhouette, but when she murmured, "Won't you come closer?" I followed her like a pirate lost at sea, drawn by the luring song of a siren.

I fell on the bed next to her and she giggled. Her laugh sounded off. A bit higher key. Must be the alcohol talking, though. I grabbed her face and leaned in to kiss her lips. "I missed you so much."

"You saw me downstairs just a few minutes ago," she teased against my lips, kissing me back. My tongue parted her mouth impatiently. She tasted like rum and smelled like lemon. Ella normally drank Vodka sunrise and swore by her jasmine and orange blossom scent.

Huh. That was weird.

We exchanged more kisses and she hesitated before laying soft pecks down my jaw and neck. Everything felt off. The fingers fisting my T-shirt. The taste of her lips. The scent of her skin.

When I threaded my fingers through her hair, her length was shorter and the strands stiff with curls. Was this her surprise? A new haircut?

Then my muddled brain registered her words. I drew away from her touch, my skull throbbing. "S-Saw you downstairs?"

"Yeah." She traced a finger down chin. "When you told me to meet you here."

I blinked, fighting the bizarre sensation moving through me. I was sweating profusely at this rate, feeling like I wanted to crawl out of my skin while simultaneously trying to find shelter within. "W-What are you talking about? I haven't seen you since yesterday, baby."

In the dark, I think she shook her head or tilted it. "What are *you* talking about?"

That's when I noticed something else. Her voice. It was completely wrong. Unlike her usual soft tone. She was slurring too. As though she'd drunk way too much.

"Ellie? W-What's…going on?" My fingers traced down the column of her throat, halting when I didn't feel the heart-shaped necklace around her neck.

Ella never, ever took it off. She promised me.

"W-Who's Ellie?"

My tongue felt glued to the roof of my mouth, unable to release a word or sound.

Who's Ellie? What is she talking about?

She reached over to the bedside table and turned on the lamp.

And that's when I saw her through a fuzzy vision.

The *her* being someone who was not my Ellie.

Tall and curvy with blond hair and crimson-painted lips. Her expression was shocked and her eyes were glazed. "O-Oh my God. You're not him."

Him?

Anger and horror caromed through my trance like a splash of ice-cold water awakening me. No. No. No. I had just made out with a girl who wasn't my fucking girlfriend. My Ella. "W-Who are you—"

I never got to finish my sentence. My door burst open. Noise from the party filtered inside my room and yanked us out of whatever warped reality we found ourselves in.

Lo and behold, my real girlfriend stood at the threshold.

Heartbreak evident all over her face. "Cade?"

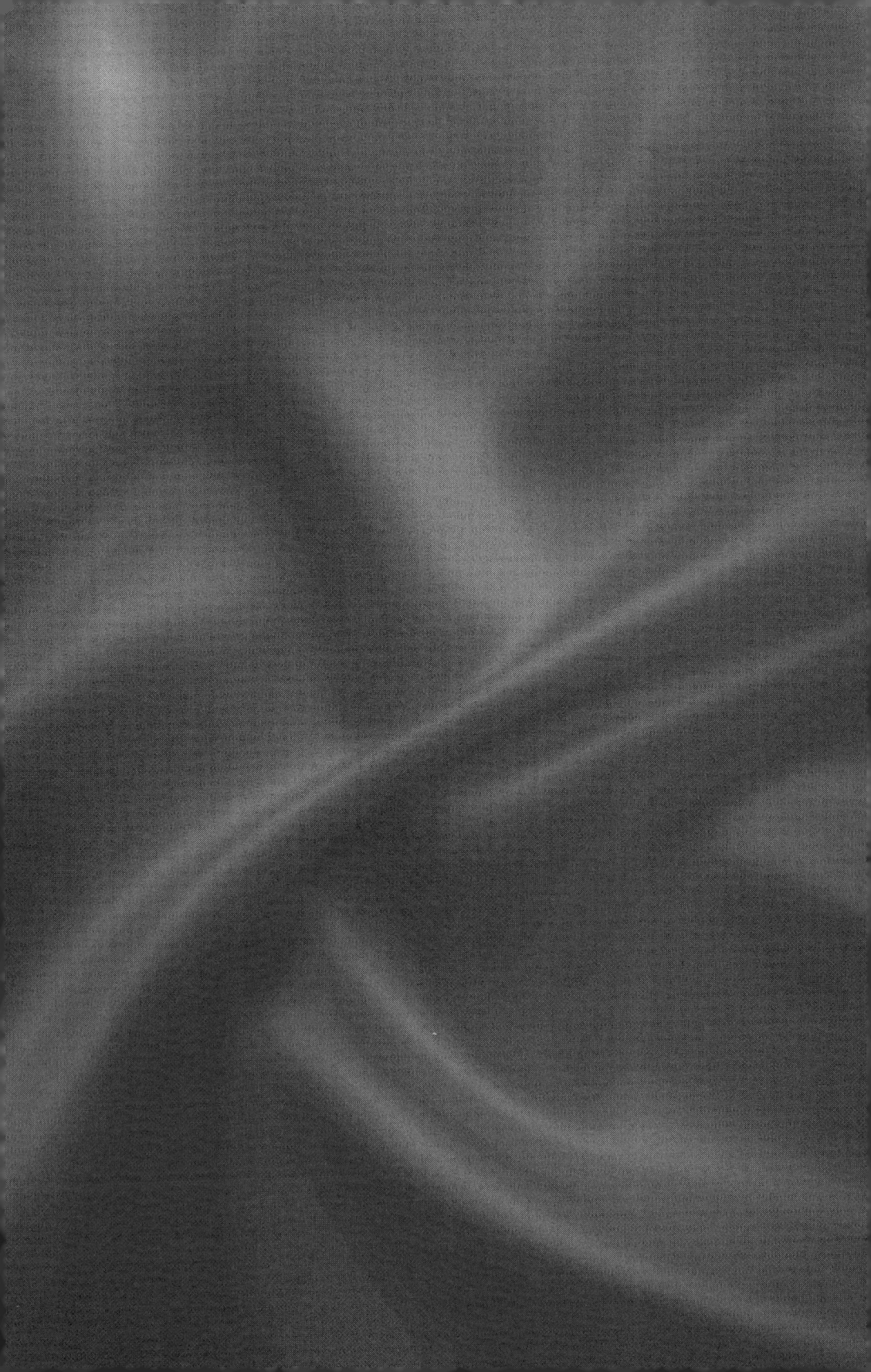

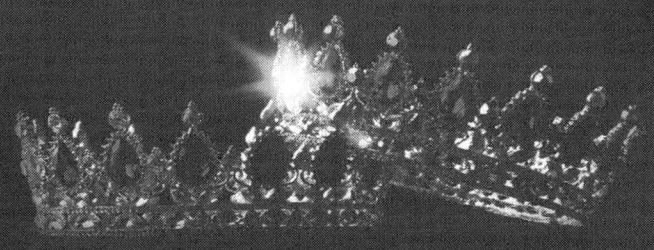

CHAPTER 22

The Betrayal

Ella

The Past - 3 months ago

There were two reasons why I was running late to Josh's party.

The first was a penis-shaped piñata. A perfect present for my future brother-in-law. Hauling it into the trunk of my orange Porsche Cayenne—an early birthday gift from *papá* and *mamá*—was a pain in the ass, since the monstrosity was five feet tall and took multiple tries before I managed to stuff it in a way where it wouldn't block my rearview mirror. I reminded myself that watching Josh beat a cardboard dick with a stick in front of two hundred people would not only be entertaining...but the highlight of tonight's celebration. So alas, totally worth the extra effort.

The second reason why I was running late?

I found out I was five weeks pregnant.

With my boyfriend's baby.

At eighteen going on nineteen.

To say the news shocked the living daylights out of me would be an understatement.

I was still wrapping my head around it.

My periods were late this month and I'd been experiencing some mild spotting, fatigue, random food cravings, and a bit of vomiting for a handful of days. In the beginning, I told myself it was just a bug. But then a few hours ago, I forced myself to go to the pharmacy and buy a pregnancy test.

When two pink lines popped up on the stick, the only thoughts swimming in my mind as I stared at my reflection in my bathroom mirror were: *oh my God, I'm pregnant. I'm pregnant and* papá *and* mamá *are going to have a heart attack and possibly—figuratively—kill me for getting pregnant outside of wedlock.*

After inhaling some calming breaths and reassuring myself that everything would be okay, happiness began to pierce the veil of my shock.

Oh my God, Ella. You're going to be a mom. Cade's going to be a dad. You're going to be a family. Just like you always wanted.

One thing was for certain: I was not getting rid of this baby.

I wanted to keep it.

While I was extremely happy, I was also nervous. Being a mom was one of my dreams, but something I'd hoped for later in life. Not before I even had the chance to complete university or start a career. Shit, Cade hadn't planned on being a dad so young either. But we weren't careful on prom night and now had to deal with the outcome.

Montardor's high society was going to have a field day when they found out the heirs of the Remington and Cordova empires were expecting a bundle of joy in less than eight months.

However, I didn't give a hoot about their opinions. The only ones that mattered were mine, Cade's, and our families. Sure, our parents may express some disappointment in us not being careful, but a surprise pregnancy wasn't grounds for disownment.

I knew we were young and the road ahead would be tough…but we could make it work, right? Cade was already like a father figure to Olivia. He would love his own child with everything he was worth. We'd be the best family ever and give this baby our all, parental and society judgements be damned.

With that pep talk, I'd driven to the grocery store to grab a bunch of supplies. My plan was to bake cupcakes and pipe the word 'Daddy' on top of them in blue frosting—the exact shade of my *querido's* eyes.

I couldn't wait to see his reaction. Cade would be surprised, yes, but content above all. He'd smile big, gather me in his arms, and kiss my forehead.

Afterwards, we'd discuss the best way to break the news to our parents.

Because we were a team.

Him and me.

Always.

The Remington residence was blazing with neon lights and teenage debauchery by the time I arrived. I parked my car near the gates and parallel to the woods on the estate. When I stepped out and walked to the trunk, a light wind sailed, causing the skirt of my sundress to flare around my hips. I wore it specifically to fend off the summer heat and for Cade, who went feral whenever I donned a short dress.

It was a peace offering to make up for the fact that I missed a series of his calls and texts.

Cade was probably worried sick. My sweet, protective, and obsessed boyfriend liked having my location and attention twenty-four seven. But I had a valid reason for not answering him. Containing my excitement was too difficult. I was too impatient and afraid I'd reveal my pregnancy beforehand.

This was a milestone for us and I wanted to see his reaction in person.

When I was in the midst of yanking out the piñata, someone shouldered into me from behind so roughly, it knocked my body against the side of the car. Pain exploded down my left arm and I gasped.

What the hell was that?

I spun around in time to see the culprit.

A tall guy wearing all-black with his hood up and face hidden stole into the party like a thief in the night.

"Watch where you're going, you fucking jerk!" I barked, rubbing my arm to soothe the ache from that hit.

I didn't have a chance to discern his features as he quickly disappeared in a sea of bodies congregating the side of the mansion.

A series of goosebumps rose over my skin. The strange sensation of being watched slithered over my frame. I glanced around, feeling uneasy. There was nothing but darkness and trees in my close proximity and yet... something felt wrong.

There was a voice in my mind chanting that I needed to find Cade. Now.

I locked my car after grabbing the piñata and crossed the courtyard, the smell of alcohol and weed assaulting my nostrils. It was triggering and I fought the urge to puke. First trimester clearly sucked. I feared it would only get worse from here.

A few St. Victorians—alumni and current students—recognized me and waved, laughing when they saw what I was dragging into the party. I greeted them back. While I would miss high school, the people, and the daily shenanigans that took place in that institute, I was more excited for this new chapter in my life. Pregnancy and starting my undergrad.

Though you'll probably have to drop out once the baby arrives, Ella. Raising newborns is not an easy fit. They need stability and routine. You won't be able to attend school like a regular student.

That chilling thought made my nausea worse.

I pushed it aside the second I entered the raging party. My stomach was in knots and my nerves were having a field day as I worked through a flock of people in the foyer, being mindful of keeping my middle shielded. I was already possessive and protective of a fetus that was barely the size of a pomegranate seed.

Searching for Cade and my friends would be like searching for a needle in a haystack. Instead of wandering around aimlessly, I figured messaging the group chat for everyone's whereabouts was the best course of action. But when I dipped my hand into my purse for my phone…

It wasn't there.

Confused, I searched through the interior frantically. Bobby pins, cash, credit card, driver's license, scrunchie…

Still no cell phone.

How was that possible?

I had it with me before I left my place.

Did I…drop it somewhere between there and here?

My shoulders drooped. Well, this was inconvenient.

I guess I'd just have to look around for Cade. Deciding to start with his room, I climbed the grand staircase, bypassing dancing bodies and a guy doing lines on a girl's tits.

The second floor was just as crowded as the ground floor, harbouring an even stronger rancid smell of weed. I was so close to vomiting and the more I neared Cade's bedroom, the more my skin prickled. There was a group of rowdy partygoers gathered close to his door, drinking liquor straight out of the bottle with no chaser.

I recognized a few of the boys and girls from St. Victoria. Shallow, vain, and most importantly: the gossiping kind.

They eyed me with interest, jealousy, and fake smiles.

I simply grinned back and waved my fingers, used to this kind of attention. At school, there were two categories of students. Those that fawned over me and my boyfriend and those that loathed us. It came with the territory of being St. Victoria's most revered. The queen bee, cheerleading co-captain, and the broody, hockey alternate captain. Children of the most affluent families in South Side, Montardor. Getting crowned prom king and queen was the cherry on top of their shitcakes.

Eventually, I reached Cade's door.

That same prickling feeling intensified when I twisted the handle and pushed, taking a step into the dark room. It was illuminated with the barest amount of light coming from a small lamp.

And suddenly, my entire world came crashing down.

I froze.

My gaze captured the scene before me in vivid details, a picture that would forever be etched in my mind under the word betrayal.

Cade.

Sitting next to another girl on his bed.

Red-stained kisses on his mouth, jaw, and neck.

Their limbs intertwined as intimately as long-time lovers.

The sharp pain in my chest had me dragging out a croaky, "Cade?"

Like I needed confirmation from him that this was a figment of my imagination. Far from reality. A fucked-up nightmare I'd somehow found myself trapped in.

I cradled my stomach, an incessant pain thrumming in my core.

Was this really happening to me?

Was the man that I loved with my whole being actually fucking cheating on me while I was pregnant with our baby?

I stood rooted in place, soaking in the situation like I was having an out-of-body experience while my dreams of a future with Cade shattered to a million pieces.

In the blink of an eye, he destroyed us.

All my love. All my trust. Instantly gone.

"Ella?" he slurred, drunk and high, appearing shocked and disoriented as he stared at me.

The girl next to him seemed intoxicated as well, watching the entire scene unfold with hints of confusion and horror on her expression.

"You fucking asshole," I fumed. "This is…This is what you've been doing this whole time? You've been…"

Cheating.

I couldn't force the word out. It was foul. Something that didn't belong in my vocabulary, much less something to be associated with Cade.

And yet the evidence was right in front of my face.

My blood boiled and tears smarted my eyes. I wouldn't let them fall. I wouldn't let him see how much he wrecked me with his treachery.

Behind me, a crowd gathered, composed of the same St. Victorians who'd stared at me with envy. Now they were gasping and guffawing at my predicament. Flashlights burst in the room as they took pictures and videos of the scene, immortalizing this juicy piece of gossip for everyone to see.

Something about my words and the people flocking around us had Cade snapping into motion. He stood up, eyes going wide with realization. As if he finally registered the depth of the situation. The utter wrongness of it.

Now he was seeing me. Every bloody and broken inch, held together by stitches of my stubborn pride.

"Ella…" Cade extended a trembling hand my way. To stop me from leaving? To provide him comfort? "It's not…It's not…wait…"

"It's not what it looks like?" I growled. "Give me a break. It's exactly what it looks like!"

"Ella…Please…I…" Cade was so far gone with booze and drugs that he couldn't stand on his feet without swaying like he was on a carnival ride.

If he wasn't intoxicated, would he have cheated on me? Or has this been going on for a while and tonight is the first time I caught him?

Bile rose in my throat. I couldn't believe it. I didn't want to believe it.

"Stay the fuck away from me, you piece of shit!" I fisted my hands to stop myself from doing any physical damage I would regret. Including clawing out my own stupid heart and throwing it at his head, blood splatters and all. "We. Are. Fucking. Done!"

Shooting daggers at Cade and the girl, I retreated a few steps and collided with a solid body. One of the St. Victorians I didn't like. He beamed at me mockingly. "Smile for the camera, babyyy!"

Anger rushed through my veins.

Taking the piñata, I whacked it against him until he fell into the swarm of people with a pathetic squeak. Squeals and curses erupted as Jolly Ranchers exploded from the penis-shaped cardboard like confetti. Then I snatched his phone and whipped it hard against the wall, breaking the screen and hopefully the device as a whole.

From his position on the floor, he yelled in disbelief. "What the fuck, bitch?"

Usually the quintessential good girl in front of these people, their shock at my outburst was palpable in the air. They'd never seen me like this. And unaccustomed to my bad side, they had no idea what I was capable of.

"Smile for this, jackass," I spat and flipped him my middle finger—a long orange claw that I wouldn't hesitate to sink into his jugular. "Now fucking move out of my way!"

People watched the drama unfold like it was a hot episode of reality TV, giggling and murmuring amongst themselves, while I sauntered out of the room, shoulders squared and head held high.

Trying to appear as unaffected as possible.

Despite the fact that pictures and videos of this moment would be plastered on social media before the end of the hour.

South Side's princess humiliated and dethroned in front of fucking peasants.

By her very own princepin.

It would be a goddamn headline.

And the coveted couple of St. Victoria falling from their pedestal would be the highlights of their summer. Not Josh's stupid piñata.

But I was one resilient bitch. I'd never allow them to see my internal scars or the magnitude of my pain. I'd never allow them to laugh behind my backs without showing them how nasty Ella Ximena Cordova could get. Revenge was a dish best served cold and I'd make sure each motherfucker here choked on every bite as I spoon-fed it down their throats.

I inhaled their cruelty, exhaled a dose of my retaliation, and adjusted my crown.

I was a queen amongst these vultures and I knew it. You could not dethrone me. I was here to fucking stay. Anyone who dared to mess with me would end up with their expensive convertibles keyed and their tinted windows smashed with a crowbar.

I ignored the taunts and gossip as I descended the grand staircase. Behind me, another pair of footsteps followed and Cade incoherently mumbled a warped, "W-Wait."

Warm hands grabbed my arm and attempted to pull me back. Unhinged. Disbalanced. Furious. That's how I felt when I spun around and yelled, "Get away from me!"

"P-Please," Cade panted with bloodshot red eyes and a sheen of sweat decorating his skin. He barely stood straight, his hold on me fragile as a feather. This wasn't like the other times he got drunk or high at parties. This was tenfold worse.

But I killed the small nugget of worry dancing in my system.

He didn't deserve that from me.

Not anymore.

I slapped his hands away and sneered, "Don't touch me! Don't ever fucking touch me again, you filthy two-timing scum!"

My words sucker punched through his drunken haze and he jolted, clutching the banister for support.

I ran down the remaining steps, angry with the need to raze everything in my surroundings. The music and the flashing neon lights slowed my senses until the only thing I could focus on was the jagged sound of my broken heart thumping in my ears.

Having heard the loud commotion, a crowd gathered at the base of the staircase. Numerous faces gawked at us, like Cade and me were the main acts in a travelling circus. And unfortunately, my friends were nowhere to be found amidst this chaos.

Despite the cold-hearted bitch persona I adopted, I was crumbling on the inside, brick by brick. All thoughts of retaliation instantly fled away. I was fighting tears, the need to vomit, and the fact that the cupcakes I made so lovingly only hours ago would have to be thrown in the garbage.

Fresh air spread over my heated skin as I sprinted out the front doors and towards the woods. I doubled over and vomited on a dirt patch, tears streaming down my face. My entire body shook with turbulent emotions and the same cramps from earlier started quivering below my waist. I pressed a hand over my stomach, retching and coughing.

A branch cracked nearby, an indication that I wasn't alone.

I snapped my head in the direction of the sound and saw...Darla.

Leaning against a tree, under the moonlit night, my ex-best friend observed me quietly.

Darla stopped talking to me weeks ago, including answering my calls and text messages, for unbeknown reasons. Since our friendship ended, she went out of her way to school her expressions into something unreadable whenever we were in the same space. I could never tell what she was thinking. It was frustrating. And if I tried to talk to her, she left faster than you could say *stop*. Essentially, she avoided me like the plague. The worst part was I had no idea why, despite trying to understand how we got here.

Though right now, Darla wasn't running away. She gripped a beer bottle in one hand and her phone in the other, the screen playing the video of me catching Cade in the act.

Oh, God. How did the video circulate so quickly? Had everyone already seen the sordid situation?

"Ella?" Darla hedged, taking a tentative step my way like I was a wounded animal.

Whenever we attended parties, my ex-best friend eventually escaped to a secluded corner to charge her social battery. Darla was part introvert, part extrovert. It shouldn't surprise me to find her slinked away in the woods, recuperating from the loudness of the Remington mansion.

Wiping my mouth with the back of my hand, I glared at her. Hurt and beyond exhausted. Unable to understand how she could throw away sixteen years of friendship without an explanation and move on like we didn't have the best memories.

"What?" I hated the wavering quality of my voice.

As much as I hated the fact that I missed her so much.

As much as I hated the fact that if things were different…I'd be telling her I was pregnant and getting the emotional support I so badly needed at this moment. And now I couldn't even confide in the one girl who'd been like my sister because she removed me from her life.

There was a slight crack in Darla's armour. A softness in her brown eyes. "Are you okay?"

"Why do you care?" I straightened, pushing my hair back and cringing at the sour taste of vomit on my palate. "You've ignored me for weeks, and now you want to talk when"—I pointed at her phone—"I'm at my lowest? Are you here to gloat because I got cheated on?"

The softness was quickly replaced by resentment.

"I was here before you, getting some fresh air." She shook her head. "And you know well enough that gloating and being petty isn't my style. No one deserves…"

No one deserves to get cheated on and be made into a spectacle.

That's what she wanted to say.

"What have I done to you?" I implored against my better judgement, wiping at my remaining tears. "I don't understand, Darla. I was never bad to you."

You were my best friend, my co-captain, my sister. What happened to us?

I zeroed in on her left wrist. She no longer wore the friendship bracelet I gave her when we were eight. Why did that hurt so much?

A heart-wrenching wave of homesickness swept over me. God, I needed to leave this place and lick my wounds in peace.

"You're right. You weren't bad to me," she agreed, depositing her phone in the pocket of her miniskirt. "You were *horrible*, and you still haven't owned up to it. You're just like all of them, Ella. Mean and fake. How does it feel to finally get a taste of your own medicine?"

I'd taken so many hits tonight, but her calling me mean and fake—comparing me to the rats of St. Victoria—was a different type of pain that made me flinch like I'd been struck. "What in the world are you talking about? I don't fucking get it, Darla!"

"You never did, Ella. That's the problem." Darla chuckled bitterly. "Don't pretend to be innocent. You know why I'm done with you."

Anything I said right now would be irrelevant when her walls were up again. I couldn't reach her and she wouldn't hear me.

Physically, this was the closest we'd stood in weeks. Emotionally, I'd never felt further from her.

Everyone who entered your life had a purpose. Sometimes it was to stay forever and guide you through your journey. Other times it was for a temporary period to teach you a lesson. While people come and go, the only constant in life was the relationship you had with yourself. The only relationship worth nourishing.

In this split second, I realized that Darla's time in my life came to an end long before tonight. I just needed to accept it and move on. No matter how much it fucking hurt.

All good things come to an end and nothing lasts forever.

Not friendships.

Not romantic relationships.

And certainly not the love of dark brown-haired, blue-eyed boys with charming, lying smiles who claimed to love you until the end of time.

"I don't, Darla," I replied, backing away, my stance unsteady. My head spun and a dull ache spread through my gut. "Nor do I care anymore. I'm done with you, too."

Darla remained silent, having already made peace with our broken friendship.

I jogged out of the woods and towards my car.

As if this party couldn't get any shittier, I found my cell phone lying on the ground next to the driver's side door.

I…I don't remember dropping it.

But I guess I did, and someone stepped on it in the dark.

The screen was completely cracked. It wouldn't even turn on.

Oh, well. A broken phone could be replaced within a day.

A broken pride?

Unlikely.

I hauled myself into my car and threw my smashed phone into the cupholder.

Then I turned on the ignition, shifted into drive, and gunned it out of the Remington estate.

The last thing I saw in my rearview mirror was Cade, stumbling after me, calling out my name.

CHAPTER 23
The Aftermath

CADE

The Past - 3 months ago

"*S*tay the fuck away from me, you piece of shit! We. Are. Fucking. Done!"

"*Get away from me!*"

"*Don't touch me! Don't ever fucking touch me again, you filthy two-timing scum!*"

Those horrendous words taunted me, piercing through my chest and birthing a large void that made it hard to breathe. The venom in them sank into my muscles like poison and I choked on every syllable.

I had to tell Ella the truth.

She had to take back what she said.

She didn't mean it.

She *couldn't*.

"Ella," I called again, my voice low and slurred. I pursued her as fast as I could, but the liquor in my system slowed me down and my pace was sluggish.

Ella had to hear me out.

She had to understand that what happened in the room was a mistake.

Ella, I thought it was you I was holding, touching, kissing. I only ever want to hold, touch, kiss you. And the second I realized it wasn't you, I was revolted. It was a mistake. An honest to God mistake. You texted me to meet you there. I came for you, Ella. I love you, Ella. Please don't leave me, Ella.

My girlfriend disappeared in an ocean of silhouettes, each one doubling and faded at the edges. I stumbled after her. The air she left behind reeked of anger, dejectedness, embarrassment, and heartbreak. Every emotion that had no business occupying her beautiful self.

My head spun. Past the hazy fog clouding my senses, I think I saw people gawking, laughing, and filming the entire scene. I think I also heard the distinct sound of one of my friends hollering my name.

I kept pushing my limbs to move quicker, despite the suffocating environment. No matter how hard I inhaled, I couldn't get enough oxygen.

Fuck, I didn't recall drinking this much. I usually…had a good tolerance. Nor did I go above my limits.

Why…Why am I feeling like this?

Drowsy, no inhibitions, and moments from falling into a deep sleep.

I didn't remember how I made it outside or how I found myself standing near the gates of the estate, close to the woods, where Ella often parked her Ducati or Porsche. That connection of ours, forged the second I laid eyes on her and strengthened over the course of our relationship, thrummed like a potent instinct, telling me she'd be here.

The dark night and the strong gust of wind rustling the tree leaves made it difficult to see or focus. My breaths turned choppy and a rivulet of sweat trickled from my brow into my eye.

Everything inside of me felt off-kilter, cataclysmically wrong.

The sound of a devastated cry had me swinging my head to the left. There she was. My light at the end of the dark tunnel. Ella. *Mo chuisle. Mi vida.*

Like a hopeless fool, I staggered after her, calling out her name.

Ella didn't hear or see me.

Instead, she got into her car and drove away.

The angry screech of her tires was the last audible sound echoing in my ears. It hurt. The lacerations Ella left on my heart with her departure.

"You have me now. I'll never leave you."

Her promise. She broke it.

She said she'd never leave me…and she did.

Without even hearing me out, she tossed me aside like I was a used-up, dirty napkin.

Did she have so little faith in me that she thought I'd willingly cheat? Did I not make it clear the only girl I was crazy about was *her*?

Ella had to hear me out.

This couldn't be the end of us.

I refused to believe it—refused to *accept* it.

Numbness spread through me like a wildfire. I stood alone in the dark, panting and grief-stricken.

Out of nowhere, the back of a gun slammed against my temple and caused pain to explode all over my skull. I lost my balance and fell to my knees with a curse.

What…What the fuck was that?

Groaning, I went to grab my forehead when suddenly, my arms were yanked back in an unyielding hold.

Overpowered, I watched through a blurry gaze as four bodies buzzed around me, hushed voices erupting from their mouths. Guy Fawkes masks concealing their faces, they wore all black attire…almost like…

The stranger who bumped into me before I left to go find Ella in my room.

My senses were impaired, yet my fight and flight response still kicked in. Trying to struggle and scream was all in vain, though. I wasn't strong enough to defend myself, let alone take on four individuals.

One punched me across the face and the coppery taste of blood filled my mouth.

The second cocked a gun at my sweat-slickened temple.

The third slapped manacles on my wrists.

The fourth…crouched down in front of me.

With a gloved hand, he grabbed my chin in a bruising grip and assessed my face. I couldn't see any of their characteristics. But I knew with certainty that this one was their leader. "How much did you give him?"

He talked to the one with the gun. "Enough Benzos in his drink that he can't fight back but remembers every second of us fucking him up."

Benzos? Drink? Can't fight back?

Dread swirled in the pit of my stomach.. Too many sensations and thoughts ran haywire through me. I felt like a system about to short-circuit.

"Good." The one in front of me patted my face like I was an obedient lap dog. I couldn't see his face, but I heard the smile in his muffled voice. "How does it feel to get a dose of your own medicine, Remington? I bet you didn't see us coming, huh? We're going to enjoy exacting revenge. Even your daddy and brother won't be able to recognize you once we're through with you."

If anything happened to me, Josh and Uncle Vance would avenge me. I wasn't scared or worried. I mustered enough strength to spit at his masked-face. Some of the saliva dribbled down my chin. "K-kiss my ass, you little bitch."

"Fucking cocky bastard!" He backhanded me and rose to his feet. "Drag him into the car. We'll show him who's a little bitch soon."

Using the last bit of my fight, I grappled to be free as they hauled me towards the gates. An unmarked black Escalade sat at the curb. *Fuck.* They were going to kidnap me, beat me to death, and no one would know where I was.

A girlish shriek boomed in the air.

My captors' heads swivelled in the direction of the sound.

Through heavy lids, I spotted none other than Darla, standing near the edge of the woods. As though she just emerged from there and fell upon us. "Oh my God! What are you doing? Let him go!"

Darla's screams drew the attention of others.

More shouts rang in the air, sounding like my friends nearing us.

Darla ran towards me bravely, not realizing that these masked fuckers were dangerous and had guns. They wouldn't hesitate to shoot us both. I tried to yell at her to stay away, but only garbled sounds escaped me.

"Fuck, fuck, fuck." One of the masked men growled. "There's too many of them. Forget him and let's get out of here! Now!"

They dropped me and I crashed forward, the side of my face scraping against the cobblestone driveway. I rolled over to my back with my hands still tied, groaning from the pain circulating through my body.

Darla reached me first, falling to her knees. "Oh, God! Cade? Can you hear me?" She pressed two fingers to my neck, feeling my pulse. "Are you okay?"

I tried to speak, but my stomach churned and I gagged. Acid bubbled at the base of my throat and trickled up to my mouth. Darla automatically shifted me to my side and I retched loudly. It was long, gross, and extremely humbling.

During my vomiting episode, my friends reached us too. Shaun dropped beside Darla. "We caught him leaving the house, chasing after Ella. He didn't look fine. What the fuck happened here?" he demanded.

"I don't know," Darla rushed out, distraught, and dabbed at the blood on my face with a handkerchief. "I was coming out of the woods and I saw four guys dragging him to the gates."

"What did they look like?"

"They all wore black and their faces were covered. That's all I saw." Darla's hand trembled as it continued wiping my face. "Shaun, this is a lot of blood. Oh, God. This is bad. This is *really* bad."

"The car's gone!" I think Nico spoke. "Black Escalade. No license plate."

"Cade, can you hear us?" Shaun spoke close to my ear, brushing my forehead with his hand. "Fuck, he's burning up."

"We have to get him to a hospital."

"N-No," I protested weakly. No hospitals. That would cause too many questions. We always handled business behind closed doors.

"He doesn't look right," Sam said. "We should—"

"N-No." I cut them off then heaved.

"Fuck," I heard Nate cussing. "We need to find Josh and see if there's someone who can handle this discreetly since he's insisting on no hospitals."

I started vomiting again while the boys sought help. Darla and Shaun stayed with me. The former kept cleaning my face while the latter rubbed my back and put his hand under my head so it wasn't resting on the cold ground.

Eventually, it was all over. I closed my eyes and breathed softly when the summer wind glided over my feverish skin, cooling me down.

"Shaun, I'm going to get him some water from my car while the others go find Josh." Darla said. "Don't leave him, okay?"

"I won't," Shaun said. Now it was just us two, the sound of crickets, and the uneasy rustling of the trees. I'd never seen my best friend look this worried. "Fuck, Cade. What have you gotten yourself into?"

It wasn't uncommon to have enemies in my family's business. But it was the first time I got up close and personal with the consequences of it.

"Someone...drugged...benzos."

"You were roofied?" Shaun asked with incredulity.

I couldn't confirm or deny it, too drained from having emptied my guts until there was nothing left inside of me.

Except for one thought pulsing through my chest like a heartbeat. *Ella. Ella. Ella.*

Always Ella.

Ella

My hands trembled on the steering wheel as I arrived home and parked in my driveway. It was nearing midnight and the entire house was asleep, an otherworldly serene floating in the atmosphere, like the calm before the storm.

The second I turned off the ignition, the dam holding back my tears broke. The windshield in front of me blurred. I cried with wracking sobs, accompanied by that strange pain buzzing through my lower back and belly.

How did I even get here?

One day I was happy and fulfilled with Cade, and the next day my entire world was crushed to pieces by his unforeseen betrayal. I gave our relationship my everything, only to be dealt with this fuckery.

I didn't understand. Why did Cade cheat on me? Was I not enough for him? Did he no longer love me? Did his friends know he was cheating on me and covered his tracks? Was he seeing *her* behind my back this whole time? Or was this the first time they hooked up?

Cade was supposed to be faithful and devoted until the very end. Just like he swore many moons ago.

"Then I'll promise you that this will last past our dying breaths until I inevitably find you again in the next lifetime, Ella."

Liar.

Dirty fucking liar.

At the reminder of all his fake vows, my sobs halted and my tears dried up.

Fuck him and fuck all his promises. Cheat on me once and you were dead to me. I wasn't the kind of girl who would take back her man just because she loved him.

And the love I felt for him was dying a slow death, curling on its edges like parchment paper set on fire until a pile of ash remained in its place.

Cade Killian Remington was going to regret the day he hurt me.

He called me crazy, right?

After tonight, I'd fucking show him crazy.

I stepped out of the car, adrenaline surging through my bloodstream.

First, I ripped off the necklace he gave me and threw it into the lawn with a battle cry. Then, I smashed the box of cupcakes on the ground and stomped on it a few times, reducing the little cakes to a mushy mess. The guards patrolling the perimeters probably thought that Francisco Cordova's daughter lost her goddamn marbles.

My chest heaved when I was done.

Though I didn't feel an iota better than before.

In fact, when grief trickled through my veins again, my mind taunted me with images of Cade and the other girl. I couldn't believe it. The love of my life cheated on me and ruined us beyond repair. We'd never recover from this. Now I was pregnant, alone, scared, and in so much agony, I just wanted the earth to open up and swallow me whole.

This was the worst feeling I ever experienced.

I swore to myself that after tonight, I'd sever all physical, mental, and emotional ties with Cade.

Angry thoughts fueled by insecurity continued to tumble through my mind like a chain reaction as I entered my home. I wondered to myself what would make me feel better. A bubble bath? Reruns of my favourite sitcoms? Or a hot mug of *champurrado?*

But the latter only reminded me more of my ex-boyfriend.

I closed my eyes, inhaling shakily.

He was everywhere.

In every thing, in every memory, in every breath.

A shot of pain zinged through my core and I stumbled, holding on to the wall for support.

What…What was that?

Suddenly, I felt wetness pooling in my thong.

Followed by another cramp.

Somehow, I managed to make it to my bedroom as quietly as possible without waking up my parents or Emilio. On the next bout of sharp pain, I used my fist to muffle my gasp and threw open the door of my en suite, dashing inside.

My heart jackhammered and my frantic fingers reached under the skirt of my dress to see the verdict.

Blood.

Thick, red blood soaked the lining of my white thong.

Dread swept through me as a sinking realization pounded in my brain.

"*No, no, no, no.*" I glanced at my reflection in the mirror, a wild and terrified look in my eyes. "*Please, no.*"

Deep loss curled into my muscles, weighing me down. I fell back against the wall before landing in a heap on the bathroom floor.

No, no, no, no.

Despite chanting it, I knew with conviction that this wasn't a period. Nor was this mild spotting during my first trimester. The sharp pains in my body weren't related to my heartbreak but to *this.*

Did I…Did I actually miscarry my baby?

For the third time tonight, I cried, pulling my knees to my chest to muffle my sobs in the material of my dress.

I was wrong.

This was the worst feeling I ever experienced.

Moments trickled into solid minutes as I cried like never before. Tonight's rollercoaster of emotions shook me. From being ecstatic about my pregnancy and baking cupcakes for Cade, to fury at catching him with the other girl, to sheer devastation at my loss.

How was I going to recover from this? How would I move on from this pain? I could never tell my parents, my friends, or even Cade what happened.

The truth would remain buried with me forever.

The sound of tiny footsteps padding into my room had my head snapping up. Emilio entered the en suite in his Batman pyjamas, rubbing the sleep out of his eyes.

Oh, God.

He must have heard me wailing.

Emilio squeaked when he saw me. Defeated, body trembling, and black mascara streaks down my face.

Scared, my five-year-old brother fell beside me, all traces of sleep evading him. "Ella?"

"I-I'm okay, *manito*. Please go back to bed and don't tell anyone you saw me."

His eyes wide with fear, he rested a small hand against my shoulder. "What's wrong?"

I brushed my fingers tenderly through his hair. "Nothing, Emi. You shouldn't be awake right now. Go back to sleep." I smiled to the best of my ability. "I'm okay."

Maybe if I kept repeating it, I'd eventually believe it.

My pain seeped into him and Emilio started crying too, despite not knowing what was happening. He wrapped his small arms around my frame and hugged me tight, squeezing with all the might in his little body. As if he was trying to glue my insides, which were falling apart by the seams, back together.

In a way, it was working.

Years from now, the only comfort I would recall from this moment was my little brother's hug. Siblings really were the greatest treasure from above. Friends and lovers may come and go, but these relationships were forever. They'd stand the test of time.

"P-Please, Ella." He sniffled, hiding his face in my throat. "What's wrong?"

I pressed my cheek to his soft curls and placed his hand on my stomach. "I lost my baby."

"No." He shook his head determinedly, blinking big wet brown eyes at me. "I'm still here."

"*Emi.*" I cried even harder at his gentle innocence. Emilio didn't understand, and I didn't expect him to. He thought I meant him because he was the baby of the family. "I know. I know you'll always be here."

I crushed him to my chest and he said nothing more, comforting me by brushing kisses against my cheek and patting my face with affection.

"I'll be okay, Emi. Please don't cry anymore."

"Y-You stop crying first," he sobbed into my chest.

I sighed at how cute and desolate that sounded at the same time. Rocking us slowly, I hummed his favourite lullaby, hoping to put him to sleep.

While silently cursing Cade to hell.

When Emilio fell asleep, I put him to bed and cleaned myself up. Without anyone's knowledge, I drove to the hospital with a towel under my seat. This was a battle I needed to brave on my own. Residual aches still pulsing through my middle, I listened to the ER doctor telling me with sympathy that miscarriages so early in the pregnancy weren't uncommon. I didn't cry. I didn't make a single sound. Stony-faced, I digested the truth of my situation—sometimes these things happened and there was no concrete reason. There was nothing I could have done to prevent losing my baby.

After giving me instructions on how to care for myself—pads for bleeding, painkillers for pain, plenty of rest, and lots of proper nutrition—she squeezed my shoulder, probably taking pity on a teenager who arrived in the middle of the night looking haggard.

The drive back home in the wee hours was a blur. When I changed into pyjamas and crawled into my bed, wide awake and staring at my ceiling, still processing my loss, I knew in the deepest recesses of my soul that I'd never forgive Cade.

Even if he begged, grovelled, and offered excuses.

He humiliated me and made a mockery of my love.

Forgiving him came with a heavy price. My pride. And that was one currency I never bartered with.

If he tried to call or text me, I wouldn't know until I got a replacement phone. And even if he tried contacting me, I'd ignore him until he got it through his thick skull that we were done.

That's if he cares to apologize. He's probably having sex with that girl, Ella, while you're forgotten, alone, and no longer pregnant. Maybe he's already over you. Maybe he's been over you. Maybe he never loved you and it was all a lie. He played you. He played you so masterfully, it's hilarious. You're pathetic, crying and pining over him. You were never important. Every nickname was a joke. You are a joke. One he's laughing at right now...

I clutched the roots of my hair and screwed my eyes shut, trying to block out all these thoughts. A choked sob burst past my lips and I clamped a hand over my mouth, refusing to cry past this point, refusing to replay the moment where I caught him with her, refusing to feel anything but hatred for him moving forward.

It was an hour before I was able to pull myself together.

The lull of sleep slowly drew my body into a quiet—far from peaceful—sleep with thoughts of Cade still ricocheting in my mind.

I wanted to marry you, Cade.

I wanted to have our baby and start a family with you, Cade.

I wanted you to be mine forever, Cade.

Why couldn't you want these things too?

277

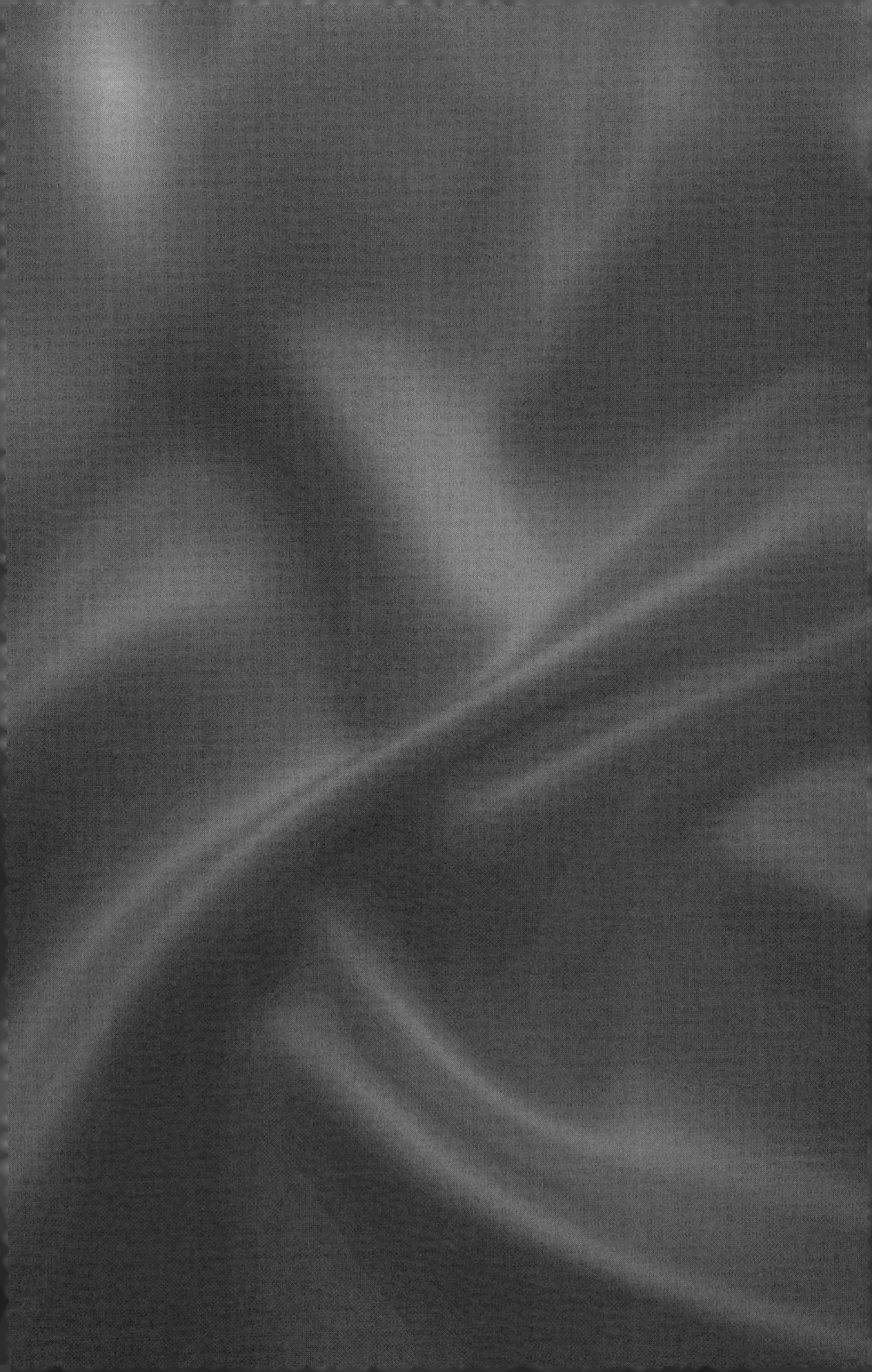

CHAPTER 24

Punish Me

Ella

The Present

3:03 a.m.

I was reeling after Cade finished recounting his version of that fateful summer night where everything between us went downhill. Then he listened as I filled the gaps and explained to him what I saw, what I thought, what I felt, and what I experienced.

Thunder struck outside like the final haunting note in a melancholic melody. In the soft glow of the candlelight, his features softened but remained an inch brittle, like the pages of a beautifully aged classical book. I longed to caress him, feel the familiar curve of his jaw, the bridge of his straight nose, the length of his long lashes, the plumpness of those full lips, and welcome him back into my arms so my heart, which never stopped yearning for its companion, could finally bask in solace.

Our gazes clashed like the rain crashing against the windows—profoundly, jarringly, and inevitably with no signs of halting. Weapons lowered and armours unfastened, we were now on the same page. There was no more secrecy and no more pain.

All our cards were on the table.

Finally, we could begin the road to healing, though I knew it wouldn't be an easy one. The past three months were extremely transformative for us. In many ways, we were still the same Ella and Cade. But in other ways, we'd changed past the point of no return.

"I'm so sorry, Cade. So sorry you had to go through that," I murmured with sincereness. "You didn't deserve it. But most of all, I'm so sorry that I wasn't there for you. I should have stopped and listened to you. Not just then but in all the weeks that followed when you tried to talk to me."

I believed every bit of his story. He'd never been a liar—despite me thinking he was for the last three months given what I witnessed at the party.

The fact that four individuals were responsible for roofying him with the intention of hurting—or worse, killing him—filled me with murderous rage. No one hurt my *querido*. No one hurt him and lived to speak about it.

After tonight, I'd do everything in my power to find those guys and show them why Montardor's fixer called me Nemesis. Cade was scary, but I could be scarier when someone put their unwanted hands on my loved ones—especially him.

Cade's shaky exhale resonated prominently between us. He'd waited so long to hear me say those words—to offer him some form of comfort. Before anything, I was his best friend and his most trusted confidante. Not being able to confide in me because I shut him out due to my own pain did a huge number on his psyche.

He once told me my touch was like a remedy. I wished I could feel the scars on his person—the ones I left knowing and unknowingly—and heal them with my feathering kisses.

"Thank you for saying that," he said thickly. "I...It means a lot, Ellie."

"Did you ever find out who those masked men were?"

A muscle in his jaw jumped. "No. I spent hours with Josh running through the security footage of that night and they were impossible to identify. None of my friends recall seeing any of them at the party. You and I were the only ones who bumped into those fuckers."

The picture was still fuzzy, but the puzzle pieces were beginning to connect. "I never texted you to meet me in your room. In fact, I think one of them snatched my phone when he slammed into me...Afterwards, I found it destroyed right next to my car door. He must have done so after sending you that message."

How they managed to unlock my phone to even send that text was beyond me.

"Do you think they're Vance's enemies?"

"At first, I thought it was some lowlives my uncle pissed off, and they were choosing to exact revenge by hurting his family. But I've spent weeks thinking about the situation and the only thing I can conclude is that it was personal. Someone clearly has a vendetta against *me* and I can't figure out who it might be. All I know is that they were desperate enough to use you and the…other girl…to get to me."

He said 'other girl' carefully to not ruffle any feathers.

I swallowed.

"Ella." Gauging my reaction, he slowly lifted his hands to cradle my face. When I didn't push him away, he laid his forehead to mine. It had always been his way of grounding himself. The way I used to touch the heart-shaped aquamarine around my neck. "I never cheated on you. Everything that happened that night was because I'd been drugged. I truly thought it was you in the room with me. And when I realized it wasn't… Baby, I'm so sorry."

"I know." He was so close that I could count every individual lash— the way I used to when we lay in bed together—and knew that the number would be close to two hundred and eight on each. Give or take a few. "I believe you and it's okay. To be honest, I feel pretty bad for the girl, too."

"Although the night is a bit of a blur in my mind, I remember her saying something like, '*You're not him,*' with a shocked expression when she turned on the lights. My guess is someone urged her to my room under the guise of hooking up. And instead of it being whoever she was supposed to meet, it was me."

"And you went back to your room thinking I was going to be there." My fingers turned to fists on my thighs. "Essentially, like me, she was just another pawn in a game none of us understand."

"Exactly."

A thought flitted into my mind and I paled. Cade said the men who attacked him were wearing Guy Fawkes masks. Just like the one who attacked me in Balthazar Building.

"Cade, what are the odds that the four masked men from that night are linked to the one from tonight?"

Surprised, he jerked back, blinking. "You think the one who pushed you down the stairs is one of the guys from that night."

It wasn't a question, rather a statement. We both didn't believe in coincidences.

"Yes, I forgot to tell you earlier, but he also wore a Guy Fawkes mask. I'm not certain if it's an actual Initiator. Maybe someone who snuck into the school and posed as one."

Cade ran his tongue over his teeth. "And you said he had the same tattoo and watch as Kian Wilson?"

"Unless the piece of shit was magically resurrected from the dead…" I trailed off and Cade's gaze rose to mine. "It's not far-fetched to assume that tonight's encounter and what happened over the summer are connected, right?"

If Kian Wilson had people who gave two fucks about him, it wasn't out of the realm of possibilities that they'd want to avenge him a handful of days after his death. What better opportunity than the night of Josh's party to get their revenge, when our guards were down and Cade and me least expected it?

"No." Realization dawned upon Cade. "It's not. It would actually make a lot of sense."

"I thought we were discreet the night we, you know, butchered Kian like a pig for slaughter."

"We were," Cade said. "It was supposed to be a clean job. Kian had no family, no friends, and no lovers. Obviously, something was amiss. I'll speak with Josh and Uncle Vance tomorrow. See if we can dig up some more information on him."

That sounded like a good plan. "Okay, well, we should probably…"

Head out was what I wanted to stay but stopped short. Right now, I wanted nothing more than to stay here, close to him. And based on the way he peered up at me, with softness and a hint expectant, I knew he wanted the same thing too.

"Ella." He dragged his knuckles down my cheek in reverence. "I'm so sorry for everything that happened to you. I assumed you were angry and resentful because you thought I cheated on you. I had no idea it was because you were also pregnant and miscarried the same night. Fuck, I wish…I wish things were different. I would have wanted nothing more than to be by your side."

I grabbed his hand and squeezed affectionately. "Let's not dwell over the past anymore or comparing our sufferings. To be honest, I don't really like to talk or think about this summer. After losing the baby and you, I turned into a shell of a person. There were many times where I drank and took drugs to numb myself. Until I snapped out of it and realized that wallowing in my misery wasn't helping. I never told my parents what happened either. They just assumed I was devastated over our breakup. I figured it was better that they didn't know the whole truth.

"It took time, but I managed to pick up my broken pieces and glue myself back together. And you know what? I like the version I am today. Tougher, unyielding, and matured from the hardships. Please know that I'm not mad—especially after understanding what really happened—and I don't have any ill will towards you. No more glancing backwards anymore. I just want to move forward, Cade."

With you.

I didn't say it out loud, but he heard the request between the lines.

With my words, I finally set us free from the shackles of our wretched past.

"No more glancing backwards." He kissed my bandaged hand. "You would have made a wonderful mom, Ella."

"You would have made a wonderful dad, too. The way you are with Livvy, I never had a doubt."

Cade's relationship with Olivia—his cousin slash adoptive sister now—was so wholesome. She still saw him as her primary caretaker, asking him to take her out for ice cream, play with her Barbies, read her stories, and braid her hair every night before bed. The latter was crucial. If anyone besides Cade braided Olivia's hair, her shoulders sagged with sadness and she adopted the sweetest puppy expression.

"Thank you," Cade mumbled. "For everything."

I gulped when he traced his thumb to the divot at the base of my throat, silently reminding me where his necklace belonged. "The competition is probably over."

"Fuck the competition," he replied huskily, watching with stark hunger as I bit my bottom lip. "I only came for you."

I mock-gasped. "You don't say."

His lips twitched in the barest smirk, soused in a cocktail of arrogance and cockiness. "Since we're being honest, I should tell you that Shaun switched my team number with Jamie Callahan so we could get paired together."

"Oh, Shaun," I deadpanned. "Our lord and saviour. What would we do without him?"

"Absolutely nothing."

We shared a small laugh that was overshadowed by the sound of the downpour battering against the walls of the motherhouse.

Cade raised our hands and slowly trickled his fingers down the length of mine like water rivulets over the slope of a leaf after a rainstorm. His strokes over my palm lines were a reminder that he was branded there, too. In my history. Past, present, and future.

"From the moment I first saw you standing in the alleyway to the moment where you first touched me, you've been in my blood," he murmured. "And from the second you called me beautiful and said you loved me even after I showed you my monstrous scars, you've owned me, Ella. I'm ruled by you and I wouldn't have it any other way, baby."

Arrows dipped in gold struck my heart and unfurled ribbons of emotions that made it difficult to speak around the lump in my throat.

When our eyes connected, I noticed how lighter his blues appeared now that his demons were expunged. This was him at peace after battling for so long. Our expressions mirrored one another.

"I never stopped loving you, Ella. Not for a single second." He pressed a tender kiss to my left wrist, over my fluttering pulse. "You're the only girl I've ever wanted. The only one I'll ever want and love. You're it for me, *mo chuisle*."

God, this man. He was as beautiful as ever with his vulnerability and poetic words. With his protectiveness and prophetic devotion. With his lowered defences and incessant love for me.

I was unable to resist him any longer.

"I've always dreamed of you, too, Cade. Ever since the first moment I saw you," I confessed. "And in the time we were apart, I still dreamed of you every night."

"You dreamt about me even when you hated me?"

"I tried to hate you. For a while, I think I convinced myself I did… But it never really worked."

One of his hands stole to the back of my neck and he tugged me closer, erasing the fictional distance between us. "How many men have you been with since me?" he asked raggedly, his breath mingling with mine. "How many do I have to kill?"

Such an unhinged mob prince. I smiled and swept my finger over his mouth, snagging his bottom lip and pulling until the inked **ELLA** was visible. I wanted to experience the feel of it as he sucked my clit. "Zero. I haven't been with anyone since you, *querido*. I only lied to toy with you."

His grip around my nape tightened. "You little brat."

I sank my orange claws into his jaw with intention. After hearing Cade's side of the story, I knew I was the only one for him. But the green-eyed envy monster residing inside of me needed to hear it aloud. "What about you?"

He arched a dark eyebrow, mirth swirling in his expression. "I've spent the last three months chasing you around the city. You think I have time for other women, sweetheart?"

"Good answer." I dragged my fingers down his throat, inciting a full-body shiver to tumble through him. His kryptonite was me running my nails lightly over his skin. It tamed him like nothing else. "Otherwise, I'd be forced to do some damage. You don't want to play with my bad side, Cade."

"Pretty girl," he whispered. "I *love* your bad side."

"It's sick how obsessed you are with me." And I loved it.

"If being obsessed with you is a sickness," he rasped with a raw, undone quality. "Then I never want to be cured. Continue to own me, to live inside of me, to never stop being mine, Ella."

A flash of coruscation illuminated our space, highlighting our hungry expressions and the fierce want rippling in the air.

With desperation, we lunged for one another.

A clap of thunder followed just as our mouths crashed together with needy sounds, two long lost lovers finally reunited after wandering forever in search of their halves.

The first kiss was titillating and my tipped world finally recentered on its orbit.

The second kiss was a dominant, reclaiming one. The kind that said *you're-mine-and-mine-alone-and-there's-no-changing-that*.

The third kiss was filled with absolution and hot lust. Every cell in my body vibrated with sheer bliss. My mind was spinning with a flurry of sensations, from his masculine cologne wrapping around me like a warm cocoon, to his bold hands chasing the curves of my body like recommitting them to memory, and to his taste melting on my tongue like sugared sin.

"*Ella.*" The sound of my name in that gravelly tone had me weak in the knees. He hoisted me up his body and I wrapped my legs around his waist. "I've missed you so much, baby."

We stumbled and landed against a wall, causing the picture frames to shake with the force. I raked my fingers through his hair and sucked his bottom lip with a moan, running my tongue over the inked **ELLA** tattoo. "I've missed you, too. So much, Cade."

We exchanged wet, greedy kisses, the salacious kind that set my entirety ablaze. It was animalistic the way our tongues met and hips ground together. We never lost the ability to drive each other wild.

His lips roamed down to my jaw and neck, leaving open-mouth kisses and love bites that made my toes curl and my eyes close as I panted. Every roll of his hips against mine was divine. My thong dampened and my clit throbbed. I wanted to surrender and let him do unholy things to my body. I wanted him to resuscitate me, make me come alive with his touch. I wanted him to leave his marks all over me so everyone knew we never stopped belonging to one another.

Cade's mouth kissed up a path up to my ear, breathing in my scent like it was his oxygen, his hands travelling from my thighs to my breasts, shaping them over my knit bralette with rough squeezes. I moaned under my breath and clenched my legs around his waist, wanting *more*.

"Do you know what it was like living without you for three months?" He licked the shell of my ear and bit my lobe. "It was torture, Ella." He wrapped his hand around my neck and squeezed, turning me breathless. "You tormented me, made me live without my heart, and now I want to fucking punish you for it."

I watched him through a pleasure-curtained gaze. "So punish me."

His nostrils flared. "What did you say?"

"Punish me for keeping myself away from you. Give me your pain and wrath. I can handle it." I licked my lips for the taste of him. "I want it, *mi corazón.*"

Cade released a strangled noise and kissed me voraciously, my plea springing him into motion. He ripped my cropped leather jacket off my body and pushed up my bralette, taking a moment to slap my tits. I used to be self-conscious of my smaller breasts, but the way he groaned while worshipping them, like I was truly perfection, bled that insecurity out. Now he was showing his appreciation by licking, sucking, and tugging them between his teeth. "Fucking hell, I've missed these little tits. Missed the taste and the feel of them so much."

"Don't stop," I begged, redirecting his face to my lips so I could kiss him senseless. "Please don't stop."

"I want to put you on your knees and shove my cock deep inside your mouth until you cry pretty tears and moan like a bad girl," he rasped, smoldering blue eyes hooded with desire. "You love having your face fucked, don't you? I know it gets your pussy wet when I treat you like my personal fuckdoll." His frantic fingers unbuttoned my high-waisted jeans as he pressed more dark promises against my swollen lips. "I'm going to do it all while praising and degrading you. And you'll only beg for more, hm?" He pinched my nipples and slapped my ass. I moaned and nodded. "Yeah, I know you will, baby. If you promise to behave, I'll even lick your pussy and have you screaming loud enough for every soul in here to know how gone you are for your princepin. You with me, Ella?"

I swayed at the imagery he spun like gold. I loved his dominance and ruthlessness in bed, and the way he always put me back together after shattering me into tiny little pieces.

It occurred to me that no matter how much time I spent fixing my broken insides, I was only ever whole in his presence.

Cade Killian Remington never stopped being the other half of me.

"*Yes.*" I trembled when his hand snuck into my thong. He found my clit and circled until I whimpered. "I'm with you, Cade."

"You can't unlove me, can you? Just like I can't unlove you, Ella."

He wanted to hear the three words. They tumbled around in my mouth. I wasn't able to echo them. Something halted me, but I felt them irrevocably. "I…"

Cade read my face and it must have been enough for him. Next second, he was grabbing my jaw with one hand and my throat with the other, applying gentle pressure. I loved when he choked me lightly. "Undress me, my dirty little princess. Come get what only I can give you."

He moved back enough for me to slide down to my feet but still be pinned between him and the wall. I made quick work of his leather jacket—the fact that it was painted with *Property of Ximena* and he still wore it like a statement was swoon-worthy—and dropped it to the floor. A trinkling sound caught my attention. When I glanced down, I saw that two wrapped orange lollipops fell out of his pocket.

The same lollipops he gifted me every month in the form of a bouquet.

"How come you have these with you?" I frowned.

Cade didn't meet my eyes. "I…I keep them with me because I miss you and in case we run into each other and…"

You take me back.

My heart twisted painfully. Why was that so incredibly sweet? And why did I feel like weeping? All our encounters from the past three months flooded my mind. I recalled how I continuously avoided and brushed him off, meanwhile he'd been carrying my favourite candy in his pockets on the off-chance that things changed between us.

"Why are you looking at me like that?" That soft edge returned to his deep voice and I almost wailed.

"You were right." I inched my fingers under his black hoodie, slowly pushing it up his muscular torso. "Although I was never with anyone else, I did search for you in every single man I met. They were never you. No one can be you. You're irreplaceable, *querido*."

The masculine moan he released when I stroked his nipples caused another pulse of wetness to coat my thong. "Did you also feel lost… without me?"

"Of course I was lost without you." I dragged off his hoodie and my knit bralette, throwing them over his leather jacket. "You're my sanctuary, Cade."

When I drank in his nakedness, I paused. Years of playing hockey and fighting in the ring roped his body with thick muscles. But now he seemed even more robust than when I last saw him. Furthermore, black and colourful ink swirled all over his skin, new tattoos that weren't there before. Wanting a better look, I grabbed the candle from the table and brought it close to him.

The warm glow melted away the shadows and allowed me to clearly see the tattoo of a realistic wolf, menacing with black fur and amber eyes, inked on his right pectoral. I tentatively drew my palm over his right arm, where he boasted a sleeve. Phases of the moon at his shoulders bled into a combination of a lion, goddess-looking twins, and justice scales on his upper arm. My breath hitched in my throat when I understood it was in honour of my zodiac signs. My sun, my moon, and my rising. His forearm was covered in orange begonias and the depiction of Nemesis, who looked eerily like myself. His right knuckles were inked with roman numerals that stated my birthdate.

And on his ribs, a pair of familiar eyes stared back at me. It took me a second too long to realize they were mine. The same long lashes, the same sharp eyeliner, and the same blue and brown swirling in my right eye.

If it weren't for the arm banded around my waist keeping me steady, I would have fallen to the ground in a puddle. "W-When did you get these?"

"During the summer." He watched me intensely, soaking in my reaction with satisfaction.

"Because you missed me?"

He nodded, pressing a kiss to my forehead when my face crumpled upon seeing the **X** on his hip bone. Exactly like the **K** on mine, in his honour. "And because I belong to you. Always."

"Cade…" This man did everything in his power to show his dedication and never give up on winning me back. He knew in this lifetime, we were meant to be. "*Eres tan hermoso.* Inside and out."

The most beautiful thing about my dark prince was his soul. It shone like the brightest star and guided me home like my very own Polaris.

"*Mi vida.*" He clutched my face, wracked with emotions. "You have no idea how much I've yearned for you."

Oh, Cade, I think I'm beginning to see just how much.

I started kissing my way down his inked body while he groaned, grazing his nipples with my teeth, nipping the hard valleys of his six-pack, and licking the **X** tattoo until I landed on my knees in front of him.

Peering up at him, I undid his belt buckle. "Are you ready to punish me, Cade?"

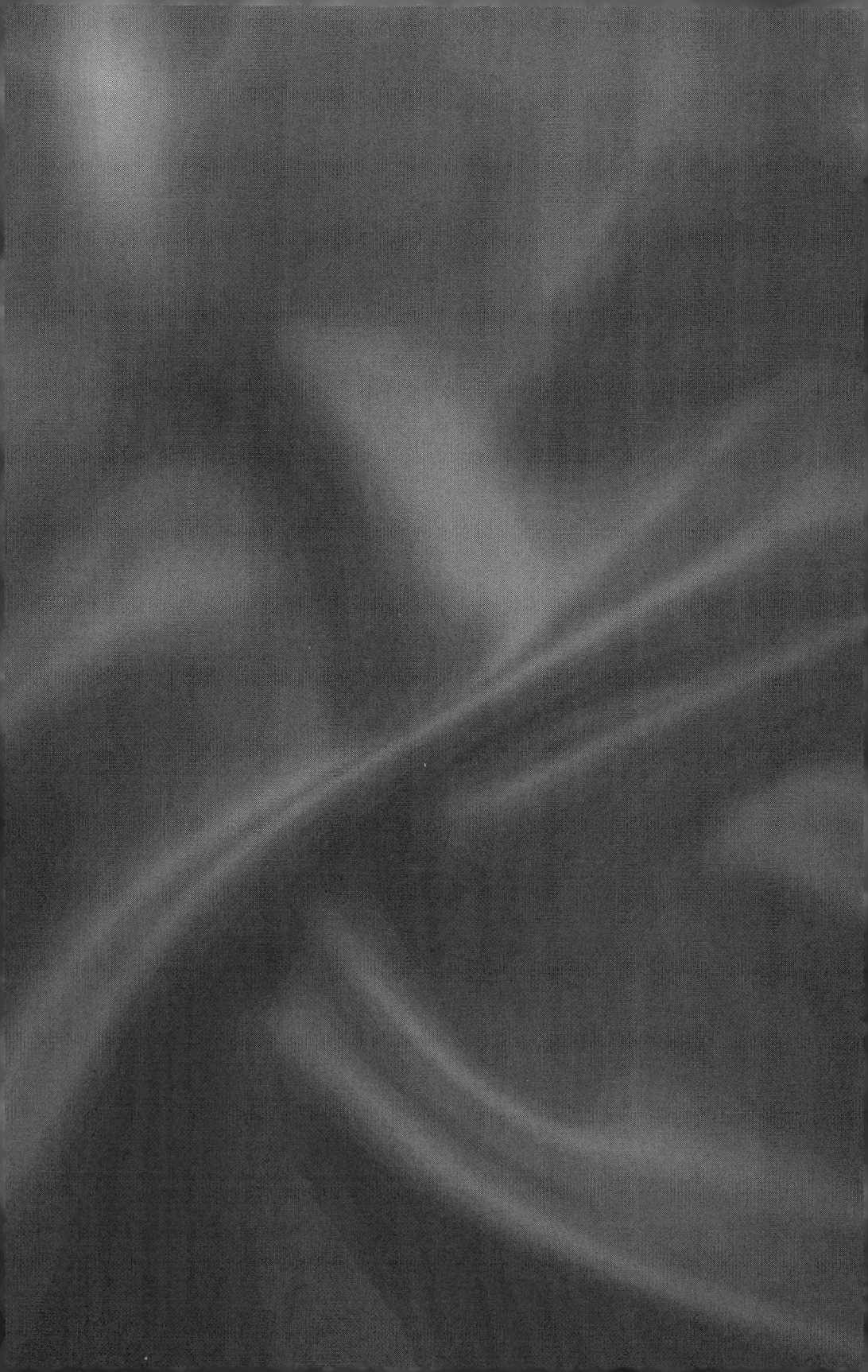

CHAPTER 25
LXIX

CADE

The Present

3:13 a.m.

G*od, if I'm dreaming, please don't ever let me wake up.*

Awestruck, I glanced down, a slight twinge travelling in my chest where my heart, formerly broken, slowly mended itself one stitch at a time.

Finally, I could breathe again after months of suffocation.

Was this really happening? Was she truly back in my life for good?

Ella was on her knees in front of me, scantily clad in nothing but high-waisted black skinny jeans, gold hoops in her ears, and the remnants of her shiny lip gloss over those plump lips.

Looking extremely innocent and submissive, a far cry from the bloodthirsty goddess I'd come to know. And I was so aroused by the sight she created that I was losing my mind.

Ella yanked off my belt and lowered my zipper before reaching inside my boxer briefs for my cock. She fisted me from root-to-tip in a tight hold that had me hissing in pleasure.

Goddamn.

Not a dream at all.

Her devil tongue wasted no time collecting the pearly drop of cum.

"Mm. I've missed your taste."

My girl lavished the underside of my cock like she was frantic to get reacquainted with her favourite treat, licking me like an ice cream cone on a hot summer day. Then her skillful mouth greedily sucked more than half of me on a hearty swoop with delicious little moans that reverberated against my wet flesh.

My eyes rolled back into my skull.

Holy fuck. Holy fuck. Holy fuck.

This was actually happening.

After months of longing for her, Ella was back like she'd never left, sucking the life out of me, slobbering all over my cock, and looking so fucking perfect in the dark with the soft candlelight bathing her figure.

She never took her eyes off me, appraising my reactions—my panting breaths, my deep groans, my gaze watching her lovely face with adoration—and letting them fuel her. I threw my head back on a growl when she took the remainder of me into her hot suctioning mouth.

Stuffed full of my cock with tears gathered in her waterline, she was stunning.

Finally, I gave in to the urge and delved my fingers into her shorter strands, pulling her head back with a rough tug.

She released my cock with a *pop* sound. "Cade?"

I wiped the lone tear that streamed down her cheek. Fuck, I hated these contacts. I wanted to see her real gaze. The blue and brown swirling together in her right eye. The one that reminded me of the sky and the earth. It was arresting.

"You asked if I was ready to punish you." I framed her jaw possessively with one hand. "Baby, I've been *dreaming* of punishing you. I've had filthy fantasies running through my mind since you left me. The kind one shouldn't have about the love of his life."

Chasing her around the city and barely getting crumbs of her attention made me insane with hunger, like a feral, unsatiated beast waiting centuries for his fated mate.

"Tell me." She scored her nails down my abs, leaving marks. "I want to know."

"I've fantasized about stealing you away from your ivory tower and taking you deep into my woods, princess." My fingers skittered to her pulse, a crude grin curling my lips when I noted how fast it fluttered. "I've fantasized about chasing you while I wear my mask—because I know it turns you on—and catching you, pinning you on your back, then pounding your sweet, forbidden cunt like an animal." I pressed my thumb over her lips and she sucked it into her mouth of her own volition. "And I've fantasized about dragging you to my cabin where I collar you, chain you to my bed, and do sinful things to your body until your voice is hoarse from begging for more because deep down…you crave those dark things, too. You want me to own you, ruin you, love you in every possible way."

The way her eyes glittered with excitement, I knew I had her number. This was one of her fantasies. Mine too.

"You promise to make it happen?"

"Do I ever break one, pretty girl?"

She smiled with affection and nostalgia. "Never."

"Now that that's settled." I tugged at her hair until she whined—giving her the pain she so needed with her pleasure—and dug my fingers into her jaw. "Open your mouth wide, sweetheart. I'm going to make you regret the day you left me."

Ella dragged her long nails over my balls, a gentle reminder that she could be lethal but was choosing to be obedient for me. "Will you let me come afterwards?"

"If you behave, I'll consider it."

"Fine."

"Don't even think about touching your pussy while I face-fuck you. Otherwise, I'll edge you all night long."

She huffed dramatically and rolled her eyes. "Spoilsport."

Fuck, I missed her.

"Open up, baby." I ran my fingers over her mouth.

She caught my hand and pressed a kiss to my knuckles, lingering on the silver rings and taking note of the one that was missing. A bout of regret flashed in her expression. She knew she messed up by throwing my promise ring out of the belfry.

"It's okay." After tonight, I'd scavenge through the grounds until I found it. "We'll get it back."

Following my instructions, Ella parted her lips, and I took it as my cue to shove myself into her mouth with no mercy, knuckling the strands at her crown like a leash.

She cried out into the empty stillness of the nurse's office.

I grinned cruelly. "Pinch my thigh if it becomes too much."

Ella blinked up at me twice, her signal for consent whenever we did this.

Then I started thrusting, pounding deep inside of her throat, gratification zinging through my system. "Fucking hell, Ella."

The sounds of our dirty act blended into a spectacular symphony, louder than the storm raging outside. They resounded in the room until I was sure someone might find us. But that's what Ella liked, therefore none of us bothered taming the muffled moans and loud groans.

Brown eyes glanced up at me. Tears streamed down her cheeks. Saliva smeared all over her kiss-swollen lips. And her wild smile stretched around my girth.

Before I met Ella, I barely had time for silly crushes. Once our paths crossed, I knew why no one caught my attention for the first sixteen years of my life. I was waiting for her. *Saving* myself for her.

Her madness and darkness mirrored mine.

She was my match made in heaven and hell.

"Good girl," I praised, moving faster and harder, revelling in the glugging noises coming from this overdue face-fucking. "You look so perfect on your knees, redeeming yourself by taking every inch of my cock like a properly trained slut."

Her response came in the form of another muffled moan. I knew what that moan meant. She wanted more. So much more.

Unable to deny this girl, I kept dirty-talking, mixing praise and degrade with every sentence, driving her crazier with each drive of my hips.

"Nasty girl, you're getting wetter with each thrust, hm? I bet you'd like nothing more than for me to bend you over and give you a few rounds of rough sex. We all know how much you loved it when I fucked you like I hated your

guts.”

“Keep the black card, baby. Use it. Drain me of every cent. I won't mind. So long as you repay me by keeping your thighs wide open so I can do all sorts of dirty things to this tight cheerleader pussy of yours.”

“I can't breathe without you, Ella. My princess, my goddess, my religion. I would die for you, kill for you, live the rest of my life worshipping you.”

It had been so long since I had this—her—and I wouldn't last long. I felt my orgasm hurtling forward, screwing my eyes shut. "Fuck, I'm coming, baby."

Pulling out wasn't an option. Ella liked to swallow, and that's exactly what she did moments later when I shot down her throat. Holding on to my hips and sucking every pulse of cum like a sexual deviant. Grazing her teeth along my cock when I pulled out of her mouth.

I was overwhelmed by the powerful release, a culmination of missing her for months and my fist being unable to do the job right. Panting, I framed her face and wiped her tears, completely speechless and spellbound by her.

Oh, sweetheart. My mind can never do your memory justice. You're even prettier up close, in the flesh. Sweet and controlled on the surface, but thrumming with fire underneath that steely armour. And it's incredible that I'm the only man to have the privilege of experiencing you this way.

Finding my voice, I ground out, "Are you okay? Was I too rough?"

"I'm okay." She held my wrists and took turns kissing each palm. "That was perfect."

I opened my mouth to agree, but the mind-numbing orgasm dulled my senses momentarily. Ella stood up after grabbing an extra lollipop from my leather jacket's pocket. She unwrapped it, stuck it into her mouth, and threw her arms around my neck. "Hi."

The feel of her naked chest against mine sent a row of shivers down my spine. I banded my arms around her waist, holding her tighter to me, vowing to never let her go. I may truly die if she walked away from me again. "Hi, baby."

"Did I behave, *querido?*"

"Barely." Once a heathen, always a heathen.

I yanked the lollipop out of her mouth. She giggled before I cupped her nape and drew her lips to mine, sucking and nipping them while that girlish, bell-like laugh chimed in my ears. It sounded like *home*.

She had a languid look when I finished smothering her with my love. For now. "You've really missed me, huh?"

"You have no idea."

Ella's face softened and she brushed gentle pecks on either side of my cheeks.

My heart beat rapidly.

She's kissing my dimples and everything in the world feels right again.

"I meant it when I said I missed you, too." She stole the lollipop and popped it back in her mouth, arching her brow playfully. "And I also miss the way you make me come."

"Of course, you do, Ella." I lifted her into my arms and strode to the single bed, depositing her on it. "Because nobody knows you like me."

"Nobody, Cade."

The reassurance patched up another wound in my heart.

She immediately raised herself on her elbows and split her thighs wide in invitation.

Ella Ximena Cordova was the most beautiful thing in my universe, hand-crafted by the heavens, and spread before me like an offering at a feast for a greedy deity.

Raven hair that barely caressed her shoulders, tan skin shimmering like gold, brown eyes denoting an intense heat, sultry lips curved in a come-hither smile, and saffron-coloured nails mapping the lines of her body, running over her pebbled nipples, down the valley of her tight middle, and disappearing into her panties with a naughty expression.

I couldn't wait any longer to have a piece of her.

"Get naked, baby," I ordered, my cock hardening again at the thought of her arousal on my warm tongue. "Now."

"Don't tell me what to do," Ella snapped teasingly. "You're not the boss of me."

"When it comes to bringing your sweet little cunt pleasure? You and I both know I am."

"You want me?" she goaded. "Come undress me yourself."

Dark amusement tipped up the corners of my lips. I'd punish her insolence by spanking her pussy and ass before I gave her a single orgasm.

Pouncing on her, she laughed when I shrugged off her booted heels and tugged her pants down her sculpted legs with impatience. Grabbing the sides of her orange thong, I all but ripped it off her pussy angrily.

"You've ruined all this pretty silk with your cum," I growled and slapped her pussy. "Horny little slut."

Ella moaned, body arching, feet digging into the mattress. "Oh, God."

I rubbed the wetness on my fingers and smirked. "You've been throwing insults and giving me attitude all night long, but it makes you fucking wet when I play back, huh?"

She glared at me, still sucking on that lollipop. "No, it doesn't."

"Let's try that again, shall we?" I slapped her pussy again, the sound marrying with her hitching moans. "Have you been wet this whole time?"

"Maybe."

"Don't test my patience right now." I slapped her tits and twisted her nipples with both hands. She gasped. I lifted her thigh and spanked her left cheek twice, pinkening the skin of her ass. "Tell me what I want to hear, Ella."

"Yes! Yes, okay? I started feeling needy since...the tunnels."

"You had a gun cocked against my jaw, but you still wanted me." I grinned deviously, trailing my fingers over her slick pussy. "Bad, bad girl."

"I hate you," she said with little conviction, panting.

I climbed onto the bed, covering her body with mine. Pulling out the lollipop, I kissed her hard, indulging in her sugary taste. "No, Ella," I whispered, our lips threaded together with a ribbon of saliva. "You don't hate me at all. Far from it."

She never answered when I said she couldn't unlove me either. But her reply was sketched over the lines of her visage. One day, soon, I would get her to utter the three words.

"What were you thinking about in the tunnels?" I dragged the lollipop down her neck and circled her nipples. Ella moaned when my lips and tongue followed suit, her nails digging into my shoulders. "When you had me on my knees for you?"

She swallowed, watching me plant open-mouth kisses all over her stomach, stopping just shy of her mound. "I…I wanted to sit on your face while you licked my pussy…and let me lick you too."

We hadn't sixty-nined in ages. But now I couldn't get the hot image out of my mind. "You want to sit on my face and make a mess, pretty girl?"

"Y-Yes, please."

"First, tell me I'm the only one for you."

Tell me I'm the only one—now and forever—and you can have anything.

"You're the only one for me, Cade." She caressed my jaw. "You've always been. I promise you."

I smiled, finishing the remainder of her lollipop in two bites. "You're the only one for me, too. You know, in case you were wondering."

She tutted. "I know. You're a little too obsessed with me."

I wasn't even going to deny it. Everyone knew it at this point. "But you love it."

"I do, *querido.*"

When I flipped us into position so I was lying underneath with Ella on top, she yelped at my lack of warning. With her back facing me, she threw a glare over her shoulder. I winked and clapped her ass. "Come get what you need, sweetheart."

I helped her scoot backwards. Now her sweet ass and ripe pussy hovered just above my face, dangling like a forbidden fruit. I licked my lips, dying to sink into it. Good Lord, this sight was a blessing. If I died right now, I'd die the happiest man on Earth.

Ella raked her nails down my abs before her hands closed around my dick. "What if someone catches us?"

Fuck the competition and fuck anyone who dared to bust through that door. "Don't worry. My gun is loaded. I'll shoot."

"Cade!"

"Relax." My palms roved over her ass, shaping and squeezing the thickness before slapping it hard. "I'm not killing anyone tonight. Now stop worrying about getting caught like that isn't your kink, you little exhibitionist."

"But—oh my God!"

Her sentence died short when I shoved her pussy onto my awaiting mouth.

Wasting no time, I flicked my tongue across her wet slit a few times until I was engulfed by her sweet and tart essence. Fuck, I was in paradise. I ate her out with zeal, my tongue alternating between circling her clit and battering it with fast jabs that had her moaning loud enough to raise the dead. "Mm, you taste so good, baby. Just like I remember."

When my lips closed around her clit and sucked, Ella screamed in abandonment.

"You like that, pretty girl?" I did it again and she quaked above me.

"Y-Yes."

"Beg me for more."

Ella panted as she jerked me off faster. "*Pleasepleaseplease.*"

I skated my hand down her back and clasped her neck in warning. "If I don't feel those lips wrapped around my cock in the next ten seconds, I'll stop."

Ella didn't need to be told twice. My girlfriend—yes, we hadn't made it official again, but *sixty-nining* was basically the definition of being back together in my book—spat on my dick and licked the entirety of my length. Then she sucked the tip before slowly taking all of my inches to the back of her throat, sans gag reflex.

My eyes rolled back into my skull and I groaned, commanding hoarsely, "Don't you dare stop until I'm coming down that tight little throat, Ella."

I resumed my ministrations on her delicious pussy and she proceeded to hoover my cock like a superstar.

The smell of our desires and the filthy noises as we pleasured each other caused pure euphoria to rush through my veins. I pistoned my hips upwards to meet each one of her downstrokes, grunting into her creamy flesh. She bounced her ass faster on my face to chase the thrusting fingers inside her hot cunt, muffling her sobbing moans around my cock.

"I'm c-close," she whined when I switched to mercilessly tonguing her hole while my thumb rubbed her clit. "I'm going to come."

"Not without me." I smacked her ass and watched it shake beautifully. I bit into it like a juicy peach. She cried out. My teeth marks looked sexy on her. One day, this ass cheek would boast my ink too. "And make sure you swallow every drop of my cum like a good girl, Ella."

My girl's reply was another trembling moan as she returned to sucking my cock and surfing her pussy over my face. Her cum glistened on my chin, lips, and tongue. She was right at the precipice, her body coiled and ready to let go. Any other night, I would have edged her—I loved eating her out for hours on end—but tonight I was a desperate man, ready to taste her soft surrender on my palate.

"*Cadecadecade.*" Ella was tightening and pulsing. "*Please.*"

"Come for me," I growled. "Drench my face, *mo chuisle.*"

Thunder and lightning struck outside as we came together. Ella orgasmed with a mouthful of cock, her cries muffled. I groaned as I emptied down her throat, lapping at the arousal pouring out of her like it was my sustenance.

Fuck, there was nothing like Ella coming undone from my touch. Wild, demanding, and so hot that I couldn't help but press lingering kisses all over her flesh in veneration.

The strong release had Ella panting like she'd run a marathon. She rolled sideways and fell on the bed next to me, completely limp and speechless.

Smirking, I trickled a finger through her wet pussy and brought it to my mouth for another taste. "Who would have known South Side's princess could be tamed with a good tongue-fucking, hm?"

"I'm sorry, but who are you, what year is it, and where are we?"

A genuine laugh burst out of me. "Come sit on my face again and I'll remind you."

Her head snapped, a lopsided smile curving her lips. She looked so cute and so much like *my* Ellie that my heart twisted. Happiness bloomed in my chest.

I think…I did it. I revived the old Ella I fell in love with.

"Is that so, princepin?"

"Princepin?" I arched my brow. "Look at you already remembering who I am."

She chuckled and crawled closer to me, kissing my lips to taste herself before positioning her knees on either side of my head.

Sifting her fingers through my hair, she gazed down at me tenderly. My breath caught in my throat. "I could never forget you. No matter how much time we spent apart. You're branded inside of me, too."

"Good." I swallowed and kissed the **K** tattoo on her hip bone. "Because I've never forgotten a single detail about you, Ellie."

Then she proceeded to sit on my face like it was her personal throne and I made her come again, loud enough for everyone in St. Victoria to know what we were doing.

And I did it all with my gun next to me.

"I can't believe you got my name inked on the inside of your bottom lip." Curled beside me in post-coital bliss, Ella traced my lips, almost in a trance. "It's so possessive. I love it."

"I'm glad you do." I burrowed her deeper into my chest, pressing a kiss to her forehead and inhaling her scent. Orange blossoms and jasmines mixed with rain. It calmed me down. "Though I hear the tat won't last long."

"Guess you'll just have to redo it in a few years."

I smiled like a fool. *In a few years.* That meant she was back and in it for the long haul, right?

Everything could finally go back to the way it was.

Well...not completely to the way it was.

Many things were different now. Yes, we were still the same Ella and Cade in some ways, though we had also changed due to the indelible marks we left on each other. Miscommunication was the root of our separation, but many external factors morphed us into the versions we were today. Ella's miscarriage was a harsh dose of reality, yet she overcame the pain and was stronger than ever. As for me? Losing her forced me to immerse myself into the family business. Lonely nights spent working alongside

Josh to build our empire and punishing dirty rats who crossed us made me colder, harsher, and more ambitious.

We grew and learned how to survive without one another.

But just because I knew how to survive without her didn't mean I wanted to *live* without her.

"Guess I will." I kissed the tip of her nose.

Now she traced the tattoos on my right arm. It was difficult to hold back my beaming grin. Ella was enamoured with all the ink in her honour. It was a way to never forget us and manifest her return.

"What else did you do over the summer, besides getting all this ink?"

"I spent a lot of time with Livvy, who made me have daily tea parties with her. She said it was the fastest cure to stop feeling sad."

Ella laughed. "Basically, a ploy to get you to play with her dolls, eh?"

"Oh, one hundred percent." I didn't mind, though. There were three girls in my life that I would do anything for: Olivia, Aunt Julia, and Ella. My mom, too, when she was alive.

Silence stretched between us. Ella was pensive. I didn't like that. I smoothed the furrow between her brows. Was she thinking about me? Was she regretting kissing and touching me?

I was afraid that once we left St. Victoria, all the magic we found tonight would be lost and her walls would go back up.

"Ella, I…"

"Yes?"

Will you take me back?

Will you love me forever?

Will you vow to never leave me again?

Tongue-tied, I was unable to echo those sentiments. Sensing my unease, Ella rose on one elbow and stared at me. She must have seen something in my transforming expression because she rushed out, "We should get going before someone finds us."

"Do you want to leave?" I whispered. *If we walk out of here, will I lose the parts of you I found in the dark?*

Ella placed a hand on my cheek. "We're way past the timer, Cade. We should leave." Glancing at my watch, she confirmed, "Crap, it's three thirty-three a.m."

I sighed. She was right. "Will you let me drive you home?"

"Did you bring an extra helmet?"

Fuck, I hadn't. "No."

"Then I'll have to go home with Callie."

"I can give you my helmet. I don't have to ride with one."

Ella shook her head and smiled like I was being silly. I was dead serious. "You're adorable." She kissed my cheek and she swung off the bed. "Can you hand me my clothes, please?"

I picked up our discarded clothing. We put our armours back on and grabbed our torches. I blew out the candle and surveyed the nurse's office, ensuring nothing was out of place.

Baseball bat in hand, Ella headed for the door, but quickly halted in her tracks. "Cade?"

I held my breath, tucking my gun into the back of my pants. "Yes?"

"Thank you for coming to Initiation Night. Thank you for telling me your truth—despite the fact that I didn't make it easy for you to be heard—and for listening to my side of the story. I'm really glad we finally aired out our dirty laundry."

Why did this feel so final? "Ella..."

She opened the door and stepped out, before letting loose a bloodcurdling shriek.

CHAPTER 26

Confessing Time

CADE

The Present

3:36 a.m.

Ella's scream reverberated through the entirety of the south wing hallway. Pulse thundering with fear, I ran out after her, barking, "What's wrong?"

Stupefied, she pointed a finger at…

Holy. Fucking. Shit.

Despite the darkness and reduced vision, what I saw chilled my insides.

An apparition, cloaked in black with an odd beam of light flickering by its side, travelled headlong in our direction.

"What the fuck is that?" I hissed.

"*Es el diablo.*" Shell-shocked, she backed up. "We need to get out of here."

"Ellaaaaaaaaa," the *thing* taunted in a garbled voice just as thunder struck outside.

We both screamed like little girls.

Then I grabbed Ella's hand and ran in the opposite direction.

"Oh my God," she cried hysterically. "It knows my name!"

"Cadeeeeeee."

And apparently mine.

"What the fuck, what the fuck, what the fuck," she chanted, trying to keep up with my fast stride. "What the *fuck* is going on?"

I wheezed, taking a right when the hallway split into two. "I have no idea, but keep running and don't stop!"

"This is what we get for sixty-nining in a haunted place," Ella wailed. "We probably pissed off some angry spirit!"

I didn't know if I should laugh or howl with the demon—in Ella's words—gaining speed on us. I wasn't one to actually believe in ghosts, but she genuinely believed in the paranormal. And you know what? Tonight might be the first night I actually turned into a believer. St. Victoria was rumoured to be haunted *and* sentient, resting over one of the gates of hell. All those unexplainable deaths may be due to the fact that it fed on souls, tormenting them when they were alive and then binding them to it during the afterlife.

I was truly beginning to lose my mind if I was entertaining all these speculations.

"*Cadellaaaaa.*" The thing behind us called out our names again, a monstrous growl that had goosebumps breaking over my skin. Ella wasn't moving quick enough in those booted heels. Grabbing her around the waist, I hauled her up the side of my body and she instantly wrapped her legs around my middle.

I gunned it down the hallway like the hounds of hell were nipping at our feet.

Ella started praying in Spanish, but deftly broke off in a strangled, "Oh my God! It's getting closer. It's fucking getting closer!"

"Should I try to shoot it?" I panted.

"The solution to everything can't be a bullet!" she chided, yelling. "It'll go right through it! And you might just anger it more!"

The hallway before us was like a never-ending black tunnel where the sounds of our heavy footsteps, thudding heartbeats, and the rain furiously crashing against the mosaic windows was magnified.

"Hey, remember that time you wanted to audition as an extra on a horror movie set?" I struggled to keep the teasing tone out of my voice as I ran. "Now you're in your very own."

308

She dug her fingers into my shoulders and glared, unamused. "You're not funny."

"I'm hilarious." And that thing was still stomping behind us. "Admit it."

"If we make it out alive, I might."

The thing behind us continued calling our names.

Ella screamed like a banshee.

Fear slickened my palm. I almost dropped her and my flashlight, which was no longer working, on the ground. "Fuck, fuck, fuck."

From past experience, I knew the end of the hallway morphed into one of the staircases that descended straight into the crypt. However, this one was said to be cursed. No one used it. Too many incidents. The kind that involved people tumbling down and injuring themselves. In one chilling case over three decades ago, someone died too.

Short on options, I took a gamble and went in, hoping Ella's torch gave us enough light to get down safely.

"Cade, no!" Ella protested. "Not here!"

"We don't have a choice," I bit out, trying to outrun whatever chased us.

A musty smell swirled in the atmosphere as I descended the stone stairwell. It was tight like the one in the belfry. I shuddered when my gaze roamed over the brick walls.

Do you pledge your allegiance was streaked along the surface in faded blood.

I cursed under my breath and Ella gagged into my neck.

Veni, Vidi, Mortus was the last saying we saw as we entered the crypt.

I came, I saw, I died.

A morbid spin on Julius Caesar's famous proverb.

I lowered Ella to her feet and inhaled a few breaths to recenter myself. Ella wobbled and I grabbed her elbow to steady her. "You okay?"

"Barely," she panted. "Something is really fucking wrong with this place."

"I think we're the only people left in the school." We hadn't seen any Initiators in over two hours. Initiation Night was supposed to be complete by 3:00 a.m. and now we were pushing the 4:00 a.m. mark.

"And now we're being chased by a spirit like it's ghost fucking busters!"

"Don't cuss, Ella. We're among saints." I canted my head to the far right, where the graves of Sister Victoria and the other nuns lay to rest. A sole light hung from the ceiling, casting an eerie glow over the coffins on the ground.

"Please." She rolled her eyes and walked further into the crypt. "Like we haven't done worse, blasphemous things in the presence of saints."

Touché. There was that time we snuck to the crypt a few months ago and…screwed in the confessional. Easily one of the hottest fucks of my life. I'd gotten down on my knees to show her how I worshipped and she'd creamed my face in blessing. Then I completed the service by pounding into her body six ways to Sunday. Sacrilegious of us, but we never claimed to be perfect.

The crypt hadn't been renovated since St. Victoria's olden days. It was probably one of the few places in the establishment that never lost its horrifying, unsettling charm.

This place was supposed to be a sanctuary, yet it felt like the devil's lair.

I followed Ella as she paused in front of the graves, tension radiating from every line in her body. "Cade…"

"What is it?"

"The crowns." She gulped. "They're here."

I froze, staring where she pointed.

Two gold crowns, encrusted with blue stones, were poised over Sister Victoria's coffin, gleaming under the light like ceremonial relics.

"There's no one left in the school and the crowns are still here."

I grimaced. "That means nobody won."

Ella shook her head. "None of this makes any sense."

Something went awry during the competition and we had no means of communicating with the outside world. Everyone had vanished and we were stuck here, hallucinating an apparition.

Foreboding ticked into my system like a swinging pendulum. "Ella, I think we should—"

310

A creak resonated and Ella nearly squeaked before I clamped a hand over her mouth. Above us, another call for our name resonated and then heavy footsteps started descending the stairs.

Panicked, I grabbed Ella and dragged her to the confessional booth tucked in the corner of the crypt. I shoved us in and closed the curtain behind us so we remained hidden. I brought my finger to my lips in a 'be quiet' sign and turned off her flashlight.

Our breaths mingled with how close we stood. The baseball bat was stamped between our fronts. I could sense her fear and she could sense mine. Wordlessly, we wrapped our arms around each other, embracing the way we had a thousand times.

Only this one felt more monumental.

Was this the surge of life before death?

"Cadellaaaa. Come out, come out, wherever you are."

We both perked up. I could feel Ella's skeptical expression in the dark. "I...I don't think it's a demon anymore."

That taunting voice sounded too human. I gritted my teeth. "I don't think so either."

"What if it's the masked guy?" she whispered.

After everything we discussed tonight, it was possible the bastard came back to finish the job. "It could be."

"Okay, so I have a baseball bat and you have a gun. Together, we can take this motherfucker down."

"Didn't you just tell me that not everything can be solved with a bullet?" I spat incredulously. "Now you want me to shoot?"

"Keep your voice down," she hissed back. "And if the situation calls for it, yeah."

"What if it's not the masked guy?"

"I'm like ninety-nine percent sure it is."

"And the one percent chance that it's not?"

"Do you want to go with my plan or not?" she asked, vexed.

"It's a bad plan. Let's wait for whatever that *thing* is to leave, then we'll make our way to the North Wing where there's an exit."

"Fine," she mumbled sullenly. "We'll do it your way."

"Good."

A few seconds later, the sound of footsteps faded away like whoever was on the other side decided to retreat back upstairs. We stayed put for another moment.

Ella rubbed herself against me. "You're hard."

I clenched my jaw, staring up at the wooden ceiling. "I know."

"You're insatiable. I sucked you off twice."

My cheeks reddened. "It's not my fault. You're pressed up against me and—"

"You can't help yourself?" She snorted. "This is so not the time, Cade."

"You think I don't know that—"

The curtain of the confessional was ripped open.

We screamed.

The *thing* screamed.

Then Ella released a battle cry and swung out the bat like a pro baseball player.

It bashed against the intruder, who fell to the ground with a groan that was very masculine and very…familiar.

Oh, fuck.

Ella heaved like a warrior as she stepped out of the booth.

Please, don't tell me it's…

When I switched on her flashlight and shone it over the unconscious big body, my suspicions were confirmed.

Ella gasped, cupped a hand over her mouth, and dropped the bat.

My eyes widened in disbelief and I doubled over, yanking at the roots of my hair.

It couldn't be.

She didn't.

"*Ella!*" I yelled at her with a ferocious quality. "What the fuck!"

Lying on the ground, cloaked in a black cape with a plague doctor mask, was Shaun.

"Oh my God." Ella started hyperventilating. "Did I just kill Shaun?"

I fell to my knees beside my best friend. The mask was practically knocked off his head and his temple was slick with a splatter of blood.

"What were you thinking? We had a plan!"

"I-I don't know!" she cried. "I panicked and reacted, thinking it was a demon, or the masked guy, or fuck, a serial killer! I thought we were going to die! Oh my God. I'm going to fucking jail. I just killed Shaun Jacobsen the III."

Shaun could not die. I wouldn't allow it.

While she had her freak-out session, I felt for his pulse with shaky fingers. Thankfully, he was alive but breathing faintly. I shoved the butt of the flashlight into my mouth and unzipped Ella's little purse, digging for clean tissues. I bundled a wad and held it to Shaun's bleeding temple.

Ella fell to her knees beside me, doing the cross before clasping her hands together in prayer. "*Padre nuestro que estás en el cielo, santificado sea tu nombre...*"

I drowned out the rest of Ella's words, concentrating on wiping Shaun's blood before slapping his cheek lightly. "Shaun? Please open your eyes."

I already lost my parents. I couldn't risk losing another person who mattered to me.

Done with her prayer, Ella cradled his face. "Shaun, I'm so sorry. I'll never be able to live with myself knowing I killed you. You're a pain in the ass, but I still adore you. Please don't die. You're too young and you have so many things to accomplish—like marrying Hera. That's one of your life goals, right? If you don't wake up now, she'll marry someone else and we can't have that. C'mon, Shauny boy. I swear I'll never pull another prank on you if you just open your eyes. Please, I'm begging you."

At the mention of the girl he was cuckoo about, Shaun's fingers twitched to life. "W-Who is Hera marrying?"

"Shaun!" Ella gasped. "You're alive!" She smacked a noisy kiss on his forehead. "I didn't kill you! Oh, thank God!"

He grabbed his head, groaning. "My skull's made of metal. I'm good, babe."

I sighed in relief and dabbed at the sweat on his forehead. "Yeah, but you might have a concussion, so you need to stay awake. Ella's got one helluva swing."

"Speaking of..." Ella stared at him accusingly. "Why were you trying to scare us, you lunatic?"

Shaun chuckled weakly and sat up with my help. "I'm sorry. I saw you both in the hallway and couldn't resist. Although, I didn't think you'd actually smack me with a baseball bat. Otherwise, I'd have reconsidered."

Leave it to Shaun to find joy in chasing us in a haunted school while roaring like a B-movie style monster.

"I'm sorry about that again." Ella hugged him. "Do you forgive me?"

"Already forgiven." Then he shot us a conspiratorial look. "You both look cozy for exes who hate each other."

Ella huffed. "Cade, mind handing me that baseball bat? I don't think I did enough damage the first time."

I threw it her way and she caught it, pretending to jokingly bash Shaun's head again. Like a good sport, he feigned dying by falling back with a hand on his heart.

I shook my head with a small smile. He was such a clown. "Since we have you here, want to tell us why it looks like everyone is gone?"

Shaun winced. "Yeah, about that…Someone called the cops. They didn't make it past the gates because it's private property, so they must have left after checking the outskirts. As instructed, no one parked their cars on campus, which gave us an advantage. Darla and me were able to sneak out everyone except for you guys since you were nowhere to be seen. That was more than an hour ago. I came back to school in hopes of finding you."

Thank goodness he didn't find us a few minutes before. Otherwise, he'd have gotten an eyeful of our extracurricular activities.

"Appreciate you coming back for us, Shaun." I squeezed his shoulder. "Do you know who called the cops?"

"No." He frowned. "Darla thinks it's one of the Initiators. But why an Initiator would call the cops and risk getting caught is beyond me."

I shared a look with Ella. Could it have been the masked guy?

"We need to get out of here." I helped Shaun to his feet with an arm around his torso. He swayed. "And we need to get you to a hospital. Pronto."

"Before I forget, Darla has your phones." Shaun winced again, taking a step with my aid. "Everyone collected theirs on the way out. You'll have to get them from her."

"Great," Ella said absentmindedly.

"I don't get it," Shaun grumbled. "You were like sisters, Ella. What happened between you two?"

Her jaw clenched. "We had a falling-out. Darla stopped talking to me. The end."

"Darla wouldn't do that," Shaun defended. "There's got to be more to the story. You should talk to her."

I agreed with him. If there's one thing I learned tonight, it was that most issues stemmed from miscommunication. And they could also be resolved by simply talking to the other person as well.

"I'll think about it." Ella's tone made it clear that she was done speaking on this subject. "Shaun, if the crowns are still here, does that mean nobody won?"

"Nobody." Shaun's eyes narrowed on the crowns. "Though I'll have you know, the crowns, along with the other prizes, were locked upstairs in the janitor's closet by the foyer. Unless Sister Victoria or some other ghost magically summoned them to the crypt, I'm not sure how they got here."

Huh. Weirder things had happened in the ancient motherhouse, but the thought of these crowns showing up here unceremoniously creeped me out in ways I couldn't explain.

"I guess it's fate." Ella smiled at me. "This means we won, *querido*."

I smiled back. "And you created history, sweetheart."

Shaun's gaze bounced between us. "Wait a minute. You're both using pet names again and I'm not sensing any hostility. Are you back together?"

Neither of us confirmed or denied.

It hurt me a little because I wanted to say '*we're back together for good*,' but I didn't know where we stood anymore. Ella never outright said she wanted to rekindle our relationship, despite everything that transpired in the nurse's office. And I didn't want to make any assumptions.

We took a lot of steps in the right direction tonight by speaking about the past and our feelings. But maybe she needed more time to think about our future before letting me know her final decision.

Whatever the case, I just hoped her answer was *yes*.

Shaun and I watched Ella march over to Sister Victoria's coffin.

She picked up her crown and set it down on her head, relishing the celebratory moment with an insightful inhale.

When she turned around to face us, she looked every bit my goddess of revenge and retribution. The bandaged hand, the faint traces of mascara tears, and the fatigued but determined expression that didn't take away from her beauty.

Ella swiped the other crown and headed my way. Gently, she deposited it on my head with a flourish. "We did it, Cade. King and Queen of Initiation Night."

The universe worked in mysterious ways. Three years ago, I wanted nothing more than to get paired up with Ella and win this competition. Now that I had the accomplishment, it paled in comparison to what I already won.

Freedom from my demons and the possibility of being with this girl again.

Ella

I lit the way with my torch as Cade helped Shaun up the stairs of the crypt. Regret and shame gnawed at me whenever I glanced at the latter. He was in pain but doing a great job at hiding it with jokes and easy smiles. I couldn't believe I actually whacked him with the bat. I was terrified when the confessional's curtain ripped open that I stopped thinking and reacted first.

I knew Shaun forgave me, but I'd still send a fruit basket to his place as an apology. Maybe playing Cupid for him and Hera, one of my really good friends, would help make amends too. Shaun had liked her for years and sucked at making it abundantly clear.

My posture sagged the closer we got to the main foyer. Now that the adrenaline was wearing off, I slowly registered the dull throb in my ankle, the cut in my palm, and the prickling in my heart.

I couldn't remember the last time I felt this exhausted.

I realized both guys were notably quiet too, staring out the windows lining the hallway. The storm was still going strong and tumultuous as ever.

"I'm guessing you and Darla didn't have a chance to clean up?" I asked Shaun, considering how everyone basically escaped to avoid getting caught by the cops.

"No." He sighed and palmed his forehead. "We're going to come back tomorrow to ensure everything is spick and span so Principal Hill doesn't lose her shit Monday morning."

Principal Hill was part of the initial group who started this tradition decades ago. She knew Initiation Night could get rowdy and would definitely cut Darla some slack if certain things weren't in their rightful place.

"Oh, by the way." Cade clicked his tongue. "I shattered a glass globe in Room 208 on the third floor."

"Bro," Shaun said exasperatedly. "You had two jobs. To win the girl and not break shit on campus."

"You know said girl can hear you, right?" I said with dry amusement.

"Since your ears seem to be in perfect working condition, why didn't you answer my question earlier?" Shaun hedged. "You know, the one where I asked if you two were back together."

Cade and I both remained silent.

Shaun muttered under his breath, "Stubborn idiots. After all the effort I put in."

No other words were exchanged as we reached the front doors. Shaun leaned against the archway for support and yanked out keys from his pocket. "Darla gave them to me so I could come back for you both."

I thought back to what Shaun said in the crypt.

I had no choice but to go see Darla if I wanted my phone back. However, I'd take Shaun's advice and try talking to her. One last time. I would put my pride aside for the girl who'd been like my sister.

We both deserved that, right?

And maybe this time she'd finally tell me what went wrong between us.

After being trapped for hours, we stepped out of St. Victoria and we're greeted by another chorus of rain, lighting, and thunder. Shaun locked the doors and then we crossed the courtyard, wet grass wilting beneath our shoes.

Our plan was to take Shaun to the hospital. I'd drive his car while Cade trailed behind in his motorcycle, which he actually parked near the woods on campus.

"I'm sorry again, Shaun," I said sheepishly. "I really didn't mean to hit you."

"It's okay, Ella." He attempted a wink, but in his state, it resembled a grimace. "I kind of deserved it, and I'm not mad at all. Plus, it makes for a funny story. I'll never forget the way you both screamed and ran away like chickens. Totally worth it."

While he cackled, Cade and I glared at him.

Moments later, we arrived at the front gates of the school.

And were welcomed by a flurry of red-blue lights and police sirens. A group of cops stared at us with menacing expressions. "Put your hands up! You're under arrest for trespassing on private property."

Cade cursed under his breath, clutching onto an injured Shaun.

The next few minutes felt like an out-of-body experience. We were forced to our knees, slapped with handcuffs, and shoved into the back of a squad car in spite of our protests. One of the cops kicked my hurt ankle and I growled in pain. Cade thrashed and threatened the cop, digging us deeper into this mess.

As we drove off, an odd sensation of being watched had me swivelling my head towards the school.

Amongst the shadowed trees, two figures stood side by side.

The same masked man who pushed me down the stairs in Balthazar Building, Guy Fawkes mask covering his face.

And next to him?

A familiar girl.

Pixie blond hair. Blue eyes. Red Riding Hood costume.

Callie.

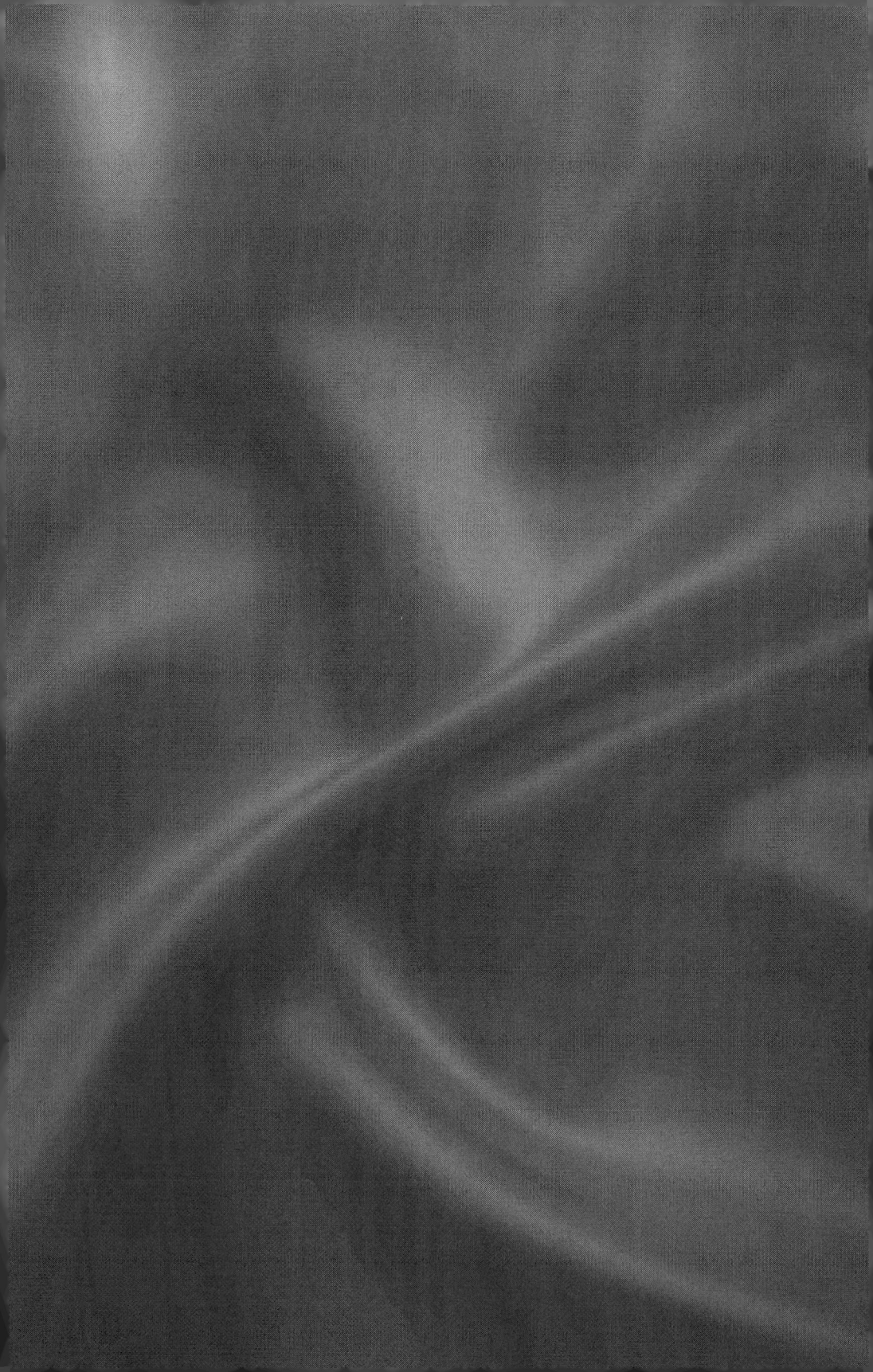

CHAPTER 27

Forever Yours

Ella

The Present

Smirking, I flipped my middle finger on the last picture of my mugshot, holding a sign with my details displayed. Despite looking haggard with my mascara staining my under eyes, I still held onto my pride with enough smugness to piss off the cops.

I was a Cordova. We didn't bend a knee to anyone.

On the outside, I appeared calm, collected, and arrogant.

On the inside? I was seething.

Long story short, the cops came to St. Victoria after receiving an anonymous call about a 'disturbance' during Initiation Night, but left when they found nothing. They came back once they received a second call around the time Shaun returned for us. Cade and I got cuffed and dragged to the police station, while Shaun, luckily, was rushed to the hospital after we scrambled to shout about his injured state.

The MPD tried interrogating us. We remained silent except for when we asked to call our lawyers. Afterwards, we spoke to our respective parents. My *papá* sounded like he was having a heart-attack when he found out his 'goodie two-shoes' daughter got arrested.

Once that was done, they took off our cuffs and threw us into a holding cell with more than half a dozen individuals.

A biker with tattoos and a wiry beard gave me a crooked smile full of invitation. I scrunched my face and looked away in a dismissive manner.

Cade glared at him. "Keep your fucking eyes to yourself."

The biker balked under his scrutiny. The Remington boys were familiar faces in the underworld with notorious reputations. No one wanted to cross them. Or invoke Vance Remington's wrath.

I leaned my head against the bars of the cell, taking note of the irritated skin around my wrists. On the way to the station, I concluded that the only cuffs I enjoyed were the ones Cade tied me with when we fucked.

"How did we even get here?" I mumbled more to myself than anything.

"Do you really want the answer to that?"

"No." I groaned. "But tell me how your uncle took the news?"

"Uncle Vance sounded annoyed at being woken up at four thirty a.m., but he wasn't pissed per se. More worried." Cade leaned against the bars too, facing me. "How did your parents take it?"

Not great at all.

"My *papá* was the one who answered. He lost his shit and *mamá* tried to calm him down in the background." I sighed. "I'm probably never allowed to leave the house again unless I'm supervised."

Like I once said, it didn't matter that I was nineteen. In my parents' eyes, I was forever a little kid who needed to be sheltered. Maybe that's why I rebelled harder over the years.

I was going to have to work for decades to get back into their good graces. Probably until I was old and grey and had one foot in the grave.

"It's going to be okay, Ellie."

I smiled weakly. "Promise?"

Cade snagged my pinky finger with his and kissed it. "I promise."

My heart swelled. He never forgot the way we promised.

We contemplated our situation in quietness for the next few minutes. The cops contacted Principal Hill to ask her if she wanted to press charges, which she swiftly declined. Initiation Night, as everyone in the inner circle knew, was a sacred tradition and once you pledged your allegiance, you were bound to it the same way mafiosos were bound to their omertàs. Plus,

Principal Hill—while strict and a bit scary—was not a snitch. St. Victoria's reputation was a direct reflection of hers and she couldn't risk throwing us under the bus, as that would affect her and her daughters as well.

I wondered how Darla was faring with this news. Her mother must have told her that we got arrested. Was my ex-best friend worried? Did she even care?

Speaking of best friends, I was once again bombarded with the image of the masked guy and Callie standing beside one another, like a villain and his heroine, watching the world burn to ashes after they set it on fire.

Who was the masked guy?

Why was Callie with him?

What were they doing together?

Was she...in cahoots with him this whole time?

No.

No, I couldn't—didn't want to—believe it.

This was Callie. The girl I'd known since fourth grade. We'd been friends for years. What reason could she possibly have to hurt me? She'd always been so kind, sweet, and gracious.

But why was she there, Ella? Your eyes weren't playing tricks.

You. Saw. Her.

Many questions bounced in my skull, completely unanswered.

Sensing my inner turmoil, Cade tucked a short strand of my hair behind my ear. "A penny for your thoughts?"

I swallowed. "I...I saw something when we were driven away from St. Victoria."

"What did you see?"

I wanted to tell him the truth. But part of me was afraid that once I uttered it out loud, it would change everything. Because if Callie was truly implicated in this...I sucked in a deep breath. "I saw Callie standing by the woods with the masked guy."

Shocked, Cade faltered a step. "What?"

"I saw them, Cade. It was *her*. She was wearing that Little Red Riding Hood costume, and he was wearing all black with that Guy Fawkes mask."

"Why would she be with him?"

"I don't know," I grated. "But I'm beginning to suspect that everything that's happened…"

I couldn't finish my sentence.

Cade understood me regardless. "There may be some truth to Darla's theory of an Initiator calling the cops."

Translation: it could have been Callie.

But *why* would she do this? It didn't make any sense.

"Ella, is Darla still friends with Callie?"

"Why are you asking?"

"Humour me."

A shard of suspicion sank into my mind, giving rise to more dread and vexation.

"No, she isn't," I mumbled. "After Darla stopped talking to me, Callie claims that Darla also stopped talking to her. We never figured out why Darla cut us out and by the time university rolled around, I stopped caring about the possible reasons."

"I don't want to stir the pot, but I think it's worth talking to Darla," Cade hushed. "Shaun's right. It's not like her to cut out anybody—especially you—from her life without a valid explanation."

Anxiousness simmered in my core. "Okay, I'll talk to her soon."

He smiled and thumbed my cheek tenderly. "Good."

"Cade, I've been thinking about something, but I'm not sure how you'll react."

His brows furrowed at my tone, body straightening with alertness. "What is it?"

"I think you should also talk to the girl you were"—I gulped—"*with* the night of the party. She might know something we don't."

"No," he said vehemently, shaking his head. "That's a dead end. I don't even know her name."

"Cade," I said softly, catching his hands with mine. "Think about it. She was intoxicated and in your room, thinking you were someone else. Just like you. She's a victim in this situation and maybe she holds another missing piece of the puzzle."

He knew I was right too.

With a resigned sigh, he nodded. "Okay, I'll try to get in touch with her."

"We'll figure this out together, okay?" I smiled and clutched the lapels of his leather jacket, drawing him closer to me. "We're a team. Ride or die."

"Ride." He kissed my right eyelid. "Always ride, Ella."

We stayed like that for a moment, fixed in place, the world around us blurring to nothingness when we were in each other's orbits.

"Before I walk out of here." Cade's mouth trickled over my cheek, kissing the skin with the gentleness of a plume. "I need to know where I stand with you."

Barely able to keep my eyes open due to exhaustion, I couldn't have this conversation right now. Much less in front of strangers crowding the jail cell with us. "Cade..."

"Tonight was a lot for both of us. Mentally, emotionally, and physically." His hands rose to cup my cheeks. "But, baby, I'm hanging by a thread. I need to know that we can make this—us—work again. Otherwise, I don't know what I'll do with myself. I need you. In every definition of the word. And I hope you need me back the same way, Ella."

There was no use lying when the writing was on the wall.

I needed him too. In every definition of the word.

"Cade, I want you to know that—"

"Cade Remington and Ella Cordova?"

We both turned to glare at the cop who interrupted us.

"You're free to leave," they said, unlocking the cell.

With no choice but to follow after the cop, I grabbed Cade's hand and squeezed. "I promise, this isn't the end. We'll talk soon, all right?"

"All right." He looked crestfallen.

I kissed his left cheek.

The corners of his lips hitched up in an adorable smile.

Then we came face-to-face with our father figures, looking overtly disappointed.

Cade and I were suddenly interested in the grey-painted walls.

When the cop left and it was just us four, *papá*, despite buzzing with anger, asked, "Are you both okay?"

We nodded like good sports.

Vance tutted, shaking his head with a mocking smile. "You two just can't stay out of trouble, huh?"

Francisco Cordova rarely played the doting father role. He didn't wear his heart on his sleeve, nor was he the super affectionate type. But he loved his children dearly and was present throughout every one of my milestones: first cheer performance, school graduations, teaching me how to drive, and so much more. If it weren't for those moments, I'd think my *papá* was nothing more than a cold businessman without a heart.

And for this moment, when he came to bail me out at 5:00 a.m. with worry and fear etched in the lines of his face. His dress shirt was haphazardly buttoned, his slacks weren't pressed, and I was certain he wore shoes without socks. A telltale sign that he rushed over to the police station the second I hung up. *Papá* was never unkempt.

Birds chirped in the early autumn morning as we walked to his Benz. He hadn't said another sentence after asking us if we were okay, and I was gearing myself for a lecture. I was self-aware enough to say I deserved it.

"On a scale from one to ten, how mad are you right now?"

Papá didn't break a stride as he replied, "The scale is currently broken, Ella."

Well, *shit*. "Tell me what I can do to make this right."

He hadn't looked at me once since we exited the station. "You're a big girl. A strong, empowered, *independent* woman, as you always say." I didn't miss the emphasis on the *I* word. "I'll let you figure it out."

Okay, so that wasn't the answer I was expecting. Which meant he was extremely furious. Normally, *papá* didn't hesitate to give me a piece of his mind if he disagreed with something I did. This cool, composed façade wasn't a side of him I was accustomed to.

It scared me.

When we reached his car, I understood there was only one course of action. Apologizing with all the sincerity I could muster.

Regardless of my up-and-down relationship with my parents, one thing was for sure. Come high or hell water, they were always in my corner. Protecting me, providing for me, supporting me. Considering we were a family that avoided dealing with our emotions while perfecting our outer image, I wasn't able to always convey my gratitude...But I did need *papá* to know how thankful I was. Right this instant.

I grabbed his arm before he could go to the driver's door. "I'm really sorry, *papá*. For everything."

I'm sorry for not being the perfect good girl daughter you want. I'm sorry for making decisions you deem bad. I'm sorry I'm not the best version of myself yet. I'm sorry for a lot of things.

The only thing I would never apologize for, however, was loving Cade.

He was the best decision I ever made.

"I'm not perfect," I continued when *papá* kept watching me with intent, as though hearing the thoughts rattling through my mind. "I do try for you and *mamá* so you never feel ashamed of me, but sometimes I fall short. Like now. I didn't mean to worry you both and I acknowledge that what happened tonight was not okay. I'm sorry for being a disappointment—"

"Ella," he croaked and for the first time, I saw his exterior crack. His blank expression fell and the crinkles by the corners of his eyes grew prominent. "You're not a disappointment. Far from it."

I peered up at him nervously. "Really?"

"You're human, *mija*. And part of being human is making mistakes and learning as you go. Even when those mistakes land you in jail and you have to call your *papá* in the middle of the night to come rescue you."

I rushed into his arms. He hugged me back and kissed the top of my head. "Ella, you have no idea what thoughts went through my mind when I got that phone call. I thought you were hurt or worse—"

His shaky voice abruptly halted, overcome by emotions.

I buried my face in his chest, his homey smell comforting after a whirlwind night.

"I'm sorry if I ever made you feel like a disappointment." He enunciated each syllable with care, making sure I understood his message. "I admit that I'm not the greatest at expressing myself. The truth is you're my firstborn and my only daughter. I want to protect you from the harms of this wretched world and I want you to receive every blessing this life has to offer, which is why I can be adamant and domineering. But I'm not heartless, *mija*. I love you very much and the thought of you in any pain kills me. I need you to be more careful and more honest with us moving forward. *¿Lo entiendes*, Ella?"

"*Sí, papá.*" I nodded. "And I love you, too."

He kissed my head again, his own eyes shining with moisture. "Good. Now let's go home."

Saturday afternoon, after sleeping a handful of hours, showering, and eating a quick meal, I was summoned to the study. I dragged myself to meet *mamá* and *papá*, mentally preparing myself to get an earful about last night—er, earlier this morning.

When I stepped over the threshold, my parents stopped their conversation.

I smiled awkwardly and lowered myself to a couch before them. "Hi."

"How are you feeling, *mija*?" *mamá* asked tentatively, taking a sip of her café. There were dark circles under her eyes that hinted that she barely slept—a combination of hosting the fall soirée and my disappearance. Though she still looked put together in her linen attire and her midnight black hair, like mine, combed back into a neat ponytail.

"Tired," I said truthfully and reached for the plate of Mexican cookies on the coffee table, grabbing two. "And hungry."

"You must be out of it after the night you had."

I'd snuck out of our home many times to go raise teenage hell with Cade during our relationship. Successfully too, without my parents or the guards' knowledge. Who knew the guilt at finally being caught would be so profound?

Often, I saw life divided by a tightrope with two sides: good and bad. Most individuals went above and beyond to stay on the former, while I constantly found myself straying to the latter.

I had a propensity for dancing with the devil. It coursed through my blood and the more I fought it, the more it manifested itself. Nothing could be done to tame that side of me. It's why I learned to accept my nature.

Good girls kept the status quo. Bad girls made the rules.

And I was someone who always created her own rules, the world be damned.

"I want to start off by saying I'm really sorry for last night, *mamá*," I said genuinely. "I never meant to cause you any panic. Or you, *papá*. It's the last thing I wanted."

Mamá and *papá* exchanged a look. I was waiting for the verbal thrashing. It never came. Upon closer inspection, they both just seemed resigned. And perhaps they knew that yelling would seldom get us nowhere. Whereas in the past, they would have blasted me for the slightest indiscretion, now they were silent.

Was this growth?

Instead, *papá* poured more café into his cup and cleared his throat. "Tell us everything from the beginning, Ella."

It was a small price to pay to get back into their good graces. Therefore, I explained everything from going to St. Victoria, participating in Initiation Night—yes, I pledged my allegiance to the inner circle, but fuck it, it's not like my parents would gossip to others about this—and how we got caught by the cops. For obvious reasons, I didn't relay any details about me and Cade because they didn't need to know what happened in the nurse's office.

That was between me, him, God, and whatever spirits witnessed the act.

Safe to say, my parents were shocked to hear the entire situation. No screaming match ensued, except for—finally—a lecture on how reckless and irresponsible we were with a calmness that was worse than fury in my opinion. I listened patiently. I knew it was well-deserved. Furthermore, I lived under their roof and ate their food. While I made my own rules, occasionally I had to adhere to theirs too.

Plus, sneaking out of a high society party to go partake in a hazing activity was pretty scandalous according to my parents' standards. Their concerns and fears were valid. They asked me to be more careful and never do anything so rebellious again. I didn't add that Cade and I had done so much worse in the past. No point in sullying my reputation any further in their eyes.

Papá mentioned that my record was clear—most cops were dirty and in the pockets of Montardor's elites—and that Principal Hill was sweeping this situation under the rug. No charges, no investigation. Moreover, the latter had plans of one day debuting into the political scene. She'd need all the support with her mayoral campaigns. The last thing Diane Hill wanted was to be on the Cordovas' and the Remingtons' shit list.

"I don't even want to know what kind of trouble Emilio will cause us." *Papá* sighed. "You kids are a handful."

Mamá inched him a teasing look. "And to think, at one point, you wanted more."

"I take it back," he barked half dryly, half playful. "These two are more than enough."

"Hey, where do you think we get it from?" I pipped in. Emilio was an angel of a child, but the Cordova bloodline was filled with rebels and my little brother would probably follow suit when he grew up. "*Abuela* said you were a demon's spawn as a child."

"Don't listen to your *abuela*." *Papá* scoffed. "She's spouting nonsense."

I chuckled, eating my cookies as *mamá* ribbed him good-naturedly, recounting old stories that *papá* pretended not to remember. Seeing them banter—seeing them less distraught and more playful—eased my guilt for putting them through the ringer.

When *papá* had enough, he groaned and stood up, taking his café with him. "I've got work to do." He leaned down to kiss *mamá's* cheek. "I'll see you later, *mi corazón*."

Mamá smiled and squeezed the inside of his wrist, where he had her name tattooed.

My parents were still sickeningly in love with each other. No matter how much Emilio and I gagged at their displays of affection, I knew deep in my heart I always longed for their kind of love. *Papá* treated *mamá* like gold.

Having seen that kind of love my whole life, I never wanted to settle for less.

It was why finding Cade felt so monumental.

He treated me like I was his whole universe.

Once *papá* left and the door of the study clicked shut, *mamá's* smile dropped. She stared at me like I took ten years out of her life. "No more secrets, *mija*. You can tell us anything, okay? We're a family. We support and confide in each other. Never forget that."

These past three years, it felt like there was entirely too much space between us. A lot of it was my fault. It became harder to share my secrets with them, as was the case for most kids who entered adolescence. And the nature of my secrets was quite dark and not the kind you casually divulged to your parents.

There was one secret, however, that I could tell her.

I went to sit beside her and grabbed her slender fingers with mine. "*Mamá*, there's something I want to tell you."

Her undivided attention was on me. "What is it?"

When I met her gaze, tranquil and comforting, it gave me all the courage I needed to say my piece. "I was five weeks pregnant in July and I miscarried the night of Josh's party."

Mamá went saucer-eyed at the unexpected revelation. "What?"

"I was afraid of your reaction before so I kept this to myself. But I'm not afraid anymore and I feel healed enough to talk about what happened," I said. "Will you hear me out, *mamá*?"

She appeared on the verge of fainting, but still nodded.

I went on to tell her the whole dreadful tale from the summer. How I found out about my pregnancy, how I was excited at the prospect of becoming a new mom, how I baked cupcakes for Cade, and how Emilio was the one to find me when I lost the baby. I also added why I broke up with Cade…and how I found out twelve hours ago that he never actually cheated on me.

When I finished my monologue, *mamá* crushed me to her chest and wept, mourning for me, my unborn baby, and all my suffering. She planted kisses on my face, whispering words of comfort in a teary voice. Feeling her visceral reaction made me weep alongside her. A mother's love was eternal and this was the comfort I had needed months ago. I should have known that regardless of my actions, *mamá* and *papá* would never stop loving or being there for me.

"You shouldn't have gone through that alone, *mija*," *mamá* whispered. "I wish you'd told me the truth sooner."

"I wish I had too."

"What will you do now?" She wiped my damp cheeks.

Sighing, I rested my head on her shoulder. "After visiting Shaun at the hospital, I'm going to drive over to the Hills and retrieve my phone from Darla."

"I meant what will you do now with *Cade*?"

Oh.

Straightening, I brushed my hands down my old Batman logo T-shirt, the one I stole from Cade when we were sixteen. Then I glanced at my palm lines—my love one, in particular. There was only one person meant for me.

"We will find our way back to each other. He's the only man I want to be with, *mamá*. The only one who understands me, protects me, loves me beyond measure. And I love him, too. I never stopped," I said with conviction. "I know he wasn't yours and *papá's* first choice for me, but he is mine. In every way that matters."

My words were firm, leaving no room for argument. Cade would be their future son-in-law. They just needed to accept it.

I once said that the universe was pulling my strings and having a laugh. But I didn't realize it was for my own benefit. After everything that unfolded on Initiation Night, one thing was crystal clear to me.

Cade and I were written in the stars.

He was my destiny.

And I'd follow him until the ends of the earth.

"I want to apologize on behalf of myself and your *papá*," *mamá* began with a remorseful tone. "It's no secret that we preferred Josh, but it doesn't excuse the fact that we never gave Cade a fair chance when you both started dating. Yes, we were disappointed that you chose him, but over the years, it became clear to us why. He's kind, polite, smart, and most of all, treats you like a *princesa*. Anyone with a pair of eyes can see how much that boy loves you, Ella. Although we didn't outright give our blessings the first time, you have them now. I know he'll continue to make you the happiest girl in the world."

"Thank you," I whispered. "You have no idea how much this means to me."

I wanted them to accept him for so long that it felt a weight was finally lifted off my shoulders.

Mamá cupped my face and smiled. "Now go to your room. There's a surprise waiting for you. It was delivered an hour ago."

Autumn sunlight filtered through my sheer curtains, casting a warm glow in my room. I padded over to my bed. There sat an enormous white box with…a bouquet of orange lollipops wrapped in a blue ribbon.

The same bouquet Cade used to send me every month until we broke up.

My heart soared in my chest like a flock of birds. I set the bouquet on my bedside table and gingerly opened the mysterious box.

I gasped when I saw the stunning, blue silk gown inside.

An envelope tucked in the wrapping fluttered to the floor. My name was written on the front in a familiar masculine scrawl. I dove for it, nearly ripping the letter open in my haste.

And when I read the contents, I swooned, overcome by so much love for Cade.

Ella,

I hope you slept well and are not too tired from last night's shenanigans (although if you ask me, getting sent to jail is not only a rite of passage but an accomplishment for heathens like us). I also hope your ankle doesn't hurt too much. Put some ice on it. When I see you, I'll kiss it better.

I know we never got to finish our conversation, but I've made it clear what I want.

You.

Now and forever.

For I love you with every inch of my beating heart. I always have. I always will.

There will only ever be you for me, princess. You're my ride or die, the other half of my soul, and the girl I will someday make my wife.

We swore that this would last past our dying breaths, until we inevitably find each other in the next lifetime.

Let us uphold that promise.

Don't make me live without you anymore, mo chuisle.

Tomorrow, when I see you at the gala, I'll be expecting your answer.

I hope you want me, need me, love me, as much as I do you.
Forever yours,
Princepin

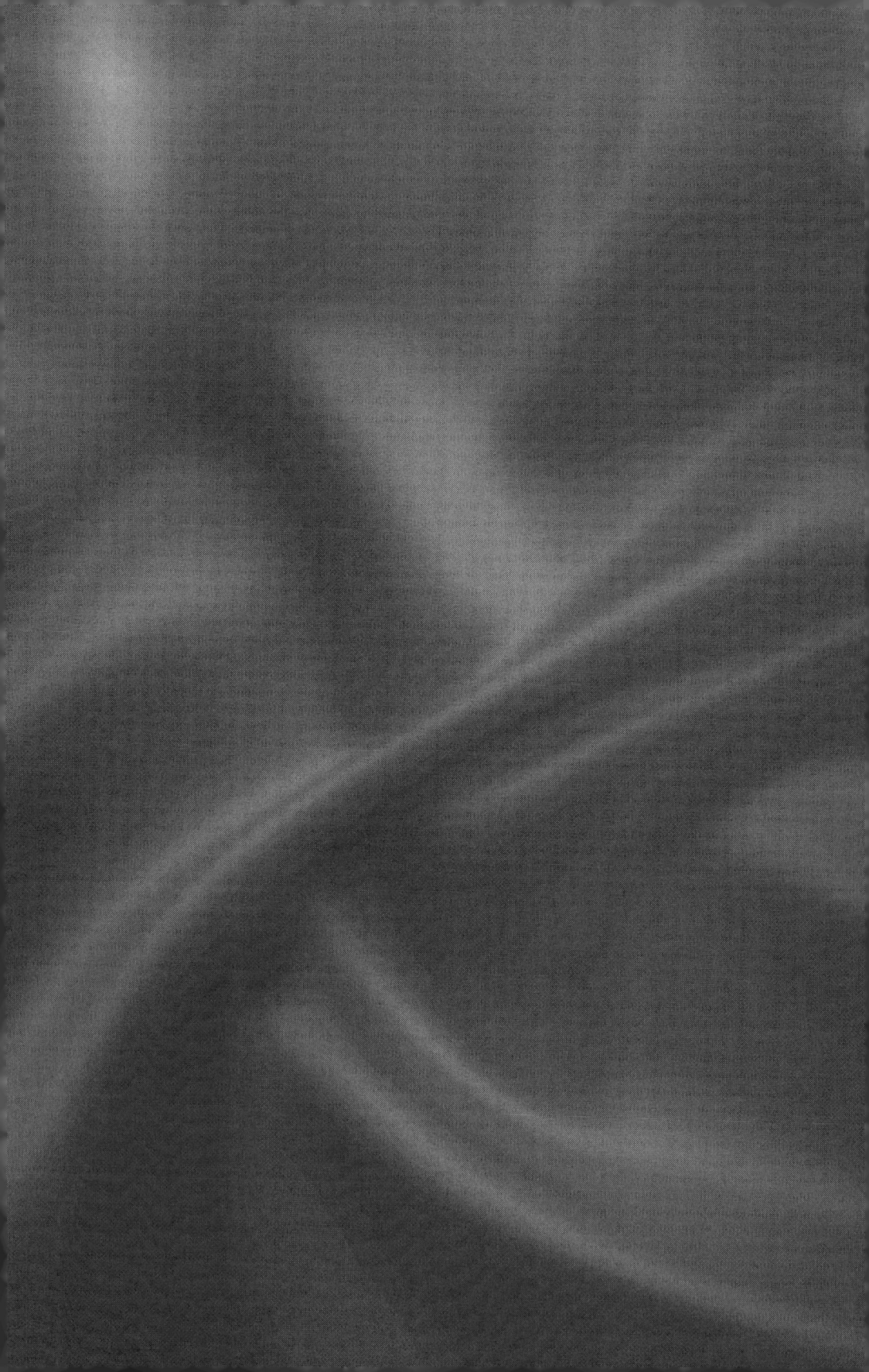

CHAPTER 28

Revenge à la Remington

The Present

"Are you going back to j-jail?"

I paused in the middle of brushing Olivia's hair, glancing at her expression in the mirror of her baby pink vanity. It was crumpled and sad, her shoulders drooping.

"No, Livvy. I'm not going back to jail."

"Good." Her chin wobbled, but she gave me a smile. "I was s-scared, Cadie."

Olivia was an eavesdropper, tiny and able to hide in places where the adults couldn't find her. This morning, she hid under Uncle Vance's office desk and overheard him and Aunt Julia discussing my predicament. Apparently, kids gossiped because somehow Olivia knew jail was a bad place. She burst into tears and begged them to save me. They had to reassure her that I was back and safely sleeping in my room to get her to stop crying.

"I didn't mean to worry you." I pressed a kiss to her temple. "I'm sorry."

"I forgives you."

I smiled. "*Forgive*. And thank you. I'll make it up to you. Next week we'll watch a movie and I'll take you to your favourite ice cream parlour. Deal?"

"And Joshy, too?"

337

"Yes. Joshy, too."

She gave me a toothy grin in the mirror. "Deal."

In general, Olivia wasn't much of a talker, unless she was conversing with me. Her lack of speech raised Uncle Vance's and Aunt Julia's concerns, and led them to consult a child psychologist three years ago. They thought Olivia had trauma from having her status quo shifted. But her behaviour was deemed normal. She was just shy by nature.

There was also the fact that Olivia saw me as her guardian. I wasn't just her cousin or adoptive brother. In her eyes, I was her mother and father figure as well. As long as I was there, her surroundings didn't matter. Despite being mostly dependent on me, Olivia adjusted a lot better than I expected since the adoption. She'd come to accept Aunt Julia, Uncle Vance, and Josh as her family too. They spoiled and treated her like their own.

Every day I was grateful for them.

Sometimes, I felt like it was my parents who orchestrated the entire thing from above, ensuring that Olivia and I found a home that cherished us.

Finishing braiding Olivia's hair, I tied a little bow at the tail. "All done, Livvy."

"Thank you." She turned around in her chair to give me a hug. This morning must have really spooked her—the possibility of losing me—and I understood why she needed to hold on longer than usual.

I hugged her back and gently patted her back. "You're welcome. Did I do a good job?"

"The best!"

Every evening, my little sister demanded I do her hair. It was a daily ritual whenever I wasn't occupied with urgent work. I knew Olivia wouldn't be a kid forever and one day she may not need me—which was a scary thought—so I was making the best out of these moments.

When we pulled away, she mumbled, "I miss Ella."

I sighed. "I miss Ella, too, kiddo."

"Is she coming back?"

Early this afternoon, I drove to her place and dropped off some gifts. I poured all my love into a letter and hoped it was enough to get through to her.

Because I didn't think I could survive any longer without Ella.

"Yes." I smiled at Olivia. "She'll be back soon."

Late into the evening, I strolled down the hallway to Uncle Vance's office. There was an overdue conversation I needed to have with him. It wouldn't be easy, but he deserved to hear the truth.

I knocked twice on the closed door.

"Come in," he replied.

Entering his office always felt like walking into the lion's den. The mood was dark and always felt a little predatory. He continuously remained on the edge of squandering any enemy who threatened his reign.

His mancave was adorned with black walls housing numerous paintings, a skylight ceiling, a mahogany bureau with pictures of our family and, behind his vintage throne, an entire wall encasing his coveted knives collection.

As South Side's kingpin, Vance Remington was known for having quite the notorious reputation. You didn't want to cross him. My uncle made killing look like a sport and was still ruthless at forty-five years old, the way he'd been two decades ago when he took over the family business.

Currently, he sat on his throne like a heedful monarch, playing with a switchblade between his scarred fingers, his Oxford-clad feet crossed and resting at the edge of his desk.

Uncle Vance's sharp eyes watched me close his office door. "What can I help you with, son?"

I took a seat in one of the leather chairs before his desk. "I need to talk to you. Is this a bad time?"

Sensing the severity in my tone, he straightened his posture and smoothed a hand over his three-piece black suit. It was wrinkled after a long day, his tie discarded somewhere, and the top three buttons of his dress shirt open, showcasing the small pendant he wore around his neck. It was a gold square with all our initials engraved. "No, I just finished some paperwork for the new art gallery. I'll need you and Josh to go over there next week and help with the incoming shipment."

"Sounds good." The incoming shipment would no doubt contain a few priceless paintings with pounds of cocaine strategically hidden within the packaging.

"Oh, before I forget." He yanked open a drawer and threw the De la Croix gun in my direction. "They confiscated it, but Officer Tate gave it back."

"Tate's really out here doing the Lord's work, eh? Sorry, I meant the Devil's."

Uncle Vance let loose a tired chuckle and the blade between his fingers did an impressive flip. "You can say that again."

"Is everything okay?" I asked. "After you came to pick me up, I saw you exchanging heated words with some of the cops."

"Everything is fine." He cracked his knuckles. "Though I forgot to mention that I have a copy of your mugshot. I've framed it and now it's sitting on my mantel."

My head whipped towards the fireplace to our right and I barked out a short laugh. True enough, my mugshot sat like a proud trophy alongside other family photos. "No way. I can't believe you actually kept it."

"Of course I did." He smirked proudly. "I keep all my children's accomplishments."

My children. He never failed to remind us—Olivia and me—that we were his in every way that mattered. My throat tightened before I whispered, "I know I don't always say it, but you mean a lot to me, Uncle Vance. I want you to know that."

I loved him and Aunt Julia like my own parents. They would never replace my mom and dad, but in a way, they *were* like my mom and dad.

The hard-layer that usually lacquered his stony features gentled and he whispered back, "I know, Cade. And I want you to know that me and Julia will always be there for you. No matter what. Understood?"

I nodded.

He placed the blade on the desk and perched forward on his elbows, his fingers forming a makeshift bench beneath his chin. "If this is about Initiation Night, Julia and I aren't mad. Was it reckless? Yes. But you're

340

young and mistakes happen. I do not hold it against you. But swear to me that you'll be more vigilant moving forward."

"I will." Uncle Vance knew I was always careful. Yesterday was my first slip-up. "But I'm not here to talk about Initiation Night—"

"Wait." He raised his hand and appeared horrified for a second. "If this is regarding your romantic troubles, I will advise you to see Julia instead. She'll have a better game plan on wooing your ex-girlfriend."

My jaw slackened. *Did the entirety of the household know I was pinning after Ella?*

"Yes, you're quite obvious," he said dryly. "We all know about your late nights where you drive around the city, searching for—sorry, I meant stalking—Ella. You reek of obsession, son."

"I-I'm not stalking her," I stammered, a bit flustered.

Uncle Vance deadpanned, "Please, I wasn't born yesterday."

Okay, so maybe there were some times where I followed her closely, making sure she got home after a night out with her friends.

"You can't judge me." I threw him a pointed look as I reached for the tray on his desk containing a decanter and crystal tumblers. I hadn't drunk a drop of alcohol in over three months. But I felt safe enough in Uncle Vance's presence. I poured myself two fingers of whiskey and let go of one more demon. "Aunt Julia said you were unbearable before you both got married. Obsessed, possessive, and jealous."

In fact, he still was the same where Aunt Julia was concerned. It was a trait the Remington men owned. Alongside loving their significant others until the end of time.

"That is true. I do love my wife very much. Actually, I killed the man she was supposed to marry so I could have her."

I choked on my sip of whiskey with the casualness of his statement. "I—You know what? I won't even ask you to elaborate."

"Good, because I won't," he tsked. "Now the longer you keep me here, the less time I have with my wife. So tell me what business you'd like to discuss?"

I drained my whiskey like a shot. Then my eyes roamed to the fireplace again. Over the mantle, there was another picture frame housing a photo of Uncle Vance and my mom. Vera Remington looked happy, healthy, and vibrant. The smile and gown she wore was a reflection of her upper-class upbringing. She'd been the depiction of a real-life Canadian princess.

Seeing her smiling face, I heard Mom's timeless voice from my memories. The same encouraging lilt when she taught me to be brave, to speak my mind, to do right by me and others. She was always there like a shadow, supporting me even when I didn't believe in myself. *"You can do anything you want if you just put your heart and mind to it, lovebug"* she'd say.

Finally finding the courage I needed, I addressed my uncle, "I know these last few months I've been…different. Everyone noticed it. You, Aunt Julia, and Josh all tried to ask me on multiple occasions if I was okay. I said yes, but I was lying."

"I assumed it had to do with your breakup. We didn't want to push you too hard. I figured you'd talk to us when you were ready."

"You're not wrong. The breakup was a part of it, but losing Ella isn't the only thing that changed me."

His eyes narrowed, tension coiling deep in his muscles. "Go on."

I swallowed thickly. "The night of Josh's birthday party, when you and Aunt Julia were away for the weekend, I…I was drugged and physically assaulted by four guys."

The climate in the room turned stormy, borderline suffocating with the bitterness of my truth. The flames in the fireplace crackled loudly, the blade sitting on the desk fell to the floor, and Uncle Vance's breathing turned uneven.

"What did you say?" he asked low, clipped.

"You heard me right."

The last time I saw Uncle Vance's expression this dark and volatile was when he came to see me at the hospital, after Julius's attack. It was my first encounter with such stark anger—and one that wasn't directed at me but *for* me.

"Tell me everything," he bit out with a growl. "Every. Fucking. Thing. Down to the last detail."

I avoided his gaze while telling him the entire situation from beginning to end. Waiting for Ella at the party, getting accosted by one masked man who roofied my drink, going to my room under the impression of meeting Ella...When I got to the part where Darla and my crew saved me before the four masked men could drag me away, Uncle Vance looked seconds from exploding.

"Soon enough, Dr. Smith arrived and handled the situation discreetly, away from the prying eyes of those attending the party. Thankfully, I had already vomited most of the drug. After my treatment, he instructed me to rest as much as possible. The next day, Josh and I went through the security footage. None of the four individuals could be identified," I concluded. "The only people who know about this situation are my friends and Josh, who swore that he wouldn't tell you or Aunt Julia until I was ready to talk."

The silence after my words was packed with tension.

"My first question to you," Uncle Vance finally started in a menacing tone, piercing me with his blue eyes that were identical to mine. "Is why the fuck did you not tell me this before?"

My head hung in shame. "I was embarrassed at what happened to me. It was perhaps the most humiliating moment of my life. I didn't want you to know unless it was necessary."

And with what happened at Initiation Night, I knew the elephant in the room couldn't be ignored any longer.

I expected Uncle Vance to yell at me.

Instead, something close to sorrow blanketed his features.

"Don't," I pleaded. "I don't want your pity."

Uncle Vance shook his head. He stood up and came to sit in the chair next to mine. I hated the way he was looking at me—like I was that same broken teenage boy confined to a hospital bed. Even though I wasn't anymore.

For three years, I morphed myself into the version I was today. A loyal soldier. A powerful fighter. An heir fitting of ruling his kingdom in the underworld.

I was tougher, stronger, and more resilient than ever.

I felt untouchable and invincible for so long, reigning alongside my family in the South Side, that being outnumbered and defenseless stripped away a part of my armour—my identity—as the fixer.

What happened the night of the party emasculated me.

Uncle Vance squeezed my shoulder. "Cade, there's nothing to be embarrassed about. What happened to you was not your fault. You were a victim."

"That's what I hate," I choked out. "I've never been a victim. Not since..."

Not since I lost the fight against Julius. It was the last time I succumbed to another's will. It was a shitty feeling and I wasn't fond of relieving anything remotely similar.

"I don't have many regrets, Cade, but I do regret not taking you in the moment Vera and Ronan passed away," he said gravely. I'd always suspected that was the case, but hearing it aloud fortified it. "Your mom wanted you to have a normal life. Julia and I thought it was best to honour her wish. We figured you'd be safe living with Julius, away from our violent world. But had we known the sick fuck would do what he did, I'd have never allowed you or Olivia to live with him. Not for a single second."

"I know, and I understand your reasoning. I don't fault you for it." I cleared my throat. "Thank you for listening to me."

"Thank you for feeling brave enough to tell me. Though I wish you'd come to me sooner so I could've helped you." He cupped the side of my head in a fatherly gesture before tugging me into his arms. I hesitantly rested my forehead against his shoulder. We weren't huggers, therefore it felt awkward at first. But with every passing second, I relaxed, finding comfort in his strength. The last person I hugged like this was my own dad. "Do you know what I see when I look at you?"

I smiled. "A failure?"

He kissed my head and his arms trembled slightly, like the emotions in his frame were too much to contain. "I see my younger self. A little arrogant, a little cocky, a little guarded, but loyal to a fault. The world has a hard time understanding individuals like us. You're soft with the right people, tough with the rest, and do not take anyone's shit. You act like nothing fazes you, but that's the furthest thing from the truth, isn't it? When you allow yourself to feel and self-reflect, every flaw and wound hurts too much. So you hide it until it doesn't hurt. One thing I've learned as I've grown older? It's okay to seek help and depend on your loved ones. It doesn't make you weak or pathetic. There's no judgement here, Cade. Even the strongest people can crumble. It's not about how many times you break down. It's about how you build yourself back up from those broken pieces."

He was right. It's better I learned this lesson now rather than later. If I allowed myself the grace to acknowledge my pain, I'd be able to power through and rebuild myself stronger than before.

"I appreciate it, Uncle Vance. I needed to hear that."

"Promise you'll come to me in the future when you have problems. I swore to protect you and Olivia from the minute I brought you both into my home. I need to know what's going on in order to keep you safe. You're my son, too." His Adam's apple rifled up and down with a rough swallow. "I know you haven't always had it easy, but you have people who love you—people you can depend on. You don't need to hide your pain anymore. Let Julia and I be there for you. It's what Vera and Ronan would have wanted, too."

"I promise," I said hoarsely. "I will."

"Good." He stood up and adjusted his diamond cufflinks. "Now let me talk to Josh and run through this security footage. I also want to question every guard who was on duty that night and figure out what the fuck they were up to when this whole thing transpired."

"All three guards who were supposed to be at the gates were found with syringes in their necks," I said. "They were made indisposed at the right time."

"Fuck," Vance muttered. "Regardless, we're going to find the men who did this to you and make them pay."

I stood up, too. "I have a request."

Uncle Vance poured himself some whiskey, arching a brow. "What?"

"When we figure out who they are, let me handle the situation myself. I want to deliver the killing blow."

"Of course you do, my little fixer." He grinned wolfishly and sipped his whiskey. "But you won't deprive Josh and me of our fun. We'll participate in the carnage. And if I'm in the mood, I might display their blood splatters on a canvas at our next art exhibition."

I laughed. Goddamn. This man really was nuts. "Sounds good to me."

"Get some rest, kiddo. You've had an exhausting day."

I turned to leave but paused for a moment. The thought of carnage and blood splatters reminded me of something. "What ever happened to Julius? I heard he died in jail, but the details were unclear."

"Oh, I killed him."

Well, fuck. My eyes widened. I had my suspicions. But I was still shocked. "Why?"

Uncle Vance picked up his knife again, tossing the blade between his fingers. "Simple. He put his hands on you, so I put my hands on him. As a final lesson."

"And what lesson is that?"

He fixed me with a levelled gaze. "Don't ever touch my family."

The most important lesson any enemy of ours should know.

"Thank you again for everything you've done for me. It means a lot...Dad."

The smile that broke over his face was almost blinding. Josh and Olivia called him dad. Uncle Vance had probably, secretly, wanted me to call him that too, even though we knew the title belonged to another. But he was like a dad to me and deserved to hear it. I was lucky to have been blessed in this life with two remarkable father figures.

"You're welcome, Cade," he said warmly, watching me walk to his door. "Where are you going?"

"To find Aunt Julia so I can 'woo my ex-girlfriend'."

His throaty laughter was the last thing I heard on my way out.

As I ascended the grand staircase, my phone—which I retrieved from the Hills this morning—buzzed with a text. I unlocked it and stared at my wallpaper for a few seconds, soaking in Ella's face. It was a picture I took a year ago when we finished racing one summer night. She sat astride her motorcycle, helmet tucked under her arm, head thrown back in laughter over something I said. She'd looked so pretty, wild, and reckless. I'd needed to immortalize the moment forever.

Fuck, I adored this girl so much.

I opened my recent text from Josh.

I did some digging today and found the girl's name. — Josh

What girl? —Cade

You know, the one that was in the room with you… —Josh

Ah. That girl. I was nervous to speak to her, but filled with anticipation at the thought of potentially getting some real answers.

Continuing my ascent, I texted him back.

What's her name? —Cade

Mabel Garcia. She's a year younger than us. Senior in high school. I already contacted her. She's willing to meet with you tomorrow to talk. —Josh

CHAPTER 29

Twin Flames

Ella

The Present

The Hill residence was an imposing beauty with a Greek Revival architecture, flanked by tall pillars, weeping willows, limestone fountain, and white and red roses across the courtyard.

My stomach flipped when I pulled into the driveway. I hadn't been here in months, and I didn't expect to be hit with such a strong wave of nostalgia. This place was like a second home for me. I grew up here with Darla and her sister Dacia, who was two years older than us.

I remembered playing with Barbie dolls as little girls on a picnic blanket, while Alberto—their butler and the closest thing to a father figure for the Hills—waited on us with iced tea. I remembered driving the staff wild with worry as we spent the day playing hide-and-seek, holed up in the kitchen cupboard with fluffernutter sandwiches and giggling amongst ourselves because nobody could find us. I remembered practicing cheerleading routines in the backyard when Darla and I first joined the team in high school. I recalled so many memories with fondness—the smiles, the laughter, the tears—and I couldn't believe I let it all go without a fight.

I should have come here long before now.

And I should have tried harder to communicate with Darla to figure out what went wrong between us.

As I jogged to the front doors, a pair of crows cawed. Either a bad omen or a sigh of good luck. Regardless, I wasn't leaving Hill residence without my cell phone and some form of closure.

I didn't even have the chance to ring their bell when the doors opened and a curious Alberto regarded me. "Miss Cordova?"

"Hi, Berto! Long time no see. How are you?"

"I'm fine." He smoothed his white-gloved hand over his greying hair. "And yourself?"

"Great." I smiled sheepishly. "I'm here to see Darla."

"Is Miss Hill expecting you?"

A little white lie never hurt anybody, right? "Yeah, she is. We're supposed to hang out tonight and watch a movie."

His features perked up with joy. "I'm very glad to hear it. I've not seen you here for quite some time and was worried you were no longer friends."

My smile wavered. "We…We've just been busy with our respective lives. You know how it is, Berto."

Seeming to sympathize with our situation, Alberto let me inside and I kissed his cheek in gratitude before climbing the grand staircase two steps at a time. Eager to see Darla and adamant on avoiding Principal Hill.

When I reached Darla's room, her door was shut.

I gingerly knocked three times.

A faint, "Who is it?" came from the other side.

"It's Ella."

Silence echoed for six seconds before I heard footsteps. The door swung open to reveal a stunned Darla. "Ella?"

I tried to remain calm and steady. "Hey."

She assessed me the way you would a serial killer on trial. "What are you doing here?

The sharp tone, so unlike her, caused me to flinch. I steeled myself quickly. "I just want to talk. Please, *darling*."

When I was seven, I learned that Darla was named after the affectionate term. I found it so adorable that I spent the better part of second grade refusing to call her anything but 'darling.' The same kids who occasionally bullied me for my sectoral heterochromia were the same ones who teased her for loving bright colours and making eclectic fashion choices. I called her darling incessantly because I wanted my best friend to know she was dearly beloved. And that it was okay to be different. It's what made us unique and special.

Plus, I'd threaten to beat those kids with tree branches and push them off slides if they ever dared to bully her in my presence.

The term of endearment softened Darla. She hesitated for a split second before allowing me entry. "Fine. Come in."

Her room was as I last remembered it. Crème and gold accents, floor-to-ceiling bookshelves, canopy bed sitting on a dais, and a work desk fitting for a queen. A laptop was opened on a page of her manuscript.

Darla had been writing romance novels secretly for a few years now. I had the honour of reading her first drafts and she was extremely talented. Fear of the unknown and Principal Hill's reaction—who was very harsh and strict with her daughters—held her back from publishing. I wished she'd take the leap. Last time we spoke, I was encouraging her to do so.

"What are you currently working on?"

She ignored me and retrieved my phone. "Here. That's what you came for, right?"

"Thanks." I grabbed my phone and watched Darla shift awkwardly on her feet, pushing her glasses up the bridge of her nose. She was in silk jammies and her hair was tied in a ponytail. "When did you get glasses?"

She gave me a bewildered look. Fair enough. I was asking her about her optical accessories when I should be asking her a million other questions. "Over the summer. I usually wear contacts, but since I'm home…"

"Ah." I pocketed my phone. "Well, they suit you."

Darla's shoulders sagged with a drawn-out sigh. "Why are you here, Ella?"

I needed to sit down if we were going to have this conversation. I parked my ass on her bed and said, "As you may already know, I was in jail this weekend."

"Yeah." She folded her arms across her chest. "I heard from my mother. Are you…okay?"

Darla acted indifferent with me these past few months, yet whenever I was in distress—like Josh's party and now—her caring side shone through. I knew my ex-best friend like the back of my hand. She may walk around with a tough exterior, but she was a softie on the inside. Moreso where I was concerned.

I hoped, with every fiber of my being, that our time in each other's lives wasn't over.

"I'm fine, but I've had one helluva twenty-four hours." I rubbed my forehead. "I think I'm still wrapping my head around everything that happened on Initiation Night."

"I tried contacting Shaun, but he hasn't answered yet. He was supposed to return me the keys to the school this morning."

"Um, about that." I cleared my throat. "Shaun is currently indisposed."

She blinked. "Pardon me?"

I winced. "I might have smacked his head with a baseball bat."

"Ella!" She screeched, momentarily forgetting that we weren't on speaking terms and sounding so much like her old self. "What. Are. You. Talking. About?"

"I swear I didn't mean to, okay?" I wailed.

A case of word-vomit possessed me and I proceeded to recount everything that happened, from Shaun chasing us in the hallway, to us terrified and hiding in the confessional booth, to me whacking him across the head accidentally. And how the only thing that woke Shaun up was the thought of Hera potentially marrying somebody else.

Darla expelled a huge breath and took a seat next to me. "This is a mess. I thought for sure he'd get you both out sans getting caught."

"On the bright side, Shaun is alive. Before I came here, I stopped by the hospital to check on him. He's going home soon. Although I'm probably going to be sending him a fruit basket as an apology every month until the day I die." Then I added as a joke, "The only silver lining in this situation is that I look really cute in my mugshot. Oh, and technically, I won Initiation Night twice and created history."

"Well, I'm glad everyone is all right." Darla smiled. "And that you won Initiation Night."

Seeing her smile at me after months was a rare sight. It incited my own. We watched each other quietly, before I decided to say, "There's something I need to tell you."

She frowned at my somber tone. "What is it?"

"Shaun mentioned that you think an Initiator is responsible for calling the cops."

"Yes, and once we find out who did it—"

"I know who did it," I rushed out. "Or at least I think I do."

Darla arched her brow. "Who?"

I didn't hesitate. "Callie."

Darla reared back like she'd been slapped. "*What?*"

"When we got arrested, I saw her and a masked guy standing by St. Victoria's woods, watching us get taken away."

"That doesn't make sense." Darla stood up and started pacing. "I know Callie is a bitch, but I don't get why—" My ex-best friend stopped herself short. "Never mind."

'Callie is a bitch.'

Well, that was a hot take.

I stood up too. "Darla, I have tried to figure out, over the last few months, why you'd remove us—*me*, in particular—from your life without a reason. I've gone over every single one of our exchanges and I don't understand if I hurt you or—"

"Cut the act, Ella." She scoffed. "You know why I stopped talking to you both. I've seen your conversations with Callie."

Huh? What was she talking about? "I'm sorry, but I'm not following. What conversations?"

Darla braced her hands on her hips, practically shooting me daggers with her eyes.

"Darla," I hedged calmly when she remained silent, apprehension swirling in my gut. "What conversations are you talking about?"

She inched a disgusted expression my way. "The ones where you're insulting me and talking shit about my family."

I felt like I was going to collapse.

What was she talking about? Why would I insult her or her family?

I loved the Hill women—and Alberto—like my own. "I have never, in my life, spoken a bad word about your family, Darla. *Never.*"

My vehement tone jolted Darla. She recovered quickly and scowled. "I have proof. Don't even bother denying it."

"Show me," I challenged. "Show me this so-called proof you have."

Usually classy and collected, Darla looked like a bomb about to detonate as she pulled out her phone, unlocked it, opened her gallery app, and thrust her device against my face with an angry huff. "There you go."

I grabbed her phone, glaring at the screenshot. It was a private conversation on social media between Callie and me.

Reading through the contents, I blanched.

It was horrifying and extremely disturbing.

I scrolled through all the screenshots and read one lie after another, feeling my blood boil, my heart rate skyrocket, and my need to break something grow increasingly stronger with every second.

In the conversations, it was made to look like I was calling Darla a pathetic bitch for being afraid of her mother, calling Principal Hill a cunt for giving us detention after we pranked the boys on the hockey team, and the worst of them all? I was made to look like I hated Dacia for being bi and calling her all sorts of derogatory terms I'd never heard in my life. And Callie was seen 'agreeing' to all these messages. But fuck, none of this was actually me. I'd rather cut off my own fingers than to hurt—*insult*—anyone like this. The Dacia one slashed the deepest. She was like the older sister I never had and I adored her with my whole heart. She didn't deserve to be spoken about in such a horrible light.

"This is fake." Repulsed, I shot the phone back at Darla. "I swear on my *abuela's* grave that I would never fucking say anything like this. Not about your family or anyone else's, Darla. That isn't me."

My ex-best friend bristled. "Then how do you explain this?"

With jerky fingers, I unlocked my phone, which thankfully still had some juice, and went into my conversation with Callie. I scrolled up to the same time stamps as those screenshots and turned my phone towards Darla. "Look at this. Read through my *real* conversation with Callie. It's just memes and the occasional text about where to meet up for our hangouts."

To be honest, I wasn't a big texter. I preferred to call. Typing up long messages—let alone the kind Darla showed me—wasn't my style. Nor was shitting on my childhood best friend and her family.

The colour leeched from Darla's face as she read through our conversation. The truth was right there. "Are you…Are you trying to tell me these texts are fabricated?"

It was the only logical answer because I sure as hell hadn't written them. "Darla, you have to believe me. I would never say those horrendous things. You know me. You've known me my whole life. I'd never utter such despicable words about you or your loved ones."

"But…you think Callie would?"

Nodding, I stared at the floor. "Unfortunately, I'm beginning to realize that Callie may not be the person I thought she was."

Considering she hasn't even left a single call or text on my phone asking me if I'm okay after Initiation Night.

Now I was certain that Callie had a hand in this whole fake screenshots situation. On top of her and the masked guy being involved with our arrest.

The *why* still remained to be discovered.

Darla gazed at me like she finally saw through the lies. "The evidence was there, Ella. How was I supposed to think otherwise?"

"I know, Darla, and I don't blame you. I just wish you had more faith in me. You should have talked to me the minute you received these. I could have shown you the truth then. Fuck, I too should have tried harder to talk to you. All I know is we shouldn't have wasted months being angry at one another. That's not you and me. We're supposed to be stronger than this."

Her hardened shell slowly broke, my words having the desired effect. "Before receiving these screenshots, Callie spent weeks rudely throwing it in my face how close you two had gotten—more than you and me. I'm ashamed to say all those comments got to my head. I wished it didn't bother me, but I felt sad and angry whenever I saw you both laughing together because it felt like an inside joke that I wasn't in on. It also made me feel like a third wheel. Like dead weight, Ella, that you were unable to shed since you felt some type of loyalty to me given our past. And after I received these screenshots, it was the final nail in the coffin. I was appalled by you and Callie. That's why I distanced myself without a confrontation. I didn't want to waste my energy on people like you. It wasn't worth it. I believed karma would do its thing, and you'd get what you deserved for being horrible friends to me."

Before Callie, there was Darla. I'd known her since we were toddlers. No one meant more to me than her. Callie knew it, too. Now I knew that everything she said was to drive a wedge between me and Darla.

She must have been jealous of us.

Darla and I had the kind of bond that was akin to sisterhood. She was my twin flame. Everybody knew it. No matter our differences, our friendship had always been tight. We were always seen together, talking and laughing, walking down the halls of St. Victoria in our matching cheer outfits and pompoms.

Nothing could break us apart. Or so we'd thought.

Nevertheless, Darla and I wouldn't let this destroy us anymore. We'd come back stronger than ever. I knew it.

"I'm sorry, Darla. I'm so goddamn sorry." I closed the distance and hugged her with all the strength I possessed, needing her to know that without her a part of me was lost. "You're not a third wheel. You're not dead weight. And there's no inside joke. Callie was wrong. You and I have always been the closest. She knows this, too. You're my best friend, you're my sister, you're my co-captain. No one could ever replace you. Your presence in my life is priceless. I'd never want to hurt you. You mean too much to me. I love you and I'm so fucking sorry again that this happened to us." My voice was ragged with emotions. "I've missed you so much. I've had one of the worst summers and all I wanted was to pick up the phone and call you. To come over and see you. To just have you by my side. And I'm so saddened that we lost this much time."

Halfway through my admission, Darla wrapped her arms around me just as tight. A teardrop touched my collarbone. "I missed you and I love you, too." Her voice was watery. "This has been the worst summer of my life as well. All I wanted was you by my side, but I was so hurt and furious. I should have confronted you so we could have resolved this earlier. I believe everything you said, Ella, and I'm not mad anymore."

We hugged each other, breathing in this newfound truce, and pulled away only when a knock at Darla's door alerted us of a new presence.

Dacia Hill leaned against the doorframe, watching the scene with a cool smile. Long blond hair. Blue eyes. Periwinkle minidress. Looking every bit the ice princess she was renowned for being. "Well, if it isn't my favourite duo reunited once more."

"Have you been eavesdropping this whole time?" Darla asked accusingly.

"Mhm." Dacia sauntered in and took a seat on Darla's bed, crossing her legs. "Berto let me know Ella was here, so we listened to the entire conversation with our ears pressed against the door. We wanted to know the juicy details on why you stopped being friends and hear your mend your friendship once and for all."

Alberto, bless his soul, had the bad habit of eavesdropping on everyone's conversations. He was here for one thing only: the tea. I wasn't surprised he dragged Dacia with him. "Where's Berto now?"

"In the kitchen, helping the staff prepare dinner for us." Dacia clasped her hands together and rested them on her knee. "Now tell Ella who sent you the screenshots, Dar."

Darla cleared her throat. "They were sent to me by the Secrets of St. Victoria account a few days after prom."

Secrets of St. Victoria was a social media account run by an anonymous individual who shared dirty secrets of the institute's populace. It was known for stirring the pot and pitting people against one another. Till this day, no one was able to figure out who was behind the account.

"And you think Callie is involved in all of this, right?" Dacia asked me.

I brought a fist to my mouth, debating how much I should let these two know. "Okay, so here's the thing. Cade and I did something bad over the summer." For their own safety, I wasn't going to tell them about Kian Wilson. "A few days after that, Cade was drugged and assaulted the night of Josh's party by four guys wearing Guy Fawkes masks. Obviously, Darla, you know this last bit, because you helped save him, which I cannot thank you for enough. Then on Initiation Night, a guy wearing a Guy Fawkes mask attacked me in Balthazar Building."

They gasped, spitting curses.

Then I gave them a rundown of my entire Initiation Night, talking about our dares, what happened between Cade and me, and how we ended up in the confessional before getting arrested. By the time I finished, both sisters gaped at me.

"With all that being said, you can probably understand why we came to the conclusion that both of those attacks are linked." I shrugged. "And somehow, Callie has a hand in all of this."

They were still silent. I knew it was a lot to take in.

"I'm sorry, Ella, you did *what* in the nurse's office?" Darla finally spoke, covering her mouth in a scandalized fashion. "In the middle of a competition?"

"First of all, it was towards the *end* of the competition when I was convinced we'd lost anyway." I blushed under their scrutiny. "Second of all, I was overcome by passion after hearing how much Cade still loves me, okay? The setting didn't matter!"

"Personally, I'm still stuck on the fact that you've already fucked in the confessional booth." Dacia looked impressed. "Damn, that's... blasphemous."

My entire face probably resembled a tomato. "Can we move on from my sex life and talk about the real situation at hand?"

"That you're into sixty-nining without locking the door?" Darla side-eyed me before her and Dacia cackled, ribbing me good-naturedly.

"I hate you both, truly." I ran a hand over my face. "I can't believe I've missed you two menaces."

Their laughter soon faded and Dacia shook her head with a smile. "No, you love us. Just as we love you. And for what it's worth? We've missed you continuously over the summer."

I joined them both on Darla's bed. "I saw online that you spent some of August in Europe."

Dacia nodded, playing with her blond strands and casting Darla a meaningful look. "Yeah, we decided it would be good to get away from Montardor for a bit."

Darla bit her bottom lip. "I have to tell you something, Ella."

"What is it?"

She touched the pulse at her wrist with her thumb, taking a deep breath. "I hadn't been feeling well for the last few weeks of senior year and I got diagnosed with a small benign tumour shortly after graduation. I ended up getting surgery for it and it was relatively quick and successful. After that, Mother suggested we take a vacation before university starts to reground myself. Get a change of scenery. All that jazz."

My throat was tight. I wanted to cry. "Darla, are you serious?"

"Yes." She smiled sadly. "The doctor said it could have been caused by stress and inflammation. Anyways, I was lucky it was small and non-life threatening."

I hated the way she was downplaying this. I hugged her again, kissing her temple. "Darla, I don't know what to say except that I'm so sorry to hear you went through this. I wish I was there for you."

"It's okay." She patted my back. "You're here now and that's all that matters."

She was right. We were back. That's all that mattered.

"While we're being honest with each other, I want to tell you both something." I played with the strings of the friendship bracelet Darla gave me eleven years ago. "I was five weeks pregnant and miscarried the night of Josh's party."

More gasps and curses echoed in our little circle. Suddenly, I was enveloped by both sisters. They hugged me as I recounted my miscarriage and how I recovered slowly, one day at a time, after that night.

Darla's voice trembled as she pressed a kiss to my head. "I'm so sorry, Ella. This is heartbreaking. I know how badly you've wanted to be a mom."

It would happen one day when the time was right. I wasn't worried.

But hearing these words of comfort after spending the entire summer dealing with this on my own filled me with warmth and healing. For the first time in weeks, I felt good on the inside. Like everything would finally work itself out.

Dacia wasn't one for emotions, but she did caress my shoulder in an affectionate gesture to show her support.

"Thank you for hearing me out," I said. "And thank you to Berto for letting me through the doors."

We shared a short chuckle.

Growing up, I never felt the lack of sisters because I had these two. I was a firm believer in counting my blessings. The Hill women were probably one of the best gifts the universe had given me.

I was grateful that we got this second chance.

Before I left for Initiation Night, I begged the universe for a reprieve. This was it. Divine timing. It threw many obstacles my way but look at me now—a better version of myself than when this entire mess started.

"All right, that's enough emotional talk for today." Dacia stood up and stretched her arms. "It's Saturday night and we should do something fun to celebrate."

"What do you have in mind?" Darla asked, going over to her vanity to fix her appearance.

Dacia and I shared a knowing look.

There's only one thing we'd be doing tonight: gathering dirt on Callie.

Before setting her aflame.

"How about we pay a little visit to the Mackowski household?" I offered with a grin.

"You read my mind, Ella." The thing nobody knew about Dacia? Behind her ice princess front hid a ball-busting bitch.

"I'm texting Hera." Darla typed on her phone. "Whatever we're doing, she'll want in on the fun."

"Good." I stood up and adjusted my cropped leather jacket. Tonight, the back of it was adorned with justice scales, stitched carefully with a gold thread. "And I know just the person who can help us execute this plan."

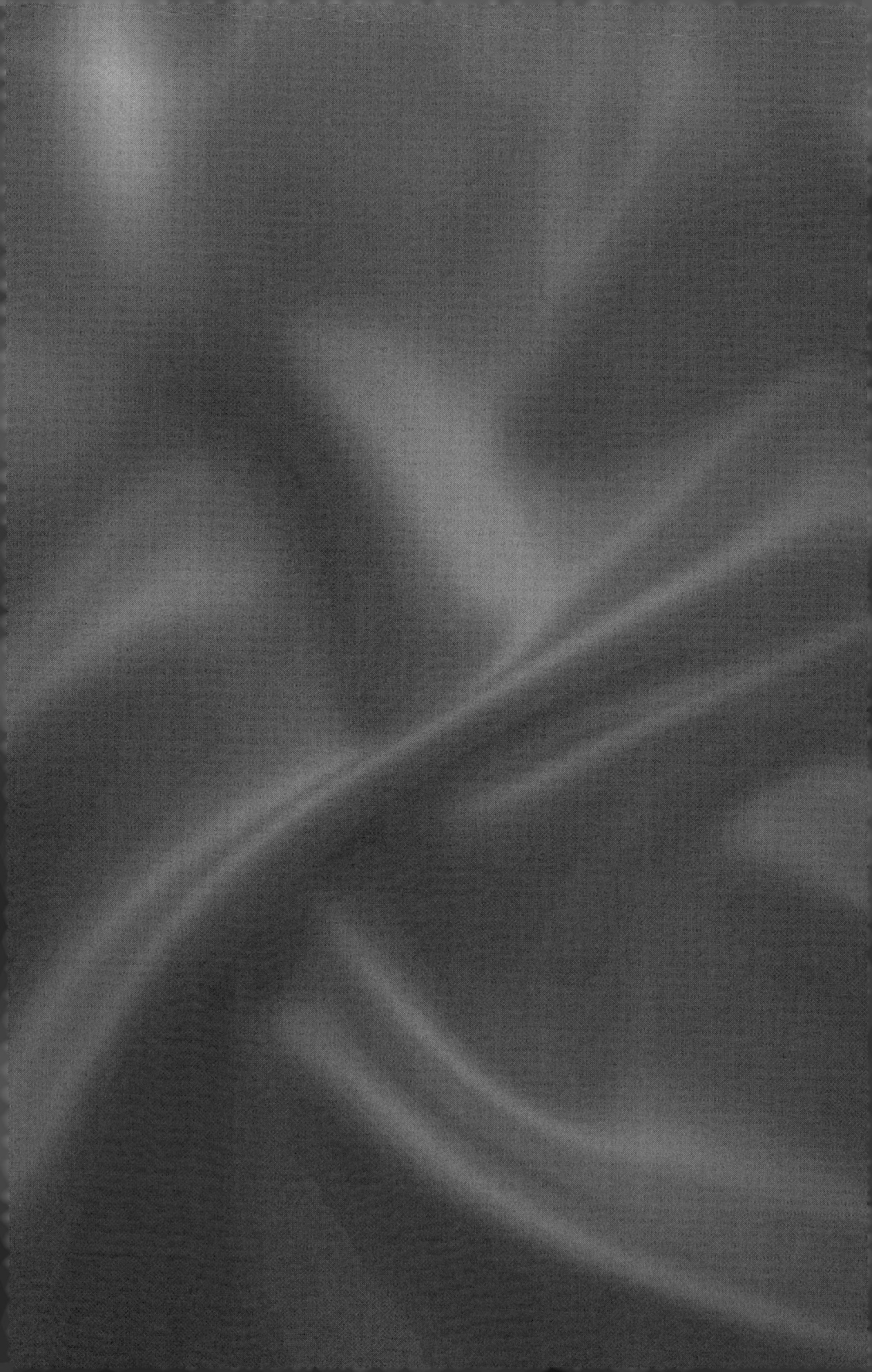

CHAPTER 30

Kidnapped Heir

Ella

The Present

"So why exactly am I being kidnapped?"

All four of us turned to glare at Josh, who was sitting in the backseat, sandwiched between Hera and Darla, twiddling his thumbs and appearing confused.

"You're not being kidnapped," I said testily from the passenger seat. Dacia was driving the getaway vehicle tonight, a black fully tinted jeep that was inconspicuous. "We're just *borrowing* you. For an indefinite amount of time."

Once we'd finished dinner, Darla, Dacia, and I gunned it over to Hera's place. She ran out with a small duffel bag, looking slightly worried—because we drafted this plan within the hour—and slightly excited—because we hadn't been reunited in months. Nothing like detective work to bring the girl gang back together again.

We all made sure to dress up in black to fly under the radar.

After that, we picked up Josh. Well, 'picked up' was putting it nicely. I texted him to come outside, saying it was urgent. When he reached the gates, we basically shoved him into the car and drove off while he shrieked for help.

Now we headed over to the Mackowski household to break in, spy-movie style.

"Okay, and why am I being 'borrowed'?" He did air quotes on the last word.

Honesty was the best policy, right? "We need you to hack into someone's laptop and help us gather some intel."

Josh was a genius with computers. If there was one person who could help us solve this fake screenshots and Secrets of St. Victoria account mystery, it was him.

"Sure, but fair warning..." he drawled with a lopsided smile. "I'm kind of stoned."

The girls groaned in unison.

Shit, I knew something seemed off about him. I assumed he woke up from a nice nap and that's why his eyes were red. The last thing I expected was for him to be high. He wasn't a smoker at all.

"Great," Dacia said sarcastically, smacking the steering wheel with her palm. "This plan is going to tank."

"So, Plan B?" Darla prompted.

Hera's green eyes were wide with concern as she tied her dark hair up in a bun. "Um, do we even have a Plan B?"

No, we did not.

I turned around in my seat to inch Josh a frustrated look. "Since when do you smoke?"

"Since Layla is ignoring me over something stupid and I'm sad, okay?" he hissed. "And my dad produces grade-A Kush, so why shouldn't I be allowed to drown my sorrows in drugs?"

"For legal reasons, I'm going to pretend I didn't hear anything." Hera covered her ears.

"Me too." Darla chuckled.

Dacia shot him a glance through the rearview mirror. "Trouble in paradise, Joshy?"

Josh grumbled, crossing his arms over his chest. His big body looked comical stuffed between the smaller frames of Darla and Hera, who were practically smothered against the windows because his muscular build took up all the space. "Layla thinks I don't love her."

We all gasped jokingly. Josh not loving Layla? Impossible. This boy

364

was professing his undying love for her at every opportunity.

He nodded exaggeratedly, pointed at us. "See? See! Everybody knows I love her. So why doesn't she believe me?"

Layla and Josh were the definition of black cat and golden retriever. She shied away from emotions while he practically dove head-first into them. But Layla had to know he loved her. It was so glaringly obvious unless...

I narrowed my eyes. "Did you do something, Josh?"

Everyone swivelled their heads in his direction, almost accusingly. Except for Dacia, who pinned him with a frosty stare through the rearview mirror.

"I didn't do anything, I swear!" He threw his hands up in surrender. "But it's like she's got these fears...about us. She's afraid to become more than friends."

Layla definitely knew how Josh felt about her. And it was clear to everyone that she was equally smitten with him. However, Remington boys were intense and loved wholeheartedly. She probably just needed more time to make sense of how their relationship was progressing before taking the next step.

"How are you going to convince her to take a chance on you?" I asked.

Josh let out a long sigh. "I'm going to get her name tattooed so she knows we're a forever thing."

"Oh my God," Darla gushed. "That's so romantic."

"Yes!" Hera agreed, clapping her hands together. "Where will you get this tattoo?"

"Right here." Josh smacked his right pec over his shirt. "*Lay.*" And his left. "*La.*" Then he giggled. "You think I should get it, show up to her doorstep, and rip off my shirt in surprise?"

We burst out laughing. Josh was kidding. Sort of. And while Layla was used to his prankster self, she'd most likely be spooked out by that gesture.

"You're a nutjob." Dacia chuckled. "Don't do that. She'll go running for the hills. Pun intended."

"So no to ripping off my shirt?" he asked, still giggling at his own joke.

"Absolutely not." We shook our heads.

"But after we complete our mission, we'll help you brainstorm other sane ideas to prove your undying love," I amended.

"Deal."

Dacia floored the gas as we entered the highway. "By the way, what excuse did you give to your parents, Hera?"

"Um, I said I'm sleeping over at your place." She glanced around the car. "What excuse did you give to your mother?"

Darla winced. "We said we're sleeping over at Ella's."

"Ella, what excuse did you give to your parents?"

I grimaced. "I said I'm sleeping over at your place, Hera."

"And I didn't give my parents any excuse because I've been kidnapped!"

"You're not being kidnapped, Josh!" we yelled at him in unison.

He giggled again, high as fuck.

"Okay, so we're all sleeping over at each other's house." Darla was on the verge of panicking. "It's fine. It's okay. No one's going to find out what we're really doing, right?"

The car was silent, except for a Beyoncé song playing quietly in the background.

"Right?" Darla reiterated, louder.

"Totally." Dacia, Hera, and I said solemnly.

"Oh, I forgot to ask. Whose place are we breaking into?" Josh chimed in.

Darla started explaining the whole story to Josh. He listened attentively—as best as he could in this state—and actually looked offended on our behalf. "No fucking way. She's a snake! What are you going to do if you find proof that Callie is behind all of this?"

The question was mostly aimed at me.

A mean smirk curled my lips. "Show her that she messed with the wrong bitches."

Josh whooped. "That's my girls!"

The Mackowskis lived in a modest two-story home in a quiet, family-friendly neighbourhood. Dacia parked near the edge of the property, hiding the car along the tall trees. With a sole flashlight to guide us through the dark night, we slinked towards the side of the house, where Callie's room was located.

The plan was to climb to her window, get into her room, and grab the necessities before dashing out of there.

It was now past midnight, which meant Callie and her whole family would be asleep. Luckily, they were all deep sleepers. Unfortunately, they had a shitty home alarm system. Both aspects that would work in our favour. Moreover, Callie liked to sleep with her window cracked open. Breaking in was going to be easy peasy lemon squeezy.

It was the not getting caught part that would be difficult.

Glancing around the group conspiratorially, I whispered, "We'll need two people to reach her bedroom. Her window is already unlocked, therefore getting in shouldn't be hard. Her work desk is on the right-hand side and that's where she keeps her laptop and diary. Those are our targets. If there's anything else that looks useful, grab it too. We should be able to execute this within a few minutes."

"Sounds good." Darla drew on a pair of black gloves and squinted up at Callie's window. "Though, I'm not sure Dacia and I will be tall enough to reach her window. It seems pretty high."

Upon closer inspection, Darla was right. My ankle was still tender from Initiation Night and Hera wasn't a former cheerleader, ergo she wasn't familiar or comfortable with our stunts. Dacia could be the base and Darla a flyer, but we'd still need a bit more height to reach the window.

An idea struck me.

My head snapped in Josh's direction, who stared up at the sky, mouth agape, counting the stars.

Feeling our calculating gazes, he blinked. "What? Why are you all staring at me like that?"

"How did I get roped into this?" Josh moaned from underneath Darla and Dacia. He was currently on all fours while the sisters used his back as a stepping stone to climb up to Callie's window. "I'm too high for this shit."

Hera cried of laughter, muffling the noise with her palm. I too attempted to keep it together between silent fits of giggles, hoping we didn't get caught prematurely by the neighbours.

"I didn't volunteer to play horsey tonight." He glared at me. "Ella, come take my spot!"

"As the mastermind behind our operation, I'm currently busy ensuring everything runs smoothly."

"Hera, you come!"

"I'm sorry, Josh," she said, not sounding apologetic at all. "I would if I could."

Dacia's body trembled while she held Darla up by her feet. "Josh, stay still!" Dacia spat through gritted teeth. "You're shaking too much."

"Oh, God." He neighed. "I'm trying!"

"I'm almost in!" Darla whisper-shouted, adding encouragingly, "Hang on, Josh. Just a couple more seconds!"

"First, you kidnap me. Second, you abuse my back. Third, you expect me to break into this girl's laptop to find dirt, and none of you have offered to buy me food!"

"We'll go get food after," I said. "We promise!"

"Fuck your promises in the ass with no lube." He cursed, torn between anger and laughter. "I'm never helping you girls again."

Darla managed to enter through the window and Dacia hopped off Josh's back before giving him a hand. He got up with a grunt. "I can't believe I got dragged into this mess. I should have gone to the gym with Cade instead of letting you girls kidnap me."

"Oh, come on, Josh!" I whispered excitedly, nudging him. "This is so much more fun than watching sweaty boys beat each other up in the ring."

His deadpan expression melted away when his lips twitched and he chuckled. "Okay, fine. I am having fun."

"Atta boy."

Two minutes later, Darla texted the group chat to say she secured the goods. Her head peeked out of the window in signal. She threw out a pink diary first that Hera caught. Then she waved the laptop, still in its case. I got closer to the window. "Throw it!"

"Are you sure?" she mouthed.

"Positive," I whispered reassuringly. "I got this."

Darla threw it down gently and I caught it.

Then Josh got into position and caught Darla when she jumped out the window.

Once her feet hit the ground, Darla's brown eyes were bright with glee. "Oh my God. We actually did it!"

Barely able to contain our squeals and giddiness, we ran for the car.

After picking up takeout from our favourite Mexican restaurant—an abundance of fajitas, tacos, churros, and frescas con crema—we drove back to the Remington estate.

Josh's room was dark, messy, and spacious with his impressive computer setup tucked in the corner. He devoured four tacos in two inhales while powering on Callie's laptop. At least now he was less high. Enough to be able to dig through her stuff.

The girls sat on the floor, using a small hammer to break open the diary's lock.

I stood by Josh's windows, staring into the courtyard. Cade wasn't home yet. He usually stayed out late on the nights where he was at the underground gym with the boys. I wanted to see him. I missed him. Bad enough that I almost texted him, though I refrained myself. Cade's letter stated he wanted my reply at the gala on Sunday evening. He would get it. In person.

"He's missed you a lot, you know?" Josh bit into a chocolate churro. "Cade's not the same without you."

I'm not the same without him either.

I gave Josh a weak smile. "I've missed him, too."

"Are you back together?"

"We will be."

"Good. You guys are your best versions when you're together," he said. "Anyone with a pair of eyes can see that you're soulmates."

"Thanks, Joshy." I ruffled his hair affectionately. He was always team Cadella.

While Josh hacked into Callie's laptop and scarfed down more churros, I went to join the girls. They finally broke the lock and were flipping through the pages, reading the entries.

It wasn't long before everyone was cursing with aghast expressions.

I couldn't believe what I read.

My heart pounded fast and my vision turned red.

Hundreds of pages filled with her talking shit. Saying the vilest things about her own friends. Me. Darla. Dacia. Hera. And so many other people from St. Victoria.

It was baffling and surprising. None of us saw this shit coming.

Callie Mackowski was a narcissistic, homophobic bitch riddled with issues.

She was 'friends' with us for years while simultaneously loathing us behind our backs.

"You all need to come here," Josh suddenly demanded in an alarmed tone. "Right now. I found your proof."

We rushed to Josh, crowding his work desk with eagerness.

He showed us everything we needed to see.

Callie was the one who photoshopped all those screenshots to end my friendship with Darla.

Callie was behind the Secrets of St. Victoria account, spreading nasty rumours about everyone at the school.

And Callie was in a relationship with the masked guy, based on the amateur porn they filmed on her laptop where you could see the skull tattoo and sapphire-encrusted watch on his hand.

His face was hidden. Hers was not.

One final thought pounded through my mind with raging intensity.

My ex-bitch of a best friend was going to pay for this.

CHAPTER 31

Last Puzzle Piece

CADE

The Present

The best way to describe this meeting was awkward.

I was at a café that doubled up as a romance bookstore with an overwhelming amount of pink, girlish laughter, and flowery décor. I sat in a velvet tufted chair across from Mabel Garcia.

She looked exactly as my hazy memory recalled. Except now she sported black hair instead of the dyed blond from that night.

Josh was responsible for picking this location, saying it would help Mabel feel at ease. Spoiler alert: she didn't look at ease. In fact, she looked as nervous as me.

I felt seconds away from breaking out into hives. Unable to find the words to commence this overdue conversation.

"Thanks for, uh"—I cleared my throat—"coming. I appreciate it."

Mabel stared at me with questioning brown eyes and a pinched smile. "Yeah. Uh, thank you for the latte."

I bought her one when we arrived. It was the right thing to do after she agreed to take an hour out of her busy Sunday afternoon to meet with me.

I took a sip of my own drink, wincing when the scalding black coffee burned my tongue. "I won't keep you for long. I just wanted to talk to you about what happened over the summer in…my room."

She tensed, a blush climbing over her face. I almost cursed under my breath. I was unequipped to deal with my own feelings from that night, let alone this poor girl's, who must have been just as humiliated as me.

"I'm so, so sorry," she rushed out. "I usually never go to parties, much less get drunk—actually, I've sworn off alcohol completely after that night—and nor do I hook up with random strangers. It's not my vibe. But I was in your room—which, I'm sorry about that as well—because the guy I was flirting with said that he wanted to uh, well, you know, and to meet him upstairs, specifically *there*, and I really liked him and thought I'd take a chance on him and—"

"It's okay," I assured her as she grew flustered, her words coming out more incoherent after the other. "Don't worry. I know it was one big misunderstanding and I'm not mad. I simply wanted to talk to you, even though this is months late, to get some proper closure."

The last part wasn't a complete lie. She just didn't need to know that closure for me came in the form of killing the motherfuckers responsible for that night.

I wanted to pick her brain. See what she knew. Try to fill the plot holes in the story.

Mabel nodded, taking a sip of her latte. "I-I understand."

"The girl who found us in my room was my girlfriend. I thought you were her. With the lights off and having drunk as much as I did—" *Having been drugged, was more like it.* "It was momentarily hard to tell the difference."

Mabel winced. "Yeah, I figured she was your girlfriend based on her reaction and what she said to you. I'm truly sorry. I had no idea and like I said, I thought you were someone else and—"

"Stop apologizing." I gave her a faint smile to ease her anxiousness. "It's okay. It wasn't your fault."

"I hope everything with your girlfriend is fine," Mabel said gently, seeming so miserable and genuinely hurt on Ella's behalf. "Will you extend my apology to her, too?"

Fuck, I felt so bad for this girl. She had no reason to feel guilty and it was clear what happened over the summer took a toll on her as well.

"I will," I replied. "And everything between us is fine." Or, at least, it would be soon. "Can you walk me through your version of that night?"

Mabel sighed, her gaze bouncing around the café, collecting her thoughts. I drummed my fingers against my thigh, feeling fidgety like a caged animal. The entire mystery of that night—of those four masked men—seemed to depend on her answer.

"I've blocked a lot of that night from my mind." She paused to take another sip of her latte. "But I do remember that I was there with a few girls from my high school, playing beer pong. This guy had been watching me for quite some time before he finally approached me. He seemed sweet enough and we started chatting about all sorts of things. Eventually, he poured us drinks, saying it was a party after all and that I should loosen up. Under his peer pressure, I kept drinking everything he handed me until I was practically shitfaced. One thing led to another and we kissed. I was really...into him. He said to go to the second floor, four doors down the right, and wait for him in the room. Keep the lights shut too. And I naively went ahead with his instructions."

It sounded like whoever this guy was, he spent time scoping out his victim before finally deciding on Mabel. Having spent a few minutes in her presence, I could tell she was extremely kind, sweet, and trustworthy. The last attribute was probably what he banked on. And unfortunately, she fell right into his trap.

"Do you remember what he looked like?"

"I remember him having blond hair and I think he was a jock?"

Fuck, that wasn't enough information. There were nearly two hundred people present that night. A lot of them were athletes from different schools in the city. However, *blond* and *jock* did help narrow down my search.

It wouldn't completely feel like a needle in a haystack.

"I see." I drained the remnant of my coffee, mulling over who this could be.

A flash of insecurity sliced over her face. "Do you think this was all a sick joke...just for the fun of it?"

I knew what went through her mind. *Why me? What did I do to deserve this?* The simple answer was that Mabel was a convenient scapegoat for this person. Nothing more, nothing less. Therefore, I offered her a nugget of the truth in hopes of giving her some peace. Make her realize that what happened had nothing to do with her and everything to do with Ella and me.

"I was roofied that night and led upstairs under the pretense that my girlfriend was waiting for me in the room. All so I could be caught in a compromising position and look like a cheater."

Her eyes widened. "T-That's horrible. Why would anyone do that to you?"

"Sometimes people like to hurt others for the sole reason that they can."

And for retaliation in my line of work.

"I'm sorry, Cade." Mabel reached forward to squeeze my arm in a platonic manner. "You didn't deserve that."

I decided right this moment that once I caught the masked fuckers, I was going to make the designated one write an apology letter to Mabel before I killed him off.

"Thank you," I rasped. "I'm okay now. It took some time, but I'm in a better place than I was three months ago. You can understand why I wanted to meet up and get some answers, right?"

"Yes, of course." She smiled sadly. "It makes sense."

"Do you remember the guy's name?" I egged on. "Maybe what he was wearing?"

"If he gave me a name, I don't recall. I was very drunk." She tilted her head in a calculating manner. "Although I do remember him saying he played hockey."

My blood ran cold.

Blond. Jock. Played hockey.

It could be anyone. It was a big city. There were many hockey players in different schools. Many blond ones. And yet I fumbled for my phone, my pulse quickening as I opened up my gallery app.

"Hey, Mabel?" I found last year's Rangers' team photo and turned my phone towards her. "What are the chances you recognize any of these guys as the one you spoke to that night?"

She leaned forward, studying the image for a minute. "Cade, I'm sorry. I don't think it's anyone from here."

Well, shit. It was worth a try. Regardless, I had three clues to continue my search.

I was about to pull my phone away when Mabel made a sound of distress and zoomed in on a particular player. "Oh my God. Wait! It's him. I recognize *him*."

Gazing down at the familiar face, I froze.

Gavino Ricci.

CHAPTER 32

You and I

Ella

The Present

Sunday evening rolled around and I arrived at the banquet hall with my *mamá* and *papá*. The gala was being hosted by another renowned family in South Side for a non-profit organization that my parents often donated to.

I wrapped my fur stole around me tighter as I stepped out of the town car, the cold autumn air nipping at my bare skin.

I wore the offerings Cade sent over yesterday. A stunning blue silk gown with a slit that exposed my thigh with every step, and a two-tiered diamond and blue sapphire necklace that made me feel like a queen.

Over twenty-four hours since I saw Cade and my heart ached, wanting to see its soul companion in the flesh. To hold him. To talk to him. To finally give my reply to his heartfelt letter.

I didn't want to live without Cade anymore either.

This lifetime was ours.

It was about time I told him.

Upon entering the ballroom, it was filled with guests, gold and black décor, waiters walking around with trays of champagne flutes, and the low whirr of conversation blending with the orchestra's classical music.

My friends spotted me before I saw them. Cutting through the crowd, Darla and Hera reached me and threw their arms around my shoulders in hugs. "You made it!"

Darla was in a black gown with her signature red lipstick, sharp winged eyeliner, and pearl jewelry. Hera was in a hunter green ensemble with soft bronzy makeup and an impressive diamond necklace that I remembered Shaun gifting her for her eighteenth birthday. He was obsessed with her and she was too blind to see it. Shaun invited her to all his hockey games, took her out for café dates, tried to learn words in Urdu for her, and she thought he only liked her as a friend.

"Oh my goodness," I said to them. "You both look beautiful."

"Look at yourself!" Darla returned. "Stunning. Ten on ten. Marry me."

I chuckled, my cheeks warming under the praise.

"C'mon, give us a twirl," Hera encouraged and I did. "Damn, girl!"

"Thank you." I preened while they oohed and aahed. "Cade gifted me the dress and necklace. Speaking of him, is he here?"

They shook their heads. "We haven't seen any of the Remingtons yet."

My shoulders sagged. "Oh, I guess they should be arriving soon."

We decided to take some selfies, and I made sure to send a full-length picture of Hera—discreetly—to Shaun, who wasn't attending tonight due to his concussion.

Christmas came early —Ella

He replied within seconds.

Good GOD. —Shaun

I'm drooling. —Shaun

Holy fuck. Is that the necklace I gave her?? —Shaun

Yup!—Ella

Send me more pictures throughout the night. You owe me. – Shaun

👍 —Ella

For the next few minutes, we chatted about Darla's publishing plans—she was finally going to do it, Principal Hill's opinion be damned—

and me reopening my online store for my knit creations. I'd taken a break over the summer and the first semester of university was extremely hectic, leaving me no time for my art projects.

In the midst of our conversation, I noticed Dacia on the other side of the room.

She had an unreadable look on her face. Holding a champagne flute in her hand, she gazed at a painting of a starry night with two lovers standing on a bridge wrapped in purple roses. The world around her buzzed, yet Dacia was rooted in place, spellbound by the image before her.

I'd never seen her like that, lost in a trance.

Dacia snapped out of it and finally left, coming to join us. She smiled and gave me a hug. "You look amazing, Ella."

"Right back at you." She wore a skin-tight white gown and enough diamonds to blind anyone who looked in her direction. "What are your thoughts on the painting?"

"Exquisite."

Darla recently told me her sister was into collecting art, paintings in particular. "Who's the artist?"

A wistful smile flashed on Dacia's lips, before she hid it around the rim of her champagne flute. "Somebody I used to know."

I didn't understand her cryptic tone. Before I could pester her for more information, I felt a familiar pair of eyes on me.

I turned around, searching for him.

My dark prince leaned against a pillar, that signature heart-melting smile on his face as he watched me like I was the answer to all his prayers.

The corners of my lips tipped up in a reciprocating smile.

Our gazes spoke while our words could not.

You're a vision to behold, mi corazón.

You're my favourite memory and I would relive you a million times over and then some more, mo chuisle.

That magnetic force yanked our bond and we crossed over to one another, pushing past a crowd of people and meeting halfway, hope and love in our expressions.

"Hi, pretty girl."

"Hi, *querido*."

"You look breathtaking."

I melted, my hands flexing by my sides, longing to clutch him. "So do you."

That smile of his morphed to a full-blown grin, flashing me those dimples I loved.

Tonight, Cade was dashing in a navy blue suit, the top three buttons of his dress shirt undone, showing hints of his tattoos and the gold chain around his neck, threaded with my promise ring. He must have gone back for it after I threw it away, making sure to wear it so everybody here knew that he was irrevocably mine.

"I was worried for a second that you wouldn't come tonight."

"I can't stay away from you, Ellie. After all, you have something that belongs to me."

I swallowed. "What?"

"My heart."

Warmth filled my chest and a hundred butterflies unfurled in my stomach.

I had his heart…and I was never giving it back.

Before I could kiss him senselessly, Cade extended his left hand, the one with the Serch Bythol knot tattooed across the back. The silver rings at the base of his knuckles glinted under the chandelier lights. "Do you want to dance with me?"

Without hesitation, I grasped his hand, swearing to never let go of him after this moment. "I would love to."

He swept me into his arms just as the orchestra began a new ballad. My left hand rested on his shoulder and my right twined with his as we moved slowly to the music.

The feeling of *home* rocked through me.

Cade lowered his forehead to mine. "I've missed you."

"I've missed you, too," I murmured.

Everyone watched us. Our families. Our friends. Our foes.

Though we didn't care. Nothing mattered except for him and me.

Dancing together after being separated for months was a statement.

A way of letting the crowd know we were together again. You could tear us apart, but we'd still find our way back to one another.

We were meant to be. Now and forever.

"How's your ankle?" He glanced down at my heels.

"It's feeling okay. I iced it. Still a bit tender, though."

"I'll kiss it better soon."

"You promise?"

"Have I ever broken one, Ella?"

"No," I whispered. "You never have."

"I never will either."

It was spoken with such strong passion. I smiled and rested my head in the crook of his neck, inhaling his calming scent.

"There's something I want to say," he rasped. "Will you hear me out?"

I couldn't deny him when he implored with all the humility he possessed.

I nodded in a silent *yes*.

The familiar calluses of his palms tickled me as he cupped my face, tilting it back so I could see all the affection swirling in his eyes. "Ella, meeting you changed the course of my life. I've never known true yearning until I laid eyes on you. Not only were you the most beautiful girl I'd ever seen, but you became the embodiment of all my dreams. Becoming your friend first was one of the greatest joys of my existence. You showed me the meaning of friendship, love, and cared for me like no one ever had. I fell hard for you and became exceedingly restless with every passing day because I wanted you as more than a friend. I wanted you as my girl."

I smiled, remembering how desperate I was to add the word *boy* before *friend*.

"And when I finally had you, Ella, that yearning was never fully satiated. Days, hours, minutes, seconds. None of it was ever enough with you. You consumed my every thought, every breath, every heartbeat. And you still do. I never thought I'd have to experience life without you—the only girl who made me feel like all my parts, no matter how dark and broken, were worth loving—but I have and I can say that I've hated every moment of it. I know I can survive without you, but I will only *live* if I have you by my side. You strengthen me. You challenge me. You make me feel alive, happy, and whole. Now that the past is behind us, will you give me the honour of having you once more? Because you're it for me. I love you with every piece of my heart, Ella."

I swooned from his confession.

"*Mi corazón*." I caressed my fingers over his chiseled jawline. "I love you too. I never stopped loving you, despite how hard I tried. It's impossible. You're etched in every corner of my soul. And I wouldn't have it any other way. I don't want to survive without you either, Cade. I want to live with you and I want to uphold every promise we made to each another."

Cade's blue eyes were vivid with emotions. Still holding my face, he kissed my forehead and reminded me of our most important vow. "You and I, in this lifetime and all the ones to come, *mo chuisle*."

"You and I. Always."

We kissed on it.

A maelstrom of tender feelings erupted like confetti inside of me as we righted every wrong in our story.

Breaking away, Cade whispered, "Are you ready to get out of here?"

In case my family asked about my whereabouts, I knew my girls would cover for me. "Yes."

The second we stepped outside, Cade unexpectedly swung me into his arms. I laughed with delight as he carried me to his Ferrari like a dark prince from a twisted fairy tale, stealing his princess away forever.

"Cade, where are we going?"

We weren't taking the usual route to his home.

"It's a surprise, Ella."

I loved surprises. "Okay."

My gaze fixed on the rushing scenery, I settled more comfortably in my seat, recalling the moment from twenty minutes ago with perverse pleasure.

Cade had opened the car door for me and just as I sat down, I noticed **ELLA** stitched in the leather headrest. It was a new addition.

Cade chuckled boyishly, seeing the stars in my eyes. "You like that, huh?"

I nodded shamelessly. "I love it. No one gets to sit in this seat but me, okay?"

He'd kissed me and murmured against my lips, "No one else ever will, Ella. It's yours."

It pleased the territorial monster inside of me.

I missed being a passenger princess, as much as I missed watching Cade drive. There was something so attractive about him behind the wheel. The way he handled such a powerful car with ease while holding my hand, pecking my knuckles like he was starved for my touch.

It wasn't long before Cade pulled into an underground parking lot of a sleek building.

"What are we doing here?" I asked when he helped me out of the Ferrari.

He grinned. "You'll know in a minute."

We walked towards an elevator. Cade swiped a keycard and we headed to the top floor. A few seconds later, there was a loud ping and the doors opened. He ushered me inside with a hand on my back.

It was dark inside, save for the moonlight seeping through the floor-to-ceiling windows lining the entire loft-style penthouse. A conversational pit sat in the middle like a centerpiece and an unlit fireplace to our left.

"Did you…buy this place?"

"I bought this place for you, Ella." Cade kissed my cheek. "For us."

I gasped. "When?"

"A few months ago. After you mentioned wanting to live together one day."

I felt undone by the love this man bore for me. I wished I had more words to convey what I felt for him—what I would never stop feeling for him.

"Cade." I threw my arms around his shoulders and he immediately placed his hands on my hips, tugging me deeper into him. "I don't know what to say."

"Do you like it?"

This was exactly how I pictured our first place. He put in the work and gave us our dream home. "It's perfect."

"Remember when I sent you gifts for your birthday this past summer? There was a keycard in there. It was for here."

I did remember seeing a keycard in those packages. It was probably stuffed somewhere in my drawers with the rest of his offerings.

Cade and me were both August babies with his birthday a few days prior to mine. I felt awful that I hadn't gotten him anything. Granted, I was overcome by my grief and pain. And I didn't know the truth about that night like I knew now.

But still.

"I didn't get you a birthday present," I said regretfully. "I'm sorry, Cade. Tell me what you want—anything—and it's yours."

"Everything I want is right here." He kissed my right eyelid. "My whole world is in my arms. I don't need anything else, Ella."

"I love you so much." I buried my face in his chest, tightening my arms around him. His heartbeat was my personal lullaby. "No more time apart, Cade."

"I love you too." He kissed the top of my head. "No more time apart, Ella."

With our vow floating in the air, he led me through the penthouse, showing me every corner of the place. Was this truly happening? Did he really buy us our own home? My excitement ramped up seeing each new room, appliance, and feature. For a girl who loved to cook and eat, the kitchen was a wet dream. And for a girl who loved art, the studio he built me upstairs nearly had me weeping.

"Now you'll have more room to create and fulfill orders for your online store." He proudly gestured to the work table and the shelves filled with all sorts of paints, yarns, threads, and tools.

God, I loved this man. I smothered his dimples with kisses until the only sound ringing in the penthouse was his infectious laugh.

"We're going to christen every inch of this place," I announced as he dragged me down the hallway of the second floor, towards what I presumed was our bedroom.

"Sounds like a plan, Ellie."

The bedroom was straight out of my fantasies, housing a canopy-style California king-sized bed, dark colours paired beautifully with pastels, an en suite housing an incredible jacuzzi, and an enormous balcony encased by a stone balustrade.

I loved everything about it.

I touched the cold glass window, staring at the night view, made even more beautiful when Cade's reflection entered the picture.

His arms went around my waist and he tucked his chin in the crook of my neck. "What do you think?"

"It's amazing, Cade. I love it."

"I'm happy to hear that."

My attention was diverted to the crystals strategically laid out on the floor next to the windows. "What are these doing here?"

"You left them at my place months ago." He kissed my nape. "Tonight's a new moon. I wanted to charge them for you."

There I went, falling deeper in love with this man.

Such a simple gesture but so meaningful.

I stared at his reflection, noting the hunger in his eyes. The lust sketched in the lines of his face. The desire coursing through his body and seeping into me slowly like an aphrodisiac. I trembled with the need to become one with him.

"I know we have a lot to talk about." I whirled around to face him, placing my hands on his muscular chest. "But there's only one thing on my mind right now."

"Mine too." He grasped my face and leaned down, planting little kisses along my jaw until he reached my earlobe. "I want to make love to you, *mi vida*."

I moaned, holding on to the crooks of his elbow. "Yes."

"I want to touch every inch of your body. I want to leave my imprint all over your heart," Cade whispered, his voice raspy like smoke and sin. "I want to sink so deep inside of your soul until all you see and feel is me, Ella."

"Please, *mi amor*," I begged. "I want that too."

We were never leaving each other ever again.

"Are you going to be a slut for me tonight?" He caressed his lips along the shell of my ear. "Are you going to show me how much you've missed me, baby?"

There he was.

My princepin. My gangster. My bad boy.

Shivers cascaded down my spine as he layered kisses down the column of my throat. "Y-Yes. I'll be anything you want me to be."

"Good girl." His dark smirk, filled with naughty promises, stamped over my pulse, feeling it beat madly for him. "Now take off your dress for me."

CHAPTER 33

Moonlit Goddess

CADE

The Present

I made my way down Ella's body as she removed her dress, worshipping every expanse of moonlit skin I could reach with open-mouthed kisses and love bites.

When I landed on my knees, I glanced up at my prize.

My princess. My goddess. My religion.

She was an arresting sight to behold.

Her face with that imperfectly perfect gaze. Her stunning body donned in nothing but stiletto heels, thong, and lustrous jewels. Her fiery heart on her sleeve, showing every emotion she felt for me. Want. Love. *Need.*

Finally, all her walls were down.

The Ella I loved was back.

And she was all mine for the taking.

"Lean back against the window, baby," I instructed and she obeyed. My fingers unstrapped her heels, cupping her tender ankle carefully. I brought it to my mouth, gently kissing around it a few times. "All better?"

She nodded with a playful gleam in her eyes. "Mhm."

My girl once told me that my touch was a remedy for her, the same way hers was for me. I was ready to bleed exoneration into our beings once and for all.

"Where else do you want to be kissed, Ella?" I grazed my palms over her calves, thighs, waist, my mouth following suit, not leaving any inch of her untouched.

She bit her bottom lip, speared her fingers in my hair, canted her hips, and guided my face closer to her heaven. "Here, please."

I stopped just shy of her cunt, my mouth drooling at the way her lacy thong stuck to her swollen flesh. She was drenched and I barely touched her. "Tell me exactly what you want."

"I want you to lick my pussy and…"

"And what?" I growled and threw her left leg over my brawny shoulder, opening her for my ministrations. I grasped handfuls of her thick ass and dragged her closer to me, my nose running along the slit of her thong. Goddamn, her scent, pure sex mixed with jasmine and orange blossoms, turned me into a madman. "Talk to me, Ella."

She gasped when I dragged my lips along the wet material. "I-I want you to fuck me."

Good girl.

"You're going to get fucked, sweetheart. Hard. Fast. Deep. Slow. All night long." With my teeth, I tucked her thong to the side. "Until you can't breathe and can't come anymore. Understood?"

"Y-Yes. Please."

Grinning like a savage, I licked the entirety of her slit, eliciting the sexiest half moan, half whimper from her. I did it a few more times, letting her taste melt on my tongue before devouring her like a hungry man whose only nourishment existed right here, between these tight thighs. I went from fucking her hole with my tongue, to inserting two fingers in that slippery heat, to lavishing her pearly bud with licks and sucks. The sloppy noises of her arousal, her begging cries, and the tightening of her fingers in my hair made me feral.

"*Cadecadecade.*"

Her pleas were like hymns to my ear.

"Mm. I love your taste." I smirked around a mouthful of pussy, my lips, chin, jaw smeared with her wetness. My blood heated and my cock ached in the confinements of my pants. I wanted to be inside of her, pounding her sinful body in every angle until her voice was hoarse from pleasure.

"Cade, please. I'm—" She broke off on a sob when I sucked her clit hard.

She was right *there*. I could feel it.

"Come for me," I commanded, digging my fingers into her ass cheeks. "Come for me so I can give you more, baby."

My girlfriend didn't last long, quaking as she orgasmed with sweet noises, praising me like I was her everything.

Her dark prince. Her God. Her salvation.

She slumped against the window, her chest heaving up and down with uneven breaths.

I licked my mouth for more of her taste and stood to my full height.

Ella watched me through glazed eyes. I shrugged out of my suit jacket and chest holster. They joined her gown on the floor. My fingers worked each button of my dress shirt deliberately slow. She feasted on my naked torso as it was revealed to her, stark hunger and greed pulsing in her features.

When I yanked my belt off, she jolted with excitement.

I smirked. "Would you like me to use it on you?"

"Later, yes."

After lowering my zipper, I pulled out my cock. Thick, swollen, and leaking at the tip. For her. Always for her. I hissed, giving myself a few strokes with the hand that was still coated with Ella's arousal. "How do you want it first?"

She licked her lips. "From behind."

Bad fucking girl. "Then that's what you'll have."

She appraised me from head to toe as I jerked off, taking in every scar, every wound, every tattoo. "You're so beautiful, Cade. I can never get enough."

Ella was my undoing.

My heart twisted in my chest and I leaned down, stamping my mouth to hers, pouring everything I was worth into the kiss.

She tasted like moonlight, jasmines, and mine.

Ella gasped, her lips and tongue meeting my demanding strokes with equal fervour. Like she was just as insatiable as me. Like she needed this just as much as me. Like she would goddamn die without me.

I was no longer alone in my solitude.

My first and forever love was back.

I nipped and tugged her bottom lip. "Turn around and put your hands on the window."

"Bossy man."

"Yours."

"Mine."

Ella turned around and peered at me with a coy glint, her dark lashes drooping over that stunning gaze in a provocative manner. A flirty smile curled her lips as she braced her palms against the glass window and jutted her ass for me. "Like this?"

Good Lord. I could write a hundred odes to that backside. Tight, perky, and thick. I wanted to bite it. Lick it. Suck it. Tattoo *Property of Cade* on her ass cheek so whenever she paraded around in a little swimsuit, every motherfucker in the vicinity knew this girl belonged to me.

"Just like that." I barely recognized my own guttural voice, fisting my cock harder and faster. "Fuck, the things I'm going to do to you tonight."

"Tell me." She started playing with her nipples and clit, moaning as she eyed my erection. "I want to know."

"I'm going to ruin you, tame you, own you." I dragged heated kisses up her spine. "I'm going to remind you why I'm the only one for you, Ella."

"What are you waiting for?"

I was going to fuck the spoiled attitude out of her.

Pressing up against her back, I whispered, "Do I need to wear a condom?"

"No." She moaned when I sucked a hickey on her neck. "I've been on the pill for two months. I want you bare."

I groaned at the thought of her hot silk wrapped around me like a vice. "Are you sure?"

"I've been dying to feel you without anything between us since the last time."

Fuck, me too.

Dropping my slacks, I kept lavishing her shoulders with kisses. "Have you touched yourself to the thought of me over the last three months?"

Shivers wracked her body. My effect on her was imminent. I loved it. "All the damn time."

My hands squeezed her small tits and travelled south, where I slapped her pussy twice, relishing her squeals. Despite trying to hate me, she'd fucked herself to the thought of me. I smiled and murmured in her ear, "Ditto."

Ella ground her ass against my cock in invitation. "Cade, please. Put it inside of me."

Fisting the short strands of her hair, I tugged her head back until she whimpered in pleasure-pain. I guided my cock to her awaiting pussy, coating my inches with her slickness. "First show me what a good slut you are and beg for my cock, baby."

"Please, I'm going to lose my mind. Give it to me. I want it. I need it. I—"

I slammed into her in one harsh thrust.

She screamed, clawing at the window for purchase. "*Cade.*"

I threw my head back on a groan. "*Ella.*"

So good, so tight, so wet, so mine.

Her pussy felt divine.

Being inside of her was akin to a religious experience. Nothing made me feel as complete as this girl. She was my sanctuary and my kingdom come.

"Hold on." I collared her throat with one hand and choked her lightly the way she liked. "This is going to be fast and rough, baby."

My words were the only warning she received before I pulled out and thrust back in, harder and deeper than ever.

I turned into an animal with her next scream, establishing a brutal pace as I thrust my cock with a vengeance, fucking her within an inch of her life. Her cunt stretched obscenely around my thickness. I pounded into her with no finesse. Treating the love of my life like my personal fucktoy.

Pure, filthy need had our bodies colliding together frantically with flesh-smacking noises.

"Remember when you said you'd never scream for me again?" I taunted with a strained, dark chuckle. "Who's a liar now, huh?"

Ella only cried out for more, growing wilder with every thrust.

"You were made for me," I growled, my stomach muscles flexing as I pumped my hips faster, my rhythm almost a blur. "Look how your greedy pussy swallows my cock whole. You're gripping me so good. Like you never want me to leave. Like you want to be filled with all the cum I've got stored for you, sweetheart."

The dirtiest noises escaped Ella's parted lips as she backed her bouncing ass against my lap, fucking back on my cock like a depraved slut. I shoved two fingers into her mouth, the same ones I fingered her with, and she sucked with a hum.

"Does it turn you on?" I whispered in her ear. "Knowing that anyone can look up and see your hot body getting fucked raw like I'm paying a couple grand for it?"

"*Yes.*"

I grazed my teeth along her jaw. "Knowing that they'll want a taste but will never have it because I'll kill them for even breathing in your direction?"

She sobbed, playing with her clit faster. "Y-Yes. Turns me on."

The admission sent me into a frenzy. "Naughty girl."

"Yours."

"Mine." I screwed her harder, watching in the window's reflection as my upward drives caused her tits to sway and her ass to shake. Damn, she was perfect, meeting me thrust for thrust, nails digging into my thighs, her arousal sloshing over my dick and her ass. "Fuck, are you close?"

"Y-Yeah," she panted.

I groaned, my thrusts increasing in speed. "Now let go, Ella. I want to feel your pretty cunt coming around me."

When I pinched her clit and murmured more dirty words into her dewy skin, she finally orgasmed with a loud scream, giving a show to anybody who dared to look up.

I followed suit and finished inside of her, my groans ringing in the air.

Without letting Ella catch her breath, I pulled out, swung her into my arms, grabbed my belt from the floor, and took us to the California king in three strides.

I threw her onto the bed, loving the way her gasp dissolved into a giggle. She rose up on her elbows, tilting her head as she watched me standing by the foot of the bed, drinking her in with dark lust coursing through my veins.

Ella Ximena Cordova was a goddess with the moonlight caressing her beautiful form, decorated with love bites, teeth marks, and diamonds worth millions of dollars.

She was priceless to me.

I would die for her, kill for her, live for her.

My girl beckoned me closer with a sultry smile. "Won't you come closer, *mi corazón*?"

"Spread your thighs," I commanded, climbing in after her. "I'm not done with you."

Like the cheerleader she was, my girl split her legs wide open. Her bare cunt glistened wet. An erotic mixture of her arousal and my cum dripped out of her hole in a hypnotizing sight.

So fucking sexy.

Based on the way Ella rubbed her slit teasingly, she liked it too. "You made a mess."

"And I'm going to make another one." My hands held her thighs as I lowered my mouth to her pussy. "Soon as I finish cleaning this one, pretty girl."

"Cade..." Ella held her breath in anticipation when my tongue licked along her slit, tasting *us* for the first time. She emitted a soft cry when my fingers dug into her skin and my tongue collected every drop. I kept my eyes on her the entire time as I French kissed her pussy, using two fingers at the same time to hit her spot. Her third orgasm was fast. She came like an insatiable little thing who just couldn't get enough of me. My tongue, my fingers, my cock.

She needed me like air.

I crawled over her until I hovered just above her lips.

We stared at one another with panting breaths.

"Do you want a taste?" I rasped.

She parted her mouth in response.

Seizing her jaw, I dribbled spit before kissing her almost angrily, shoving my tongue into her mouth. She moaned at our essence and kissed me back with the same passion, her palms roving over my arms, spending extra time caressing the scars on my left one in the most affectionate manner. Telling me silently how strong and beautiful she found me. Telling me silently how grateful she was that I was alive and with her right here, right now. Telling me how much she loved every bit of me, even the parts that were wretched.

I grabbed her waist and rolled us over so I was underneath with her on top.

Ella gasped, but understanding quickly flickered in her eyes.

"Come ride me so I can fill you up with more cum," I crooned darkly. "You want that, don't you, sweetheart?"

<hr />

Ella

Good Lord, Cade's mouth should be illegal.

I was still recovering from the three orgasms and the way he dirty-talked to me. But seeing him lick my pussy, overflowing with his cum, like a filthy motherfucker before having me taste *us*, was the cherry on top of the cake.

"Yes, I want it." I straddled him and rose up enough to grab his hard cock and lodge it at my entrance. "I want you so bad, *querido*."

"Needy brat." Cade clutched my throat with one hand and squeezed. He yanked me down to his face, kissing me desperately. "*Eres mia*, hm?"

I licked the **ELLA** tattoo and bit his bottom lip. "*Sí, soy tuyo*."

Cade quickly cracked the flat of his belt against my ass until I broke away with a moan, pain and pleasure coalescing in my core.

"Now ride me," he demanded. "Fuck that pussy over my cock and make yourself come, Ella."

He didn't need to tell me twice.

I lowered myself onto him, inch by inch, whimpering because he was so long and thick and filling me perfectly.

"Good girl," he praised. "All the way down—fuck." He barked out a curse, drops of perspiration glimmering on his skin as I sank to the root. "That's what I'm talking about, baby."

My clit throbbed and my heart fluttered, loving the way he slowly unravelled for me, one stitch at a time. I kissed Cade, allowing myself time to adjust to him again.

Using his big muscular chest for leverage, I rocked up and down on his length, working him torturously slow, wanting to see him lose control and just *snap*. Cade knew what I was doing, but he was letting me have my fun.

"Do you like it?" I licked the sweat from his jawline and bit into his skin like a wildcat. "When I ride your thick cock like a horny slut?"

On a particular downstroke, I clenched around him and raked my fingernails over his abs with wickedness. Cade threw his head back on a beastly groan, looking like a famished dirty prince coming home and finally having his lover service him. God, he was so fucking hot in the midst of pleasure, his fingers digging into my hips with a bruising quality.

"You dicktease," he growled and slapped the leather belt against my ass in warning. "I said to fuck me." *Slap.* "Not play games." *Slap.* "Get to it." *Slap.* "Or I will punish you."

I cried out, clenching around him. I loved his wrath on my skin. It turned me on like no other. Leaning forward until my pebbled nipples brushed against his chest, I whispered, "Maybe I want to be punished."

His eyes flashed with a menacing gleam. With a cruel smirk, he grabbed my waist, braced his feet against the bed and pulled me off his cock. "Who am I to deny the love of my life, hm?"

Next second, I was slammed back onto his cock and then he started

399

fucking into me from below. Fast. Deep. Fucking ruthlessly. The sheer force of his pounding had my body bouncing on top of him with each savage thrust. I had to hold on to the banging headboard and grip the silk sheets so I wouldn't fall off his lap. "*My, God. Cade, Cade, Cade.*"

"That's right, Ella." He punched his cock inside of me brutally. "Your God." *Thrust.* "In." *Thrust.* "Every." *Thrust.* "Goddamn." *Thrust.* "Way."

He was selfishly using me for his pleasure, battering my pussy with no remorse, igniting a flurry of sparks every time he hit *that* spot inside of me. I loved every second of it. I screamed for more, my voice raw from begging him to never stop.

The angle was doing wonders for my clit. I had missed this, him, us so much.

Closing my eyes, I moaned as I neared my peak.

"*Mo chuisle,*" he murmured in a soft tone, despite our rough love-making. "Open your eyes. Let me see all your shades and colours."

I gave him what he wanted.

Cade's sky blue gaze locked onto mine as he ruined, tamed, owned me. This was my forever, my happily ever after, my lifetimes wrapped into one. I loved him, I loved him, I loved him.

"Don't come yet," he warned, despite being close himself. "Not until I say so."

He was killing me. I was so close. "No, no, no. Cade, *please.*"

"Answer me first." He slowed his thrusts to slow, deep ones to edge me. I whined from frustration, sinking my nails in his inked torso. "Who gets to treat you like his dirty little princess?"

Only you. "*Cade.*"

"Who gets to fuck you until the day we die?"

Beautiful, jealous, possessive man. "*Cade.*"

"Who gets to have this pussy sitting on his face whenever he wishes?"

I nearly squirted. "*Cade.*"

"Who gets to tattoo his name on your skin?"

If this pop quiz didn't finish soon, I was going to die. "*Cade!*"

"Good girl." His intense expression softened a hint as he kissed me tenderly. "Let me give you your reward now."

Cade started thrusting faster and harder, working us to a fevered pitch again. An old familiar rhythm that always drove us crazy. Our little bubble rang with harsh breaths, naughty promises, and the sensual noise of our sweat-slickened bodies making war.

"I'm going to steal you away." *Thrust.* "Marry you." *Thrust.* "Spoil you rotten." *Thrust.* "Make you my queen." *Thrust.* "And rule together." *Thrust.* "You with me, Ella?"

"With you, Cade." I moaned, holding on to him with all my might. "Always."

He pressed frantic kisses all over my skin like he was desperate for me to understand the depth of his feelings, while making love to me like never before. "I love you. *Te amo. Mo ghrá thú.*"

My heart glowed, hearing him say he loved me in three different languages. I returned the three words against his warm lips.

My confession sank into the waters of his soul like an anchor and he gazed at me in utter rapture like I was the personification of all his desires.

It wasn't long before we came together, wrapped in each other's arms and echoing more words of love.

Cade was created for me.

And I, for him.

After a few more rounds of lovemaking, I was completely spent. A delicious soreness pulsed through my muscles as I lay on my stomach in the silk sheets. Basking in post-coital bliss and feeling extremely sated and languid.

"What's got you smiling, Ellie?"

I beamed into the pillow. "You, and how much I've missed us."

"Me too." Cade pressed a kiss to my hip.

Currently, my boyfriend was propped on his elbow and using my ass like a table as he rolled a joint. Glancing over my shoulder, I caught him smiling and extending it towards me. I grabbed his Zippo from the nightstand and lit the tip.

Cade took a deep puff and exhaled, weed smoke curling out of his mouth.

"You want some?" he asked, handing it over.

I took a drag while he moved up the bed, propping his back against the headboard. He started sifting his fingers through my hair.

"Do you have pictures of Knight on your phone?" I exhaled and passed the joint back to him.

"Yes." Cade's eyes lit up and he grabbed his phone. The fact that he still had my picture as his wallpaper turned my insides to mush. Turning his screen my way, I saw a shot of a Doberman puppy.

"Oh my God. He's so cute." I squealed, going through each picture and video. The one of him and Olivia rolling around in the living room really did it for me. "I can't wait to meet him."

"He's the sweetest boy. I've shown him your pictures on multiple occasions. At this point, he basically knows you're his mommy."

I pouted. So adorable. "Can we bring him to the penthouse?"

"Yes. Though fair warning, my family is really besotted with him. We might have to split his time between here and there."

"Sounds like a plan." I was imagining us taking Knight for drives with Emilio and Olivia to get ice creams and pup cups for him. "I went over to your place last night, but I didn't see him. Me, Josh, and the girls were kind of busy doing detective work."

"Yeah, Josh told me you all kidnapped him and wouldn't set him free until he helped you find evidence."

Josh made it sound like we held him at gunpoint. "Did he tell you the part where we made him get on all fours so we could use his back to climb up to Callie's window?"

Cade was in the midst of inhaling smoke when he burst into a half cough, half chuckle. "No, he did not." His face scrunched up. "But I read Callie's disgusting diary entries and I need to wash my eyes with bleach after seeing clips of that amateur porn."

"Same." I cringed, remembering the video.

Suddenly, Cade's features darkened. "I need to tell you something, Ella."

Not liking his grim tone, I sat up. "What is it?"

"I met with the girl from that night. Her name is Mabel. Josh found

402

her and arranged for us to meet." Cade handed me the joint. "We talked. She was very friendly and kind. Sorry too, although she had nothing to apologize for, considering she was a victim in this situation."

"I'm sensing like there's something more." I placed my hand on his naked chest. "What is it, Cade?"

Anger flashed in his eyes and his jaw clenched. "I know who the masked guy is."

Every line in my body froze, the joint halfway to my mouth. "Who?"

"Gavino Ricci."

Profound shock tunneled through my system, robbing me of any sound.

Cade saw all the questions swimming in my wide eyes. "It's been him all along, Ella."

Gavino Ricci, Callie's so-called crush, was the masked guy?

Why the fuck would he do this?

Moreover, I didn't see a single diary entry from Callie stating that Gavino was the masked guy, or that she was sleeping with him.

The puzzle was almost complete, but I needed a few more answers. "You need to elaborate. Help me better understand. Please."

"Mabel said she was talking to a blond hockey player at Josh's party. He pressured her into drinking until she was basically drunk. Then he asked her to meet him upstairs. In my room specifically. When I showed her the Rangers' team picture from last year, she recognized Gavino."

"Taking advantage of a girl like that—forcing her to drink—and then letting her be humiliated is fucking despicable," I spat. "Why would he do that? Why would he hurt you and me? It doesn't make sense." I shook my head. "What motive could Gavino have for all of this?"

"I texted Josh and Uncle Vance the minute I found out about Gavino. By the time I got home, they did some more digging and found out that… he used to be Kian Wilson's foster brother."

I closed my eyes on a bone-deep sigh.

The final puzzle piece fell into place.

"He was Kian Wilson's foster brother and he wanted to avenge him," I concluded. "And somehow he knew we were the ones responsible for killing him."

"Exactly." Cade exhaled more smoke. "How he figured out that part is yet to be known, but one thing's for certain…"

He trailed off but I knew what he meant.

In the Remingtons' world, there was only one way to deliver justice. Gavino Ricci had to pay for his actions and suffer the consequences. He had to die.

"Callie must have given him my passcode." She'd seen me type it in a million times—my boyfriend's birthday. "I bet you he's the one who bumped into me the night of the party, stole my phone, and sent you those text messages."

Cade nodded. "I think that's what happened too."

With that settled, I crawled into Cade's lap. He held my hips, thumb brushing over the **K** tattoo on my hip bone. "How are we taking him down?"

Cade's smirk was packed with dark mischief. "I thought you'd never ask."

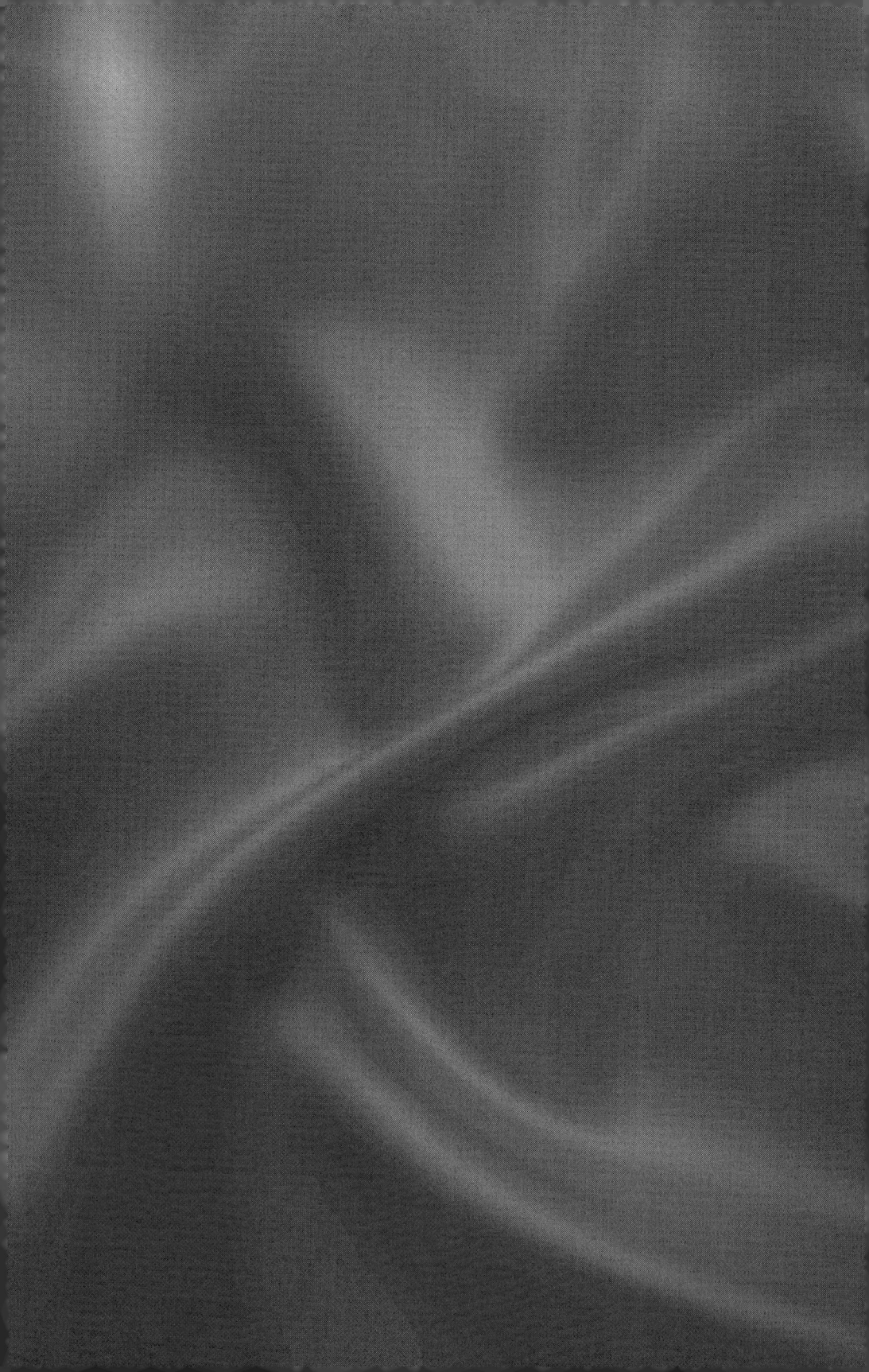

CHAPTER 34

Clown Shit

Ella

The Present

Forty-eight hours later, we were ready to execute our two-part plan to take down the traitors.

The first person on the list was Callie Mackowski.

She worked part-time as an apprentice in the hair and makeup department at Deos Theatre, an old establishment in the city owned by the Remingtons, that played shows twice a week. As the curtain call for tonight's *Othello* came to a conclusion, I clapped alongside the crowd with only one thing on my mind.

Revenge.

I shared a conspiratorial glance with the girls—Darla, Dacia, and Hera—sitting in the same row as me. The crowd tonight was thin, so it wouldn't be long before they left the auditorium. The security cameras had been disabled—thank you, Josh—and all the guards would ignore what would take place in the next few minutes. Vance ensured of it.

Moments later when the spectators and most of the crew had left, a guard by the backstage signalled us. Four pairs of heels clicked loudly as we descended the stairs and followed his trail.

The hallway was dark and bore the smell of sweat and cheap fragrances. We walked to the dressing room and the guard unlocked it,

407

ushering us inside. The door closed behind our backs with a soft click.

As per Vance's order, he'd stay planted outside until we finished.

The room had a spacious layout, wide and long in a rectangular stretch. One wall was covered with vanity mirrored desks that were littered with brushes and makeup kits. Another wall housed a multitude of costumes, accessories, wigs, and other props.

Callie was cleaning one of the desks when she heard the sound of our footsteps.

Her head snapped up and she blanched.

"H-Hey." At least her surprised tone, with a hint of uncertainty, was genuine. Unlike the rest of her. "What are you girls doing here?"

Hera inched her a frown. Darla threw her a glare. Dacia was blank-faced. And I gave Callie a Cheshire cat grin as we circled her like vultures, forcing her to remain rooted where she stood, a rag in one hand and her other gripping a foldable chair's arm with a knuckle-whitening quality.

I ran the tip of my finger over the edge of a makeup kit innocently, pouting. "Can't some friends come say hi to another...*friend?*" I pushed the kit off the table and it fell to the floor with a loud clatter. "Or are we not friends anymore, Cal?"

She sensed the shift in the air as her gaze bounced between us, understanding dawning upon her.

This wasn't a friendly visit.

Now we were all on the same page.

"What are you trying to say, Ella?" Her posture inflated with annoyance. "Get on with it."

"Are you surprised to see me here, Callie?" I leaned my hip against one of the desks and crossed my arms over my chest. "You probably thought I'd still be in jail, huh? Considering you and Gavino called the cops on Initiation Night."

My sentence hung like a sword over her head.

Callie's eyes flared, shocked that we knew.

Quickly, she sprang into motion.

I blocked her way. "Sit down. We're going to have a nice chat."

Callie tried to push past me before Dacia grabbed the hem of her shirt and yanked her back, growling, "Sit. The. Fuck. Down. You incompetent idiot."

Despite her struggles, Callie was steered into the chair, fearful and tense, while Hera and Darla duct-taped her hands and feet to it. Realizing that her fight was in vain, she finally whispered, "Are you going to hurt me?"

Ah, so she did know what *I* was capable of. I tsked at her. "You're not worth dirtying my custom couture outfit, sweetie."

I had no desire to spill her blood or even physically hit her. None of us did. What we did want, however, was to teach her a lesson she'd never forget.

We were sweet until you betrayed us. Then God have mercy on you because there was no escaping our wrath.

Now that she was tied to the chair and looked helpless like a wounded animal, I began her retribution. "I've got to hand it to you, Callie." I perused the various makeup on the counter. "You had us all fooled. Who knew underneath your girl-next-door act was a goddamn snake?"

She sucked in a breath and froze.

"You probably noticed your laptop and diary are missing." I picked up a face-paint kit and a spare brush nonchalantly. "We stole those, by the way, and you're not getting them back."

"Fucking cunts, you had no right!" she snapped and lurched in my direction, but the binds jerked her back. "Those are my things! Give them back!"

The girls braced their hands on her body to hold her steady.

"No can do." I clicked my tongue and gave her my most apologetic expression. "Oh, and we read every single diary entry you've ever written. Not to mention, saw your amateur porn. We have all the proof with us. And you know what that means, don't you?"

Her silence was answer enough.

For a few seconds, Callie met my glare head-on, not backing down. I treated this girl like my family and all this time, she'd been talking shit and planning vile things for us behind our backs. It was a shame it came down to this.

I pushed aside every good memory I had with her. Birthday parties. Sleepovers and movie nights. Coffee and study dates. Seeing the fireworks every year at the Halloween carnival. After school cheer practices, especially the one where we accidentally broke Sister Victoria's statue in the foyer and burst into giggles before remembering that Principal Hill was going to punish our asses for such a big fuckup.

All those moments filtered through my mind like a film and slowly, one by one, I lit them on fire like I did Kian Wilson's car, erasing Callie Mackowski's existence from my mind the same way I did him.

I couldn't forgive her transgressions—hurting me, my family, my friends. Unacceptable. She'd give me my pound of flesh and then fuck out of our lives.

Picking up the brush, I dipped it in white paint. "Do you mind if I practice my makeup skills while we have this conversation, Cal?" I hit her with a shark grin. "I'm no expert, but I'm sure you'll look beautiful by the time I'm done."

The girls sniggered.

Callie stayed painfully silent, holding her breath as the first stroke touched her cheek.

I painted her entire face white first. "You pretended to be our friend for years, while secretly loathing us. I don't get it. We were only ever kind and sincere to you. Why all of this hate? What have we done to you?"

Once I began painting blue on her eyelids, she understood where this was going and shook in her seat, raging. "You all act like you're better than everyone else—me! All four of you bitches. Hera, you always thought you were the smartest in the room! Ella, you and Darla paraded around the school like you're queen bees and everyone should kiss the ground you walk on! And you," she spat in Dacia's direction. "You ruined my chances of becoming the captain of the cheerleading team by picking these two nepo sluts as your successor, you fucking *dyke*—"

Out of nowhere, Darla grabbed her designer purse and swung it so hard against Callie's body, the latter almost toppled over. We all shrieked and tried to stop Darla, who absolutely lost her cool.

Chaos ensued in the dressing room as limbs and curses shot everywhere.

"I dare you to insult my sister again!" Darla looped her purse strap around Callie's throat and tried to choke her. Callie croaked like a frog. "And I'll make you regret ever talking, you classless, tasteless, insufferable red riding witch!"

"Darla, no!" We couldn't murder the bitch no matter how tempting.

410

"Stop!"

Dacia managed to drag her sister away from Callie, wrapping an arm around her and whispering words like 'It's okay,' and 'She's not worth it.' Hera let loose a winded breath and pulled out the phone Josh gave us with *full access* to Callie's personal social media account.

Which had thousands of followers to witness her downfall.

"Listen up, you two-faced, idiotic, homophobic, lying bitch," I spoke calmly, but with barely concealed fury. "Your jealousy and insecurities are not our fault. Our only mistake was befriending you and treating you with love and kindness, while you harboured one-sided resentment towards us. Just because someone has something you want doesn't mean you have the right to insult them. Especially when those people did nothing to warrant your anger or judgemental thoughts." I continued painting Callie's face, adding a red nose and an exaggerated red grin. "If being in our presence— our accomplishments—intimidates you and makes you realize your own failures, then that sounds like a *you* problem. Because the truth is we've only ever supported and celebrated you, Callie. It's not Hera's fault that she is the smartest in the room. It's not Dacia's fault that she picked us as her successors, considering we earned our fucking place through hard work and sheer perseverance. As for Darla and me? We can carry ourselves however we goddamn please. It's just like Darla said…You're a classless, tasteless, insufferable *bitch* with a spectrum of issues…Absolute garbage in our book. And we no longer associate with you." I tipped her face towards the mirror with a flick of my fingers. "Do you like it? I think I did a good job at capturing your truth."

Callie looked like a fucking clown.

She fumed, seeing her reflection—seeing her ugliness. "There you go talking like you're once again better than everyone else, Ella."

Callie still didn't get it. "No. I don't think I'm better than anyone. But you do, based on the utter crap you wrote in your diary about your 'friends' and peers."

Hera launched the phone my way and I caught it. "Since you're so fond of talking shit about everyone else, we thought it was fitting to share your words with the world. See what they think of that, eh? I reckon they'll have the same opinion as us."

Callie barred her teeth, agitated. "What the fuck did you do!"

Wiped out all her previous pictures on her social media account to give us a clean slate…and then posted snapshots of her diary entries.

"Exactly as I said." I angled the phone's screen her way. "Showed the whole world your true colours."

The magnitude of her situation crashed down on her. She panicked, her breaths choppy, as I read out loud the rude and disgusting entries.

*"Dear Diary, Lori is trailer trash and a goddamn skank. She's got **gold digger** written all over her ass. The only thing she's good at is getting on her knees to suck rich boys' cocks. Hate whores like her. I can't wait till someone catches her and she gets expelled. Maybe I'll be the whistle-blower (pun-intended) and let Principal Hill know.*

Callie.

"Dear Diary, Cassidy apparently fainted in the crypt when she was cleaning it during detention. Claims she saw 'Sister Victoria.' My foot! She's got a penchant for fucking the loser nerds without a condom. I'm sure she's pregnant. That's why she's been having all those nausea and fainting spells. Though the Sister Victoria thing was a good cover-up, I'll give her that.

Callie.

"Dear Diary,

Bobby and I fucked. Anal, to be precise. He said it would be soooo much fun. It wasn't. He didn't use enough lube and he creamed in my ass. The worst part? He called me by Ella's name when he came. Guess he likes her and only got close to me for one reason. Fucking asshole. Fucking bitch. Hate them both.

Callie.

"Dear Diary,

I'm sick and tired of all the girls on the cheerleading team. Four years of this BS. Especially Ella and Darla. Who the fuck do they think they are? Co-captains? More like Co-cunts. I don't want to take orders from them. I worked hard to be on the team. I deserved to be captain. Dacia, the ex-captain, graduated St. Victoria two years ago and passed the torch to those two whores. Like they earned

it. Hah. I can't stand any of them. They ruined everything for me. So I'm going to ruin everything for them. They act like they're tighter than a nun's vow, but I'll drive a wedge between them. Make them regret ever getting in my way.
Callie."

By the time I finished reading, my skin crawled from relaying her nasty thoughts. They were all lies about others and situations she warped to better fit the narrative that pleased her sick mind. Safe to say, Callie wasn't a girls' girl and had internalized misogyny.

An anal creampie would be the least of her worries by the time we were through with her. "Sounds like you need professional help, Callie. In fact, we'd be more than happy to refer you to a few therapists. What do you say?"

"Fuck. You." Her posture deflated and her voice was weak. "Fuck all of you."

With our actions, she was now a social pariah. It was over for her.

The posts had thousands of likes already. People were going off in the comment sections. She'd never recover from this. Her reputation was beyond tarnished. A fitting punishment for someone who wanted to be revered by the masses.

"Smile for the camera, Callie." I brought the phone in front of her face with an obnoxious grin. "Say 'cheese'."

She didn't say cheese. Just stared at me with a hateful glare.

The thing I didn't understand was why Callie remained our 'friend' if she hated us? Why waste your energy on people you had no care for? Was there a deeper lying issue we weren't aware of?

I guess some things would remain unanswered. Based on her demeanor, it was clear she wouldn't say anything more as she marinated in her sheer humiliation.

Posting the image on her social media, I captioned it '**I'm a clown** 🤡' and attached the link to the Secrets of St. Victoria account, making her identity known there too. Then I turned the screen her way so she could see her picture one final time. "Beautiful, no?"

The girls gathered close, chuckling at the shot.

413

"I hate you," she spat, but there was no more power in her words.

"The feeling is mutual, Callie," I returned. "This is your karma. You created Secrets of St. Victoria to insult your peers and spread fake rumours, you photoshopped screenshots to ruin my friendship with Darla, and you gave Gavino my phone's passcode and helped him drug and assault Cade this past summer. You made your bed and now you have to lie in it." I put the phone in my pocket. "For the last offense alone, I'll fuck up your entire life. Do you hear me? No one lays a finger on my Cade and gets to walk away without a single consequence."

Callie paled, stammering out, "D-Drugged and assault? I-I don't know anything about that."

"Did you give Gavino my passcode or not?"

"If I did…I don't remember." Gavino may or may not have told her the intricate details of his plan but regardless, this idiot was an accomplice to what happened to Cade and Mabel. Unforgivable by all my standards. "I didn't know that Gavino hurt Cade over the summer. We only started sleeping together a few days ago. All I know is he asked for my help on Initiation Night, saying he wanted to rough up you and Cade a bit."

This, I believed. Their porn video was dated just this past Thursday. She hadn't written about it yet in her diary either. Otherwise, we'd have seen Gavino's name mentioned as the masked guy. So for the most part, she was kept in the dark about his plans. Still guilty, though.

The only laughable aspect of this situation was that these idiots actually thought going to jail would knock Cade and me down a peg.

"Are you trying to tell me that if you knew about all of Gavino's plans, you wouldn't have helped him?" I sneered.

"It doesn't matter." She glared at all of us. "Because you won't believe me. Are you fucking happy now that you've ruined my whole life?"

"You ruined your own life, Callie." I shook my head. "We're just the ones delivering justice."

I was a Cordova. My *papá's* daughter. Cold and ruthless if you crossed me. I would make you sorry until the day you took your last breath.

"Now that everything is said and done, *this* is the only mercy I afford you." I grabbed the arms of her chair and lowered myself until we were at eye level. "Once we walk out of here, three guards will come to retrieve you. They'll take you home so you can pack any necessary belongings. Then they're going to drive you to the next city. After that, you're on your own, but you will never, ever set foot in Montardor again. Do you understand me?"

"You can't do that! This is my home!" she growled. "You have no right, Ella!"

"I've got the strongest man in South Side backing me up, and let me tell you...Daddy Remington was furious to hear that you and Gavino tried to hurt his son." I tutted and she trembled. "Should you even try to contact the authorities, your family, or whatever friends you have left for help, there are people with strict orders to put a bullet through your head."

Callie started to cry, blue-stained tears cascading down her white cheeks.

Now she understood.

She fucked with us so we fucked with her career, reputation, and happiness.

It was all up in flames.

"You're done, Callie." I retrieved her cell phone from the front pocket of her jeans. "Have a nice life, bestie."

We bid her our farewells and spun around, walking out of the dressing room the same way we came in. Meaning business and total destruction.

Justice in Cade's court was poetic.

In mine? It was driven by pure fury.

Now that my scale was balanced, the Nemesis in me quieted down, satisfied with the end result of this carnage.

Once we reached the parking lot, we said our goodbyes, promising to see each other soon. For the first time in months, I felt relaxed, the burden on my shoulders lifting now that I had my girls back in my life.

They piled up in Darla's car while I straddled my Ducati and texted Cade.

It's done, querido. —Princess

Good girl. —Princepin

Now come meet me. —Princepin

Slipping my helmet on, I gunned it to our next destination.

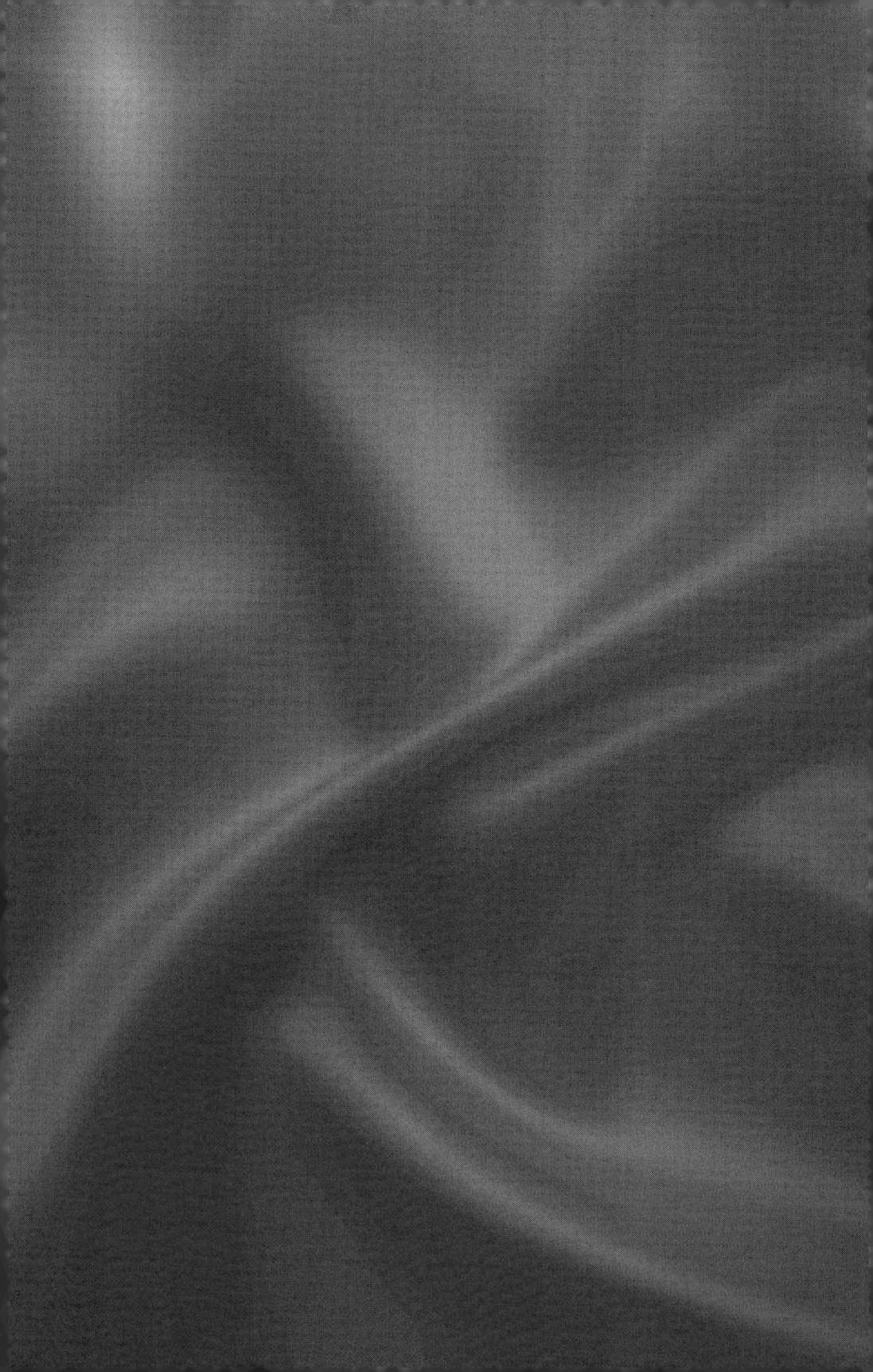

CHAPTER 35

Bloodthirsty Principin

Ella

The Present

Late at night, I was riding down the road when I heard the rev of another motorcycle. I didn't have to look back to know it was my boyfriend.

Cade's matching black Ducati slowed once it reached mine. We shared a quick glance and fist bumped, our grins hidden under our helmets. Riding alongside each other, we finally pulled up to the private property owned by the Remingtons, parking our motorcycles strategically behind a heap of trees.

Located between South Side and East Side, this old property once served as an amusement park in the early 2000s. Now it was abandoned and resembled a ghost town with most of the rides defunct, except for the carousel. Cade mentioned that Vance had plans of gutting it soon and rebuilding something new in its place.

Which meant it was the perfect place for our escapade.

As soon as I kicked down my bike stand and removed my helmet, I jumped Cade's muscular frame, climbing him like a tree. His deep laugh rang in the night like a symphony, muffled when I stamped my mouth to his in a lip-lock.

"Hi, baby," he murmured when we pulled away.

"Hi." I pressed tiny pecks all over his face. "I missed you."

His hands tightened on my waist as he lowered me to my feet, leaning into every little kiss. "I missed you too, Ella."

I pulled Callie's phone out of my pocket and handed it to him. "Here you go. Her passcode is 0000."

He unlocked her phone and perused the contents. "Did everything go smoothly?"

If painting her face into a clown, giving her a piece of our minds, posting her diary entries online, and revealing her identity on Secrets of St. Victoria counted then yes, *very* smoothly. "Oh, yeah. We got our revenge and I'm satisfied."

"Good." Cade smirked, pulling open the text conversation with Gavino. "Josh let me know the guards are with Callie and she's being driven to the next city."

Good riddance. "One down and one more to go, *querido*."

Cade kissed my forehead. "I'm going to text Gavino to meet us."

I hugged his arm and watched him message Gavino, pretending to be Callie.

Gav, we need to talk. It's urgent. —Callie

His reply came instantly.

What is it? —Gavino

Cade and Ella. I think they're onto us. —Callie

What the fuck?! —Gavino

He called and Cade automatically declined.

Callie…PICK UP. —Gavino

I can't answer right now. Can you meet me somewhere? —Callie

Fuck. —Gavino

You're joking, right? —Gavino

I'm not. But maybe we can sneak in a quicky afterwards?

◐ —Callie

"He's going to fall for it," Cade mumbled and I hummed in agreement.

Okay, fine. Where? —Gavino

Cade texted him the address.

The abandoned amusement park? —Gavino

Baby, you're a freak. —Gavino

Gavino sent a smiling face with heart eyes emoji.
We gagged.

I'll be there in an hour. —Gavino

Can't wait for you to fuck my pussy HARD. <3 —Callie

Cade and I cackled like villains when he pressed send.

See you soon, babe! —Gavino

"The unassuming idiot has no idea what's coming his way." Cade scoffed and pocketed Callie's phone before grabbing my hand. "C'mon. The boys are already here and they're helping us tonight. Let's go meet them."

We walked through the lot, taking inventory of the dirty ground from years' worth of pollution, rusty rides, and a broken-windowed concession stand until we finally arrived at the back of the outbuilding that once served as the public restrooms.

Wearing all black attire, Nico, Nate, and Sam were there, making graffiti on the brick wall before spotting us. "Lovebirds, you finally made it!"

I smiled good-naturedly at their teasing. Boisterous greetings echoed in our circle as they did that thing boys did whenever they saw each other—half handshake, half back claps.

Nico came to hug me first, brown eyes warm and dark inky curls whipping in the wind. "Hey, Ella. Good to see you again."

"You too, Nico." I hugged him back. "I hope you've been well. I'm sorry I haven't been to any of your races lately—"

"Hey, what about me?" said another familiar voice.

I glanced over my shoulder at Samuel, relieved to see his mischievous smile and green eyes without an ounce of contempt. Unfortunately, I cut ties with these guys, who were also my friends, after my breakup with Cade. I appreciated them acting like their usual welcoming selves, proving that the past was water under the bridge.

"You haven't been to any of my fights either," Samuel rasped, crossing his arms over his barrel chest. "I'm butthurt."

I grinned at his playfulness and ruffled his dirty-blond hair. "I'll make it up to you guys. I swear."

"Deal. Now that you're back with Cade—thank fuck, by the way, we were getting tired of his moping ass—will we be seeing you at the gym again?"

I learned how to fight courtesy of Cade and these boys. I missed the gym and wanted to start bringing my girls for self-defence lessons as well. "Yes." I gave him a hug too. "I'll be there next week."

"All right, time to talk business," Cade announced and we gathered in a circle. "Gavino is arriving within the hour."

Unlike the other boys, Nate didn't say anything except for throwing a brotherly arm around my shoulders in a silent greeting...and an olive branch. Considering our last exchange ended with me yelling at him for interrupting a situation I had under control. Whenever I ran into Nate after that moment, the mood between us was hostile. I regretted it. So I squeezed his hand back and we smiled, calling it a truce.

I felt much more at ease now that I knew I was back on good terms with all of them. I didn't realize how depressing it was to have my entire support system reduced to Callie after that summer night. Especially when I used to have so many people in my life who loved and championed me.

Another burden slowly lifted off my shoulders.

Everyone listened carefully as Cade provided updates on the whole Callie/Gavino debacle. "Callie's out of the city and Gavino's coming to meet 'her'—AKA us—soon. The property has three entrances, therefore we'll split up to stay on the lookout. Ella, you'll be with me, while the boys cover the rest. The minute Gavino crosses into the lot, we're all over him. Beat him. Taser him. Shoot his leg if necessary. But do *not* kill him. That's my job."

Of course it was. Nobody but Cade was allowed to deliver the killing blow.

After a few more instructions, it was go-time.

Ski masks slipped into place, Cade towed us towards the entrance closest to the carousel.

"How do you feel?" I asked him as our strides ate up the distance.

I heard Cade's smile in his voice. "Thrilled at the prospect of ending that motherfucker's life."

CADE

Exactly an hour later, a gunshot rang in the air, followed by Gavino's pathetic shriek. The boys' footsteps echoed in the lot as they brought him to us.

Baseball bat resting on her shoulders, Ella sauntered next to me, face covered in her ski mask and booted heels clicking loudly on the pavement. I cocked my gun as we met them.

They threw Gavino's trembling body at our feet. Blood poured out of a bullet wound in his shin. "P-Please, stop!" he wailed. "Who are you people?"

Ella lowered to her haunches in front of him and used the end of the baseball bat to tip his chin up. "We're your worst nightmare, Gav."

"W-What do you want?"

I shared a secret smile with Ella. Gavino grew more distressed, blue eyes teary, blond hair mussed. "Where's Callie? What have you done to her?"

"Your manipulative fuck buddy is far out of reach," Ella drawled. "She left the city and you at our mercy."

Callie hadn't, but nothing wrong in painting her as the bad guy after everything she did. He'd die thinking she betrayed him.

Gavino panted with little whimpers when he realized he'd walked right into a trap. "Who are you people?" he asked again.

I crouched down and patted his cheek condescendingly the way he'd done to me all those months ago. "I bet you didn't see us coming, huh, Ricci? We're going to enjoy exacting revenge. Even your dead brother Kian won't be able to recognize you in hell once we're through with you."

His blue eyes flared in recognition. "C-Cade? Ella?"

"Bingo!" My girl raised the baseball bat and thwacked him.

Gavino fell back, momentarily losing consciousness.

"Let's get this show on the road, pretty girl?"

Her eyes gleamed with wickedness. "Yes."

I tilted my head, signalling to my crew. They nodded and backed off, receding into the shadows until we were through with this traitor.

Grabbing Gavino by the scruff of his neck, I dragged him towards the carousel. Ella skipped beside me, humming a little tune under her breath.

I threw his limp body onto a paint-chipped mechanical horse and Ella dug through our supply bag, handing me ropes and my knife. I tied his ankles and his hands together around the pole. Now he resembled a pig getting roasted over a fire.

Stepping back to appraise my handiwork, I pulled off my ski mask.

"Ready?" Ella asked, doing the same. We both wanted to be the last faces he saw before it was game over for him.

"Ready." I kissed the tip of her nose and went over to the control panel.

I came last night to test run and make sure it still worked. Turning on the switches, warped carnival music resonated from the carousel and a few flickering lights came on, giving the entire thing a creepy allure. The platform started spinning slowly with a creaking noise and the horses shunted up and down rhythmically.

Ella hopped on the platform first, baseball bat and red gasoline can in her hands. I smiled seeing the back of her leather jacket bedazzled with *Property of Killian.*

Then I stepped onto the turning platform and poured an entire bottle of ice-cold water on Gavino's head. He awoke with gasps and a coughing fit. Those quickly turned into wheezing when he noticed he was strapped against a mechanical horse with nowhere to run.

Ella and I stared at him with smirks.

"Good evening, sleeping beauty." I leaned against an opposite horse with my arms crossed. "Did you have a good nap?"

Propped against the center pole, Ella snickered and popped a gum bubble.

"Why are you doing this?" he bemoaned. "Please let me go."

"Don't act stupid. You know this is payback for what you did to me. For what you did to Ella on Initiation Night." When I remembered this asshole put hands on my girl and hurt her ankle, a new wave of anger washed over me. So I shot his ankle to even the score. Gavino howled in pain. "Now I'm going to ask you a few questions and if I'm satisfied, I'll let you walk out of here as a free man."

I was lying, of course.

He was never leaving this carousel. It would be his final resting place.

Before the hour was up, he'd know why they called me a fixer.

"F-Fine," he whimpered. "I'll do anything. Just please, let me go. It hurts."

It's going to hurt even worse, Gavino.

I loaded more bullets into my gun. "First question: *why?*"

I didn't need to elaborate. He knew what I meant. And while I knew the answer, I wanted to hear him say it.

"You killed my brother," he barely managed to growl, body straightening on the horse as much leeway as the ropes would allow. "Kian was the only family I had and you fuckers took him away from me."

"Good answer. But you should know that Kian was a piece of shit." I began listing the reasons on my fingers. "One, he stole money from us. Two, he was overly handsy with women who told him 'no.' And third, he tried to sexually assault my girl at Jared Roy's party. So while he may have been a good brother to you, he was a fucking douchebag by every other standard."

423

"N-No." Gavino gulped. "Kian wouldn't do those things. He was innocent."

Ella and I shared a look. Gavino spoke with conviction, obviously having no idea of the extent of Kian's depravity. He obviously thought brother dearest was a good person.

"Second question: how did you figure out we killed Kian?"

"Can you loosen these ropes at least?" He whimpered again. "I'm in pain."

Ella came forward to tighten the ropes.

"You are in no position to make a single demand," I threatened. "The next time you do, you'll get another bullet. Understood, Ricci?"

He visibly paled, reining in his insults and pain as best as possible.

"Don't make me repeat myself," I said through clenched teeth. "How did you figure it out?"

He struggled to find his words, the blood loss already getting to him. Glassy-eyed and swaying, he mumbled his explanation, "The night you killed him, Kian was supposed to meet me at a bar after concluding his dealings. When he didn't show up...I got suspicious and went to the location he was last at. His car wasn't there, but...I found his watch—identical to mine—bloodied and half-melted, and his chopped-off hand with the same tattoo as mine. The smell of fire still lingered in the air and he was nowhere to be found, which meant he was either hurt or dead. Some of Kian's peers helped me track down the guard who kept watch on the warehouse. We tortured him until he confessed that you and Ella were the last ones there. My brother's car was located in the junkyard shortly... with blood speckles on the paint job. It didn't take a genius to figure out you two killed Kian."

"Kian got what he deserved." Ella shot him a menacing grin. "His death wasn't quick and he cried like a beggar every time I bashed him with my bat." Ella popped another gum bubble and slid the weapon along his body, letting Gavino know that she could do the same to him. "Then Cade butchered both of his hands and shot him until he bled out."

Gavino screamed, shaking in his restraint with renewed anger. "You fucking bitch!"

Ella threw her head back on a taunting laugh.

When would these brothers learn their lesson? No one was allowed to call Ella a bitch. I aimed my gun for his thigh and pulled the trigger. "Talk to my girl with disrespect again and the next bullet will land on your dick. Just like with your brother."

Gavino cried hysterically. Snot ran down his nose, his lips, and his chin like a waterfall. At least now he wouldn't say another word to Ella.

"Who were the men that helped you?" Old Johnny was found dead in his apartment over the summer. Bullet wound in his head and a gun in his hand. Now I realized Gavino and company made it look like he shot himself.

Whimpering, he snitched, "Vinnie, Douglas, and Bruno."

All low-ranking associates. Already dead. Meaning Uncle Vance and Josh wouldn't be able to partake in the fun like they initially wanted. "Were they the same masked men who helped you in the summer?"

To fucking drug and assault me.

"Y-Yes."

"Why did they agree to help you?"

"They didn't want to work for the Remingtons anymore," he cried. "They were part of Kian's circle."

The three fuckers probably thought they could either A, kill me for petty revenge or B, use me as a bargaining chip to obtain their freedom. "Vinnie, Douglas, and Bruno all died late July in a deal gone wrong. Is that why you waited until Initiation Night to try exacting your revenge again because you had no backup or brains, you idiot?"

Instead of answering, Gavino wept from the pain of the three bullet wounds and the tight ropes around his limbs.

I'll take that as a yes.

"P-Please, I've answered all your questions. Let me go. I'm getting d-dizzy from this stupid merry-go-round!"

I couldn't believe this was the same jackass who got into St. Victoria through a scholarship—the same one I played hockey with for years. Clearly, he was only book-smart and not street-smart. He'd failed both times at getting his revenge. And while his execution was nearly successful the first time, the fact remained that Gavino Ricci was an amateur who bit more than he could chew.

"What did I say, goldilocks?" I shot his left shin to match the right one. "You don't give me orders."

Over his pleas and cries, Ella said loudly, "How did you convince Callie to help you?"

"N-Not hard," he hiccupped. "She's wanted me for months. Willing to do anything. Plus, it was a bonus that she didn't like you guys."

"Did you bump into me the night of Josh's party?"

"Y-Yes."

"Did you send Cade the text messages to meet upstairs in his room?"

"Oh, God!" Gavino panted from the pain. "Yes, it was me!"

"How did you unlock my phone?" Ella asked her final question.

His hiss broke into another pitiful wail. "Callie gave me your passcode the night before. I met her at a bar, she was drunk, and it was easy to coax any information I wanted out of her."

I waved my gun at him. "So not only did you want to drug and assault me, but you wanted to drive a wedge between Ella and me by making it look like I cheated on her in the middle of a crowded party?"

When Gavino just cowered under my angry gaze, I barked at him, "Answer me, you lousy fuck!"

"I-I did, okay?" he wheezed. "It's not my fault it worked—ah fuckkk!"

I shot his right arm because he pissed me off. "The next bullet is going in your left one unless you give the gloating a rest."

I promised myself that once I caught the asshole behind the entire shitshow, I was going to force him to write a letter of apology to Mabel Garcia for implicating her in this mess. Unfortunately, Gavino wasn't in any state to crawl, let alone write, which meant I'd have to create a fake letter on his behalf to give her some form of closure and justice.

"Please," he slurred. "Can you just let me go? I've given you all my truths. I won't tell anyone about this night. I-I'll fuck off to another city."

I glanced at Ella.

She was already staring at me.

We got all our answers.

The puzzle was finally complete.

Gavino Ricci stupidly messed with us to get revenge for his good-for-nothing foster brother—someone who wasn't even a decent human being—and now he'd pay the price.

Wordlessly, Ella grabbed the gasoline can and started walking around the spinning platform, dousing the entirety in layers of slick oil.

I placed my gun back in my chest holster and cracked my knuckles.

Gavino, through a hazy gaze, watched me wearily.

"You want to know why they call me the fixer?" I smirked. "I *fix* pesky little problems like yourself, Gavino. And I'm damn good at it too. You should have done your research before choosing to fuck with me. I'm not a merciful man. I'm even less merciful where my girl is concerned. Fuck with her *or* me...and you're a dead man walking."

"B-But you said I could walk away if I answered all your questions!"

I tilted my head, my cold smirk turning into a frightening grin. "I lied."

Then I cocked my fist back and smashed it into his face, breaking his nose, his teeth, and the skin of his cheeks. Blood poured out of his orifices as I punched him to a pulp and shoved his head against the pole repeatedly until his cries were a distant sound compared to the vivid heartbeat rushing in my ears. "This is for putting drugs in my drink." *Slam.* "This is for trying to paint me as a cheater." *Slam.* "This is for messing with Mabel." *Slam.* "This is for touching my Ella." *Slam.* "And this?" *Slam.* "This is your final lesson: You *never* fuck with a Remington."

I bashed his face against the pole one final time, but he was already dead, his skull cracked open, oozing out like an egg. His body slumped like a puppet with its strings cut, his blood covering the once pastel-coloured mechanical horse. Some of his blood had landed on my face during the assault.

When I glanced at my reflection in one of the little carousel mirrors, I looked like I was bathed in his life force. The beast inside of me finally received his pound of flesh.

I was sated.

My eyes cut to my girlfriend, standing next to us with the gasoline can.

I looked like a monster.

She gazed at me like I was her saving grace.

"My bloodthirsty princepin," Ella said with awe and stars in her eyes, throwing her arms around my neck. "How I love you."

I smiled down at her. "And I love you, *mi vida*."

She wiped the blood on my face with her handkerchief and then I doused Gavino's dead body with the remaining petrol.

We stepped off the spinning platform.

I handed her my Zippo.

Ella shook her head. "No, Cade. This one is all yours."

Flicking the flint wheel, a small flame ignited. I lowered it to the trail of gasoline licking the ground and leading straight to the ride.

Within seconds, bright fire burst all around the merry-go-round, engulfing Gavino Ricci's corpse and the horses in a diabolic sight.

See you in hell, Gavino.

"How are you feeling now?" Ella asked.

"At peace."

"Good." She smiled. "I'm at peace too."

I extended my gloved hand towards her. "Let's go, princess."

Hand in hand, we sauntered away like thieves in the night.

Leaving absolute unhinged chaos in our wake.

Just the way we liked it.

CHAPTER 36

Forbidden Fantasy

CADE

The Present

On the night of Halloween, I finally made mine and Ella's fantasy come true.

I once said I practically lived to indulge this girl. All her whims, wants, needs, kinks.

And I was a man of my word. I never flaked on a promise. Especially one to her.

Fall leaves crunched beneath my shoes as I crossed the woods in the Remington estate towards the cabin where Ella waited for me. It was late night and the full moon was high in the sky, gleaming bright.

The night breeze swirled with notes of danger, sin, and forbidden pleasure.

Uncle Vance and Aunt Julia were at the Cordovas' with Olivia. Josh was out, too. Maybe still at the Halloween party we were previously at. Maybe getting a tattoo for Layla. Maybe showing up to her place and ripping off his shirt in surprise. Or something in between. And our guards on the graveyard shift were given clear instructions not to patrol anywhere around the woods so my girlfriend and I could have time for our extracurricular activities.

I entered the silent cabin with unhurried, measured steps. The lights were off and the only illumination came from the moonlight, filtering through the glass windows and coating the inside furniture with a silvery glint.

The door to the bedroom was left ajar by me.

After I'd collared and chained Ella to the queen-sized bed, I kissed her red lips, asked her to repeat her safe word—Orange—just in case, and then said I'd give her a few minutes to get into character.

Now when I crossed the threshold, I wasn't her tender-loving boyfriend.

I was playing the role of her fantasy. A cruel enforcer here to collect a debt.

Cracking my knuckles, I lowered myself to the chair set before the foot of the bed, where I had an eyeful of my girl's delectable body.

Tonight, she was dressed like a bloody bride. A white veil with a glittering tiara, white corset mini dress, white sheer stockings, white stiletto heels, and speckles of fake blood covering her ensemble from top to bottom. She looked both innocent and unholy.

Although she feigned sleep on her back, a slight tension radiating through her frame let me know that she was aware I was here and ready to play our game.

I relaxed into my chair and grabbed the crystal decanter on the table next to me, pouring two fingers of Irish whiskey into a tumbler. I smirked when I noticed Ella shifting in the sheets like she was 'waking' up.

"Did you sleep well, my bloody bride?" I rasped, leaning forward with my elbows perched on my knees, my drink cradled in my hand.

Ella yelped, her eyes finding mine in the dark. "Oh my God!"

"Is that a yes?" I chuckled darkly before taking a sip of my whiskey. "Or a no?"

She didn't answer at first, licking her lips nervously—*excitedly*—as her eyes roved over my silhouette.

I was in a black suit, black gloves, black shoes, and black ski mask. The only parts of me visible were my eyes, my lips, and the knife I twirled between my fingers.

"W-Why am I here?" The chains rattled as she tried to break free, kicking her legs and arms in every direction, causing the silk sheets beneath her to susurrate and the hemline of her already short dress to ride up so high...I saw a peek of that delicious pussy, barely covered by her joke of a lace thong, already wet. "Let me go!"

I unbuttoned my suit jacket and leaned back in the chair, my pointer finger tapping against the armrest in time with her laboured breathing. "You know why you're here, *Ximena*."

She shivered at the way I said her middle name. "I...I think I recognize you. From the Halloween party."

I nodded slowly, deliberately not saying a word.

"You..." Her eyes trekked down to the noticeable bulge in my pants. "You were watching me. When I was drinking and dancing with my friends."

We'd gone to a club for a Halloween party. That's where our fantasy began. As Ella danced and laughed with her friends, I'd stayed in the shadows, watching her like an obsessed stalker. She pretended to shoot me bashful glances and smiles, blushing innocently when my eyes never wavered from her form.

Every single minute had helped build the anticipation so when I 'kidnapped' her and brought her to my cabin, we'd fall effortlessly into our game.

"Did you like it?" I asked huskily. "Having my undivided attention all to yourself?"

Her thighs clenched in response like that needy pussy was already primed and ready for a few rounds of hardcore fucking. "*No.*"

I tutted, finishing my drink. "Little liar. I'll make you eat your words before you know it."

The chains rattled again and Ella released a half whine, half growl as she exerted more force to free herself. "Please let me go! I haven't done anything to you!"

"Mm, but you have." I stood up and tilted my head, watching her calculatingly. "All night long, you've *provoked* me with your come-hither smiles and your flirtatious glances. You made me insane with want and now you're going to be punished for your sins, Ximena."

Ella's chest heaved and down with her inhales and exhales. Her little tits were practically bursting out of her corseted bodice and my mouth watered at the thought of tasting her brown nipples—licking, sucking, tugging until she was a wanton, writhing mess beneath me. "Who are you?"

I climbed onto the bed with the grace of a predator, relishing the way she trembled as I loomed above, my hands and knees caging either side of her body. She was caught in the lion's den and her body language told me she lived for the thrill of it, despite the mock fear expression she tried to adopt.

Lowering my face, I soaked in the way her eyes darkened when I brought my lips just an inch over hers, my minty breath caressing her.

"My name's Killian," I rasped. "*Kill,* if you prefer." I dragged my mouth to her ear. "Also known as the man who's going to ruin you for anyone else."

Ella pretended to freeze, but I saw the undertone of excitement in her expression.

"Has anyone ever told you"—I trailed a finger across her lips, smearing some of her red lipstick—"that you have the most beautiful gaze in the world?"

She nodded, acting afraid of my interest in her. "Y-Yes."

"I've done my research on you, Ximena," I said softly and mapped my finger to her pulse, beating fast for me. "Spoiled heiress with a bad shopping habit. Marketing major at Vesta University. Loves lollipops, knitting, and anything orange. And my favourite? Ex-captain of the cheerleading team in high school. How am I doing so far?"

"Get away from me!" Ella squirmed under my touch. "Have you been stalking me this whole time?"

I brought my knife between us, placing the handle under her chin and tipping it up to meet my eyes. "And if I said yes?"

"Then I'd say you're crazy."

"I am," I promised in a dark tone. "For you."

Another shiver coasted down her spine. "Please…What do you want from me?"

I skimmed the dull side of my blade down her neck. "You owe me a

434

debt, Ximena, and I'm here to collect."

Without waiting for her reply, I used the sharp end of my knife to rip down her dress in one clean swipe while she gasped and squealed. The torn garment gaped and fell down on either side of her body, leaving her only in a veil, tiara, panties, garter, stockings, and those sexy heels—God, those heels that would be digging in my back as I fucked her like a beast.

I dragged my fingers from her throat down to her smooth pussy. "You are a literal goddess."

I lowered my mouth to her right nipple, blowing over it before flicking my tongue across the hard bud teasingly.

Ella cried out, loving my touch but pretending not to want it. "Fuck, fuck, fuck."

"Yes, you will be *fucking* me soon." Her cries turned to throaty little moans as I alternated between her nipples. Lavishing them with desperate licks, sucking them into my mouth until the pleasure bordered on pain, and grazing them with my teeth to remind her that I was holding back from giving her every bit of my dirty, ruthless side. For now. "Before the sun comes up, you'll be riding my cock like a dirty little princess begging to have her cunt filled with my cum."

"Please, you have to let me go!" she whimpered in pleasure, struggling to maintain character as I clutched her waist and spread noisy, open mouth kisses down her luscious body, pausing to trace the tip of my tongue over the **K** tattoo on her hipbone. "I'm rich! I can give you lots of money! Name your price!"

I shoved the black ski mask above my mouth, allowing her to glimpse my jaw and lips, which would be drenched in her arousal soon. "The only currency you're paying with tonight is this"—I ripped her soaked lacy thong and thrust two fingers knuckle-deep inside of her—"tight little pussy."

Ella's back arched on a breathy moan and her thighs fell open for more, the chains rattling as her hands pulled at the restraints. "Oh, God!"

"You're very wet," I praised, moving my fingers in and out of her slowly, making sure to crook against the spot that always made her sob in ecstasy. "Warm and sweet, too. I'm going to enjoying devouring you, my bloody bride."

435

She was panting, her heels digging into my shoulders as though trying to push me away from her. "I'm a virgin."

"You won't be for long," I vowed, my tongue flicking out against her wet cunt. "Hmm, you taste like heaven, baby."

"N-No, please!" Ella glanced down her body at me, a mixture of a bewildered and naughty look on her stunning face. "I need to stay pure for my future husband."

God, she played the fuck out of her role like a perfect actress. My girl was far from a blushing virgin, but my cock still hardened from her words and this fantasy.

"Fuck him," I growled, giving her pussy a hard slap before rubbing the sting with my fingers. "I'm the only one for you. Now and forever."

"P-Please, Kill. I'm a good girl. I'm—"

"You'll be a *filthy* girl by the time I'm done with you." I grabbed her ass when she tried to scoot away, dragging her closer to my mouth. "Remember to scream my name when you come. Otherwise, I will punish you."

"I—Ahhh!"

Eating Ella's pussy was one of my favourite hobbies. My tongue licked and sucked her clit until she whined and trembled in her chains. I stretched her tight opening at the same time with one, two, three—*four*—fingers. She bucked her hips for more while pretending to be shy, like she'd never had anything inside of her. I grinned wickedly into her flesh at her little porn-worthy noises, all the *please, more, ah, yes, ohs* making me harder than ever. I'd mastered the ability to make her come quick with a good tongue fucking, so it wasn't long before Ella let go, shattering wonderfully against my mouth.

As she recovered with panting breaths, I crawled over her until we were face-to-face.

Clasping her jaw, I smashed our lips together in a crude kiss, making her taste herself. Ella moaned, kissing me back and tangling her tongue with mine.

Then she bit me hard.

I pulled away with a growl, touching the drop of blood pooling at my bottom lip. With a disapproving noise, I hushed, "Naughty Ximena, that's no way to thank a man who gave you an orgasm."

In retaliation, I bit her neck. Right over her pulse.

She screamed. "*Pleasepleaseplease.*"

Satisfied with my blood smeared on her, I fisted the hair at her nape and tugged. "You didn't scream my name when you came. I'm going to have to punish you for your disobedience."

I rose over her and unbuckled my belt, pulling down my zipper and freeing my cock. Hard, swollen, and needing her so bad.

Ella licked her lips salaciously. She always loved a good face-fucking.

Remembering our game, she squirmed again and asked haughtily, "If I do this for you, will you let me go?"

I will never let you go, sweetheart.

I pretended to consider it for a moment as I jerked off. "Maybe… Or maybe not."

She opened her mouth of her own volition, zeal sparking in her gaze, as I brought my tip to her lips. Before she could suck, I yanked on her hair to the point of pain, halting her. "Say you wanted me first. Say you danced for me, smiled for me, eye-fucked me in a room full of people because you wanted the night to lead right here, Ximena."

Ella batted her lashes innocently, gulping. "No. I didn't mean for—"

I thrust into her warm mouth in one go, muffling her protests. I pulled out and she gasped, a saliva ribbon threading my cock to her lips. Smiling cruelly, I shoved back inside of her throat, feeling it flex around my flesh. Fucking hell. I groaned. "Can't admit it yet?" *Thrust.* "No problem." *Thrust.* "You may think of yourself as a virtuous princess." *Thrust.* "But I know a sinner when I see one." *Thrust.* "You're just like me, baby." *Thrust.* "And tonight?" *Thrust.* "You wanted to be at my mercy, getting your tight little holes fucked brutally by me."

No more words were exchanged as I pounded without finesse, giving her the rough, throat-stretching, face-fucking she goddamn adored. Ella quaked underneath me with a series of glugging noises. The headboard banged against the wall with the force of my drives and the chains shook as her nails dug into my torso. The rustling of the fabric let me know she was squeezing her thighs together, trying to get relief on her pussy. Her face turned into an exquisite mess as tears ran down her cheeks and her red lipstick feathered around her mouth.

"Tight little brat," I rasped, pumping faster, the sound of my belt buckle swishing echoing in the room. "You're going to make me come so fucking good!"

She hadn't earned my seed yet, so I pulled out at the last second, making her cry out in disappointment. She loved drinking me down and being filled with my cum. She wasn't getting any of those things right now. "*Killian!*"

That spoiled diva tone just did it for me.

I shuttled my inches in my fist, groaning as I shot spurts all over her wet face and body, painting her like a masterpiece.

Ella stared at me with shock and awe.

Laughing devilishly, I tucked my cock away and zipped myself up. "I'm not ready to let you go yet." I wiped my cum from the corner of her lips and fed it to her. She sucked my fingers automatically. "However, if you please me next, I might grant you your freedom."

"What do I have to do?" she whispered all soft and innocent.

Fuck, no one turned me on like this woman. I couldn't wait to be inside of her.

"Do you want to play with me, Ximena?"

We both knew what that sentence meant to us.

Her breathy inhale was a telltale sign. "What are the rules, Kill?"

I walked two fingers up her leg and towards the heaven between her thighs. "I want you to run. I want you to try your best to escape me. There's an unlocked car with keys at the edge of the woods. If you get to it first, you're free. But if I catch you?" I smirked. "I'm going to fuck you. As hard, as deep, as long, and as many times as I please. And if you satisfy me with your cheer pussy—the one you've been taunting me with all night long—maybe I'll let you go, Ximena."

Ella couldn't disguise her elation at the thought of being fucked in the woods. "Okay."

Taking the key out of my pocket, I unlocked her cuffs and collar from the headboard. Still role-playing the shy virgin, she shielded her private bits with her hands.

"You look even more beautiful covered in my cum."Tipping her chin with two fingers, I leaned close, brushing my lips to hers. "Now *run*."

Ella scurried from the bed and shot out of the door, her sheer veil floating behind her like a white flag.

Grabbing my knife and belt, I followed after my prey.

Ella

My heart beat extremely fast as I ran out of the cabin and straight into the woods. The wind caused the trees to rustle and a pair of crows cawed in the distance, yet the only sounds I could concentrate on were my hurried footsteps and those of Cade...slowly stalking after me.

This dark game with fear and primal play wrapped together in a pretty red bow filled me with so much exhilaration, I could barely think straight. And while I was far from a damsel in distress, I was having so much fun role-playing the part.

The leaves beneath my feet nearly caused me to slip. I debated taking off my heels, but that would only slow me down. Fighting the light chill nipping at my naked, cum-stained skin, I kept running, feeling Cade's shadow closing in on me like a hunter cornering its prey.

I knew these woods very well, therefore navigating through them wasn't difficult. Cade's black Ferrari shouldn't be parked too far. My debt collector was giving me a head start even though he could have easily caught up to me. He wanted me to reach his car. He wanted me to touch the door and feel my freedom. And then he wanted to snatch it away from me until I was screaming and giving him what we both desired.

My veil whipped in my face with the next gust of wind. I pushed it back and eased my pace when I finally spotted his sports car, gleaming under the moonlight like a beacon of hope.

Cade's footsteps grew louder.

I glanced over my shoulder, seeing his big body nearing. Panicking, I lurched forward and my fingertips grazed the door handle.

Then I felt the heat of his presence behind my back.

"Looks like you're not escaping me tonight, Ximena." Cade grabbed my hips and yanked me back. I collided with his muscular front. "Time to cash in on my prize."

Banding his arm around my waist, he lifted me up and away from the Ferrari.

"No, no, no!" I screamed and pretended to struggle as he dragged me deeper into the woods, encasing us in more darkness. "Please!"

I was having the time of my life and trying not to let my real grin shine through.

Cade tossed me down in the middle of an opening surrounded by tall trees. Instead of finding dirt and leaves beneath my hands and knees, it was a soft blanket. He didn't want me to get a single scratch as he'd said earlier tonight. My boyfriend was so sweet.

When Cade fell to his knees behind me, I tried to crawl away. It was in vain. He grabbed my ankles and tugged me back to him, his strength overpowering mine. "Caught you," he murmured. "Now you belong to me, baby."

Clutching my neck, he pressed my face down and hiked my ass up before spanking me with his belt. I cried out. That same belt was then looped around my neck and tightened like a leash. "Killian—"

"Quiet," he commanded. "Don't act like being chased and pinned in the woods doesn't turn you on, you kinky little slut." He clapped his hand—sans leather glove—hard on my ass. I whimpered from the sting. "You're dripping down your thighs with the need to be ravaged."

Good God, was I ever.

Cade thrust his fingers in my soaked pussy and fucked me to a maddening rhythm, tugging on the belt and causing my back to arch. I loved when he asserted his dominance.

"Do you like having your virgin cunt fingered?"

I shook my head, but my breathy moan revealed the truth.

He tsked. "I told you I'd make you eat your words." He brought his fingers in front of my face, sticky with my arousal. "Seems like you *love* it, little cheerleader. You're drenched for me."

Cade shoved those same fingers in my mouth and I sucked greedily.

He groaned, loving it when I tasted myself.

He pulled out his fingers and went back to thrusting them into my pussy. I throbbed, needing to be filled by something more than his fingers. But he was being a tease, purposely denying me.

I rocked my hips back and forth, chasing his fingers and my pleasure desperately.

Cade gave my ass another slap in appreciation. "Goddamn, I'll never be done with you. Keep fucking my fingers like that and I'll drag you to the altar and make you my Mrs. before you know it."

I broke character for two seconds to say over my shoulder, "Don't threaten me with a good time, *querido*."

Surprised, he chuckled, a twinkle appearing in his blue eyes.

It was no secret that one of my life goals was to drag Cade to Vegas and marry him.

We fell back into our roles as Cade continued fingering me, hitting my G-spot and inciting my screams. I was certain I scared away all the ghosts and birds in the vicinity.

Before I could come, he removed his fingers and rolled me over.

"Killian!" Frustration spiked at having been denied my second orgasm. I barely had time to curse at him when he suddenly shoved my thighs open and lined my knees with my shoulders until I was folded in half.

"Do you want to come?" he asked in that deep voice that caressed me intimately.

Shivering, I nodded shyly.

He unbuttoned his black dress shirt, slowly revealing every expanse of his beautiful tattooed frame. My mouth watered seeing those bulging muscles, so thick and hard from years of work. I wanted to sink my teeth into them. Taste the fragrance of his skin on my tongue. Trace every ink he had in my honour while he made love to me in the roughest way possible.

He dropped his shirt and lowered his zipper, pulling out his hardened cock again. Seeing him fist it with his right hand, the same one with my birth date tatted in roman numerals on his knuckles, had my breaths quickening. It was so sexy.

Cade meant it when he said I was branded in every corner of his being.

He was in mine, too.

My mind, my body, my soul.

"Now tell me what I want to hear." He seized my jaw with one hand and used the other to guide his tip to my pussy, slowly gliding through my wet folds. I bucked my hips in a silent demand for more. "Say it. You wanted me. You wanted me to steal you away and do dirty things that make you feel alive, Ximena."

I threw my head back on a moan when he rubbed his cock against my clit, sending a flurry of sensations through my core. My toes curled and my nails dug into his shoulders with intent. "Yes," I whispered. "I wanted you at the party and I want you now...and forever."

It was all he needed to hear.

Cade rammed all eight inches inside of me in one deep thrust.

I screamed and he groaned gutturally, my muscles clenching around his thickness. He gripped my hips and started slamming his cock into my cunt, his masculine grunts echoing in my ear. "Tight little virgin, all mine to sully, hm?" he taunted, licking the shell of my ear. "You're taking it so well." *Thrust.* "Squeezing me so good." *Thrust.* "Fitting me so perfectly." *Thrust.* "You were made for my cock." *Thrust.* "Made for *me.*" *Thrust.* "You like it, don't you?" *Thrust.* "Getting fucked in the woods after being chased like a prey?"

I moaned in agreement, wrapping my legs around his waist.

"I knew you were a sinner," he grated. "Just like me, baby."

Raw. Animalistic. Dirty. My dark fantasy fucked me for all I was worth. He bounced his thick cock inside of me with savageness, treating me like his personal fuckdoll. I was his to mold, his to use, his to break. Every breath in my lungs was laced with the taste and smell of him. Earth, leather, wood, sin. Like a maestro, he played my body to a tune that never

442

failed to bring me straight to euphoria.

A hunger like nothing I ever experienced before clawed at my insides. Under the sway of the full moon, carnal lust spread through me. I licked the tattoos on his right arm. Sucked the skin on his shoulders. Bit the chain housing my promise ring. Squeezed the muscles of his ass in encouragement. Raked my nails along his back and broke skin. I did all of that while being reduced to a whining, incoherent mess. "*More, more, more.*"

As he worked himself to the hilt over and over again, he brushed the spot inside of me that broke my dam, causing a small burst to rush out of me and cover our slapping sexes.

Cade went feral when I squirted, fucking me faster, harder, and deeper than before, wrapping his hand around my throat. Holding me in place as he forced me to just *take, take, take,* until I was breathless from his grip and on the verge of my release.

A fine sheen of perspiration glittered on his inked body as drove into me, the sound of our skins smacking against one another amplified in the woods. Cade looked magnificent under the moonlight, succumbing to our passion.

"My beautiful bloody bride," he growled, tightening his hand around my throat. "Play with your clit. Make your pussy come around my dick. I want to feel you milking the cum out of me like a filthy girl."

Trembling, I snaked my hand down to rub my sensitive clit and glanced at the erotic picture of his fat cock pushing into my small cunt. His length glistened with my arousal and a smear of blood, a telltale sign that I got my periods since I was due.

"Do you like the way we look, Ximena?"

"Y-Yes."

"Good. Get used to it." He slapped my tits with both hands. "Because from now on, you'll be spending every night on your back servicing me until we're both satisfied." Then he twisted my nipples until I moaned from the pleasure and pain. "Until we take our dying breaths, baby."

"Until you find me again in the next lifetime?" I murmured vulnerably, heart pounding fast for him.

He gave me a wolfish smile and leaned down to whisper against my lips, "Promise, pretty girl."

With my teeth, I frantically tugged his ski mask over his mouth and latched onto his lips with a needy noise. Kissing him wildly. Licking the **ELLA** tattoo. Sucking on his tongue. All while he braided his fingers with mine and brought them above my head, reciprocating my demanding kisses as he gave me more of his cruel lovemaking.

Skin on skin, breath with breath, heart to heart, we watched each other as we neared our completion. The way he gazed at me in reverence undid me. I thrived being the center of his universe. He made me feel cherished, powerful, and untouchable.

It wasn't long before we came together, our shouts and groans resounding in the air.

Panting, Cade laid his forehead to mine, a shudder moving through his muscular body. I held him to me, removing his mask and caressing my fingers over his face in gratitude.

He created this whole fantasy for me.

I was truly the luckiest girl in the world.

"Ellie?" he mumbled, eyes still closed, chest bowing against mine with every breath. "You okay? Was I too rough?"

Why did he sound so cute and spent? Now I was the one going feral, smacking pecks all over his face. "I'm more than okay. That was perfect. Who knew you'd play the role of my obsessed, stalking, psychotic admirer so well?"

"I mean, it's not like I didn't have practice over the summer."

I burst out laughing.

His dimples came to life.

Naturally, I showered them with more kisses.

Cade gently pulled out of me with another groan. Now that our game was over, I felt sore everywhere.

"Fuck, that's so hot." He watched his cum dribbling out of me. With two fingers, he scooped it back inside my pussy. "Mm. I want to keep filling you up. I never want to stop."

My dirty *querido*. How I adored him.

I looped my arms around his neck and pulled him back down to me. We'd have to clean up soon, but I just wanted to feel him like this a bit longer. "Thank you for tonight. I had fun. In fact, I think we should make this a yearly tradition."

"I'm game." He pushed aside my white veil and tucked the stray strands of my hair behind my ears. "Anything you want, Ella."

The gold chain around his throat glinted in the moonlight.

Slowly, I removed it from his neck and unthreaded the promise ring. My full name was engraved in cursive along the twenty-four-carat gold band.

Understanding dawning upon Cade, he extended his right hand to me. Filled with anticipation, he held his breath as I slid the ring on his finger again.

When it sat at the base of his knuckle, he finally exhaled with relief.

Bestowing a soft kiss on my lips, he whispered tenderly, "I love you, Ella."

No longer was there yearning in his eyes.

All I saw was love for me and hope for the future we once created together.

I smiled at him. "And I love you, Cade."

With those words, I remembered the truth of our existence.

There was no Ella without Cade.

And there was no him without me.

He was my beginning, my middle, my end.

In this lifetime and all the ones to come.

CHAPTER 37

The Greatest Gift of All

CADE

The Present

I had been celebrating *Día de Muertos* for the last three years with Ella. It was a special traditional holiday in her culture to honour their ancestors.

The night after Halloween, me, my family, and some close friends were gathered at my girlfriend's home to partake in the occasion. The Cordova mansion was decorated in bright festive colours, *calaveras*, *papel picado*, and an enormous *ofrenda*—home altar—in the foyer. We had dinner, drinks, and listened to their family share funny anecdotes and stories of their dead loved ones.

Francisco and Silvia Cordova kept giving me warm smiles throughout the evening, as I sat next to Ella at the formal dining table. Somewhere in the last two weeks, they'd come to genuinely accept me as their daughter's boyfriend. Ella told me they saw the errors in their ways. In the past, I'd said that nobody's opinion mattered to me, but I'd be lying if I said that having their blessings didn't fill me with gratitude. It was a silver lining and made me feel even more comfortable about the future Ella and I would create.

"You should join us next week on our hunting trip, Cade," Francisco offered politely.

Uncle Vance stared at me with pride from across the table.

Although I wasn't into hunting innocent animals, I gave him a nod. "I'd like that."

It was the closest we'd come to a truce. The relief in the room was palpable. Aunt Julia was teary but hid it by taking a sip of her tequila and Ella's *mamá* just seemed plain happy.

My girlfriend squeezed my hand under the table with a soft smile.

"You're beautiful," I mouthed to her when nobody was looking.

Ella was dressed in a rich orange gown that made her tan skin glow, her black hair was straightened, and she wore the aquamarine heart-shaped necklace I gifted her over the summer. The one she swore to never, ever take off again.

"So are you," she mouthed back with a playful wink.

A lopsided smile bloomed over my lips at her compliment.

After dinner, I was headed to meet Ella when I suddenly found myself tucked under the grand staircase with Olivia. Apparently, she and the kids were playing hide-and-seek. She saw me walking by with a glass of *champurrado* and *pan de muerto* and ushered me over with a whispered, "Cadie, come here!" Now I was on my knees next to her little form, dunking pieces of sweet bread in the hot chocolate and feeding it to her. Turns out, she wasn't excited to see me. She just wanted my dessert.

"Thank you." Olivia munched on the last bite with enthusiasm, then brought her finger to her lips in the universal *shh* sign. "Don't tell Emi I'm hiding here."

"I won't, Livvy." I chuckled. "All done or do you want some more?"

She patted her full belly. "All done."

Olivia was adorable in her pink ruffled dress with a skull painted on her face. I couldn't resist kissing her chubby cheek and ruffling her hair. "Don't get into too much trouble while I'm gone, okay?"

"'Kay," she whispered cheekily and went back to her dark hiding spot.

Shaking my head, I left with a smile, no more *pan de muerto*, half a glass of my favourite *champurrado*, and towards Ella. I walked down a hallway, passing by a few giggling kids, past the formal family room where all the adults had migrated with drinks, before reaching the foyer.

My girlfriend stood in front of the *ofrenda*. It boasted clusters of marigolds, candles, water, candy sugar skulls, favourite foods of the deceased, and picture frames housing photos of those passed on, allowing their spirits to crossover.

Ella's back was to me, so she didn't see me approaching. She fussed over the altar and adjusted the flowers and copal incense.

Just as I came to her side and wrapped an arm around her waist, she placed a little hand-knitted onesie on the altar.

"Is that for..." My throat tightened.

Ella turned to me with a sad smile. "Yes, for our *angelito*."

For our little angel. My heart gave a painful twist.

I kissed her forehead. "One day, we're going to have that family you always wanted. I promise."

She sifted her fingers through my hair, kissing my jaw. "And you never break one."

"Never."

Her blue-brown gaze was warm tonight, glowing in the candlelit space. "I want to show you something. Will you follow me?"

I would follow you until the ends of the earth, sweetheart.

Nodding, I let her wordlessly guide me to the solarium, my hand twined with hers.

"Close your eyes," she said with a tinge of mischief.

We walked deeper into the room and she pressed on my shoulders, silently asking me to sit down on one of the couches. I obliged and kept my eyes closed, feeling her move around the space and set some things into place.

I heard the flick of a Zippo and the smell of fire wafted in the air.

"Open now, please."

When I saw a cake sitting on the coffee table before me, lit with nineteen candles, I grinned wide.

Ella took a seat next to me and murmured, "Happy belated birthday, Cade."

She missed mine and this was her way of righting some of our wrongs.

"Thank you, Ella." I kissed her knuckles. "This is so sweet."

"I made you your favourite yellow cake with chocolate frosting." She laid her head on my shoulder and gazed up at me. "Make a wish, *querido*."

"What should I wish for?" I cupped her face and polished my thumb over her chin. "When I already have everything I desire?"

Her expression softened and her silence spoke volumes as she caressed my wrist, over my pulse, in understanding.

Now that I had her in my life again, I didn't need anything else.

Regardless, I still made another wish and blew out the candles.

She cut a thick slice and handed it to me on a plate. I fed her the first forkful before taking one for myself. "It's delicious, Ella. Even better than the *champurrado* and *pan de muerto* that Olivia stole from me."

That made her laugh. "I caught Olivia and Emilio sneaking chocolates behind the kitchen staff's back."

I fed her another bite of the cake. "Those two are going to be a handful when they grow up, huh?"

"Yes, they will." Smiling, she stood up. "Wait here. I have some more surprises for you."

"More than one?" I arched an eyebrow. "You're spoiling me."

"I'll always spoil you from here on out."

She repeated my own words back to me three years later and I beamed.

Ella dragged out a gift-wrapped square frame from behind the couch. I didn't like her lifting heavy things even if she could. I grabbed it from her and laid it on the coffee table. "What's this, Ellie?"

"Open it." She practically bounced up and down with excitement.

I cut through the tape using my knife. Wrapping removed, I glanced down at the painting in awe.

The initials **V.R.** were painted in the corner.

Ella snaked her arm with mine and kissed my bicep over my suit jacket. "Your mom painted this before you were born. Your uncle helped me find it."

Strong emotions coursed through me. I couldn't breathe or speak. Only stare at one of the few artworks I had left of my mom.

Vera Remington had been a talented painter and renowned artist in the city. Her paintings used to be displayed in many art galleries. Most of her creations were already sold or had burned down in our last home, forever lost to me. Uncle Vance and Aunt Julia had some rare gems hanging around the Remington estate.

But this painting?

It invoked a maelstrom of feelings inside my chest, all warring between happiness and sadness.

The landscape was lush greenery with a sunset sky. A cottage style home on the left and the backs of three figures on the right, standing hand-in-hand, facing the glimmering water.

Ella pointed to the figure on the left. "That's Vera." To figure on the right. "That's Ronan." And then to the small figure in the middle. "And that's you as a toddler." She glanced up at me, noticed the moisture in my eyes, and grazed her knuckles along my cheekbone. "Julia told me your mom painted this after she had a dream...when she was pregnant with you. This is the kind of life she wanted for you all."

Quiet. Peaceful. Away from this wretched world of ours.

I missed my parents now more than ever.

A tear unexpectedly fell down my cheek. Ella gasped under her breath and kissed it away gently. Unable to utter a single sentence, I crushed her to me, silently thanking her for giving me such a thoughtful gift.

Ella rested her head on my chest, hugging me tighter.

We stayed locked in an embrace for what felt like an eternity.

The world could end this very moment and I would be fulfilled with her in my arms.

"Thank you, *mo chuisle*." My voice was thick when I found it again. "My parents would have loved you."

It was the very truth. Mom and Dad would have adored the ever-loving hell out of Ella.

She wiped under my eyes with her thumbs and kissed my lips. "And I would have loved them too."

Ella picked up a manilla envelope from the coffee table. She extended it my way. "This is also for you."

I weighed it in my hands. It was thick and heavy. Ella watched intently as I opened it and pulled out a slew of documents.

It took me a minute to register the surprise.

And when I did, I felt speechless once again.

Deed to a property in Ireland under my name.

Questions buzzed through my mind, but all I could focus on was the four-by-six-inch photo tucked in between the papers.

It was a vast land with a beautiful home.

Just like the one from the painting.

Stunned, I just stared at Ella, my heart expanding in my ribcage with all the affection I felt for her. "Is this the exact place my mom painted?"

Ella nodded. "Yes. After I found the painting, Julia told me Vera was inspired by a particular place she'd seen on a family vacation in Ireland. I did some research, found it listed, and bought it for you. I hoped it would make you feel closer to your mom and dad."

My voice was raw as I whispered, "Ella…"

"I wanted to gift you something meaningful and memorable. You always do so much for me and sometimes I don't have the words to convey how thankful I am. But this? This is my way of *showing* it to you." She framed my face with both hands, peering up at me with so much tenderness, my chest constricted. "You once mentioned that your parents had planned a trip to Ireland for your sixteenth birthday and you were looking forward to it…before they unfortunately passed away. They may not be here physically, but I like to think they're still here spiritually. And while I didn't have the privilege of meeting them, I also like to think that they would have wanted you to go on that trip." She smiled at me. "So I say let's do it. Go on the vacation you always wanted and stay at this very place, Cade."

I was floored by the depth of love this girl possessed for me.

"I think that's a fantastic idea." I tightened my arms around her waist. "Thank you for giving me one of the greatest gifts."

She kissed my dimples. "And what's the greatest gift you've ever received?"

I smiled and kissed her right eyelid. "You, Ella."

EPILOGUE

Ella

A few years later...

The sound of a pebble hitting my balcony doors had me placing the romance book I was reading face down on my blanket. With a frown, I headed out of bed and towards the source of the noise.

Cade was away for business with Vance and Josh. I decided to visit my parents' home with Knight so I wasn't alone in our shared penthouse.

The summer wind blew through my long black strands as I stepped out on my balcony, the skirt of my dress flaring behind me. It was a beautiful evening with the sun slowly begging to set, colouring the sky's canvas in remarkable shades of gold, pink, and blue.

The balustrade was overflowing with orange begonias, their sweet scent bringing forth a bout of nostalgia. An adorable pair of hummingbirds flittered around the blooms, drinking their nectar.

"What are you smiling at, Ella?"

I jolted at the unexpected, familiar voice ringing so close.

"Cade?" Frowning, I peered around, seeing him nowhere in my surroundings.

Was I beginning to imagine Cade because I missed him?

"Down here, pretty girl." His tone was laced with mischievousness.

Oh, God. No, that wasn't my imagination at all.

I ran to the edge of the balcony and glanced down, my mouth falling open in surprise. A chuckle escaped me when I realized he'd positioned a ladder against the structure and was slowly climbing the rungs towards me.

"What are you doing here?" My cheeks hurt from how hard I was smiling. "I thought you weren't coming back until tomorrow."

"Business concluded early." He finally reached the last step and paused, placing his hands on the balustrade and leaning forward to kiss me. "And I was desperate to get back to you."

I kissed him back, grasping fistfuls of his dress shirt. "I missed you."

"I missed you too," he mumbled against my lips. "So much."

I nuzzled his cheek. "Is there a reason why you're climbing up to my balcony like Romeo?"

"Yeah, actually, there's a reason for it, Juliet."

"Oh?" I hiked a brow, feeling giddy. "Tell me."

The breeze mussed his dark hair and he pushed it back, smiling at me heart-meltingly with those dimples on display. Even after all these years together, he never failed to take my breath away.

He was so handsome, my dark prince.

"Ella, the first time I saw you standing on this very balcony, you looked like a goddess to me. I was awestruck by you. I'd never seen a more beautiful girl in my life and your sweet smiles and playfulness revived something inside of me that had been dead for so long. You brought me back to life." He grasped my cheek with one hand. I turned my head to kiss his palm, warmth unfurling in my chest. "Falling in love with you was inevitable. I knew since we were sixteen that I wanted you to be mine forever. Every year since, I've fallen deeper for you. I could write an entire book to express how much I love you and it still wouldn't be enough to convey my feelings. You're my ride or die, my soulmate, my pulse, *mi vida*. I would die for you, kill for you, live for you. In this lifetime and all the ones to come." A tear trailed down my cheek as I watched him flip open a small velvet box, revealing a stunning orange diamond nestled in a yellow gold band. "Ella Ximena Cordova, will you marry me? Will you be my wife and make me the luckiest man on earth, *mo chuisle*?"

It felt like I waited my whole life for this moment.

"Yes, Cade." I grabbed his face with my trembling hands, sniffling. "Yes, I will marry you!"

456

"Thank God," he joked. "Not that I had a doubt, of course."

I laughed, but it was watery.

He slid the ring on my finger, taking a second to admire it.

"It's perfect. I love it." The unique diamond glittered under the setting sunlight. I glanced at him, full of love and hope and excitement for our future. "I love you, Cade."

He leaned forward to kiss me again. "And I love you, Ella."

I finally got my Vegas wedding.

Cade looked devilishly handsome in a navy three-piece suit poured over his tall, muscular body, his dark brown hair styled artfully, and pure reverence shining in his sky-blue eyes.

My white dress was short, ending just above the knees, with a sweetheart neckline that awarded it an elegant and timeless look, created by Maison Sereno. My ensemble was complete with my long black hair curled to perfection, a veil with both our names embroidered, a crown and jewelry made of endless diamonds and pearls, and a white leather jacket resting over my shoulders—the same one that I'd bedazzled years ago with the words *Mrs. Cade Killian Remington.*

All our friends and families were present. My girls looked gorgeous in matching orange bridesmaids' dresses and the boys all wore matching blue ties. Including Shaun, who was Cade's best man and doing the most, clapping and whooping the loudest. If he hadn't paired us together on Initiation Night all those years ago, maybe Cade and I would not be here today.

Darla was my maid of honour and I was so thankful that the universe brought us back to each other. The last few years were filled with joy, laughter, and many girls' trips around the globe, and I wouldn't have it any other way.

And despite how happy she looked for me, I couldn't help but notice how her smile was laced with a bit of wistfulness. It broke my heart that she may never have this. Her marriage was recently arranged to one of the most corrupt men in Montardor. Zeno De la Croix reigned the city's underworld and I was afraid he'd eat my best friend alive.

If I could have done something to prevent it, I would have. I was forever protective of Darla.

"You look incredible," Cade whispered to me, holding on to my hands as a fake Elvis Presley officiated our wedding. "I can't take my eyes off you."

The look on his face when he'd first seen me in my dress was seared in my mind. I'd remember it even when I was lying on my deathbed.

"Thank you." I blushed under his praise. "You look incredible, too."

We finally said our vows and exchanged our rings. The matching gold bands were engraved with the words *You and I* on top. Except the underside of mine was embossed with **CKR** and his with **EXC**. If ever we removed our rings, the initials would still be creased in our skin. Another way of branding ourselves as belonging to one another. On top of the tattoos we already possessed. Including the one I got years ago on my ass cheek that said *Property of Cade*. That was perhaps my *querido's* favourite one on me.

"You may now kiss the bride!" Shaun hollered before Elvis Presley got a chance.

Cade closed the distance and kissed me with eagerness. Banding an arm around my waist, he dipped me back, causing me to giggle and wrap my arms around his neck.

Everyone cheered as we basked in the moment of finally being married.

Even though we didn't need a piece of paper to certify that we belonged to each other.

We always had.

We were soulmates. We were fated. We were written in the stars.

"We forgot to sign a prenup," I murmured when he straightened us and rested his forehead on mine.

Cade Killian Remington, my husband, smirked in that bad boy manner that was so reminiscent of our teenage years. "There's no end for us, Ella. Remember?"

"How could I forget?" I teased and kissed his lips. "I'm trapped with you."

"Forever," he promised.

The End

ACKNOWLEDGEMENTS

Thank you so much for reading Trapped With You (Remastered). I sincerely hope you enjoyed Cade and Ella's love story. It was a wild ride and I'm so excited I got to share it with you all. These crazy, devoted, obsessed, and morally grey characters will always have a special place in my heart.

I wrote this book over the course of a year while taking breaks in between since I suffered through really bad burnout from my day corporate job—which I've thankfully quit not too long ago to pursue my dreams of becoming a full-time romance author—and I could not have completed it without the support of so many incredible individuals.

To Annie, you were truly my rock throughout this entire journey. There aren't enough words in the English language to express my gratitude. For the hours you spent alpha reading and giving me all your detailed feedback to ensure that this was the best possible version of Cade and Ella. For the hours you spent going over all the covers and illustration designs with me. For the hours you spent listening to my chaotic voice notes when I was spiralling during the writing/editing process. For all the time you spent empowering me and reminding me of my wins. I don't know what I would do without you and you already know how much your stamp of approval means to me. Everyone deserves to have an Annie in their life and I'm so lucky to have you in mine.

To Armita, thank you so much for alpha reading during your busy schedule. It means a lot to me. I appreciate your medical expertise, the time you spent going over the story's outline, and all that you've done for me from the start of my publishing career. I won't forget it.

To Alicia, thank you for beta reading with all that you have going on, for always being in my corner, for giving me advice like my big sister, and for uplifting me with your kind words. I adore you so much.

To Ellie, I know Cade and Ella are your favs and I hope I did you proud with this version. Thank you so much for beta reading and for helping me with the release of this story via LoveNotes PR.

To Emma, thank you so much for beta reading and being so thorough. Your insight was extremely valuable and I appreciate you answering all of my questions. Forever grateful that our paths crossed. I cherish our friendship more than I can ever convey.

To Emily, thank you for editing Cade and Ella's story again and for providing all your feedback. You're absolutely lovely and it's always such a pleasure working with you!

To Manuela and Gabriele, once again, thank you for creating such beautiful illustrations for Trapped With You. Especially the cover illustration. You brought my vision to life with Ella depicted as the goddess Nemesis and Cade as her dark prince. Absolutely stunning. I can't wait to work together on more art pieces!

To my graphic designing team at Qamber Designs, I love working with you ladies. Najla, thank you for creating such a beautiful special edition cover. Still obsessed with it. Nada, thank you for creating such beautiful interiors for my books. You've worked your magic yet again on Trapped With You and I hope you're proud of yourself. Whenever we finish working together on a project, I'm always in awe of your dedication, professionalism, and kindness. From the bottom of my heart, thank you for everything.

To my Mom, I love you. Thank you for always praying for me and supporting my dreams. I couldn't be here today without your blessings.

To my best friends, you know who you are, thank you for always believing in me and encouraging me. I'm so grateful to have you in my life. The kind of friendship we have warms my heart. We may not talk everyday, but I love that we pick up where we left off whenever we do. You all mean so much to me.

To the ladies from Instagram's book community (Danni, Eden, Ellen, Himani, Leah, Mahbuba, Marie, Meena, Niss, Norhan, Ria, Sahra, Sasha, Sil, Smiqa, Yas, Zahra and so many more) thank you for being so amazing and supportive!

And finally, to my wonderfully readership, I would not be here today without your unconditional love and support for my characters and stories. I love you to the moon and back <3

If you enjoyed reading Trapped With You (Remastered), I would appreciate it if you left a rating and review on Amazon and Goodreads. It's a huge help for indie authors!

Love always,

Marzy

OTHER WORKS

If you'd like to read more from me, you can also check out the books of
the other couples in my story world:

Mabel & Liam: **The Guy For Me**
Darla & Zeno: **Corrupted By You (Sins of Montardor – Book #2)**

ABOUT THE AUTHOR

Marzy Opal is a romance author who writes steamy and swoon-worthy romances. Her stories always contain dirty-talking heroes, empowered heroines, everlasting love, and lots of spice. Aside from writing, Marzy has a strong passion for lattes, entrepreneurship, women empowerment and leadership!

CONNECT WITH ME

Enjoyed Trapped With You? Make sure to stay connected for
upcoming books and series! My social media handles are @marzyopal
and you can find me on:

Goodreads | Instagram | Facebook | Marzy's Queens Readers' Facebook
Group | Newsletter | Pinterest | Spotify | TikTok | Twitter

www.marzyopal.com

Made in the USA
Columbia, SC
24 April 2025

57115657R00261